THE ROYALS OF ACUNIEL

The Love of a Princess

THE ROYALS OF ACUNIEL

ASHTON E. DOROW

Life & Lit Press
www.LifeandLitblog.com
@Life.and.Lit

Cover and interior by Roseanna White Designs
Cover images from Shutterstock.com

ISBN: 979-8-218-05267-6

To my Pawpaw....

Words fail me when it comes to how much I miss you.

Thank you for loving Mawmaw the way you did and being an example of true, lasting love for over 56 years.

Prologue

Adelaide

A PRINCESS MUST PUT HER KINGDOM FIRST. I SMOOTHED trembling fingers over the pale blue silk of my wedding gown, willing my roiling stomach to settle and repeating the familiar mantra for the hundredth time this morning.

A wedding day should be one of rejoicing. Yet all I felt was fear.

"You are a vision of loveliness, Your Highness." My head lady's maid beamed at me, admiration in her softly wrinkled eyes. "The prince shall not be able to take his gaze off you!"

I swallowed at the mention of *him*–Prince Miles Alexander Wesley of Trilaria. My betrothed for the last eight years, and in little more than an hour... my husband.

We met once–at the signing of our betrothal contract when I was ten years of age and he, a young man of fifteen. Since then, the prince had been little more than a memory. That is, until just a few weeks ago, when he and the Trilarian royal entourage arrived.

He was pleasant enough, kind, handsome, and we had enjoyed several amiable conversations since his arrival. But a few days of acquaintance did not change the fact that he was a stranger to me. And the very thought of leaving behind all I had ever known for a foreign land with this unknown husband was… terrifying.

To say the least.

'Twas certainly not the sort of marriage I dreamed of as a girl. After all, one cannot help but dream of finding true love when one has parents as enamored with each other as King Rowan and Queen Arabella. Yet arranged marriages are the way of royals; and after my Father wrongfully accused the kingdom of Trilaria for the murder of my grandparents and warred with them for nearly a decade, in truth, this alliance was more vital for the good of Acuniel than my happiness. No matter how much my parents loved me.

"'Tis nearly time to leave, my darling."

I turned at the sound of Mother's voice, finding her crossing my chamber. Queen Arabella, the people's beloved peasant queen, always radiated with grace and beauty, and today was no different. Her ruby red silk gown flowed around her figure, still eye-catching even in her maturing years. Her gold and ruby crown sparkled in the sunlight filtering through my window, and her dark eyes radiated with love.

She wrapped loving arms around me, nearly breaking my carefully controlled dam of tears. "I can hardly believe this day has come. It seems only yesterday your father and I presented you to the kingdom!"

Shorter than I by a few inches, she had to pull back and lift her chin to see my face. Her eyes instantly narrowed. Mother missed nothing. I should have known she would see straight through my attempt at a brave face.

"Adie… are these tears I see? Please, do not cry, my darling." She held my face in both her hands.

"I am trying, Mother. I only wish… If only Trilaria were not so far away."

She clucked her tongue and hugged me again, tighter than before. I relaxed into her embrace, hoping the comfort of a mother's hug would ease the coils of tension winding through my body. "I know, darling. I know." Her voice cracked as she released me and braced her hands on my shoulders. "I understand the fears plaguing your heart. I have often felt them myself. But listen to me—I feel at peace with this… in my heart."

She laughed softly, the sound choked with tears. "Your father struggles with it more than he admits, but only because he dreads the thought of you leaving us. He has dreaded it since the day you were born. Of course, I do not wish to see you leave either, but I feel certain about this. Your marriage to Prince Miles will unite our kingdoms and finally bind the rift made between us and Trilaria for good." She gave me a squeeze. "Not only that, but if you allow it, this union can strengthen *you* as well. In time... I am certain you will find love with your husband, just as I did with your father."

A knock sounded at my door. One of the maids peeked out into the hallway before opening the door wide to reveal my father, King Rowan. His eyes found Mother first–as always. Then they slid over to me, widening at the sight of me in my wedding gown. I could almost hear his heart breaking.

"Adelaide... I have not seen such a beautiful bride since your mother."

Mother giggled like a young maiden and gave Father a teasing nudge. "You and I both know you cared little for my beauty at the time."

"I would not be so sure if I were you, Wife." Father pressed a kiss to her cheek. "You know not what sort of struggles took place in my mind that day. Mayhap even *then* I thought you the most beautiful woman my eyes had ever beheld."

I blushed at their open affection, yet could not help smiling over the interchange. In truth, I would miss seeing the way they loved each other.

Father gave Mother another kiss before pressing one to the top of my head, his large hands cradling my cheeks.

I had heard stories of how Father used to be, before my parents married, and in the early days of their union. Hard, cold, and volatile were the words most often used. My mind had never been able to wrap around that image of him. All I had ever known was *this* man before me. Mother said it was the grace of God which had changed him so drastically, but even that was hard for me to comprehend at times.

"The procession awaits us in the courtyard, my loves. I do not wish to rush you, but we must not keep the people waiting. They already line the streets and cheer for their beloved princess."

The people of Acuniel–they were the only thing keeping me

determined to fulfill my duty. I loved my kingdom with all my heart and would do anything to benefit it.

Even marrying a stranger I did not love.

"I am ready, Father. Let us not tarry a moment longer." The words nearly sent my tears spilling again, but at least I managed to get them past the lump in my throat.

He smiled, tucked my arm in his, and led me from my chamber, which would no longer be mine after today. Together, the three of us walked in silence until we reached the courtyard, where that silence broke with the cacophony of voices echoing over the palace walls. Father had spoken true. Our people *did* already clamor for a glimpse of their princess and treaty bride.

The sound of revelry sent my heart into a gallop, nerves straining further. *God in Heaven, give me strength.*

Because this was no time for weakness.

I *had* to be strong. I had lived my entire life to love and serve my kingdom, and I would not stop now, even in the face of such overwhelming uncertainty. I would marry my stranger prince. I would sacrifice my happiness for the sake of protecting and serving my people. And I would pray that somehow, someway, the Lord allowed me to find peace and happiness of my own in the process.

I squeezed Father's arm before taking my place in the wedding processional, accepting a bouquet of fragrant blooms as I went. When the palace gates opened moments later, I whispered another prayer, the sound of my people's celebration ringing in my ears, and stepped forward into my destiny.

PART 1

Chapter 1

Three years later...
The Kingdom of Trilaria

Adelaide

February 15th

Dear Mother,

The plague continues to tear its way across the kingdom. King Wesley has ordered all town and village gates be closed, and traveling between them is strictly forbidden without written approval from a local lord or the king himself. I am more grateful than ever for the messenger birds you and Father gifted to Miles and I upon our marriage. The ability to communicate with you during this time is a great comfort.

I have never seen the likes of this, Mother. It fills me with such dread. I know you would say the Lord has all of this in His hands, but I cannot help being fearful. So many have died already, suffering with fevers and the most grotesque sores. I do not foresee this plague slacking in its attack any time soon. Please be in constant prayer for Trilaria, and ask Father to do the same.

Give my siblings my love. Roland, Gareth, and Matilda... how I miss them all! And of course, you and Father, and dear old Uncle Matthew.

When this dreadful scourge is past us, you must all come for a visit.

Prithee, write me back as soon as you receive this letter. I must know if you all are well. I pray daily that this plague does not make its way into Acuniel.

With my love,
Adelaide

February 28th

Dear Mother,

It is with trembling hands and a heavy heart that I inform you King Wesley has fallen ill with this grave disease. While some of the sick have recovered, the vast majority do not live past a few days to a sennight after their symptoms begin. Please keep him in your prayers.

Queen Nerissa is sequestered in her chambers, away from the king. I and Miles keep to our chambers as much as we can, and Prince Carac and his new bride, Ophelia, are doing the same. Lord willing, we will not follow the king to a sickbed.

Also, I am relieved to hear Acuniel remains untouched and all of you are well. I pray that it continues to be so.

With my love,
Adelaide

March 5th

Dearest Mother,

There are many things to say.

First, King Wesley has died. I know… I feel the

same shock and horror that you must feel at reading this dreadful news. *The kingdom is heartbroken. As you know, King Wesley was a good, wise, and righteous ruler.*

Of course, this also means Miles is the acting king, though it will not be official until a coronation can be held. Such must be delayed because Miles is now ill as well. And—please, do not panic when I say this—I awoke feeling ill myself. I fear the plague has found its way to me also.

We covet your prayers in the deepest way. Pray for the Lord's will and His peace and comfort to be upon our hearts.

Give all my love to Father, Roland, Gareth, Matilda, and Uncle Matthew.

Your Daughter,
Adelaide

"*SHH...* JUST REST, MILES." I SMOOTHED THE DAMP RAG across my husband's face. Fever wracked him, sending chills and tremors along his body. The sores swelling beneath his arms, around his groin, and even beneath his chin reeked of infection, while his fingers and toes had turned a horrid black.

"Leave me, Adelaide..." Miles' words wheezed between his cracked lips. He attempted to jerk his head away from my touch. "You—you should be... in bed yourself."

"Nonsense. I am well now. But you are not, and my place is here." I steadied his face with gentle fingers and ran the cloth over his heated brow. Miles opened his mouth as if to say more, but a cough seized him, cutting off his words. He struggled for breath until a bloody spittle sprayed across my wrinkled bodice.

I snatched up the already stained cloth from his bedside table and held it over his mouth until the coughing ceased.

Somehow, I had beaten this ruthless plague, though it sapped my strength significantly. Miles, on the other hand, still languished in his sickbed after a full week of illness, only getting worse by the day.

Our three years of marriage had yet to result in both children and the sort of romantic love my parents shared, but we were friends, companions of the truest form. I had no wish to see him die.

God, please. Spare my husband's life. I know not what I will do if...

I rubbed my forehead with my fingertips, attempting to massage away the tension there. My eyes felt gritty and dry, heavy with the desire to sleep. How many hours had I been at my vigil? I had long ago lost count, and now my still-weakened body cried out for reprieve. But my duty was to my husband, the acting king of Trilaria–and therefore, to the kingdom as a whole.

There was no time for sleep.

Another coughing fit seized Miles. He hacked so hard he lost his breath. I surged forward, struggling to elevate him further and whispering calming words into his ear. "*Shhh...* I am here, Husband. You are not alone." I pressed a kiss to his sweaty head, unbidden tears welling in my eyes.

He finally settled and relaxed back into a mound of pillows. I breathed a shaky sigh. "Just close your eyes and rest. Shall I read to you? Mayhap sing a song?"

He shuddered through another wave of chills, eyes slipping closed. "Nay... Nay, Adelaide... Thank you."

I sank against the back of my chair, shaken. In the silence, I watched my husband struggle to breathe and offered up desperate prayers–for him to find rest, for comfort, for a miracle.

If God did not intervene and Miles died, his younger brother, Carac, would take the throne, alongside his new bride, Princess Ophelia of Galiel. But Carac developed a fever himself earlier this morning, and if both he *and* Miles were to pass... what would we do then?

My lack of children long ago became a source of great pain, and even shame, for me. I knew well the whispers of courtiers–that I was a failure as the Crown Princess. It was my duty to produce an heir. Yet for whatever reason, God had not allowed me to conceive, and I began to wonder if motherhood would always remain out of reach.

Since Miles and I had no son, and Carac and his bride had only been married two months and showed no sign of bearing a child yet, who would be next in the royal line? I knew nothing of the line of succession beyond our immediate family. No one ever expected that the entire royal family could be eliminated all at once.

Nay. I had to cease such negative thoughts! That would not, *could not*, happen.

Right?

I sighed, pillowing my head on my arms along the edge of Miles' bed. The fatigue grew ruthless now, insisting I take a moment of rest. Would it truly do any harm to close my eyes for a few minutes?

Nay, stay awake, Adelaide! I fought to keep my lids open, dozing then shaking myself awake over and over.

The final time, I bolted upright with a gasp. The dreary sunlight leaking in from cracks in the shuttered window was gone now. The candle on the bedside table had melted down to little more than a stump, wax dried around it in messy globs.

Alarm pricked like needles from my scalp down to my toes.

I had not merely dozed, but fallen asleep for *hours*!

"Forgive me. I did not mean to fall asleep." His body lay still, with his head lolled to one side, away from me. He must be sleeping deeply now, for he had not looked so peaceful in days.

I leaned forward to smooth his sandy brown hair back from his face. His forehead felt surprisingly cool, the sweat vanished. Had his fever broken?

"Miles? Are you feeling better?" If he was finally resting well, I hated to wake him. But it had been too long since I was able to get him to eat or drink, so it might be best to wake him and try again.

I stood from my chair, needing to stretch my aching back. Then I leaned over my husband, once again smoothing a gentle hand across his forehead and cheek.

Suddenly, in the dim light of the dwindling candle, I noticed his gray pallor.

My blood ran cold.

"Miles?" I shook him, hard. "Miles, wake up."

He did not budge… In fact, his chest did not even move with breath.

"Miles!" I collapsed on top of him, desperately feeling for a heartbeat. It had to be there. It had to! He could not be gone.

Yet I could feel nothing save my own pulse hammering in my temples.

"Help! Someone, please!" I spun away from the bed, tripping over my skirts in my haste for the door.

Before I could reach it, the door flung open and the King's Guard on duty barged in. "What is—"

"Prince Miles—he—he— Get help! Please, quickly!"

The guard spun on his heel and ran to do my bidding. How anyone was supposed to help, I knew not. But I had to do *something*. Anything!

I raced back to the bed and took my husband's hand, gripping it, willing him to respond. It was stiff and cold. Too cold.

My knees turned to water. I sagged onto the mattress' edge, staring with horror at the ghostly pale form of my husband. Any help that might come was already too late.

Crown Prince Miles Alexander Wesley of Trilaria… was dead.

Chapter 2

Adelaide

March 14th

Mother,

I am well.

However, Miles has died. He passed late last night in his sleep. It was peaceful, as deaths go, yet I cannot help but feel guilt. Mayhap if I had done more, been more vigilant, pushed him to eat more, drink more, found a different physician to tend him—the possibilities constantly spin in my head. I know you would say not to blame myself, but I cannot help but feel as though I failed my husband... in more ways than one.

I PAUSED THE LETTER, RESTING MY HEAD IN MY HANDS. Tears blurred what I had written thus far, and one rebellious drop spattered onto the parchment, luckily missing the wet ink. Should I tell my mother the truth about my relationship with Miles? That we were friends, companions, but not in love? I could count very few occasions when he kissed me simply because he wished to show affection. And his eyes certainly never sparkled when he saw me after a long absence, as Father's had always done with Mother.

Yet, we cared for each other in our own way. We had found contentment in our friendship. And knowing he was gone left me feeling empty and confused and...

Lost.

What would come next for me, now that I was a widow?

I wiped my face with the sleeve of my white mourning gown

and continued writing. Each word felt like a ripping of my soul, a humiliating revealing of the private places of my heart. I had always been able to speak to my mother about anything, but this… This was different.

> *I have never spoken of this to you, for I had no wish to upset or worry you—or, God forbid, disappoint you. But Prince Miles and I never did love each other the way you and Father do. Our relationship was always amiable, yet shallow, reserved. Not exactly what I had expected, or hoped.*
>
> *That is another of my regrets. Mayhap if I tried harder, we could have had more in our relationship. Mayhap he would have fought harder to live if he had loved me.*

Another tear splattered onto the page, this time smearing the last word written. It would be best to finish this letter later. I could not afford to dissolve into another fit of tears at the moment, sitting in my mother-in-law's chambers as I was.

Having fallen sick shortly after I did, Queen Nerissa was much improved and expected to make a full recovery. But the loss of her eldest son, especially following so closely after the loss of her beloved husband, had devastated her. Ever since receiving the news, she had done nothing but sit in her bed, rotating between hysterical tears and silent despondency.

The queen's attendants—the few that were not also ill—asked if I would keep her company and try to ease her grief. They insisted I possessed a calming presence, though I was not so sure of that. But I happily heeded their request and appreciated any opportunity to prove helpful.

My new sister-in-law, Ophelia, on the other hand, remained locked away in her chamber, barely even bothering to check on her new husband as he, too, fought for his life.

Swallowing a sigh of frustration, I blotted the ink on my letter, blew on the script to ensure it dried, then folded the parchment. I would have to finish this in the privacy of my own chamber, where any resulting emotions could be released freely.

"Mother?" With only one blood daughter, who was married and living far away in England, the queen relished having another daughter with whom to share a relationship. She insisted on my calling her "Mother" from the start, and our bond had grown strong through the years, not even waning when I failed to produce an heir for her son.

I prayed our relationship would not dissolve now that Miles was gone...

"Mother?" It took a second time of my calling her name before she came out of her glassy-eyed trance and looked at me.

"Yes, Adie?" Once the queen had learned of my childhood nickname, she insisted upon using it. At that moment, it was a relief to hear the familiar name. Perhaps my mother-in-law—or more accurately, my *former* mother-in-law would not disown me after all.

"Are you hungry? It has been several hours since you ate anything. If you like, I can request something for you."

She sat silently for a long moment before finally nodding. "Yes, dear. I think I could stomach a cup of broth, and mayhap some bread. Though only if you stay and eat with me. You are looking too thin, Adie."

I smiled, warmed by her unnecessary concern. "Of course."

"Also, would you mind staying with me tonight?" Her expression turned sheepish. "Sleep in here, I mean. I—I cannot bear the thought of being alone just yet."

I rose from her small desk, tucking my half-finished letter into the hidden pocket of my gown before moving to the small chair beside her bed. "I would be happy to stay with you, Mother." I reached out and squeezed her chilled hand, hoping the gesture communicated my love.

She squeezed back, gripping me like a lifeline.

The arrival of our evening meal took longer than what it would have before the plague, since the number of palace servants had dwindled significantly. But eventually, we sat in companionable silence, enjoying the simple fare. Later, I requested a cot be brought to the queen's chambers and positioned near her own bed.

While the servants set up my new sleeping arrangements, I got the feeling I would not return to my own chamber any time in the near future and would have to find the time and space to finish my letter another way.

Before retiring for the night, I read aloud from the royal psalter, translating the Latin text as I went. "I will extol thee, Oh Lord; for thou hast lifted me up, and hast not made my foes to rejoice over me. Oh Lord my God, I cried unto thee, and thou hast healed me. Oh Lord, thou hast brought up my soul from the grave: thou hast kept me alive, that I should not go down to the pit. Sing unto the Lord, Oh ye saints of His, and give thanks at the remembrance of His holiness. For His anger endureth but a moment; in His favor is life: weeping may endure for a night, but joy cometh in the morning..."

The passage struck something deep inside. Tears stung my eyes and I cast a furtive glance at the queen to ensure she had not noticed. She slept peacefully, her face finally relaxed and free from the creases of despair.

I slowly closed the psalter and placed it on the bedside table, easing out of the chair and crawling onto my small cot. 'Twas far from the most comfortable bed, but it was enough. In truth, the company was as beneficial to me as it was Nerissa. Although Miles and I kept separate chambers throughout our union, it felt strange to sleep in mine, knowing he was no longer on the other side of my wall.

I settled under the covers, snuggling them close beneath my chin. The words of the psalm played over and over in my head. *Weeping may endure for a night... but joy cometh in the morning.*

It seemed all I and the queen had known lately was weeping. Even with the lack of romance in my marriage to Miles, my heart felt broken at the loss of him. At the loss of all that could never be. The future we could no longer hope to have together. The pain was suffocating, like a wound deep within me that no physician could staunch, and if I suffered so, how much greater must my mother-in-law's pain be?

Could God truly turn all that sorrow into joy?

I pray it is so... For her sake, especially.

I rolled onto my side, watching Queen Nerissa sleep. I realized she technically no longer held claim to the title, yet I could not bring myself to stop using it.

It finally sunk in that *I* had been Queen of Trilaria myself for a little over a week, before Miles' death brought our reign to a shockingly quick end.

Yet another loss to grieve…

I never wished to be queen for the sake of power or anything else so ignoble, but for so long I had known my fate, preparing for my future role and treating my responsibility with the utmost respect. To say it was disorienting to have that future suddenly taken away was an understatement.

Serving our kingdom had been the one thing truly uniting Miles and myself. We talked for hours about our plans for our future reign and how we could help the people I had come to love over the last three years. Now, Miles' brother, Prince Carac, was the acting king, and my less-than-selfless new sister-in-law held the role I was quite literally raised to fill.

How on earth had life taken such an unexpected turn?

Chapter 3

Adelaide

THE UNEXPECTED TURNS IN MY LIFE PROVED FAR FROM being over yet, for Prince Carac followed his older brother and their father into the grave just three days later.

If I had thought Nerissa's grief great before, 'twas nothing compared to now. The queen was inconsolable, causing worry to hang like a millstone around my heart. Though fully recovered from her plague symptoms, would she now give up all will to live and waste away?

I could not let that happen. My husband may no longer be here, and my future altered, but my duty still belonged to what family of ours remained. I loved Queen Nerissa like my blood kin, and I would not sit idly and watch her die of a broken heart.

I could not lose anyone else.

"Please, Mother. Sip some of this. The physician said it will help you regain your strength." I desperately held the potent cup of tonic to her lips. The woman had fought me on taking the foul-smelling medicine all afternoon. "*Please*, Mother. For me?"

Finally, her shoulders drooped in defeat and she slowly opened her mouth to sip the tonic. She gagged as she finished, and I quickly handed her water to rinse away the repugnant taste. After taking her fill, Nerissa sagged against her pillows, hair spreading around her in wild disarray. In her grief, the normally well-composed woman had completely given up on her appearance, and I winced at the snarls and tangles forming in her long tresses.

"Would you like me to plait your hair for you, Mother?"

She nodded weakly, offering no further response. Relieved, I hurried to her dressing table and found her ivory hair comb, which had a row of fine teeth on one side and thicker teeth on the other, separated by an intricately carved design in the middle.

I sat on the edge of her mattress, gently pulling her long hair to one side and working at the tangles with careful strokes. With so much hair that was constantly having to be combed and coiffed, she had long ago learned not to be tender of head, but I still had no wish to cause her discomfort.

"You have such beautiful hair. So long and thick, and the silver color that is coming in is so becoming on you."

Nerissa gave a quiet scoff. "I am glad *you* think so. I remember shedding a few tears when the first sign of gray appeared." She looked at me askance, her face still forward so as not to hinder my work. "My hair was much like yours when I was young. So dark one could almost call it black."

She lifted a petal-soft hand and touched my cheek, hazel eyes welling with sudden tears. "You are so beautiful, Adie. My son was a blessed man. Not only because of your beauty, but your heart." She lovingly patted my face. "You have been too good to me. Better than a daughter even!"

I laughed, despite my discomfort at her unmerited praise. "'Tis good Elsebeth is not present to hear you say that."

The worry lines etched deeper into Nerissa's forehead at the mention of her daughter. "Oh, I do miss her terribly… but I am thankful she should be safe from this scourge in England. And what of your family? Have you heard anything new from your mother?"

I shook my head. "They remain well, last I heard. But nay, nothing new as of yet." I painstakingly finished my letter concerning Miles' passing and sent it with our swiftest carrier pigeon, but I had yet to receive a response. The birds had never failed to reach their destination unhindered, but I began to fear something happened to the bird this time.

Just in case, I would need to write another letter this evening to inform my mother of Carac's death—and to beseech her continued prayers for Trilaria in the unsteady days ahead.

The uncertainty of our future troubled me greatly, though I had yet to speak of it to Nerissa for fear of exacerbating her already fragile state. As widows, both us and Ophelia sat in precarious positions. Not to mention, without a ruler, our kingdom grew weak and vulnerable in a way it had never been before. An enemy nation could sweep in and overtake us with little fight if they so wished.

I had yet to hear if the Royal Council located another relative eligible to take the throne, and for the sake of our personal futures, I would need to make inquiries regarding the matter as soon as possible. Preferably on the morrow.

"Have you seen Ophelia today?" Nerissa's gentle question interrupted my stressful thoughts.

I shook my head, finishing my combing and starting to weave her hair into a thick braid. "Nay. I heard from a maidservant that she is still shut away in her chamber."

Nerissa sighed. "She must be so distraught. To have one's marriage end after only two months..."

I finished the braid and tied it off with a piece of ribbon I fetched from the dressing table. When I sat back in my seat to admire my handiwork, Nerissa reached out and touched my arm. "I know Ophelia has proven to be... *frustrating* at times. But prithee, go ensure she is well on the morrow. See if she needs anything."

I suppressed a sigh and instead nodded obediently. "Of course, Mother. If you wish."

My knuckles rapped softly on my sister-in-law's door the following morning. "Ophelia? May I come in?" After penning my latest letter and watching the messenger bird dart off into the chilly morning, I had delayed this visit for as long as I could. Ophelia's petulance grated on me like few other things in this world, but she was still family. And more than that, Nerissa wished for me to do this.

After no response, I knocked again. "Ophelia? I promise I will only be a moment."

Silence. Then at last, the sound of someone removing the bar from the door before it opened a crack. Ophelia's pale face and bloodshot eyes greeted me. "Oh, 'tis you." She stepped away from the door, allowing me entrance.

When I entered her chamber, I noted the canopied bed still in disarray and her dishes from the morning meal cluttering a table in one corner. Ophelia paced away from me, plucking at her mourning gown. "Ugh! I *despise* white! It does nothing for my complexion."

"Nonsense. You look beautiful in anything."

She cast me a rancorous look as she spun to face me again. "What do you want, Adelaide?"

I folded my hands at my waist, remembering all of my mother's lessons on showing kindness even to those who did not deserve it. "I only wished to inquire after your welfare. Is there anything you need?"

"To be out of this god-forsaken land–*that* is what I need!" She huffed fiercely, hands braced against her hips. "I am going positively mad here. Oh, I *knew* this marriage was a mistake, but my parents would not listen!"

I blinked at her harsh words. When they first wed, the foreign princess had seemed enamored with Carac. Clearly her acting skills were exceptional, for I now glimpsed the true Ophelia. She had never held any sort of affection for Carac at all–not even friendship.

Poor Carac... He deserved so much more than this glaring resentment.

"Ophelia..." What could I say without inflaming her anger more? The thought of a confrontation made my insides squirm. At times I wished I had more of my mother's penchant for boldly speaking her mind, the consequences be hanged.

"'Tis a pity you feel that way," I said at last. "I will leave you to yourself and not bother you again, if that is your wish. I only sought to ease our mother-in-law's mind. She has been worried about you."

Ophelia sneered. "That woman is nothing to me now. Why should she bother to concern herself with me?"

My mouth fell slack. "Because she loves you. Loves us."

Again, Ophelia sneered, this time scoffing as well. "*Love?* She barely knows me."

My blood boiled in my veins. How hurt Nerissa would be if she heard Ophelia's cold words.

I swallowed a frustrated sigh. Nothing worth saying to her remained.

Without another word, I turned and left the chamber and the haughty, selfish woman within.

The members of the Royal Council had little to do with me beyond communal meals or social events, but the head of the Council, Lord Raynard, had always been the kindest of them all. After leaving my sister-in-law's chamber, I sought the man out. Last I heard, he remained in good health and had not yet fallen ill—though one councilman was sick, and another had already died.

I prowled the palace in search of Lord Raynard, unnerved by its silence. Before the plague hit, the palace buzzed vibrantly with activity and life. Now, the rooms and corridors felt cold, darkened by shadows and the looming spectre of fear. The place that had once felt like home now felt more foreign than the day I first arrived.

At last, I spotted Lord Raynard exiting the late king's study. "Ah, just the man I was looking for. May I beg a moment of your time?"

"Oh, Your High—Your Ma—I mean, Your *Highness*." The man blushed as he bowed to me. Apparently, I was not the only one feeling confused by all of the rapid changes in titles. "How may I be of service, Princess?"

I glanced up and down the corridor, ensuring we were alone. "I am hoping you can enlighten me as to where matters currently stand. Has it been determined who shall inherit the crown?"

His graying brows knit close together as he sighed. "Ah, yes… I wish there was a simple answer to give, Your Highness. This entire situation is so unforeseen, truly unprecedented. With further deaths in the extended royal line, we must go farther down the family tree than anticipated to find a suitable candidate. We hope to determine who should rightfully inherit and locate the man before any more tragedy befalls us."

Without him saying so, I knew he feared an enemy invasion as much as I did. In this moment of political and economical instability, anything could happen.

"Do you suppose word of the king's and the princes' deaths has made it past our borders yet?"

"I dearly hope not, but I know word spreads faster than one might expect, even in times like these, so 'tis certainly a possibility. 'Tis only a matter of time before our enemies know. We are a small kingdom, but ordinarily rich in trade. No doubt, many kings would love to overtake us."

My heart stuttered at the thought. "And what of us? The queen, Princess Ophelia... Myself?"

The nobleman's eyes grew heavy with sympathy. "All three of you will, of course, remain where you are until a king can be appointed." He cast a furtive glance at our surroundings before pitching his voice lower. "If it were up to me, I would suggest Queen Nerissa, or even you, take the throne. But unfortunately, our laws do not allow for such. Only a male can inherit. And once a new king is crowned, your situation could change... He may decide to send all of you away."

Lord Raynard leaned closer, looking as if he wanted to reach out and pat my shoulder. "You must prepare yourself, Your Highness. 'Twould even be wise for you to arrange to return home."

"Nay!" The response left my tongue without thought. Lord Raynard's eyes widened in surprise at the outburst, so I softened my tone. "In all due respect, my lord, while I love my home kingdom of Acuniel, my place is here."

His keen eyes searched my face for a silent moment. Then he nodded. "Of course, Your Highness. I must confess, many would be saddened to see you leave us. But... you must be prepared for the possibility that you may have nowhere to go *but* Acuniel."

Deep down, I knew he spoke the truth. I *should* prepare for such a possibility, but I could not bring myself to think in those terms just yet. In the first few months after my marriage, I may have seized the opportunity to return to my beloved home in Caelrith, the capital city of Acuniel. Now, however, I knew beyond doubt that I belonged in Trilaria.

That night, over our evening meal in the queen's chambers, I shared what I learned with Nerissa. I still feared distressing her further, but the queen deserved to know the truth of the situation.

"So we are able to remain comfortably as we are, for the time being." I forced cheerfulness into my tone. "And who knows—mayhap the new king will allow us to stay here. In different chambers, of course. But surely we will not be thrown out into the streets."

The queen frowned, her countenance deeply troubled. I reached out and took her hand in both of my own. "Fret not, Mother. Please... I am certain all will be well."

But *was* I certain? How could I offer such assurance when I knew full well that everything about our life was so terribly *uncertain*?

She patted our clasped hands with her free one, atop the small table where we sat, and nodded solemnly. "Did you check on Ophelia as I asked?"

I stiffened and slowly pulled my hands away, sitting back in my seat. How much of my conversation with the princess should I share? "Ah, yes. I did."

"And she is well?"

"Well enough... She was... very distraught. The emotional toll of this plague seems to be wearing on her." It was as much of the truth as I could bring myself to say. It would wound Nerissa deeply if she knew the girl not only resented her marriage to Carac but abhorred *everything* about living here.

Even with what little I shared, the queen's face fell. "Oh, the poor dear." She shook her head, eyes growing glassy and distant. Moments ticked past until she finally lifted them back to me. "Adie, I believe I will retire now. Take your time with your meal and whatever else you would like to do before bed. You should not have to worry yourself so much with an old woman like me."

Nerissa pushed up from the table and moved toward her changing screen. One of her maids—one of the few not currently ill—hurried from the shadows to attend her. I stared after them both, watching the pair disappear behind the screen.

"Mother, I would not consider you an *old* woman. Do not speak of yourself that way."

She laughed dryly. "Well I am a *young* woman no longer–that is certain."

Several minutes later, she emerged from behind the screen in a linen nightdress and climbed into bed.

I pushed away my partially eaten bowl of stew, no longer hungry myself. Instead, I had the maid to assist me into my own nightdress before sitting at the dressing table while she brushed my hair. The woman's strokes were gentle, experienced from many years in the queen's service, but I could not help missing my own maid, Gretta. The young woman currently lay abed with the beginnings of the plague, and I could only pray she survived the ordeal.

"Thank you, Abigail," I said when the woman finished her work. While the maid gathered the soiled dishes from our meal, I curled up on my small cot and picked up the royal psalter, turning to the comforting passage from the other night. Mayhap the words would soothe the queen's troubled soul as they had mine. "Weeping may endure for the night, but joy cometh in the morning."

Chapter 4

Adelaide

March 19th

My Dearest Adelaide,

My heart is broken with you over the loss of Prince Miles, not to mention that of his father and brother! How horrifying this entire situation is! Your father and I have spent many an hour in the palace chapel, beseeching the Lord on behalf of you all. We may never understand the ways of God, but we must trust that He is working all for our good, even so. This is a lesson I have had to learn and relearn many times in my life.

My heart also aches to know the truth of your marriage with Miles. Why did you not tell me sooner? I have been so distraught over it, and 'tis why I took so long to send my reply. While I know such a lack of tender feelings in a marriage is common among people of our rank, I had hoped and prayed for more for you, my darling. You deserve someone who will love you for everything you are. But I can be thankful that you and the prince shared a pleasant relationship, at least, and that he was good to you in the ways that matter most.

I hesitate to mention this, for I do not wish to pressure you or seem as though I am attempting to dictate your life, but… mayhap you should consider returning home to us? We all miss you so, and we would be more than happy to welcome you back into our midst. Your father has been most anxious to see his beloved girl again, and I long to hug you and see with my own eyes that you are safe and well.

But the decision is up to you, Adelaide. You willingly submitted to this marriage treaty for the sake of Acuniel, and we would like to now leave the decision about your future firmly in your own hands.

With all my love,
Mother

I LOOKED UP FROM THE LETTER THAT HAD JUST AR-rived, blinking away tears.

They wanted me to come home.

Part of my heart longed to meet that desire and return to my family right away. But a deeper part knew I could not. I could nev-er abandon the woman who was neither my relative by blood or even by marriage anymore, but remained the mother of my heart.

"Adie?"

I turned at the sound of Nerissa's voice. "Yes, Mother?"

She stood by the window, looking particularly pale this morn-ing in her stark white gown as she stared out at the world. A slow drizzle dampened the earth below, fitting the sullen mood hanging over the former queen. "Will you please go to Ophelia and ask her to come visit me? I must speak with her. And you."

My nerves stretched tight at the nearly ominous tone of her words. "Of course. I will go straightaway."

I folded my letter and tucked it within a drawer of the queen's desk. A reply to my mother would have to wait.

At Ophelia's door several minutes later, she again took an age to answer my knock. When at last she peeked out at me, she looked in no better mood than the day before. "You are here *again*? I thought you said you would leave me alone."

"The queen wishes to speak with you—with both of us, togeth-er, it seems."

She waved a dismissive hand. "Tell her I am too tired or some-thing of the sort. I am not coming." She started to close the door in my face.

I caught it with my hand. Hard. "Ophelia. Please. You can

spare a mourning woman one moment of your time. You *will* come with me, whether you like it or not." It seemed some of my mother's fire had found its way into me today.

Ophelia stared at me as though I lost my mind. "How dare you speak to me that way?"

"How dare *you* disgrace the mother of your husband this way?"

She clamped her mouth shut and clenched her jaw, green eyes sparking fire. "Very well, Adelaide," she finally consented, chin set at a proud angle. "I will come. But *only* for a moment."

"Very good." I nodded, moving aside so she could leave the room. Her white gown trailed behind her as she stomped down the hall with me at her heels.

Back in the queen's chamber, we found our mother-in-law still standing by the window. She turned upon our entrance, her expression shadowed in the rain-dimmed light.

"Ophelia, thank you for coming." She motioned us forward and took each of our hands when we drew near. Her sad eyes focused on Ophelia's face first, and then mine. "I feel blessed to have two such lovely daughters-in-law. My sons, though they did not have much time to spend with either of you, were blessed as well."

Tears filled her eyes. "We have found ourselves in quite the predicament here. But this land is not your own, and 'tis not fair of me to hold onto you both and force you to endure this hardship with me." She squeezed our hands, her tears beginning to drip down her cheeks. "You must leave this place. Both of you, return to your father's house and your true mother. May the Lord deal kindly with you, as you did with my sons... and with me."

Ophelia's eyes widened and she opened her mouth to speak, but I interrupted. "Mother, nay. Surely, we must stay here with you. We cannot abandon you at a time like this!"

She shook her head, dropping our hands. Taking a step back as though beginning to sever her ties with us. "Nay, you must go. You are both still young—you can easily find new husbands elsewhere and be happy as you deserve." She laughed bitterly. "The Lord has clearly put His hand against this kingdom. We are cursed! You should not have to suffer alongside us."

"You are most wise and gracious, Queen Nerissa," Ophelia interjected. "I will send a messenger to my parents posthaste and have them send a company of soldiers to meet me at the border of

Trilaria and Galiel." She surged forward to hug the queen and press an emotionless kiss to her cheek.

My heart hammered in my chest as I watched Ophelia turn in a whirl of silk and hurry out the door. I did not care how much Nerissa wished me to leave, I *would not* go.

"Adelaide, please do not argue with me on this. Go home to your family as Ophelia is doing."

"Nay! Nerissa, you *are* my family, and I will not abandon you."

The tears were small rivers down the queen's face now. "You owe me nothing, child. Your vows to my son were until death do you part, and death has come. You have no further obligation to me. You have already been too good to me staying as long as you have, and I have been too selfish, wanting to keep you here. You deserve to live a full life, full of love and happiness. Do not waste the remainder of your youth with a depressed, cursed old woman."

"Listen to me." She backed away from me, but I followed, gripping her by the shoulders. "Please, do not tell me to leave you. I love Acuniel and my family there, but *this*? This is my home now. Trilaria is my kingdom. *You* are my family. And if vows are of such importance to you, I shall make one to you today."

I looked her firmly in the eyes, struck by their similarity to her son's. "As God and you are my witness—" My voice quavered, but I would not let myself break. Not now. "Where you go, I will go. Where you live, I will live. Your people, the people of Trilaria, are and shall forever be my people. Where you die, I will die there also. As only death could separate me from your son, only death shall separate me from you. And may the Lord deal with me severely if I break this vow."

The queen sobbed and fell into my arms. "Oh, my dear girl! What did I do to deserve you?" Her knees buckled, her weight bearing down on me as I lowered us gently to the floor. I held her close, and there we wept together until we had no tears left to cry.

PART 2

Chapter 5

One week later...

Nicholas

PLAGUE IN TRILARIA. KING WESLEY, DEAD. THESE WERE the rumors that had reached Lord Nicholas of Aguilar on his travels around the continent and sent him rushing home. This panic residing in his chest was what spurred him on day after day for well over a week and brought him to this night-shadowed border of Trilaria.

He had pushed his faithful steed, Castor, far harder than was right in his haste. Nicholas' own body ached all over from the hard riding and sleeping no more than a few hours each night. But he could not rest until he reached home and discovered what had become of his family and their people in the region of Aguilar.

Up ahead, a group of Trilarian soldiers blocked the wooden bridge spanning the River Arlith, which divided Trilaria from Galiel. Nicholas brought Castor's pace down to a trot. The early spring chill made a shiver trace down his spine, despite the heavy cloak he wore.

What were these soldiers doing here? Were circumstances truly so bad that the king–or whoever succeeded him–ordered a halt to travel?

"Who goes there? Halt, in the name of the king!"

Nicholas drew in his reins a stone's throw from the bridge's edge. "I am Lord Nicholas of Aguilar, son of Prince William, the king's second brother and Duke of Aguilar."

One of the soldiers edged nearer, ahead of his companions. "The crown has ordered that no one is to enter or leave Trilaria without written consent."

"I have heard of this plague, and our good king's unfortunate passing–may his soul rest in peace. Are circumstances so dire that you would keep even native Trilarians from returning home?"

The soldiers shared a look, though it was hard to make out much of their countenance in this light. "My apologies, my lord," the first man said, "but we have our orders and must not go against them. However," he pitched his voice lower, as though someone might overhear their conversation, "we can only guard so much of this border. Who knows what sort of people may cross beneath our notice?"

Nicholas fought down an amused grin, schooling his features into a solemn expression. "I understand and appreciate your loyalty to your post, good sirs. I shall leave you be then and pray for the swift departure of this scourge."

The men bowed in their saddles and Nicholas reeled Castor around, heading back into Galielian territory. The soldier's message was clear. They could not let Nicholas across the bridge, but there was nothing stopping him from finding another way over the border.

The River Arlith flowed north and south for many miles, so there was no way to get around it. The best Nicholas could hope for was to find a narrower section, shallow enough to cross safely in the dark.

Once out of sight of the soldiers, Nicholas turned north and forged into the dense forest. It was slow going, weaving Castor safely in and out of the trees and underbrush, but at last, Nicholas emerged onto the river's edge. The waters shimmered in the moon and star light, flowing south in a gentle current. But if he remembered correctly, this section of the river was still too deep to cross. Nicholas nudged Castor further upstream, searching through the darkness for a shallow point.

Finally, he reached a place where the ground sloped gently down into the water, forming a small, pebbled beach. A moderate distance from shore, a tree grew in the water. It did not appear to be submerged more than a few feet.

This was as good a place as any.

Nicholas patted Castor's neck. "Come on, old boy. You can do this." Horse and rider waded into the chilled waters. Castor neighed a protest, and for a moment, Nicholas second-guessed his decision. Mayhap it would be wiser to wait until morning? Even if they made it safely across, they could catch their death with the cold after getting soaking wet.

But that sense of urgency nagged again, at the back of his mind. He *had* to get home. And there was no time to waste.

With a bracing inhale, Nicholas kicked Castor forward into the river. It stayed shallow until nearly halfway across before the ground dropped suddenly. Castor stumbled with a shrieking neigh. Nicholas clutched his reins, fighting to stay in the saddle as the horse struggled for footing. The water crept up Nicholas' calves, invading his leather boots and freezing his toes.

Finally, Castor righted himself and Nicholas released a pent-up breath. The water was much higher now, but still navigable. "Come, boy. Almost there." He nudged the horse onward, and a few minutes later, they emerged from the water onto the opposite shore. Inside Trilarian territory at last.

Chill bumps dotted Nicholas' skin and stiffened his muscles, but they had to keep moving. He dug his heels into Castor's flanks, spurring the horse across the moonlit meadow that edged this side of the river. From here, it would be less than a day's journey to Aguilar if they could ride uninterrupted.

Nicholas only prayed he was not already too late.

"Brother!" The door to the keep of Aguilar Castle banged open and a flurry of white barreled out.

Nicholas slid from his saddle, nearly collapsing at the impact of his aching body against the hard earth. He scarcely regained his balance before his half-sister, the product of his father's second marriage, slammed into him. He stumbled back, bumping into

Castor's foaming side and wrapping his arms around the fourteen-year-old girl to steady them both. She sobbed against his chest, great gut-wrenching sounds that sent his heart into his throat.

Clearly, she was alive and well–but she wore a mourning gown.

He grabbed her shoulders and held her slight frame away from him. "Eleanor, tell me. What has happened?"

Her blue eyes stood out like sapphires against her flushed face and golden blonde hair. Even being half-siblings, one would think they would share some resemblance; but after six months away, the stark contrast between her fair coloring and his black hair and dark eyes struck Nicholas all over again.

"It–it… Father! He–" She choked on a sob and fell forward to bury her face in his shoulder, despite his sweaty state. Confirming his worst fear.

Nicholas wrapped his arms back around her, one hand cradling her head, and fought to keep his own emotions under control. His heart galloped as fast as Castor's hooves, and he could feel his nerves unraveling at a rapid rate. But he could not give in to it right now. Not in front of Eleanor.

He sucked in a calming breath. "What of your mother?"

"She is well. She has not been ill."

Nicholas' shoulders sagged in relief. His stepmother, Lady Clarice, had always been kind to him, even if she could never replace the mother he lost at the age of nine. "And Mericus?"

As if on cue, another figure emerged from the castle.

"Brother. You have returned." Nicholas' twin ambled towards him as though their entire world had not just turned upside down.

Nicholas' jaw tightened. In the past six months, he had missed his father, Eleanor, and even his stepmother. But not Mericus.

It never ceased to amaze him how two men born of the same womb, at the same time, could be so wholly different.

"Yes, I have. And Eleanor has just told me about Father."

"You should have been here instead of gallivanting around the world." His twin threw the words at him like a javelin, but they missed their mark. After so many years of verbal barbs, Nicholas had learned to deflect them–for the most part.

"I shall regret not being here through this horrifying ordeal for the rest of my days. But I am here now. That is what matters at this moment."

Mericus' glower remained in place, his posture rigid. Why did they always have to be at odds? It was part of the reason Nicholas left home in the first place–to get away from the constant tension. That and the fact that Father *told* him he should go and experience the world for a time.

It had not always been this way. They were friends once, as brothers should be. But everything changed when Father declared he would choose his heir at the time of his death. Mericus, older than Nicholas by a couple minutes, had never been able to move past the perceived betrayal.

With their father... dead–Nicholas could hardly stand to think of the word–one of them was the new Lord of Aguilar.

However, now was not the time to ask which son their father chose. There were even more important matters at hand.

"How long has it been since...?"

"A week on the morrow."

Eleanor squeezed closer to Nicholas at their brother's words, whimpering softly. The poor dear...

"Was there a service?"

"In the middle of a plague?" Mericus scoffed. "There has been no time for formal services. Most bodies are being dumped in mass graves."

Nicholas winced at the coarse phrasing, arms instinctively tightening around his sister. "Surely Father was not placed in such a grave."

"Nay. He was given a hasty, but proper, burial in the family cemetery."

Nicholas swallowed and nodded, relieved to know his father did not have to share a grave with the masses. Still, he deserved a true Christian burial service.

The unraveling began again in earnest. Nicholas would need time alone before long, away from the eyes of those for whom he must be strong.

Movement in his peripheral vision brought his head around–a stable boy, coming to take Castor. Nicholas passed him the reins and wrapped one arm about his sister's thin shoulders. He gently steered her toward the castle entrance, sending Mericus a meaningful look as they passed. "We shall speak more soon. But for now, I must tend to our stepmother and Eleanor."

Nicholas stared at the mound of dirt that was his father's grave. The disturbed earth still looked fresh, and only the most rudimentary of markers signified that a prince of Trilaria lay buried here.

Tears welled hot in Nicholas' eyes. He raked his hand back through his disheveled curls.

I never got to say goodbye. I would have been with him to the very end, if I had my choice.

Even now, he could feel his father's warm embrace and see his encouraging smile from the day Nicholas left Aguilar. After one too many arguments with Mericus, and too much strain on their household, Father thought it best that Nicholas leave for a time, go see all of the places he read and heard about. Nicholas consented *only* because Father was so insistent about it. Prince William, the Duke of Aguilar, had been in perfect health, after all. None feared he would pass before his son returned.

Nicholas heaved out a heavy breath, lifting his face to the night sky. Their family had already experienced so much death. First his mother and the babe she was in the midst of birthing–another son. Then the son and second daughter of his father and Lady Clarice, when they were still infants.

Why did Father have to follow them to the grave *now?*

His poor stepmother was just as inconsolable as Eleanor. When his sister led him into Lady Clarice's chamber, the woman–much younger than Father and still very beautiful–ran into his arms, sobbing out her grief. Nicholas had done his best to comfort her, along with Eleanor, and kept the two of them company until supper.

'Twas a relief to now be alone for a time, where he could process these unsettling events in peace.

Footsteps shuffled behind him.

Nicholas stiffened and turned. "Hello, Brother."

So much for peaceful solitude...

Mericus stopped beside him, keeping his face toward the piteous grave. "What brought you home? I expected you to be gone longer."

"I heard rumors of the plague, and that King Wesley has died. What else have I missed?"

Mericus crossed his arms over his chest, which had always been broader than Nicholas' own. Not only were their personalities vastly different, but their looks were markedly different as well. Mericus had always been taller, his face fuller, eyes larger, with a beard he kept thick, while Nicholas was slightly shorter, leanly muscled, and all sharp angles in the face. Not to mention, he rarely let his beard grow beyond a short stubble. The only things exactly alike about the brothers was their hair–black as night and loosely curled–and the deep brown color of their eyes.

"King Wesley died several weeks ago now," his brother finally spoke up. "Our cousins, the princes, soon followed."

"Both of them?" Alarm spiked through Nicholas.

"Yes. Though, from what I understand, the queen and the princes' wives survived."

"Then who is king?"

"No one yet, to my knowledge. Though I expect we will receive an announcement that Uncle Charles or his son Henry has been crowned."

A sense of unease settled in Nicholas' stomach. Why had they not received tidings of the new king yet? Surely the Royal Council would have named a new monarch as soon as possible.

"I did not wish to mention this earlier, in front of Eleanor, but I must ask now…" Nicholas readied to ask the question that would alter their lives forever.

But Mericus beat him to it. "He chose me, Nicholas."

The words felt like a punch to the gut, nearly knocking the wind out of him. Of course, it was entirely possible that Father had chosen Mericus, but Nicholas' relationship with him had always been stronger. Nicholas had almost begun to assume *he* would be his father's choice. And had not that been Mericus' assumption, as well? Why else would his brother have felt such animosity towards him all these years?

"Oh." It was all he could get out for a moment. "I… I am happy for you, Brother."

"Nay, you are not," Mericus sneered. "Admit it. It grates you that Father would choose me. You just *thought* you were his pet."

"He loved us both. Equally, I am certain. Our relationship was... *different*. But I never once doubted that he loved you."

"Save your empty placating, Brother. I do not require it." As quickly as he had shown up, Mericus departed, leaving Nicholas alone with their father's grave.

Chapter 6

Nicholas

NICHOLAS ABSENTLY TAPPED AGAINST THE BOILED EGG before him. Although there was little time for meals in his rushed journey, now that he had arrived home, his appetite was non-existent. Everything he swallowed tasted of ash in his throat. The ashes of death and disappointment and regret.

I wish I had never left…

How could You let him die without me, Lord?

Even being back in his own familiar bed, Nicholas barely slept. Every time he closed his eyes, he either dreamed he still raced through forests and valleys on Castor's back, or he relived a memory of his father from childhood.

'Twas the worst sort of torment.

The door to the Great Hall opened, and Lady Clarice entered. He stood from his seat. "Stepmother. I hope you slept well."

She gracefully took her seat, the white silk of her gown pooling around her. A gauzy veil framed her wan face and hid most of her golden hair that so resembled her daughter's. She sighed, all her grief and exhaustion in the sound. "As well as can be expected, I suppose…"

"Where is Eleanor?"

"She is sleeping late this morn. The girl has hardly been able to rest since… Well, everything. She finally slept soundly last night. I suppose knowing you have returned safely puts her mind more at ease."

Nicholas stared at his uneaten egg, tapping it again. Sweet Eleanor. She had always idolized him–far more than he deserved.

"Did Mericus tell you?"

He glanced up at his stepmother. "About Father naming him heir? Yes, he told me last night."

"About...? What?" Her brow furrowed and she leaned forward against the table. "Nay, Nicholas. Your father did not choose him. He did not choose *anyone*."

"What do you mean?" Nicholas sat up straight in his seat.

Clarice sighed—whether in frustration, grief, or a mixture of both, he knew not. "Your father had rallied, and we thought—even *he* thought he would recover. Eleanor felt poorly, and we feared she was catching the plague herself. So your father insisted I leave his side and stay with Eleanor. Even the servants did not feel compelled to keep so close an eye on him any longer."

She massaged her temple with trembling fingers. "When I went to see him the next morning..." Her voice cracked and she shook her head. "Oh, Nicholas, guilt has tormented me ever since. I should have been with him. Eleanor ended up not being ill at all, only feeling unwell because of so much fear and stress. Mayhap if I had been there when he—" She pressed a hand against her mouth, cutting off both her words and a sob.

Nicholas should be comforting his stepmother, searching for words to reassure her that she need not feel guilty. But all he could think about was his brother's attempted deception.

"Mericus lied to me." His heart began an angry drumbeat.

Clarice swiped at her tears. "I am afraid so. Your father never did tell us who he chose. Though I have my suspicions of who it would have been."

Nicholas pushed up from the table. His chair clattered behind him, nearly toppling. "Of all the—" He clamped his mouth shut. Fury bubbled up like a cauldron within him. He had to find his brother. *Now.*

"Pardon me, Stepmother." He stormed across the Great Hall and banged his way through the doors. His feet pounded upstairs to where the family chambers lay, but before he could reach his brother's door, the man himself emerged.

"Did you truly think you could get away with it?"

Mericus turned, surprise evident in his face.

Nicholas reached his brother, resisting the urge to throttle him. "Did you really think you could take Father's property for yourself without at least consulting me first? If Father *did* want you to be his heir, then that is well and good. I will not fight you on that. But blatant deception I will not stand for!" Nicholas swiped a hand through the air to punctuate his words.

Mericus faced him and drew up to his full height, a few fingers taller than Nicholas. His eyes narrowed in a spiteful glare. "How could I consult you when you were absent? I should be the heir anyway. I should have *always* been his first choice. And *I* was the one who was here with him in the end."

Nicholas raised his chin, refusing to back down from his brother's move to intimidate. "He *told* me I should leave! You know that very well. He had grown weary of *this*!"

Mericus shoved Nicholas out of his way with a growl, sending Nicholas into the wall.

Nicholas had never wanted to fight like this with his own flesh and blood. He never relished fighting with *anyone*. But he could only handle so much. He could only be pushed so far.

Nicholas charged after his brother. "We are not finished here, Mericus. We must discuss this. Now. No running away. No deception." He gripped his brother's tunic and yanked him to a halt.

Mericus whirled, a fist flying toward Nicholas' face. Knuckles crunched against bone. Blood spurted.

Nicholas' hand flew to his bleeding nose, fury and shock combining in a heady mixture. They had not come to physical blows since they were young adolescents, verbal sparring becoming their usual way. But now…

Nicholas' own fist flew before he could think a moment longer. Always the better fighter, Mericus deflected the punch, grabbing Nicholas' arm and twisting him around until his back slammed against the wall.

"My lords!" Nicholas' head turned to find a young servant hurrying towards them. His face was pale, his eyes wide. No doubt because he found them in the midst of fisticuffs.

"What is it, Lucius?" Nicholas pulled away from his brother's now loosened hold, chest heaving. He dabbed at the blood still dripping from his nose. It left stains on his sleeve and he could almost hear the washerwomen cursing as they attempted to clean the fabric later.

"Lord Nicholas, Lord Mericus," the servant bowed to each of

them, "a member of the Royal Council has just arrived. I was sent to find you."

The brothers shared a look. Clearly, their dispute would have to wait...

Mericus was already walking around the servant and down the corridor. "We will meet him in the Great Hall immediately."

The royal emissary rose from his bow before the twin noblemen. Nicholas stood beside his brother atop the dais in the Great Hall, resisting the urge to tap his foot in anticipation of whatever the man had to say. Did he come bearing more grim tidings? Or to announce the identity of the new king?

"My lords, I am relieved to see you are both alive and well, though I am grieved at the news of your father's death."

"We thank you for your condolences, Lord Raynard," Nicholas responded for the both of them.

"I am sure you have heard of the passing of our dear King Wesley, and the tragic loss of both Crown Prince Miles and Prince Carac." Sorrow showed in the aging lines of the councilman's face.

"Unfortunately, yes. We have heard," Nicholas said. "And we must confess we have been anxious for news of the new king. I assume it is our Uncle Charles, or perhaps his eldest son?"

Lord Raynard hesitated. "Ah... You see, therein lies our trouble. The king's brother, Prince Charles, *and* his son have also perished in the intervening weeks since the king's death–along with the prince's wife and a grandchild. As you know, his younger son died two years ago of the ague, and all other children of your uncle are daughters. Which means... the both of you are next in line for the throne."

"Pardon me?"

"Are you serious?"

The brothers' shocked responses overlapped with each other. The official's eyes shifted between them before resting on Mericus. "I expected to find your father here, not yet having heard of his death. But since he is gone, the two of you are next in the line of succession. Though, of course, you cannot *both* rule, so whichever of you your father named as heir shall stay here and the other will take the throne."

"He died before he could make his decision."

Of course, Mericus appeared eager to tell the truth of the circumstance *now.* It was all Nicholas could do not to roll his eyes.

"I see. Well, that certainly complicates things…" The official folded his hands in front of him, brow furrowing. He looked to the side and at the ground before abruptly shifting his attention back to them. "I suppose the best course of action is to bring *both* of you back to Valen. I shall discuss the matter with my fellow councilmen, and we can make a ruling on who should inherit what."

Nicholas glanced at his brother, noting the gleam in his dark eyes. The Duchy of Aguilar would be of no interest to him now. Clearly the matter of inheritance had never been about his brother's desire to serve their people or further the family legacy. It was power and wealth he cared for most.

Would Trilaria be safe in such greedy hands?

Nicholas' stomach turned with dread. He never thought he could be king one day. The only thing that ever mattered was Aguilar. Nicholas shuddered to think of his brother ruling the entire kingdom, but could *he* do any better? He felt sorely ill-equipped for such a task.

"I know this is much to take in, my lords, but we must leave immediately. Time is of the essence in this. Every day Trilaria remains without stability, it becomes more vulnerable."

Nicholas jolted himself from his troubled thoughts and stepped forward. He would worry about the logistics, even consequences, of becoming king later. Right now, he must focus on doing all he could to protect and serve his kingdom. "I will inform our stepmother and sister. Mericus, can you please instruct the servants to help us pack as quickly as possible?"

Blessedly, his brother nodded without comment and left to do as asked. Nicholas hurried down the dais steps to stand before Lord Raynard, clasping arms with him. "We shall do our duty to the kingdom and respect whatever decision the Council makes. My family and I will be ready to leave by midday."

Chapter 7

Adelaide

HOW MUCH MORE DEATH WOULD I WITNESS?

I turned away from the sight of the deceased young girl being hauled away like rubbish. My stomach churned, threatening to dislodge the porridge I ate earlier that morning. *God, when will this end?*

Nearly a fortnight had passed since Ophelia's leaving and my fervent vow to Nerissa, and today made a sennight since I managed to convince my mother-in-law, and the elite Royal Guard, to allow me to leave the palace grounds and serve the people of Valen.

Since both Nerissa and I had already survived from the plague, I did not fear catching the disease again or spreading it to her. Our people had languished too long without comfort or support from their rulers. I might not be queen, and I knew many saw my actions as scandalous, but... I could do–I *had* to do something.

So for the last seven days, I spent a few hours each morning offering comfort to the sick and dying. Many refused my help, saying a princess should not concern herself with their ilk, yet just as many received my care with gratitude. I visited bedsides and lifted prayers heavenward on their behalf. I held hands as too many passed through the veil between this world and the next.

The weight of it took a toll, more and more each day. Nightmares haunted my sleep, and even the smells were becoming too much to bear, regularly sending bile up my throat.

But I could not stop. I could not abandon these people now.

I could only keep working and pray for our deliverance.

"Your Highness, are you quite well?" A young woman with her

hair tied up beneath a faded scarf and stains marring her patched clothing stared up at me.

"Yes, quite." I waved a dismissive hand, hoping she would let the matter rest.

"You look rather pale, Princess Adelaide. I hope you are not overtaxing yourself. We would never forgive ourselves if something happened to you on our account."

Her genuine concern made my heart swell, but I would not allow any of these people to treat me as though I were made of glass. My mother's famous resilience also coursed through my veins. From a tender age, she instilled in me compassion for the peasants of our kingdom, and a willingness to serve in even the lowliest capacities.

"I assure you; I am well. You need not worry. I should be heading home now, however. Queen Nerissa will be expecting me back by dinner."

She nodded, acquiescing, yet doubt still lurked in her eyes. "Of course, Your Highness. God bless you for your kindness toward us."

I reached out to gently squeeze her arm, offering a warm smile before I left the darkly lit home. The spring sunlight stung my eyes after so long in the shadows. The sound of mourners rang across the city–a near constant dirge these days–and the scents of sickness and death, combined with the usual stench of waste, made the air nearly unbearable. I resisted the urge to press the corner of my linen veil over my nose and mouth. Instead, I clutched my hands in the skirt of my plain linen mourning gown, lifting it from the filth littering the street.

"Are you ready to return home, Your Highness?" My trio of personal guards fell into step around me. They were part of the King's Guard—Trilaria's fiercest and best trained men who protected the royal family—and had become my loyal companions over the last three years.

"Yes, Sir Arthur. Her Majesty will be expecting me soon." Though Nerissa consented to me leaving the palace grounds each day, she grew too anxious if I was gone longer than a couple hours. As much as I wished I could stay longer and do more for the people, I also had no wish to cause my mother-in-law any more distress than necessary.

We reached the palace gates a short time later. Sir Arthur, the head of my personal protectors, called up to the gatekeeper, informing him of our identity. In moments, the towering wooden gates creaked open to allow us entrance.

Inside the protective walls, the courtyard buzzed with more activity than I had seen in months. Servants worked like a hive of bees around the royal carriage and a small wagon parked in front of the palace's main entrance, unloading it of several trunks.

My heart tripped into an anxious beat. Lord Raynard left several days ago in order to bring back King Wesley's second younger brother, Prince William—the man who would become our new king. The man who would decide my and Nerissa's fate.

Apparently, the royal councilman's mission was successful, and our new ruler had just arrived.

Leaving my guards, I rushed past the busy servants and into the palace. Had Nerissa heard this news yet?

Breathless, I reached Nerissa's chamber and knocked on the door. At her soft response to enter, I opened the door and slipped inside. "Mother, Lord Raynard has just arrived! It appears he was successful in bringing back Prince William."

The queen bolted out of her chair, her embroidery project tumbling to the floor. "Are you certain? Did you speak with Lord Raynard directly?"

"Nay, not yet. But the carriage is in the courtyard and servants are busy unloading trunks, enough for several people." I crossed the room to her, pulling the veil from off my hair as I went.

Nerissa's face paled and she slowly sunk back into her chair beside the window. "It seems we shall soon learn our fate."

I knelt before her, clasping her hands. They trembled slightly within my hold. "Your brother-in-law is a good man, is he not? Surely, he will be kind to us. Mayhap he will even let us stay."

"I do hope you are right, my dear."

A knock sounded at the door, sending my gaze over my shoulder. Abigail, who had been standing like a silent shadow across the room, moved to answer it.

A servant girl stood outside. She curtseyed quickly before launching into her message. "Lord Raynard asked me to inform the princess and queen that there shall be a supper in the Banquet Hall this evening, to welcome our guests from Aguilar."

I squeezed Nerissa's hands and stood, answering for the both of us. "We will be there. Thank you for telling us."

The girl bobbed another curtsey before scurrying away. It would be strange to sup in the Banquet Hall again after so many weeks of dining on simple fare in our private chambers. 'Twould feel almost... disrespectful to return to grand communal meals when we all just lost so much.

Yet whether we liked it or not, normal life would have to resume eventually. Except, life would never be *normal* again, would it? At least, not as we had known it before. We would have to find a new type of normal, for the changes wrought could never be undone. And, with the arrival of the man who held our fate in his hands... it seemed the changes were far from over.

Nicholas

"Lord Nicholas, Lord Mericus. 'Tis an honor to have you both here with us." Lord Harold—the last of the seventh councilmen to greet them upon entering the Banquet Hall—bowed to Nicholas and then his brother.

"'Tis a pleasure to be here. We only wish it were under more happy circumstances. Our hearts are grieved by the loss of so many of our kinsmen."

Lord Harold bowed his head in sorrow. "Too true, Lord Nicholas. Too true."

When the man walked away, Lord Raynard approached. "I have spoken with my fellow councilmen and they agreed to my suggestion on how to proceed. We will interview and observe you both throughout the next week in order to determine which of you," he nodded between the twins, "would be best suited as king."

"We are at the service of the Council and the kingdom, my lord." Mericus bowed regally. "And we shall patiently await whatever decision you make." That eager gleam again shone in Mericus' eyes.

Nicholas clenched his hands behind his back. Would the

Council discern his brother's true motives, or would they be blinded by his guile and charm?

"Thank you, Lord Mericus." Lord Raynard smiled amiably before turning to speak with one of the other Council members.

"You look as taut as a bow string, Nicholas." Lady Clarice stepped close to his side, pitching her voice so only he could hear. The humor in her words were plain. "Do relax."

He smiled and rolled his shoulders. "Forgive me, Stepmother. It has been too long since I had occasion to be in the capital. And I certainly never thought to be here as a potential *king*."

She patted his shoulder in a rare physical show of affection toward him. "Fret not. You are the clear choice–in my mind, anyway. And if you are chosen, you will make an excellent king."

Nicholas opened his mouth to respond, but what could he say? Words would not come. He settled instead for placing his hand over the one still resting on his shoulder.

The doors to the Banquet Hall suddenly opened, drawing every eye. Queen Nerissa entered, graceful and poised as always, even in her white mourning garb. Behind her trailed a young woman. Her own mourning gown swished across the floor behind her, a filmy veil fluttering over her hair as she walked. She carried herself exquisitely, spine straight, shoulders back, chin up, yet without an air of pride.

Was that Princess Adelaide? Or Princess Ophelia? Nicholas had been abroad when Prince Carac married his foreign bride, so he had yet to see what the woman looked like. Nicholas *had* been present at the marriage of his cousin and Princess Adelaide in Caelrith, Acuniel, and journeyed to Valen for court a time or two since, but… the princess of his memory did not match what was before him now.

Was it possible the young woman had changed so much since he last saw her? Or was it only the stark mourning attire that made her unrecognizable?

"Stepmother?" He leaned in to address her, keeping his voice low and his eyes on the lovely young woman. "Who is the lady with Queen Nerissa?"

"Why, that is Princess Adelaide, poor Prince Miles' widow! Do you not recognize her?" Lady Clarice clicked her tongue in sympathy. "I do feel sorry for the girl. They were married three years, and yet she never bore the prince a child."

"I would not exactly count that as a mark against her, Stepmother."

He glanced over in time to see her shrug, though the gesture was so slight only he could notice it. Shrugging would be considered unladylike, and the woman was nothing if not the epitome of ladylike behavior. "Unfortunately for the princess, many would not agree with you."

"Lord Mericus, Lord Nicholas. May I present to you her Majesty, our dear Queen Nerissa."

Nicholas turned at the sound of Lord Raynard's voice. The councilman motioned toward the queen, waiting for him and his brother with expectant eyes. They stepped forward simultaneously and offered deep bows.

Technically, one could say the queen was no longer the *queen* since the death of her husband and sons, but for the woman's sake, Nicholas was grateful the title was still used as a courtesy for now.

"Your Majesty, it is an honor to see you again," the brothers said, almost in sync.

Nicholas made sure to reach for the queen's hand first, pressing a kiss to her cold fingers. "Please accept my sincere condolences for the loss of His Majesty, King Wesley. He was a good and noble king that we shall all greatly miss."

"Thank you, Nicholas. My, it has been so long since I last saw you–and your twin." The queen transferred her hand to Mericus' hold, accepting his kiss as well. Then her brow furrowed in apparent confusion. "I must confess... I expected to see your father here."

Ah… So she had not yet heard the news.

Mericus cleared his throat and stepped in to supply an explanation. "I regret to inform you our father has died of the plague as well, Your Majesty. My brother and I are next in the line of succession, and it appears *one* of us shall be chosen to take the throne." Nicholas did not miss his brother's sidelong glance and that emphasis on "*one*".

The queen's eyes widened. Her already too-pale face blanched further. "Oh my… I see. What a situation this is. I am so grieved to hear about your father. He was a good man, and always so kind to me."

She pulled her hand away and stepped back, allowing Nicholas his first clear view of the princess.

He was first struck by the startling blue of her eyes, which flitted between the brothers for a moment before coming to rest squarely on Nicholas' face. His breath hitched. Never had he seen such beautiful eyes in all his life. The color of the pale blue beryl wedding ring his mother wore

Then he noted her height–taller than most women, including the queen by several inches. Instead of seeming dwarfed beside Nicholas, she had only to tip her chin to see him eye to eye. It made her seem even more regal, her movements as smooth and elegant as a stately willow.

And her face... The lines of her cheeks and nose were softly angled, her lips full and wide. Her hair was so dark it appeared almost black, much like his own.

How did he not remember meeting her before?

Mayhap he had not bothered to remember her because she had been his cousin's bride...

Completely unattainable.

"My lords, this is Princess Adelaide, widow of our dearly departed Crown Prince Miles."

The princess stepped forward at the introduction from Lord Raynard, offering a smooth curtsey.

Blasted Mericus stepped forward before Nicholas could gather his wits. "Your Highness, 'tis a pleasure to see you again." Apparently, his brother had no trouble remembering her. "I am grieved to hear of your husband's passing."

"Thank you, my lord." Her voice sounded soft and sweet, with an underlying husky warmth that was soothing to the ear.

"Princess Adelaide." He stepped forward as soon as his brother released her, gently taking her hand and bowing over it. He lifted his eyes to her face and kissed her knuckles. His breath hitched again. Why on earth was he so shaken by this young woman? Could she see the effect she was having on him as she observed his face just now? *Lord, let it not be so!*

"I, too, was most grieved to learn of Prince Miles' passing. How I wish he were here right now, and we were not."

Her brows arched at that. Did she find the pronouncement an indicator of his lack of interest in the throne? Or as the sincere statement of sympathy he intended it to be?

"I thank you, Lord... Nicholas, was it?"

He released her hand and straightened. "Yes, Your Highness. At your service."

"Lord Nicholas, your sympathy is much appreciated." Her mouth lifted in the smallest, but sincerest, of smiles, revealing an endearing crease beside her mouth.

"Shall we be seated? The servants should be here any moment with the meal."

Nicholas did not bother to note who had spoken. Instead, he simply offered his arm to the princess. "May I?"

She dipped her chin and placed her hand in the crook of his arm. He could feel every touch of her fingertips through his sleeve. Nicholas inwardly growled at himself. What sort of wretched man was he, to be so attracted to a woman only recently widowed? 'Twas unseemly.

Lord Raynard, who took the role of host this evening in absence of the king, indicated the chair Princess Adelaide was to take, next to the queen. "And you, Lord Nicholas, why do you not sit there beside her? Lord Mericus—you, Lady Clarice, and Lady Eleanor may sit there across from them."

Nicholas pulled out the princess' chair and pushed it in for her once she sat. He took his place at her left, unsure whether to be elated or dismayed at the seating arrangement.

Princess Adelaide turned to the queen on her other side. "Are you comfortable, Mother?"

His aunt patted the princess' hand. "Oh, yes, my dear. Fret not about me."

Nicholas felt his mouth twitch up, finding the interchange endearing. Was the princess always so concerned for others?

Servants appeared with the promised evening meal, spreading a collection of roasted ducks covered in a dark sauce, bowls of preserved figs and roasted, spiced vegetables, and stale bread trenchers across the table. Nicholas took a trencher, passing it to the princess before beginning to fill one of his own.

"Like Her Majesty, I was shocked to learn it was you and your brother that Lord Raynard brought back from Aguilar." The princess placed a portion of duck on her trencher. "How ever shall they decide who will take the throne?"

"No one could be more shocked than I to be here, Your Highness. I assure you. And apparently they shall interview and observe us for a sennight to decide who they feel is most equipped for the role."

"I see." Her beautiful eyes turned sad. "I am sorry to hear of your father's death... I have not lost my own father, but I do understand the feeling of loss." From the way she carried herself, it was clear Adelaide was a strong and graceful woman. But for all her strength, sorrow hung about her like a burial shroud. She had seen too much death of late. Too much heartache.

He could relate... More well than he would like.

Nicholas lost only one relative to this plague, not three as she had, but he knew not how he would ever recover from his father's death. The unraveling of his emotions had culminated in a tearful moment in the privacy of his chamber back in Aguilar, but the throbbing ache remained, deep down. Would it ever go away?

"Thank you, Princess. These are dark times, are they not?"

"They are, indeed..." Her eyes lowered, dark lashes fanning against her cheeks. When she lifted them again, he saw the glimmer of tears in her eyes.

"I understand Prince Carac married shortly before the start of the plague, yet I do not see his wife here. I do hope she is well."

Now the sorrow glistening in her eyes morphed into a spark of fire. "My sister-in-law is quite well—as far as I know, anyway. She was the only one of our family not to fall ill. She decided to return home to Galiel nearly a fortnight ago."

"Oh. I see... And that irritates you?"

She looked at him in surprise. "Am I so transparent?" She sighed, wiping her fingers on the table linen and pitching her voice lower, for his ears alone. "I suppose I cannot blame her for being homesick—she had only been married to Carac a few months. But it still feels like a betrayal. A dishonor to her husband and his family."

"You have no desire to return to your family, even after all you have been through here?"

"Never." The sparks shot from her blue eyes, pinning him in his seat. She seemed to notice her shocking vehemence and flushed, looking away. "I will stay with my mother-in-law, no matter where she goes. I am all she has left… She needs me, whether she is willing to admit it or not."

He knew not whether to gape or smile at the princess. Such passion for those she loved… He could well relate to that. "'Twas that very same passion which had driven him home, and then pushed him to come here. And it was what would *keep* him here, even if he found himself sitting on a throne he had never wanted.

"Your dedication is commendable, Your Highness. The queen is blessed to have you."

Her blue eyes slanted to meet his gaze. A man could get lost in such eyes…

"Thank you for your kind words, Lord Nicholas." Again, she spoke only loud enough for him to hear.

He resisted the desire to lean in close, settling instead for what he hoped was a friendly smile. "You are most welcome, Princess."

Chapter 8

Adelaide

April 6th

Dear Mother,

A king has been found at last. Or rather, two potential kings. It turns out Miles has twin cousins, from his father's second brother, Prince William. The twins are next in the line of succession and one shall take the throne while the other inherits Prince William's property and title as Duke of Aguilar.

I PAUSED IN MY WRITING, MOVING TO DIP MY QUILL IN the inkwell on my desk. I finally returned to my own chamber last night–at Nerissa's insistence. It was both a relief and a torment to be back in my old surroundings, the rooms once occupied by Miles and myself.

The dark, intense eyes and stubbled jaw of Lord Nicholas flashed in my mind. Our conversation over the evening meal had been both pleasant and surprisingly comfortable, even if we had touched on painful subjects at first.

The Lords Mericus and Nicholas may be twins, but one would never guess it. They were so different, in mannerisms and build. Only their hair and eyes were identical. I would call both men handsome, but Lord Nicholas… He was unnerving in his masculine beauty.

Miles had been handsome… but not like that.

I winced, shaking my head. Placing a palm to my forehead as if to push such traitorous thoughts from my mind. My husband had been gone only a few weeks. How could I even entertain the idea of another man so soon?

Tears of shame surged in my eyes. Miles deserved better than this. He deserved to be missed and properly mourned. Not forgotten. Not by anyone, but especially not by me.

> *I have had the opportunity to converse with Lord Nicholas, but have said little to his brother thus far. It remains to be seen which of the two would be best suited for the role of king. I can only pray for God's will to be done and that the right man will be crowned. I trust you and Father shall do the same.*
>
> *With all my love,*
> *Adelaide*

After blotting the neat script lining the page, I folded and rolled the letter until it was small enough to fit within a pigeon's carrying case. I would take the missive up to the aviary in one of the palace towers before leaving for my daily trip into Valen.

Catching my reflection in my long looking glass, I smiled in amusement at the picture I made. In my simple gown and wimple, I looked more peasant than princess. Minus the white color, were these the sort of clothes Mother wore before she married Father and became queen? I would have liked to have seen her back then.

Exiting my chamber, letter in hand, I made my way to the nearest stairwell. Footsteps thudded fast behind me, coming around the curve of the stairs. I startled, stepping closer to the wall just as a large figure barreled around the corner, nearly colliding with me.

"Oh, I beg your pardon," said an equally startled male voice.

I looked up and found myself face to face with the man who had been assaulting my thoughts since the previous evening. "Oh. Lord Nicholas."

"Your Highness?" His black brows shot high. "Forgive me. I did not recognize you." He chuckled, the deep sound rumbling off the walls of the stairwell. "I thought you were a serving maid."

Suddenly self-conscious, my hand drifted to the scarf hiding my hair. "Pardon my appearance, my lord. I go into the city each morning to help care for the sick."

His brows raised further still, if that were possible. "Is that not dangerous, Your Highness?"

I shifted away from him, feeling my defenses rising. "I am not so foolish as to take unnecessary risks, my lord. I have already suffered through the plague and, fortunately, recovered quite easily. I do not fear catching it a second time, and I benefit no one by cloistering myself in my chamber doing nothing. Our people are suffering and dying in droves. Why not help them in whatever way I am able, however small it may be?"

He crossed his arms, a strange expression on his face. Was it curiosity? Wonder? Puzzlement? A mix of all three?

"Your passion and generosity do you credit, Princess. I said your mother-in-law was blessed to have you, but truly it is all the people of Trilaria who should count themselves fortunate."

My heart warmed at his praise, though I had no real need for his validation.

"I would happily accompany you, if I could. But it seems I am forbidden to leave the palace for the foreseeable future." His voice and expression rang with annoyance. "Neither my brother nor I have had the plague yet, and the Council wishes to protect us if possible."

"Understandable, my lord. If you will excuse me, I should be going."

"Of course." He bowed and I curtseyed in turn before resuming my trek down the stairs. Lord Nicholas' steps continued behind me, bound on some unknown mission of his own, and that traitorous part inside me wished he would defy orders and accompany me after all...

Nicholas

Nicholas shifted his weight from side to side, trying to ease the strain on his feet without calling too much attention to how uncomfortable he felt standing before the Royal Council. The eight remaining councilmen—two had died of the plague thus far—sat in their throne-like chairs on either side of him. They questioned him on his education, home life, and more for nearly an hour. He never considered himself shy, but standing before eight pairs of critical eyes belonging to the men who held his entire future in their hands... it was hard *not* to squirm.

He would have much rather spent the morning tending the sick with Princess Adelaide.

"And lastly, Lord Nicholas, do *you* believe yourself qualified and equipped to be King of Trilaria?"

Nicholas tucked his chin, hands behind his back. There was no need to rush his response. Such a question deserved careful consideration, especially if he wanted to give the best answer possible.

After several moments, he lifted his face and said, "I never once considered the possibility of being king. I did, however, spend the last sixteen years knowing that leading the Duchy of Aguilar was a possibility. Because of this, I made sure I learned all I could from my father about leadership. In fact, I observed the example he set in *all* areas of his life.

"I do not profess to be a perfect man by any means, and I would not claim to be a perfect king, or even a perfect candidate for the role. But... I love my kingdom and my people. I love my family." He paused, looking each man in the eye. "I never desired a position of power for the sake of power itself. Instead, I would gladly ascend the throne of Trilaria if it meant my reign would benefit the kingdom at large. I will gladly serve, protect, and even fight for the people I love."

Silence echoed in the meeting chamber. Had he said something amiss? Or was the silence a good sign?

Nicholas bowed his head in deference to the Council, awaiting their response or dismissal.

Finally, Lord Raynard spoke up. "Thank you for your time and your words, Lord Nicholas. You may be excused."

He nodded and slowly turned on his heel, exiting through the meeting chamber's double doors. He remained unsure how to feel about the Council's lack of response, though what more could he have said about his qualifications while still remaining open and honest?

Nicholas had spoken from his heart... He only hoped it was enough to save Trilaria from his brother.

Adelaide

Exhaustion pulled at my limbs. The morning visiting the sick had been a particularly difficult one. I witnessed two more deaths—an old woman and a young boy. The plague cared not for things such as social status, age, or gender. Nay… Death lay waiting without partiality.

The nausea that began my mornings as I served the city, now plagued me throughout the day. I barely ate any of the delicious supper laid out in the Banquet Hall this evening, and my discomfort dimmed even my enjoyment of Lord Nicholas' amiable conversation.

Finally, with the meal at its end, I could retire to my room without causing a scene by an early departure. I pushed up from my chair, pulling at my long skirts to not trip over them as I left the table and headed for the door.

"Your Highness?"

I paused, surprised by the sound of Lord Nicholas' voice. Stifling a sigh, I turned and found him approaching. His sister, a beautiful blonde and blue-eyed girl of fourteen, walked close at his side. "I understand if you are too tired, after your busy morning," he raised a meaningful brow, "but I promised my sister a game this evening and wondered if you care to join us? My brother has agreed to join as well."

The earnest look on his face and the eagerness peeking from behind his sister's usual forlorn expression squeezed my heart. Praise be to God that my father still lived, but the very thought of losing him… I could well imagine the dear girl's pain.

How could I say nay?

I pushed out a smile. "Certainly. I would be happy to join you."

"I promise not to keep you up too late." Lord Nicholas smiled. Why must the expression highlight the lines of his face to such advantage?

He offered me his arm and we made our way up to the suite

of chambers currently occupied by his family. In their cozy sitting room, lit by the glow of a low fire and several candles, the siblings and I sat around a table.

"I asked one of the servants if the palace had any games stored away somewhere, and they were kind enough to bring these to me," said Lady Eleanor. "We have chess, draughts, backgammon, and Fox and Geese."

"I will warn you, I am excessively skilled at both chess and draughts," I teased. "My father taught me how to play from the time I was a young girl."

"Oh, really?" Lord Nicholas narrowed his eyes at my good-natured boasting. "Mayhap we should play those then and test the truth of your claim."

"Nicholas is rubbish at chess," Lord Mericus muttered from his seat to my right, arms crossed over his broad chest.

"Not as rubbish at it as you are, Brother."

"Mericus and I can play draughts first, while you two play chess," Lady Eleanor's sweet voice chimed from across the table. "And then we can switch."

We all agreed, and the selected games were set up. My nausea still threatened to consume me, but I was determined to enjoy at least *this* part of my evening. How long had it been since I played a game of chess? Or any game, for that matter? Miles never much liked such past times.

Early into our game, it became clear Lord Mericus' statement about his twin's skill was correct. Lord Nicholas was losing miserably, but he put up a valiant fight.

"Ah… I would not do that if I were you." I gestured toward the poor move he was about to make.

"Are you attempting to trick me? Or are you actually helping me?" He narrowed his eyes, amusement curling the sides of his mouth.

I smirked and gave a dramatic shrug. My etiquette teacher would have been aghast at the unladylike gesture. "I suppose that is for you to determine, my lord."

"I win!" Lady Eleanor crowed, clapping her hands excitedly. "Now, as soon as Princess Adelaide puts Nicholas out of his misery, we can see if you have any better luck beating me at chess, Mericus."

I chuckled, glancing over at the taller, broader of the twin brothers, but he did not look nearly as amused as the rest of us. Instead, he watched Lord Nicholas with a dark gaze that left me uncomfortable. Even in my limited interactions with the pair, I noticed the tension between them. The animosity that roiled just below the surface, ready to erupt. Why were they so at odds?

Refocusing on the game, I made my next move. Lord Nicholas made his, and then it was my turn once more. I fought down a victorious smile when I cornered his king, ending the game. "Checkmate, my lord."

Lord Nicholas sighed ruefully, sitting back and clapping his hands against his thighs. "At least you are a more gracious winner than Eleanor."

I laughed, my first true laugh in far too long. 'Twas like a breath of fresh air to my lungs.

We sent a servant for drinks—ale for the men, rose water for Lady Eleanor and myself—and then switched games, with Lord Nicholas and I battling each other in draughts, while the other two siblings played chess. I won, again. But, to his credit, Lord Nicholas did not seem to mind. He laughed heartily at his defeat and bowed to me in deference. "You spoke true, Princess. You are *excessively* skilled in both games. But mayhap, with practice, I shall become as skilled as you?"

I accepted his praise with a flourish of my hand. "Thank you, my lord. And mayhap, with practice, you can become at least *half* as skilled."

He laughed again, a merry sound that made his eyes squint and crinkle at the corners.

It flooded me with warmth that pushed away all thought of my churning stomach.

Abruptly, I pushed up from the table. These reactions to this man were far too unsettling. They could not be proper. I should not enjoy his company so much, so soon after losing Miles.

"I should be going. I usually sit with the queen for a time before we retire, and she will be expecting me." In truth, my mother-in-law had likely already gone to sleep by now, forgoing our usual routine, but it was as good an excuse as any.

The twin lords stood, offering bows. "Goodnight, Princess Adelaide," said Lord Mericus. "Thank you for honoring us with your company."

I glanced back at Lord Nicholas before I reached the door. "The honor is mine, I assure you." Then I slipped out into the corridor and all but ran to my chamber.

Chapter 9

Nicholas

FEW THINGS BROUGHT NICHOLAS MORE PLEASURE than the written word. Over supper that evening, Princess Adelaide spoke of the palace's extensive library, which she said included an excellent copy of *The History of the Kings of Britain*. He heard the book contained accounts of the legendary King Arthur and his kingdom of Camelot, and he was eager to read them. No matter whether the stories were fact or merely lore, they had always fascinated him.

Nicholas found the library easily enough, using the directions Princess Adelaide provided, and pushed open the door. His momentary enjoyment of the scent of dusty parchment and leather was ruined by a female scream across the room. He jumped to attention, hand instinctively going to the silver dagger he kept on his hip.

Mericus had a young maidservant pinned against the large desk that occupied the room's center. He whirled at the sound of Nicholas' entry, but not before Nicholas saw the way he groped the woman and the disheveled state of her clothing.

"Mericus! By all that is holy, what are you doing?" Nicholas charged across the library. He grabbed his brother by the front of his tunic and wrenched him away from the servant. The young woman screamed again, leaping back from the brothers, and hastened to secure the loosened ties on the front of her bodice.

"What I do is none of your business." Mericus jerked out of Nicholas' hold. "Besides, I was not taking anything she was not willing to give."

Nicholas' fists curled tight. He cast a probing look at the maiden, whose eyes glistened with tears, her cheeks blazing red. At first glance, he had assumed Mericus aimed to take the woman against her will. But what if his brother was telling the truth, and the encounter was consensual—though still a sin in the eyes of God? 'Twas hard to tell by looking at the servant girl.

"Either way, you know Father never stood for such behavior in his home."

Mericus scoffed. "But Father is not here, is he?" The question was a punch in Nicholas' gut. "And you are neither my lord nor my king to tell me what I can and cannot do. I make my own rules, and I shall continue to do so as king."

Nicholas stepped toe-to-toe with his brother. "What makes you so certain you *will* be king?"

Mericus stared down at him, pure hatred burning in his eyes and radiating through the tense silence. Finally, he glanced at the cowering serving maid. "Be gone. We are finished here."

The girl kept her eyes averted, her face now white as milk, but she nodded and turned to leave. Nicholas watched her go, feeling certain Mericus was lying, and that he had narrowly saved the poor maiden from a horrible ordeal.

Disgust roiled in Nicholas' gut. The Council should know about this. Yet Nicholas had no proof of Mericus' attempted assault, only his own suppositions. Would they even believe him without any evidence? Not all men felt the way he did about such matters. The councilmen might all be Godly men who detested such behavior as much as Nicholas… or they may not be.

There was also Mericus' attempted treachery back in Aguilar to consider. Nicholas wanted to tell the Council, and with his step-mother's testimony as supporting evidence, that claim would be easier to prove. But Mericus would certainly deny any of these accusations leveled against him—*adamantly*. What if they believed Nicholas' claims were nothing but lies told in a greedy effort to win the throne? Would sharing this information only serve to discredit *him* instead of Mericus?

There were three days left until the Council announced their decision about the kingship. Mayhap he should wait, keep a closer eye on his brother, and think about how to proceed.

Once the library door closed behind the maid, Mericus leaned close to Nicholas' face. "You had better mind your own business from now on, Nicholas. And stay out of my way." Then he shoved past Nicholas and followed the girl out the door.

Nicholas sighed and leaned against the library desk. He had no stomach for reading anything now, so the book on Britain's kings would have to wait for another night.

I should have found the book after all...

At least then he would have something to do besides toss and turn all night.

Nicholas huffed, tossing off the bedclothes. Despite the spring chill outside, it was still too hot in his chamber. Sweat slicked his torso, keeping him from finding comfort in his bed, and it did not help that thoughts of his brother and the maidservant still plagued his mind.

He sat on the edge of the feather-stuffed mattress, raking his fingers through his sweat-dampened curls. Mayhap a time of prayer, away from this stifling chamber, would help settle his mind and body. He noticed the location of the chapel earlier in the week. It should be empty this time of night, and surely no one would mind him being there.

Nicholas dressed quickly, tossing on a simple pair of hose, a long, loose tunic, and his favorite worn pair of boots. He certainly looked nothing like a king at the moment.

The thought led him to another—the image of Princess Adelaide in her simple linen gown and wimple that caused him to mistake her for a servant. He smiled at the reminder of the passion flashing in her eyes as she defended her actions.

Eerie silence lay over the palace when Nicholas exited his room. All torches and candles sat dormant, leaving the palace in a blackness as dark as pitch. If not for the small candle Nicholas lit and carried with him from his chamber, he would be walking blind.

Finding the chapel proved harder than he expected, due to the dark obscuring his sense of direction in the veritable maze of corridors. But at last, his hand pulled open the heavy chapel door on creaking hinges.

A startled squeak from within almost made him drop his candle. "By all the–Princess Adelaide?"

Several candles illuminated the altar area, and there, at the altar rail, stood Princess Adelaide, one hand clutched over her chest. "Oh, Lord Nicholas, 'tis you." She gasped out a breath of relief, posture sagging. "You frightened me."

How many times in one day would he walk into a room and find an unexpected occupant?

"My apologies." Nicholas glanced behind him. He should not be alone with her in the dead of night. Oh, the scandal they would face if someone found them. "I ought to go..."

"Please, do not leave on my account. I was nearly finished anyway. I will leave." She took up a candle and started down the middle aisle between the wooden pews. That was when he noticed her attire… A dressing gown over what appeared to be a white linen nightdress. And her hair–every dark and glorious inch of it–fell unfettered behind her back all the way to her thighs.

Nicholas cleared his throat and glanced away.

But she stopped before him in the doorway, forcing his attention back to her. The combined light of their candles glinted in her blue eyes and made them sparkle like the gems they resembled. "You are awake awfully late, Princess."

"I could say the same of you, my lord," she quipped, arching a brow.

"True." He nodded in concession to her point. "I assume you are like me and unable to sleep?"

She looked down then, a stray lock of hair slipping forward over her shoulder. Shadows from their candles danced across her face. "I have always been one to stay up late, but recently…" She looked back up and glanced around, as if checking to ensure they were truly alone. Seeming satisfied with their solitude, she turned back to him, an earnest, vulnerable expression overtaking her face. "I have been having night terrors… about the plague. The people I have seen die. My husband… I awaken and often have trouble going back to sleep."

His heart reached out to hers. He barely knew this woman, yet he got the sense that she did not share such personal details often.

From what he observed of her in the past few days, she kept her true emotions and internal struggles close to her chest, likely only sharing them with a certain few, and only in certain moments. Much like himself.

What an honor it was to be among the few to whom she chose to confide one of her struggles.

If only there were something he could do to soothe her mind... But he could not even seem to settle his own.

"Death... It can haunt the mind of even the strongest people, Your Highness." His fingers ached to reach out and rest on her shoulder or arm, to offer some sort of comfort. But this encounter was already inappropriate enough without adding *touches* to the mix. "I will pray for you this night, that you may find rest."

The anxiety in her face softened. Her shoulders relaxed. "Thank you, my lord. You are... most kind."

The simple words did such complex things to his heart. "And you are most welcome."

"Goodnight, Lord Nicholas." She bobbed a curtsey that seemed ridiculous in this setting. "I shall see you on the morrow."

"Goodnight, Princess."

She slipped past him then, the flowing fabric of her dressing gown brushing his legs as she passed. He remained rooted in the doorway, watching her form and the flickering light of her candle until both disappeared from view.

Chapter 10

Adelaide

"YOU KNOW, YOU REMIND ME OF MY LITTLE SISTER. HER name is Tillie." I brushed the cool, damp rag across the young girl's forehead. "Well, her name is actually Matilda, after my grandmother, but we call her Tillie for short."

The girl smiled weakly, her dark-circled eyes crinkling at the corners. "Is she a princess too?"

"She is. Do you know why you remind me of her?"

The girl shook her head.

"Well, she has beautiful, chestnut hair like yours. And a smile that lights up the room, just as yours does. She is very kind and brave, also like you." I smoothed the rag down the girl's cheek, love and longing for my sister swelling in my heart. "And you know what else? When she was a few years younger than you, she got very sick. We were all so afraid, but Tillie was strong, and she fought hard to get well. And you know what happened?"

Again, the girl shook her head.

"She recovered, and she is even now living with my family in Acuniel, happy and healthy. In fact, she is so strong that she often trains in weapons alongside my brothers." I patted her cheek. "*You* will get well and be strong and healthy, too. Just you see." *Lord, let it be so. Let this sweet child live. Please… So many have been lost already.*

The girl's countenance lifted, the light of hope filling her eyes.

I could not stand to look at it a moment longer. I turned away–too quickly, it seemed, for my head swam and my stomach lurched. My hand clutched my middle. Sweat beaded on my face. *Not again!*

I rushed outside, into the street, but the scent of refuse and animal dung did nothing to help the nausea. My stomach roiled.

I braced a hand against the house, bent over, and wretched.

"Your Highness?" Sir Arthur was at my side then, concern lacing his tone. "That is the third time you have been ill since we left this morn. Are you certain you are well?"

Why must I have witnesses to my humiliation? My insides heaved again, and it was all I could do to force the bile back down. *God in Heaven, help me.*

I batted a dismissive hand at Sir Arthur once the wave of sickness passed. "Yes, I am well. Prithee, do not trouble yourself over me."

"But Your Highness, I really think you should—"

I pushed myself upright, indignation flaring. "I *said*, I am well." The world swam, swirling and twisting in my vision. My knees grew weak, and I had to catch myself on the wall to keep from falling.

"Your Highness!" Sir Arthur steadied me, putting an arm around my shoulders. "I knew you were not well. You have been pushing yourself too hard. The queen will have my head if something happens to you on my watch."

"I shall deal with the queen." My legs trembled like those of a newborn calf. Mayhap I was *not* so well after all.

"We are going home. Now." Sir Arthur swept me into his arms without waiting for permission. The sudden movement almost sent me vomiting again. Giving in to his insistence, I settled my head against his shoulder while he called for the other two guards.

My faithful protectors escorted me back to the palace as quickly, and yet as comfortably, as possible, regularly checking to make certain I was alright. I could only offer them reassuring nods, for suddenly, all I wanted was to be lying perfectly still on my bed.

When we at last reached the palace, the guards took me through the servants' passages to my chamber, to avoid notice. There was no need to cause an uproar over my condition just yet. More than likely, I was only overtaxed by the events of the past weeks, and a long, dreamless rest would restore me to rights.

My guards deposited me in bed, and before I could instruct

them otherwise, they called for both my maid–who blessedly re-covered from the plague–and Nerissa. Both women arrived at the same time several minutes later.

"Adie! What has happened?" The queen sank beside me and clutched my hand. "Gretta, bring a cold cloth and some water for her to drink."

"I am well, Mother. Only exhausted. I just need to rest."

Sir Arthur stepped forward–the meddling man. "Pardon me, Your Majesty. Ordinarily, I would not intrude, but… Her High-ness has been ill all morning, and after her last episode, she sud-denly grew weak and almost collapsed. I thought it best we bring her home straightaway."

I frowned at the knight, but knew he was only doing his job–protecting me no matter the cost. Even if the cost was my ire.

"Thank you, Sir Arthur. You were wise insisting she come home. Please, call for the royal physician straightaway."

I tried to sit up and protest the queen's words, but she stopped me with a firm hand to my shoulder. "Nay, Adelaide. You are going to rest, and a physician *is* going to examine you. I shall not have something happen to you because of your own stubbornness."

Deflating, I sagged against the pillows and nodded silently.

My mother-in-law made me drink a full cup of water brought to her by Gretta, and then she washed my face with a damp rag. I did not relish being, in turns, coddled and scolded like a child, but I understood the love from whence Nerissa's actions sprang. And, in spite of my resistance, 'twas not long until her gentle ministra-tions soothed me into a blessedly peaceful sleep.

My nap lasted several hours, until shortly before supper. But the queen insisted I stay abed and take the meal in my room. Once I finished every scrap of food on my plate, which was a struggle considering the persistent nausea, she finally allowed the physician in to examine me.

The man poked and prodded me and asked questions for what seemed an eternity. Finally, he stepped away from me and now stood with his head bowed, expression thoughtful. His chin doubled when he tucked his head like that. "Your Highness, may I ask you how long it has been since your last monthly flow?"

The question took me by surprise and sent heat into my cheeks. "Well... I suppose the last one was about two months ago. In the early days of the plague." With the trauma and stress of the plague, I had scarcely given note to the fact that my flow had not come. "But my cycles have never been... perfectly regular. I have been late before."

The physician nodded. "I see..." After a few more thoughtful moments of silence, he nodded again, as if deciding something. "Your Highness, there is nothing *wrong* with you. Nothing that shall not resolve itself in a few months, at least. You are with child."

A wave of shock, like a wall of ice-cold water, crashed over me. My mouth opened and closed, trying to form some intelligible response, but nothing came.

The queen gripped my hand. Was it me that was trembling, or her? "Are you certain?"

"If the late monthly course was the princess' only symptom, then I would reserve my judgment for the time being. But she has all the other usual signs of a pregnancy, and I have tended enough expecting mothers in my time as a physician to feel certain about this. However, it is clear this pregnancy, combined with all the recent stress, is already taking a toll on the princess' health. She must rest and limit her physical exertion when possible."

Nerissa squeezed my fingers. "Thank you. The guards will escort you out. I trust you understand when I ask that you keep this knowledge to yourself for the time being."

The physician nodded. "Of course, Your Majesty. Upon my honor, not one word of it shall pass my lips outside of this chamber."

The queen led the physician to the door and instructed my guards to escort him home. Sir Arthur and his fellow King's Guards were no doubt curious to know the outcome of my examination, but they would never press for knowledge of it. They could be trusted not to spread rumors.

I sank deep into my pillows, waves of shock continuing to soak me. Three years of marriage to Miles, and no children... Three years of feeling like a disappointment to him and the kingdom, who expected me to produce an heir… Now at last, his child grew within my womb. But he would not be here to see it.

What a cruel twist of fate.

"My dear girl." Nerissa weighed down the mattress at my side, her arms wrapping around my shoulders. "Do you realize what this means?"

It meant my child would be fatherless. And that its father died never knowing that he even *was* a father.

"Adie, you could even now be carrying the *true* heir to the throne!"

Her words brought my chin up and finally loosened my tongue. "The true heir… If I have a son, then the throne would rightfully be his."

"Yes, my dear." The queen suddenly turned to my maid, who stood to the sidelines, her face mirroring our own shock. "Gretta, I entrust you shall not speak of this to anyone?"

She bobbed a curtsey. "Yes, my queen. You have my word."

"Very good." The queen turned back to me, taking my hands in both of hers. "If this child is a boy, then he would be the rightful heir. But Trilaria needs a king *now*. One of Prince William's sons must still be crowned."

The queen's eyes lowered, brow furrowing in thought. "With a child, especially one of such importance, 'tis more imperative than ever that your own position is secure. You must have protection, a guardian to care for you and the babe."

My shock-numbed mind struggled to keep up with her flow of thought. "What can we do?"

"If you were to marry the son who is crowned king, then he will be able to offer all the protection necessary, and your son will already be in perfect position to take his place as the true king when the time comes. However, the king must be one who is willing to set aside his own power in favor of your child…"

"You want me to *marry* Lord Nicholas or Lord Mericus?"

"Do you not see, my dear? This is the only way to redeem our family, to preserve the line of my husband and yours." Tears welled in my mother-in-law's eyes and hope brightened her features for the first time in weeks. "Mayhap the Lord has not abandoned us after all!"

I sat up straight, gripping her hands. She was right. If I wanted to preserve my husband's legacy, if I wanted to protect the throne of Trilaria… this was the only way. Yet so many questions spun in my mind, and waves of fear left me quaking.

"But Mother, we do not know which brother shall be king until the Council announces it on the morrow. Should we wait to speak up until then? And how do we know either of them will even have me?"

The queen's eyes grew thoughtful once more. She tapped her chin with a slender finger. "We need the *right* brother to be chosen as king. The one who would be willing to serve as regent for your son."

The faces of the twin brothers passed through my mind. I had not spent much time with either of them yet, not enough to truly *know* either man. But from what observation afforded me, Mericus did not seem the sort that would approve the idea of abdicating his throne to another man's son.

Lord Nicholas, on the other hand… His kind words to me, his offers of prayer and sympathy–it all seemed to point to a good heart. Would that heart be willing to sacrifice power for the sake of a child not his own?

"I have known the twins all their lives," said Nerissa. "Granted, it has been a few years since I spent time with them, but I have always known Nicholas to be the humbler of the two. He has always possessed a gentle and kind spirit. I am certain *he* is the one you must marry."

Her words affirmed my own thoughts about the man, but the very idea of marrying him tied my stomach in knots. "Do you believe he will have me? And what about the Council's decision? How shall we make certain they choose Nicholas?"

"We shall take the decision out of their hands."

I resisted the urge to laugh at my mother-in-law's statement. "And *how* do you propose we do that?"

She lifted my chin with her hand, her eyes intent and focused, though mischief twinkled deep within them. "Leave that to me and do *exactly* as I say."

Chapter II

Adelaide

THIS IS MADNESS. I PRESSED MY FOREHEAD AGAINST THE doorframe of Lord Nicholas' chamber door. One hand drifted down to rest on my stomach, which yet bore no visible sign of my pregnancy. I was about to gamble my reputation, my entire future, on the chance that the man on the other side of this door would consent to my shocking proposal and marry me. *Everything* hinged on the next few minutes and my powers of persuasion.

My mother had been forced to gamble everything to save her life, *my* unborn life, and both the kingdom of Acuniel *and* Trilaria. I would lead by her example and take this bold step... Risking it all for the sake of both Trilaria and this unborn child within me.

I squared my shoulders and smoothed the folds of my deep blue and emerald gown. Nerissa insisted I put aside my mourning garb for this mission and had Gretta dress me in one of my finest gowns, fashioned in the royal colors of Trilaria. My hair she instructed Gretta to brush and curl and then leave hanging down my back, with a thin golden circlet and flowing veil covering it. According to them, I was a vision of regality and patriotism to my kingdom, but all I felt was fear.

Putting my hand to the latch of Lord Nicholas' door, I prepared to push it open. Would he be asleep? The hour was late, drawing close to midnight, but I dearly hoped he was not yet in bed... With any luck, he would be awake and still *clothed.*

No turning back now, Adelaide.

With a deep breath, I pushed open the chamber door and strode inside.

A manly shout accompanied by the sound of a weapon leaving its sheath was my greeting.

"Who goes th—*Princess Adelaide?*" Lord Nicholas stood at the foot of his bed, body poised for attack, a silver knife held at the ready. But the knife slowly lowered as he took in my appearance.

I hurriedly shut the door behind me and crossed the room to him. Blessedly, he was still dressed, though it appeared I had caught him in the middle of preparing for bed. His embroidered surcoat and belt lay across the bed, his simple under-tunic and hose remaining. Much like the other night, when he happened upon me in the chapel.

"Princess Adelaide, what in heaven's name are you—"

"My lord!" I fell to my knees at his bare feet, bowing with my hands pressed against the floor. "I am your servant. Please, have mercy and hear my request."

He did not move, whether due to shock or a willingness to listen, I knew not. And I dared not look up to see. "I am in desperate need of your help, my lord."

"What is it?" His voice strained. With shock? Irritation? "Are you in danger? What can *I* possibly do?"

"I need you to marry me, and redeem the line of your cousin, Prince Miles."

"You need me to— *What* did you say?"

Now I forced my eyes to travel from his feet up to his face. Dancing firelight cast shadows on his face, obscuring some of his features, but his shock and confusion were evident.

"I said… I need you to marry me. I have discovered I carry the child of my husband, Prince Miles, and there is every chance that this child shall be a son and the true heir to the throne. My child deserves to continue the legacy of his father and grandfather and sit upon the throne of Trilaria. However, I know the kingdom needs a ruler now, and for the sake of my child, it must be one who is willing to serve as regent until my son can ascend the throne."

"This is madness." He reached down and gripped me by the arms, pulling me to my feet. "We do not even know if I will be chosen as king."

"If you announce your marriage to me, and the fact that I could be carrying Prince Miles' heir, the Council will have no choice *but* to choose you. They must honor my child's possible claim to the throne, and they must allow you to serve as the temporary king if you are already my husband.

"You see, we benefit each other in this, in more ways than one. With me as your wife, you are practically guaranteed the throne. Not to mention, you gain valuable knowledge to aid you, since I have trained all my life to be a ruler, though you have not." I paused to take a breath. "And with you as my husband, I can secure the future of both myself and my child."

My heart hammered in my chest, so loud that he *must* be able to hear it. Would he also hear my desperate plea? Would he join me in this mad scheme? Or cast me out of his room and into disgrace?

We both seemed to become aware of the fact that he still held my upper arms at the same moment. He glanced at where his hands gripped me and then let go, gaze moving to the closed door and back to me. "Have you any idea of the scandal you could cause with your actions this night?"

"Me alone with you in your chamber, in the dead of night?" Heat flushed my cheeks, but I refused to look away. "Yes, I am quite aware."

"And is that your goal? To corner me, through this compromising scenario, into a marriage with you?" Anger sparked in his eyes like the embers even now snapping in the fireplace.

"Nay. I will not force you to marry me. If you refuse me, I shall leave this room and accept whatever disgrace may come to me should this meeting be discovered. But I *am* boldly and desperately asking you to make me your wife..." I braced myself before uttering the word that could *really* send him running. "Tonight."

"*Tonight?*" He leapt back from me. "You propose we marry *now?* Tonight?"

I took a step forward, pleading. "If we wed this very night, we can approach the Council on the morrow and essentially remove the decision from their hands. Once we inform them of our marriage and the child I carry, they will have no choice but to choose you over your brother."

His eyes narrowed at me. "And why did you not approach Mericus with such a proposal?"

"Because I knew that if I were going to risk everything to make such an audacious plea, *you* were the one I would take the chance on. I have sensed the goodness of your heart and felt certain you would be the one most willing to sacrifice the crown for a son not your own."

I dared to take another step closer, looking up into his face. His angular jaw clenched. He stared at me intensely, through the black curls that fell in disarray around his face. Silent moments ticked past, stretching my nerves taut. But I would not break his gaze.

"Very well."

I blinked. "What?"

"I will marry you, Princess Adelaide. This very night."

My heart leapt into my throat. He said yes. He would marry me.

Tonight.

Now.

Everything inside me erupted into frenetic chaos, one moment coming down from the rush of the last few minutes, and the next, surging with anxiety over the fact that I was about to be a married woman again. This time to another man I only just met. One whose sultry eyes and striking appearance had tormented me for the past week.

Somehow, I managed a curtsey that only wobbled a little bit. "Thank you, my lord. Thank you."

He only nodded, his eyes searching my face before turning away and snatching his discarded clothing from the bed. "Give me a moment to make myself presentable, and then we can wake the priest."

Chapter 12

Nicholas

WAS HE REALLY DOING THIS? STANDING BEFORE A PRIEST in the royal chapel marrying the enchanting wife of his dead cousin, who even now carried the man's child, in order to be named king of Trilaria on the morrow?

Had he gone mad? Or was this truly the right decision, as he had felt so strongly in his chamber less than an hour before?

Nicholas prayed it was the latter.

His bride-to-be stood at his left, her face placid as she looked up at the priest who was about to unite them in holy matrimony. She looked so calm, so brave. Was she not trembling inside as he was?

He swallowed hard, clasping his hands behind his back and lowering his head. He could feel the queen's eyes on him from where she stood just a few feet away. Evidently, his aunt was the princess' co-conspirator in all this insanity. She agreed to serve as a witness to their union, alongside the princess' maid and personal trio of King's Guards. The knights currently stood shoulder to shoulder before the chapel doors, with blank expressions and their Trilarian crest pendants—gifts from the king upon their entry into his elite force—glinting in the candlelight. Did they mean to keep intruders at bay? Or bar him from leaving if he changed his mind?

Nicholas smothered a mirthless laugh. Surely there had never been a stranger wedding than this.

"Let us begin." Nicholas looked up at the priest, who still appeared none too pleased about being woken from a deep sleep in order to marry two seemingly impetuous young people. "Lord

Nicholas of Aguilar, wilt thou take this woman to be thy lawfully wedded wife, to live together after God's ordinance in the holy estate of matrimony?"

The words hung in his throat. Nicholas turned and looked into the face of his bride. Her piercing blue eyes silently pleaded with him, and he was helpless to deny her. "I will."

The princess' lips lifted in the faintest of grateful smiles. Then the priest asked the same of her, and her voice was soft and low as she responded, "I will."

"Please join right hands and repeat after me." Nicholas obeyed, turning fully toward Princess Adelaide and taking her right hand in his. It was small and soft in comparison. He thought he detected a slight shaking to it, but mayhap it was his own hand that trembled.

"I, Lord Nicholas of Aguilar…"

This time the words came a little easier. "I, Lord Nicholas of Aguilar…"

"Take thee, Princess Adelaide of Acuniel and Trilaria to be my lawfully wedded wife."

The vows continued on, and he repeated every line, pledging himself to the young woman he held by the hand. This was not the marriage Nicholas had *ever* expected or wanted, but he endeavored to mean every word he spoke. For he would do his utmost to serve, honor, protect, and even… *love* her until death parted them.

She would be his now, a part of his family. And he would always take care of his own.

"Please repeat after me, Your Highness." The priest began the princess' vows and she repeated them, stating each line with a careful reverence. Would *she* endeavor to fulfill her vows to the best of her ability? From everything he had seen of her, he thought she would. She was nothing if not loyal and dutiful. But was there any chance she could learn to love him? She was marrying him for the good of her child and the kingdom, but was there any part of her that wanted him for *him*?

Lord knew there was a part of him that wanted *her* for more reasons than just duty. Even now, his heart hammered at the thought of being her husband.

Nicholas swallowed. Adelaide looked down at their joined hands when she finished her vows, her expression going shy, and he wondered if she could sense the direction of his thoughts.

"Do you have a ring, my lord?"

With his free hand, Nicholas reached into a pouch tied to his belt, withdrawing the gold and emerald ring Princess Adelaide had pressed into his hand before they left his chamber to wake the priest. Her wedding ring from Prince Miles. On such short notice, it was all they had for the ceremony.

Would she mind him selecting a new one? For he did not relish the thought of his wife wearing another man's ring… Though, if she truly loved Miles and missed him as much as Nicholas thought she did, mayhap she would not want to give it up.

Would he always be competing with his cousin for her affections?

"With this ring, I thee wed." Nicholas gently pushed the ring onto the fourth finger of her left hand, right back into the place it had rested for the past three years. The emeralds flashed in the candlelight.

She clenched her hand closed as soon he let go, lowering it to her side. "I do not have a ring for Lord Nicholas at this time."

"Yes, you do." They both turned, startled by the queen's interruption. "'Tis right here." She approached them, extending her hand and offering a ring to the princess.

King Wesley's ring.

Princess Adelaide looked from the ring to his aunt, her eyes wide. "Are you certain?"

"Yes, my dear." His aunt closed the princess' hand around the golden ring. "I want you to have it." She transferred her gaze to Nicholas and nodded, sincerity shining in her face.

As the queen retreated, his bride took his left hand and slid the ring onto his fourth finger.

"Let us pray."

A fog settled over Nicholas as they knelt for the priest to bless their hasty union. Though he understood Latin fluently, he did not comprehend a word the man prayed. The daze remained as they stood again and the priest pronounced them man and wife, and it only cleared when the man of God said to greet the bride with a kiss.

A kiss? Was she ready for him to kiss her?

Nicholas mentally shook himself, vision coming into focus on the face of his bride. She waited silently, looking up at him with calm willingness. Expecting his kiss.

His heart stuttered. Nicholas stepped closer, bridging the gap between them. He lifted her chin and lowered his lips, hesitating a moment before touching them to hers. Her lips were soft, warm, and it was all he could do not to linger there. Sudden desire flared strong in his gut. But he was *not* his brother. No matter how strong his attraction to her, he would never force himself on any woman, or coerce her into doing his will. Not even his wife.

Nicholas pulled back, wanting to see her reaction to his kiss. But his bride looked down at the floor the instant they were apart, her face hidden from his view.

"My congratulations to you both. Now, if you will excuse me, I shall take my leave." The priest hurried away, obviously eager to return to his pillow. Nicholas stifled a chuckle. The poor fellow would never forget this night, that was certain.

And neither would Nicholas.

He turned back to his bride as the queen hurried forward to wrap her in an embrace. Nicholas waited on the sidelines, giving them their space as they spoke in low tones.

He had been angry at first, when Princess Adelaide declared her proposal of marriage, feeling like an animal cornered into a trap. But the moment he glimpsed her true desperation, the passion and love and even fear driving her to these unconventional actions... How could he have said nay to that?

Now, watching her in the flickering candlelight illuminating the chapel, he knew he had made the right decision.

The women finished their conversation and his wife turned to him, expectancy on her face. "Shall we go?"

"Go where?"

Her face flushed bright pink. She cleared her throat. "To your chamber, of course."

"Oh." What a dunce he was!

Nicholas stepped forward to offer his arm and escorted her from the chapel. Outside the sanctuary, the palace was as dark and still as it had been a few nights before when they met, unexpectedly, in that very spot. He pitched his voice to a whisper as they walked back toward his bedchamber. "I confess I had thought...

Well, I suppose I assumed you would not want to join me tonight. So soon."

She did not look at him, but he sensed her embarrassment even so. "'Tis a necessity, I am afraid. We do not want the Council or anyone else to claim our union is invalid."

She was right, of course. If their union was unconsummated and the Council favored Mericus as king, they could always insist the marriage be annulled and have his brother marry her instead.

The walk to his chamber seemed interminable. By the time they reached his door and he led his wife inside, Nicholas' nerves were stretched to the limit. His heart raced and his stomach churned. *I think I am going to be ill...*

What a pathetic husband he made already.

He turned away from the door to find Princess Adelaide standing in the same spot he had been when she barged in here less than two hours ago. She removed her veil and golden circlet, fully exposing her dark hair, which had been curled into thick ringlets. The ethereal fabric of her veil fluttered down and settled on the edge of his bed.

She turned her back to him as he approached. At first, he was not sure why she did so, then he realized... She was waiting for him to unfasten the laces of her gown.

Right. Of course. Women had help with these sorts of gowns, either from their maids or, in instances such as this, their husbands.

He eased in a breath, hoping she could not sense his anxiety, and carefully, slowly, pulled at the laces holding her gown closed. He thought his heart would come out of his throat completely by the time the laces were fully unbound and she slipped out of the garment. She wore a long white chemise underneath, but it did little to disguise the beauty of her form.

Lord, have mercy upon me.

She looked up at him, once again expectant. But at last he could see the emotions she had been doing such a good job of concealing. Her eyes were glassy, and her legs shook beneath her. She was just as nervous as he was. Perhaps even afraid.

He could not do this. Not tonight.

"My lord–"

"Your Highness," he blurted out before she could say anything else. He stepped forward and hesitantly reached for her shoulders. "We do not have to do this."

"I told you we—"

"No one has to know we... did nothing. We shall share the room, the bed even, but nothing more need happen. If any questions are asked, we can truthfully state that we shared my bed. They need not know the details of what did or did not occur."

Her lips parted in surprise, but she apparently saw the wisdom in his plan. "Very well."

Nicholas breathed a sigh of relief while she turned away and went to the far side of the bed, climbing under the covers. His hands shook as he removed his surcoat. He normally slept unclothed, as men generally did, but tonight...

Nicholas climbed in beside his wife, still wearing his tunic and hose. She was his spouse, but she was also a stranger, and the thought of being unclothed in front of her felt too discomfiting at the moment.

He rolled to face her. She lay on her side, bedclothes pulled to her chin and hands tucked beneath her head. She looked perfectly innocent and sweet and... breathtakingly beautiful.

The surge of desire struck him again, but nay. Unlike with his brother and the serving maid, Princess Adelaide *was* his to do with as he pleased, according to law; but no matter what others would expect of him, Nicholas had no wish for a relationship based on fleshly desire alone, with a woman who cared nothing for him. A woman who no doubt still loved and longed for her first husband, his cousin.

He had been saving himself for his future wife, and he would continue to do so until the wife beside him was ready to take that step. He would not taint any happiness they might one day share by selfishly acting upon his flesh.

"Goodnight, Your Highness." He rolled back the other direction to blow out the candle burning on his bedside table.

"You need not call me by my title any longer. At least not when we are alone. Adelaide will do."

Her gentle voice surprised him, and he paused just short of blowing out the candle's flame. "*Adelaide*, then." Her name felt wonderfully at home upon his lips. "Please, call me Nicholas."

"Nicholas." She smiled softly, that dimple-like crease appearing beside her mouth again. Then she surprised him further by reaching out a hand and placing it on his arm. "Thank you. For everything."

He resisted the urge to cover her hand with his own. "You are welcome… Adelaide."

He blew out the candle and settled beside her. She had retreated to her side of the bed, but once his eyes adjusted to the darkness, he could see she still faced him.

Nicholas settled on his back and stared at the ceiling. He had never shared a bed with someone before–aside from childhood, when he slept next to his brother. It felt strange to have another body less than an arm's length away.

He stifled a sigh and tried to get his muscles to unwind and relax. But with this keen awareness of the woman beside him, her warmth stealing across the space between them, and the sound of her gentle breathing…

Nicholas had a feeling he would not sleep at all this night.

Chapter 13

Nicholas

MORNING LIGHT PEEKED THROUGH NICHOLAS' EYE-
lids, chasing away the dream of his father.

Apparently, at some point in the night, he *had* fallen asleep
after all.

Nicholas groaned and stretched his back. Suddenly, he became
aware of the proximity of the body next to him, the hand resting
on his shoulder. He stiffened, looking over at the sleeping form
of his wife. Her face was half-buried in the edge of his pillow, her
lashes fanned against flushed cheeks and lips slightly parted.

'Twas strange to wake with another person next to him. But
mayhap he could get used to it.

His wife stirred, sighing and flexing her hand against his
shoulder.

The smile on his lips could not be helped. "Good morning."

"Miles?"

His heart plummeted at the groggily spoken name. His suspicions must be correct… Adelaide did still care for and miss her first
husband. She assumed she slept beside him even now, no doubt
explaining why she had drawn so close.

"Ah… nay. I am afraid not."

Her eyes flew open and she gasped, bolting upright.

He sat up next to her. "Forgive me, I did not mean to startle
you."

She smoothed a hand down the side of her face before tucking
a lock of hair behind her ear. It was then he noticed the imprint of

the creases in his pillow on her face. How long had she lain there so close to him?

"No need to apologize. I only… forgot where I was for a moment."

"I cannot blame you. 'Tis an odd thing for me as well, waking to find a woman in my bed."

Her face flushed and Nicholas inwardly winced. He meant to put her at ease, and yet managed to make things between them even more awkward.

Suddenly, the redness of her face faded, exchanging itself for a sickly pallor. Her eyes bulged, hand clamping over her mouth. "Where is your chamber pot?" she mumbled from beneath her fingers.

He pointed to the corner nearest his side of the bed.

Without another word, she leapt up, running around to the chamber pot and falling to her knees. She had scarcely gotten her head over the distasteful vessel before her retching began. Horrible, wracking convulsions that made his stomach turn with disgust and his heart twist in sympathy.

This was a common symptom of pregnancy, yes? Was there anything he could do to help her? Doubtful… but he had to try.

Nicholas climbed out of bed, footsteps crunching over the dried rushes and lavender lining the floor. He knelt at her side while she vomited again. Her dark hair hung in wild disarray, puddling on the floor and almost falling into the chamber pot. Hesitating for only a moment, Nicholas gathered her hair. It was thick, and soft as the finest silk. How would it feel to explore its depths with his fingers? For now, he settled for pulling it out of the way and holding it there in his fist.

He had never tended a sick person before but remembered the way his mother soothed him as a boy. So Nicholas made shushing noises to his wife, stomach clenching with every wave of her sickness. *The poor girl…* Using his free hand, Nicholas rubbed small circles on her back, hoping it offered some measure of comfort.

Her heaving finally subsided, and she sat up, hand trembling as she wiped her mouth.

He continued rubbing her back. "Do you need something to drink?"

She nodded, face still pale, her eyes avoiding his.

He stood and hurried to his wash basin, retrieving the pitcher of water. "Unfortunately, this is all I have at the moment. 'Tis a bit stale." Her body still trembled from exertion, so Nicholas held the pitcher to her lips.

When she had drunk her fill, he sat the vessel on the floor beside them. Adelaide offered him a wobbly smile, wiping a dribble of water from her chin. "Thank you. Though I wish you had not seen that..."

"Think nothing of it."

A strange sound hiccupped from her throat and she covered her mouth. Was she getting sick again? But nay, tears welled in her eyes and dripped down her cheeks. Why was she crying? Had he done something wrong?

"Your High–Adelaide, I mean. What is the matter?" He touched her shoulder.

She shook her head, swiping at her tears. "Nothing. I just... Oh, I–I know not *why* I am crying."

What on earth? Were all women like this, or just her? Or did this also have something to do with her pregnancy?

Again, he felt so helpless, useless. But he could not watch Adelaide cry and not at least *attempt* to comfort her.

"Look at me." Nicholas cupped her cheek and lifted her face. "Worry not about my seeing you ill, or about these tears, or anything else. I know this is a... strange and unexpected arrangement, but..." He paused to gather his breath. Last night, he had made a holy vow to her, and this was his first step in keeping that vow. "I *chose* this. I agreed to this arrangement of my own volition. And we will get through all of these difficulties *together*."

Fresh tears dripped down her cheeks and he desperately wanted to make them stop.

"Do you understand me, my wife?"

She nodded, sniffling. "Yes."

"Good." He nodded, barely stopping himself from kissing her forehead as he would if it were Eleanor he comforted. "Now—we have a busy morning ahead of us..."

Chapter 14

Adelaide

I STOOD BEFORE THE COUNCIL, AT LORD NICHOLAS' side—or rather, at *Nicholas'* side, since we were on a Christian name basis now. The eight lords stared at us from their chairs, lining two sides of the room, with the king's empty throne at the far end presiding overall. Every one of them seemed dumbfounded by our shocking news. Finally, Lord Raynard spoke up. "You are *quite* sure, Your Highness? You are, indeed, with child?"

"Yes, my lord. The royal physician is certain of it." I kept my hands clasped at my waist, my posture straight and strong.

"Then there is every chance that this child shall be a son, and therefore the rightful king."

"Exactly, my lord. However, I know the kingdom desperately needs a ruler *now*, which is why…" I glanced over at Nicholas. He nodded, assuring me he was here, with me, ready to face whatever came next. I marveled again at his kindness to me, his honorable and even tender actions both last night and this morning.

It seemed my gamble paid off in even greater ways than I dared expect.

I took a deep breath and pressed on. "Which is why Lord Nicholas and I wed last night."

Gasps of shock erupted from the men.

"You what?" I thought Lord Raynard's eyes might pop out of his head from the way they bulged.

Here Nicholas stepped in, as we agreed he would. "Yes, my lord. The princess and I discussed the matter and thought it the best course of action. If I am appointed king, I will gladly serve my people as their ruler. But if the princess' child proves to be a son, then I will just as gladly surrender the throne to Prince Miles' heir, serving as regent until he is old enough to rule on his own."

"And you thought you could take this matter into your own hands, did you?" grumbled another of the councilmen, Lord Percival.

"We meant no disrespect or treachery, my lords. We only wished to act quickly for the sake of Trilaria and preserving the true royal line of King Wesley and his son."

The man harrumphed, bearded mouth drawing down.

"And who performed this ceremony? Were there any witnesses that can corroborate the union?"

"The palace priest performed the marriage ceremony. We exchanged rings to symbolize the pledging of our troth, and Queen Nerissa and the princess' maid and guards were there to serve as witnesses. I am sure you would not question the *queen's* trustworthiness, would you?"

Murmurs spread amongst the men. "Has this union been consummated?" one of them asked.

Heat burst across my face. I kept my eyes lowered, knowing Nicholas was supposed to handle this answer as well.

"We did share my bed last night, my lord." He made the statement so matter-of-factly. So convincingly.

"I see..." I braved a glance up in time to see Lord Raynard tuck his chin thoughtfully. "Then the marriage is valid. It cannot be annulled. So..." he shared a look with his fellow councilmen, waiting for their nods of approval, "it seems we have no other lawful recourse. You, Lord Nicholas, shall be our king."

My new husband bowed low—one of the last times he would have to do such. Soon he would outrank everyone in this room. "Thank you, my lords."

"We will perform the coronation on the morrow, in the palace chapel." Lord Raynard looked between us, a subtle glint of approval in his eye. Clearly the others thought our actions a bit underhanded, but it seemed he approved, at least. After all, had he not told me just a few weeks ago that he would happily have Nerissa or myself rule alone, if only the law did not require a male to be the head sovereign? "I offer you my congratulations on your nuptials. May God bless your union greatly, for the benefit of both yourselves and Trilaria."

"We thank you for your kind words, my lord." Nicholas bowed again, dark curls falling into his face.

"Your brother should arrive any moment for the previously scheduled announcement of our decision. We shall share the news with him then." Lord Raynard looked uncomfortable at the thought, and I wondered for a moment which brother they originally intended to choose. Had we narrowly stolen the throne out from under Mericus?

Nicholas leaned close to speak in my ear. "Your plan has worked to perfection."

"Well, I must confess most of it was not my idea. 'Twas Queen Nerissa's."

One thick, black brow arched high. "Oh, really? I assumed my aunt had something to do with all this, given her presence at our wedding, but I never guessed her to be the mastermind."

Before I could respond, the doors to the meeting hall swung open and in walked Nicholas' stepmother, half-sister, and twin brother.

"Good morning, Lord Mericus. Lady Clarice, Lady Eleanor," Lord Raynard offered in a friendly greeting, but Mericus ignored him. Almost from the moment he crossed the threshold, Mericus' eyes narrowed in on Nicholas and I.

"Princess Adelaide. I did not expect you to be joining us."

I purposely did not respond to his unspoken question of the reason for my presence. "Good morning, Lord Mericus."

His eyes shifted from me to his brother, who still stood close at my side. Could he see the king's golden ring on Nicholas' finger from this distance?

"Thank you all for joining us this morning," Lord Raynard spoke up, taking control of the room again. "It has been an honor to get to know both of you this week, my lords. But, upon discovery of certain… critical information, it seems the choice of who shall be king has been taken from our hands."

Nicholas tensed at my side. Was he bracing for his brother's reaction?

I glanced across the room at Lord Mericus. He looked in startled confusion between the Council and his brother. "Taken out of your hands? Forgive me if I am a bit perplexed."

Lord Raynard cleared his throat, no doubt trying to determine how to convey the situation delicately. "It seems there may be another heir to the throne. Princess Adelaide has just discovered she carries the child of the late Crown Prince Miles. She has chosen to marry your brother, Lord Nicholas, who will serve as king until such a point that her son, if she births one, can take his place as the rightful ruler."

Lord Mericus stiffened, a dark look of anger mixing with his shock. And if looks could kill, Nicholas would have fallen dead then and there.

The tension I had sensed between the two brothers stretched tight. Ready to snap.

"You cannot be serious."

"I am, Lord Mericus. Your brother shall be crowned king on the morrow, and you shall be free to return home to the region of Aguilar and assume your role as its duke." Lord Raynard stood from his seat, smoothing the folds of his clothing. "I do not believe there is anything more to discuss here. This meeting is dismissed."

As soon as the words were out of Lord Raynard's mouth, my husband turned and took my arm, leading me to the door. "Keep walking." His voice was low, close to my ear. His feet moved quickly, striding with purpose down the corridor, and I was hard pressed to keep up.

"Nicholas!" Mericus' voice boomed behind us. "Get back here, you conniving snake!"

My head snapped toward Nicholas. His face was stone, giving no hint at his current emotions.

Heavy footfalls pounded from behind. We turned a corner, nearly to the stairwell that would lead back to Nicholas' chamber, when a body plowed into Nicholas, twisting him and pinning him to the wall. A small scream slipped out before I could stop it.

"You underhanded swine! This was all your doing, was it not?" Mericus spewed the words into Nicholas' face. "You cleverly manipulated everything into your hands. You *stole* the throne, which should be mine!"

"My intentions were nothing but honorable."

Mericus growled like a beast, pressing harder against Nicholas' shoulders, but my husband did not flinch or shy away from his brother's wrath. "Brother, I assure you—I did not seek to deceive you or *steal* anything from you. I only seek the good of our kingdom, and to offer protection and assistance to Princess Adelaide and her child."

"So it was all *her* doing then?" Mericus whirled on me, his face such a mask of dark hatred that I stumbled backward, tripping on the hem of my gown—the same one I had worn last night. "Sneaky little wench. What did you do, seduce him to get him to marry you? Are you even pregnant at all? Or was that a lie?"

Nicholas' fist flew hard and fast, striking his twin in the side of the head and sending him tumbling to the ground. "*Never, ever* speak to my wife in that manner!" His chest heaved, his eyes blazing like hot coals.

"Nicholas! Mericus! *Enough!*" Lady Clarice stepped between the two brothers, hands out to halt any more blows. "Please, no more fighting. What is done is done."

Mericus rubbed at the side of his head, still on the ground. Nicholas kept his eyes on his brother as he straightened his clothing.

A soft whimper brought my head around. Eleanor stood against the wall behind me, her blue eyes wide and lip quivering. I hurried to her side, wrapping an arm around her shoulders. Her small frame trembled beneath my touch. Were these sorts of volatile arguments a common occurrence between the brothers?

Mericus rose to his feet, his anger still firmly pinned on Nicholas. "I will not forget this, Brother. I shall *never* forgive you; you have my word on that."

Nicholas' body remained tense, his eyes now sad, giving me a glimpse at the pain caused by his twin's words. "I dearly wish you did not feel that way, Brother. I truly do."

Nicholas extended a hand to me. Somewhat reluctantly, I released his sister, patting her shoulder in reassurance before moving to my husband's side. I put my hand in his, noting the blood dripping from his knuckles.

"Come, Mericus. Let us go." Lady Clarice tugged at her stepson's sleeve, pleading with him.

We did not stay long enough to see if he listened to her. Instead, Nicholas gently pulled me with him, away from the wretched scene.

The shock and fear of facing such fury… 'Twas disconcerting, to say the least. The tension between the two men had always been clear—a current of negative emotions flowing just below the surface. But I had not realized just how deep and wide those emotions ran.

From whence did they stem? Was Mericus only jealous, or were there justified reasons for his anger? Surely Nicholas had not *intentionally* tried to hurt his brother.

As soon as we entered Nicholas' chamber, I hurried to the washstand. A servant had replenished the water while we were gone, leaving a clean rag beside it. I dipped the cloth in the water and wrung it out. "Here. Let me see those knuckles."

"They are fine, Ade—"

"No arguing, if you please. Let me see your hand."

He eyed me for a moment, then sighed in defeat, extending his bloodied hand.

I took it and drew him to the washstand. With gentle movements, I dabbed away the blood. The skin of three of his knuckles was split, but the wounds looked shallow enough. I washed out the rag, wrung it again, and resumed my work.

He winced but allowed me to continue.

"What was that back there?"

"I had to defend your honor. No man, not even my brother, shall speak to you thus."

I warmed at the knowledge that he was so willing to defend me, but the display of violence was still disturbing. "I thank you, Husband. Though I cannot help but notice there is more difficulty between the two of you than this singular event."

"Mericus and I… rarely get along. As young boys, we were as close as you might expect twins to be. But after my mother died, when our father announced that Mericus was not the heir presumptive, and he would instead choose his heir at the time of his death, well… things changed. There has been little peace between us ever since."

"And do you want it that way?"

"Nay… I never wanted things to be thus between us." His expression turned pained and distant for a long moment. "But my brother seems unwilling to make amends, and over the years, he has become increasingly… Well, let us say 'tis good you approached me in the middle of the night and not him. As much as it pains me to admit it, I believe Trilaria is better off without him as king."

My hands stilled. Nerissa and I had suspected Mericus would not be as willing to follow through with our scheme, but I had not thought *that* ill of him. Then again, I would not have expected him to treat Nicholas and I as he had done this day. So mayhap there really were much darker things lurking beneath the man's surface.

"I am grieved to hear that, Nicholas… A brother should be a friend, not a foe."

Truly, my heart welled with sudden sympathy, and I could not resist reaching out to touch Nicholas' arm.

My new husband stiffened, but his gaze remained fixed on my own. For a long moment we stood like that, the silence thickening with… something that made my pulse flutter.

Abruptly, Nicholas cleared his throat and took a step back. Out of my reach. "Enough about Mericus. And I believe my knuckles are properly cleaned now. Are you hungry? It is some time yet until dinner, but I suddenly find myself famished. How about I call for a servant to bring us something?"

All I managed was a nod before he turned and hurried from the room.

Chapter 15

Nicholas

IT WAS AMAZING HOW ONE'S WORLD COULD CHANGE so drastically in such a short span of time. Less than a fortnight ago, he was racing home like a mad man in the hopes his loved ones still lived. Since then, he had lost his father and yet gained Adelaide–along with the throne of Trilaria.

Two things he never once anticipated receiving.

Of course, he always intended to marry *someone*. But a wife like Adelaide? A princess born to rule, full of grace and dignity, a woman so beautiful and pure of heart that he felt unworthy to be called her husband?

Nay… *That* he never anticipated.

'Twas nearly as astonishing as finding himself King of Trilaria– or almost king, anyway. Any minute now he would make his way to the small chapel where he married Adelaide. He would make another holy vow, this time to serve, love, and protect not just one person… but an entire kingdom.

His father's face came to mind, and he remembered the arms that held him tightly before he left for his travels six months ago. He had not realized that embrace with his father would be the last.

What would Father say if he could see him now? Would he be proud?

I dearly hope so…

His father had trained him to rule Aguilar, but not the entire kingdom. Was he truly equipped for this task? What if he was an utter failure, leading the kingdom to harm, even ruin? The Council had shared their fears of an enemy attack. What would he do if that happened?

Fear crowded in like a black cloud, threatening to suffocate him. His chest constricted.

Nicholas braced his hands against his knees, the weight of his fur-lined cape pressing on his back. Like the weight of this responsibility he was about to undertake.

Breathe, Nicholas. Breathe.

Now was not the time to panic. For there was no going back. He *had* to do this, had to take this terrifying step forward for the sake of his people. For Adelaide. And for the babe growing within her womb.

Adelaide... His heart thudded at the very thought of her. Last night had been yet another tortuous experience. She stayed in his room again, so they could appear as newlyweds eager for time alone, and Nicholas had again struggled to sleep with her so near.

After the coronation, he would move into the king's chamber and she into the queen's, which adjoined his, while his aunt took Adelaide's old room. Tonight, he would have to insist that they sleep separately so he could finally get a solid night's rest without being keenly aware of her every move.

"My lord?" A muffled voice reached through the thick wood of his chamber door.

"You may enter."

Lord Raynard slipped in, leaving the door cracked. "'Tis time, my lord."

Nicholas nodded, silently following the head of the Royal Council as he and a pair of King's Guards led the way to the chapel, where his bride waited outside the tall double doors. She was once again not attired in her mourning clothes, but in another gown styled in the royal colors of Trilaria. Her dark hair was elaborately arranged beneath a modest veil, but her head remained otherwise unadorned, in anticipation of the queen's crown that would soon grace her head.

"You are a vision, Princess," he bowed low, taking her hand and kissing it.

She curtseyed. How was she so graceful in everything she did? "You are too kind. But I must say, you are looking quite regal yourself."

He glanced down at the rich clothing covering his body. It was the same deep blue, emerald green, and gold as her gown, with the heavy royal robe suspended from his shoulders by a jeweled chain. "You mean this old thing?"

She surprised him with a laugh, something he could only remember hearing from her once. 'Twas as sweet sounding as her speaking voice and made her entire countenance light up.

"Shall we?" He extended an arm to her just as the doors opened before them. Together, they took the first steps into the chapel.

All eight Council members occupied the pews, alongside those family members currently residing with them in the palace. His aunt, stepmother, and siblings stood in the front pew on the right side. Mericus watched him with a stony expression, only his eyes communicating the depth of his true feelings.

Nicholas' knuckles still ached after that punch yesterday. But his heart ached more. Was his relationship with his brother irreparably damaged after the events of the last week?

He and Adelaide stopped at the altar. The priest they had so rudely awoken from a dead sleep two nights before stood over them, luckily in far better spirits now. Yet, as with during the ceremony, Nicholas could scarcely hear a word the man said. Everything faded into a blur and his mind struggled to keep up. Then suddenly, Adelaide squeezed his hand tightly and brought his eyes and ears back into focus.

"Please kneel."

Nicholas obeyed, sinking to his knees at the altar rail. He noticed the crowns resting on pillowed stands beside the priest, along with a ball and scepter. The priest drew a cross with anointing oil on Nicholas' forehead, doing the same to Adelaide. Then he placed his hands on their heads and began a lengthy prayer in Latin. When the prayer ended, the priest retrieved the golden ball and scepter, both studded with sapphires and emeralds, and placed them in Nicholas' hands. They were cold against his skin and heavier than he expected.

"Do you, Lord Nicholas of Aguilar, vow to uphold the ideals and laws of the Kingdom of Trilaria to the best of your ability?"

"I do."

"Do you vow to protect and serve your people to the best of your ability, working in their interest for the good of the kingdom and the crown?"

"I do."

"Do you vow to be a wise and just ruler, seeking God in all your ways?"

"I do."

"And do you vow to protect Trilaria and its people from its enemies, no matter the cost?"

With every vow, the anxiety eased out of him and a passionate determination lent fervency to his voice. Just as he had meant every vow he made to his wife, he meant every vow he made today. He would work to fulfill these promises with everything inside him. "I do."

Then the priest moved the ball and scepter to Adelaide's hands, repeating a similar set of vows that she was required to make as Nicholas' consort, able to advise and assist him in ruling, though without autonomous power of her own. Her voice was soft but sure as she made her vows, her face intent upon the priest. She would no doubt serve her kingdom to the best of her ability, just as she had been doing for years already. In fact, he realized it was that desire to serve and protect her people that motivated her proposal of marriage.

She was a brave one. A gem of the rarest degree. Exactly what a princess–what a *queen*–should be.

After Adelaide's final vow, the priest retrieved the king's crown. It was fashioned of solid gold and studded with the same gems as the ball and scepter, with its bottom edge lined in white fur.

The priest settled the heavy crown on Nicholas' head. The weight of his kingdom, officially upon his life.

God, help me to bear it well.

The smaller, daintier crown settled on Adelaide's head, and then the priest shouted across the small gathering. "By the power vested in me by God and this kingdom, I crown thee, King Nicholas and Queen Adelaide of Trilaria!"

A chorus of applause echoed off the arched ceiling. Voices chanted, "Long live the king! Long live the queen!"

Nicholas rose from the railing. He reached out a hand to steady Adelaide as she rose, to assure she wouldn't trip on her voluminous skirts. Then they turned, hand in hand, as the small crowd bowed in honor of their new king and queen for the first time.

Chapter 16

Adelaide

UNDER NORMAL CIRCUMSTANCES, THE CORONATION of a new monarch would be performed in the Valen Cathedral and celebrated throughout the kingdom with much fanfare, especially in the capital.

But this was no ordinary coronation.

Instead of a lavish feast and a ball that lasted well into the night, we celebrated my husband's crowning with a subdued affair in the Banquet Hall. The mood of the room was peculiar, one moment feeling jubilant because of the new start for our kingdom; and the next, solemn and mournful because of all we had lost.

My own heart felt strangely divided. I was queen at last, as I always imagined and expected I would be. But the king sitting at the table's head was not the man I spent the last eleven years preparing to rule beside.

Again, I felt the tilting of my world, as if the earth itself were turning beneath my feet. It left me disoriented, finding myself in this reality that was everything I had planned for and yet completely different at the same time.

That night, the world shifted even more, as I settled into my new living quarters–the chamber that once belonged to my mother-in-law. It felt wrong somehow, like I had forced her to move from the room she had occupied for decades.

I had to remind myself that I would have already replaced her in these quarters had Miles lived and become king. This move was always expected to come at one point or another.

I surveyed the trunks of my belongings that cluttered the

space. A team of servants had worked to pack everything from my old room and move it here for most of the afternoon. On the morrow, they would unpack and disperse the items, bringing order to the space once again. But for now, this chaos would have to remain.

I crossed to the chair beside the window and sank into it with a sigh, pulling the veil from my hair. Growing a human was exhausting, to say the least. Surely, I could sleep for an entire day without waking once!

Gretta would arrive at any moment to help me dress for bed. And then what? For the past two nights of our marriage, Nicholas and I had shared a bed, but nothing more. Surely that would end tonight. Miles and I had had a true marriage from the start, and while I never particularly enjoyed that side of our relationship, it had been a necessary thing, so I had, therefore, participated willingly. Why should my marriage with Nicholas be any different?

An unsettled feeling twisted inside me at the thought.

A soft knock sounded on the door that separated my chamber from the king's. I took a sharp breath. "Come in."

The door pushed open and my husband entered. His hair, no longer perfectly styled, hung in casual disarray around his face. His clothes, however, were still in perfect order, so clearly a servant had not yet arrived to attend him either.

I rose from my chair as he crossed toward me.

"I wanted to ensure you are well. You looked a bit pale last I saw you."

He stood close–close enough that I now noted how well-matched our heights were. While I had felt like a giant beside Miles, Nicholas was just the right height compared to mine. "I am well. Only a little tired."

He looked at me with suspicion. Could he read the truth on my face so easily? I thought I was better at concealing my feelings than that.

"If all is well with you, then..." His eyes searched my face. I held my breath, anxious to know what he would say next. "I bid you goodnight, my queen."

He started to turn away and I could not help the surprised question that flew from my mouth. "Goodnight? Do you not–" My mouth clamped shut before I could further embarrass myself.

He paused, turning back to me. Hesitancy flickered in his expression. "There is no need to... rush anything, Adelaide."

"Oh." My rapidly beating heart slowed to a dull thump. If he had so easily read the exhaustion in my face, surely now he could see the shock that had me reeling.

"I will sleep in my chamber, and you can sleep in yours."

"Oh…" Why would nothing else come out of my mouth?

Nicholas nodded and took a step backward. "Sleep well. I shall see you on the morrow." Then he turned and left me in my puddle of shock.

I suppose I should have been thankful that he would not require such things of me. But all I could feel was… rejected. Was I so undesirable to him that he would not even seek a true union with me as any other man in our world would? Miles and I had also only known each other a week before our wedding, but the brief acquaintance had not stopped *him* from his duty.

Of course, my mother told me some of the details about her early days of marriage with my father—how it took several months before they came together as a true husband and wife. But that was because my father had so resented his marriage to her, after being pressured into it by his advisors, that he had wanted to control at least *one* thing about the situation.

But no such bitter feelings existed between Nicholas and me. Or did they?

He claimed to have married me of his own volition, but did he secretly resent our marriage, deep down? Would he come to despise me for "cornering him" into this arrangement, as he had first accused me of doing?

I sunk back into my chair, hands suddenly cold, body numb. Tears formed in my eyes out of nowhere, surprising me. Would marriage to Nicholas prove to be even *more* lonely than marriage to Miles had been?

Chapter 17

Adelaide

April 14th

Mother,
  There is much to tell you.

I PAUSED TO HUFF A MIRTHLESS LAUGH. THAT SENTENCE had to be the understatement of the century.

> *First, I must tell you the best, and yet bitter-sweet, part of this news. After all these years of hoping and waiting, I shall finally bear a child. My heart aches that Miles will not be here to see it.*
> *Since there is every chance this child could be a son, and therefore the rightful heir to the throne, my future requires security more than ever. Tri-laria also requires a ruler immediately, to lead the kingdom until my child can rule in his own right. And so that brings me to the most shocking portion of my news...*
> *I have married Lord Nicholas of Aguilar, and yesterday morn we were crowned king and queen.*
> *I can only imagine your mix of joy and shock at all this news. I know not how to feel about it myself.*

Once again, I paused, tapping the quill's tip against the edge of my inkwell as I absorbed that truth... How to feel about this marriage, indeed?

"Do you require anything else before I leave, Your High–I mean, Your Majesty?"

Gretta's fumbling question snapped me out of my thoughts. "Nay, thank you, Gretta. I am actually about to leave as well. You are dismissed."

"Yes, Your Majesty." My maid curtseyed, looking pleased she had finally mastered addressing me by my new title, and headed for the door.

I hurried to finish my letter, jotting down a few more sentences before blotting, drying, and folding it. After pausing to let a wave of nausea pass, I exited into the corridor, intent upon my bird cote and then the courtyard to resume my usual morning routine of visiting the sick.

"Adelaide. Good morning."

I stopped and turned to find Nicholas hurrying towards me. He looked well rested... *I*, on the other hand, had struggled to sleep after his odd rejection the night before, despite my exhaustion. "Good morning."

He stopped before me, looking down at my attire with furrowed brows. "Where are you going?"

I lifted the letter. "First, to send this to my mother." He looked confused by that, and I realized I would have to explain the messenger birds to him later. "Then into the city, of course, as I always do. Though with the events of the past few days, I have been unable to go."

He shook his head. "Adelaide, you cannot go. Not anymore."

I balked at him. "What do you mean? Of course, I am going."

"Nay, you are not."

"And why is that?" I was feeling argumentative after last night. Would he insult me *and* take away something that was so important to me?

He grabbed my shoulders, looking me square in the eyes. "Because you are *with child*, Adelaide! 'Tis admirable of you for wanting to help the people—I have told you as much—but you cannot continue to risk your safety."

I resisted the urge to pull away from him. "I am no wilting flower, Nicholas. I will be fine."

He heaved a frustrated breath, hanging his head and then shaking it. "Nay, Adelaide. I will not allow it. In fact, I *forbid* it."

"*Forbid?*"

"Yes, forbid. According to your physician--"

"You spoke to him?"

He nodded, hands still holding firm to my shoulders. "Yes, I did. Just this morning, actually. I thought it appropriate for me to be apprised of your health. According to him, he said you should be *resting*. If you continue to overtax yourself as you have been doing, it could be detrimental to you and the babe."

"But—"

"Nay, Adelaide. I know not why you insist on arguing with me over this. Surely you cannot be so foolish." His voice rose in earnestness with each word. "What if you were to fall ill with the plague again? What if something happened to you? Think of your child! Think of Miles!"

I blinked at him, shaken by his words. He was right, of course. It was one thing to risk my own safety for the sake of others. Risking that of my child was a different matter entirely.

But his words, and the commanding tone with which they were spoken, still smarted. Especially when my emotions were already in a muddle.

I pulled out from his hold. "Very well, *Husband.* I will not go." Tamping down the anger fueling my heart, I stepped around him and returned to my chamber, slamming the door behind me.

Nicholas

He had hurt her—of that he was certain. He was right in his insistence that she stay within the safety of the palace, and he would not go back on his order. *But* he had seen the pain and frustration in her face. Visiting the sick of Valen, helping in whatever small way she could, was important to his wife. And it would crush her to have it taken away.

Mayhap there was something he could do, as king, to help the people. Something that would soothe Adelaide's heart.

He would have to think on it…

After his argument with Adelaide—their first, he realized—Nicholas had spent a long day in meetings with the Royal Council, being tutored in the ways of kingship. Learning things about his kingdom and its operation that he had never considered before.

His brain felt as though it had turned to liquid in his skull, and a dull throbbing took up residence in his temples. Even now, walking back to the corridor that housed the royal family's quarters, Nicholas rubbed his head, trying to ease the tension. The soft comfort of his new bed beckoned him. Even if it *was* disconcerting to know he slept in the place where his uncle died.

But he could not give in to his desire for rest. Not yet, anyway.

His steps carried him to his wife's door, and his fist rapped gently against the wood. Adelaide had hardly spoken to him at either dinner or supper, and then retired to her chamber as soon as the latter meal concluded. There was a chance she was already abed, but he hoped that was not the case.

"Who is it?"

"Nicholas."

Silence. Then soft rustling and the door opening to reveal her face. She was still in the gown she wore to supper–another white mourning gown...

He had wondered if she would return to her mourning garb after their wedding and coronation. Today he received his answer. Clearly, she would continue to grieve for her first husband for a while yet.

"May I come in?"

She said nothing, but stepped back to allow him entry. The door closed firmly behind him

"Are you feeling well? I noticed you left the Banquet Hall immediately after supper."

"I feel well enough. Thank you for your concern."

He tapped a fist against his thigh. Why was he suddenly so nervous? Was it because he feared her rejection?

"Well... in that case, I wondered if you would join me for a game of chess? Or any other game you would desire to play, for that matter."

"Would your sister be joining us?" Though Mericus had left that morning for Aguilar, his stepmother and sister chose to remain in Valen for a few months.

"Nay, it would be just you and I." He watched her face, but

it revealed no reaction. Long moments ticked past, and Nicholas struggled not to squirm.

"I would be happy to join you. Where shall we play?"

His heart sighed with relief, and he grinned. "Just follow me."

Adelaide

Nicholas opened the door to the royal family's private sitting room, motioning me ahead of him. A soft gasp slipped from my mouth. "You planned all this?"

I looked back in time to catch his smile as he followed me to where an ivory and ebony chess set rested on a table. Beside it sat drinks and a plate of iced currant cookies. Many candles flickered around the room, with a small fire in the hearth, offering us plenty of light and lending the space an overall cozy atmosphere.

"I had servants set everything up during supper in the hopes you would agree to join me."

A smile snuck across my lips—I could not seem to withhold it. And after being in such a foul mood all day, it was refreshing. I had never been so easily prone to a fit of temper like I displayed that morning. Mayhap this pregnancy was affecting me more than I realized.

My husband pulled out my chair and waited for me to sit before taking his place across the table. "Would you like a sweet? I knew not if you cared for them, but these are a favorite of mine, so I took the risk." He held out the plate of currant cookies.

"I love these as well, actually. Though I must say my favorite sweets are gingerbread and fresh strawberry tarts. We had the most beautiful strawberry patches outside Caelrith. My siblings and I would pick them in the summertime and the palace cooks would bake delicious tarts. They were a frequent birthday request of mine."

Nicholas poured us both cups of honeyed water, passing one to me. "And when *is* your birthday? And for that matter, how old are you? I am ashamed to admit I know not my own wife's age." He made the statement with a teasing tone, but it was the truth. We knew next to nothing about each other, beyond what we observed in our brief acquaintance.

"On the eighteenth of June I will be two and twenty. And you?"

"This next thirteenth of January my brother and I will be six and twenty."

One year younger than Miles then. "I have never met twins before, you know. It was intriguing to see you both together."

I took the liberty of studying him while he made his first move in the chess game. Muscled shoulders. Trim waist. A nose that had a slight bump on one side, as if it had been broken at one point—perhaps in an altercation with Mericus? A sharp jawline edged with black stubble. A mouth that pursed in concentration as he thought through his strategy.

I looked down at my hands resting against the silk skirt of my mourning gown. Miles' face loomed in my memory like a haunting apparition. I had never found myself admiring *his* looks, though he had been a fairly handsome man. How could I suddenly start to think this way now that Nicholas was here in his place?

I pushed out a shaky breath. Breathed back in. "You and your brother do not look as much alike as I would have expected. Is that a common thing with twins?"

"Quite. Or so I am told. I rather like it actually. I would not want to share the exact same face with my brother."

I chuckled and made my first move in the game. Mericus was handsome in his own right... but nothing like Nicholas.

I reached for a cookie and took a bite, relishing in the lightly sweet taste and crumbly texture.

Nicholas frowned, dawdling over his next move. "I do not mean to pry, but... I wondered if I might ask you about Miles. 'Tis been some years since I had the opportunity to spend time with my cousin. I had no chance to see what sort of husband he made."

The sweet turned to ash in my mouth. 'Twas all I could do to choke it down without causing a scene. "Ah... Miles—he..." The truth of our relationship hung in my throat. How could I admit my shame and guilt aloud?

I fiddled with an ivory pawn, refusing to meet Nicholas' eye.

"Miles was good to me. He was… a true friend, faithful confidant. A good husband, truly."

"I am glad to hear it." My new husband's voice sounded strange. Almost strained. But I still refused to look up and see what his expression might be. "Do you miss him?"

I swallowed. "Yes, of course… I am sure I will always miss him. We all will."

"Yes… We will, indeed."

Tense silence followed until Nicholas at last rapped a fist against the table. "Well, enough sad topics for one night."

I made my next move, trying to slam the door on my regrets and the pain they caused.

"You know what? I have an idea." Nicholas leaned forward against the table, hands clasped together on its edge and his expression at once eager and hesitant. "Clearly, we have much to learn about one another, seeing as we did not even know each other's ages. How about for each move we make, we ask the other a question?"

My stomach flipped with nervousness for some odd reason. Did I fear him getting to know me and disliking what he found? Or was it because the way he looked at me sent my stomach reeling? It could be the confusion over his behavior. He had no desire to make me his wife in the physical sense, yet he did such kind things as this private evening together and wanted to know more about me.

What sort of man had I married?

Truly, he was far different than any I had met before.

"That would be agreeable to me."

For the next hour or so we went back and forth, making our next play in the game and asking a question of the other. Our favorite colors, favorite and least favorite foods, favorite pastimes, and dozens of other things. My stomach filled with the sweets and honeyed water, my laughter flowed more freely, and I found myself truly relaxing for the first time in too long.

Despite Nicholas' determination to best me in our chess game, I soundly beat him in the end. "Checkmate!" I cornered his king with a flourish, leaving him no choice but to surrender.

He clamped a hand against his chest as though wounded

there. "Ahh, you defeated me again, my foe. Shall I ever be able to conquer you?"

Something about the way he asked that question sent a fluttering through my heart. "You shall have to practice often, and mayhap one day… you shall succeed."

He leaned back in his chair, smiling softly at me. Was it just a trick of the candlelight, or had his eyes gone darker?

Suddenly, he sat forward and snagged the last of the cookies. "We shall have to make this a regular habit then. Say, once a week? Or more if you would rather. Just say the word, Wife."

His proposal took me off guard. Was his desire to play chess with me rooted only in a wish to get better at the game? Or did he actually enjoy spending time with me? "Once a week sounds suitable to me."

"Perfect." He pushed up from his chair and stretched with a yawn.

I stood as well. "I ought to be getting to bed." The exhaustion that had plagued me these last few weeks was sinking down on me again. My eyes were so leaden I could barely keep them open.

"May I escort you?" Nicholas reached out an arm and I took it, allowing him to lead me back to where we had begun our evening together—at my bedchamber door. "Sleep well, Adelaide." He lifted my hand to his lips and kissed it. He had done so multiple times now, but this time, his lips lingered longer than usual, sending warmth up my arm and into my cheeks.

Startled, I pulled my hand away. "Sleep well." Then I turned and hurried into my chamber, shutting the door in his too-handsome face.

Lying in bed that night, once again very much alone, my mind turned and tumbled in a million directions. Mayhap it was a good thing Nicholas made no move to pursue a marriage beyond name-only. If he did not desire me in that way, then I was free of that particular weight of duty I felt during my marriage to Miles.

More importantly, I could avoid feeding these unsettling feelings Nicholas elicited in me. I could remain true to Miles' memory for as long as I desired, and enjoy an easy companionship with Nicholas, free of any deeper entanglements.

Yes… This was for the best. It was not an insult at all, this unconventional boundary he had placed between us. 'Twas a mercy. A measure of freedom.

Finally at peace, I snuggled beneath the bedclothes and slept more soundly than I had in months.

Chapter 18

Nicholas

NICHOLAS LOOKED UP FROM HIS CLASPED HANDS where he knelt at the chapel altar. He was expected to meet with the Royal Council in an hour, but Nicholas could not bring himself to leave this room yet. The solitude and time spent conversing with the Lord were too refreshing to relinquish.

So many thoughts and emotions swirled through his mind… His brother, the kingdom, the plague.

His wife.

He could not say he loved her yet, so soon, but he *wanted* to love her. He wanted the sort of relationship he saw his father display with his mother and stepmother. He wanted to be a good husband to her. But how did he do that, exactly?

"God, help me to love her. I want to learn to be what she needs."

He deeply enjoyed their time together last night. His wife was an intriguing creature, sweet as an angel but full of wit, with an underlying streak of iron will. He felt sure he could fall in love with Adelaide in time. But would she ever love him in return?

Could he compare to her first husband, the father of her child?

He would have to work hard to win her heart, of that he was certain. And he had a feeling their frequent chess games in the evenings were a good place to start. But how else could he get to know her, to understand her? He had lived with Lady Clarice and Eleanor for many years, and so was used to some aspects of dealing with the fairer sex. But living with a *wife*–that was something different entirely.

An idea struck. His stepmother—mayhap she would be willing to offer some insight.

Suddenly determined, Nicholas pushed up from the altar and left the chapel in search of Lady Clarice. He found her in her chamber, breaking her fast.

The maid that accompanied his stepmother on the trip allowed him entrance, and Nicholas took a seat opposite the woman who had been his only mother-figure since he was ten years old.

"Stepmother. I have a favor to ask of you. I need…" He swallowed, suddenly embarrassed to voice his request aloud. "I need you to tell me about women."

Her blue eyes, so much like Eleanor's, bulged. She turned to her maid and gave a dismissive wave. "Please, leave us for a few moments."

The woman curtseyed and slipped from the room on silent steps, leaving the pair alone at the small table. "What do you wish to know?"

Nicholas propped his forearms on the table's edge. "I wish to understand my wife, but I fear I know too little about women in general. Especially when it comes to such delicate matters as… childbearing."

He cleared his throat, shifting uncomfortably in his chair. "In the short span of time since our wedding, she has been horribly ill, wept for no apparent reason, nearly bit my head off when I was only trying to protect her, and then was as charming as one could desire mere hours later. I–" He paused, taking a breath, shaking his head. "Are all women so complicated or just my own?"

His stepmother threw her head back and laughed, a sound that she so rarely released with such freedom that it took him aback. The laughter faded on a sigh and she pressed a delicate hand against her bodice. "Oh, my dear Nicholas, that is all quite normal, indeed. I am afraid some aspects of your wife's character may always be a puzzle to you, but I have no doubt you shall learn her well. It is your nature."

"How did you and Father fall in love?"

His question seemed to take her off guard as much her laughter had done him. "Well… I had known of your father for some time, while your mother was still alive. I thought he was handsome, distinguished. But I was so young, and he was married. And because of that, of course, I never gave him any thought at all. Then when your mother passed, your father came to Valen for court several months afterward, looking so forlorn and broken... I could not help but offer him my sympathy and prayers.

"Something seemed to connect between us then, and we conversed several more times. Then one day, months later, my father informed me that Prince William had asked for my hand in marriage. I could not have been more shocked, though a part of me was also secretly thrilled by the news.

"When we married, there was an attraction there, to be sure..." His reserved and proper stepmother flushed crimson. "But it was not until months later that I knew I loved him, and he loved me. I suppose it was... a gentle unfolding between us." Her eyes grew glassy and distant all of a sudden. "Like a rose blooming in the spring."

Nicholas reached out a hand to cover hers on the table. "He loved you well, Stepmother. Until the last breath."

"And I him..." She struggled to compose herself, fluttering her lashes against the tears. "But enough about me. We are supposed to be speaking of you and the princess—or the queen, I should say."

"What would you suggest I do to earn her trust? Her affection?" He did not voice aloud the insecurities he felt, not sure he even understood them yet himself.

His stepmother turned thoughtful for a long moment. Then she turned her hand beneath his and squeezed. "I have some ideas..."

Adelaide

Gretta entered my room backward, a tray in hand. When she turned and spotted me sitting up in bed, she offered a friendly smile. "Oh good, you are awake." The scent of hot porridge wafting from the tray tantalized my senses, despite my swirling stomach

I pushed up higher against the pillows at my back. Ordinarily, I rose around sunrise; but this morning, bright rays of light were already streaming into my chamber when my eyes opened just minutes ago. "I fear I have overslept. What time is it, Gretta?"

My maid brought the tray to my bed, not even bothering to suggest I dress first and take the meal at the table across the room, as was my usual habit. "Why, 'tis nearly midday, Your Majesty!"

"*Midday?*" I smoothed stray tendrils of hair from my face. The exhaustion of this pregnancy truly was taking its toll.

"Yes, my queen. I came in at the usual hour and you were still sound asleep, so I quietly left. I know how tired you have been lately and had no wish to disturb you. But the kitchen is already beginning preparations for dinner, so if I was to bring you anything to break your fast, I needed to do so now."

Gretta finished settling the tray in my lap and I finally looked down at it. A bowl of porridge indeed rested in the center of the tray, as I had assumed by the scent permeating the room. Alongside it were a bowl of fresh strawberries and a steaming cup of some sort of drink. "Gretta? What is this?" I lifted the cup and sniffed it, hoping the scent would not roil my stomach. Many smells had begun to do so of late.

"Oh, 'tis a tea made of boiled ginger root and lemon and sweetened with honey. His Majesty instructed me to have it sent up to you along with your meal. Apparently, the ginger is good for queasy stomachs."

She shared the information so matter-of-factly, but my ears perked up at the mention of Nicholas. *He* had thought of the drink? And after our conversation over the chess game last night, he could also be responsible for the strawberries.

I took a sip of the tea, letting the hot liquid slide down my throat. It was strong but pleasant, and thankfully agreed with my capricious palette and stomach. Snuggling deeper into my pillows, I alternated between bites of the porridge and sips of tea.

It seemed my new husband was a puzzle—one moment pushing me away, the next trying to draw close.

And I knew not what to make of that...

From that day on, every morning with my breakfast and every evening after supper, Gretta entered with a cup of ginger tea in tow. And never once was it by my request. Further surprises sometimes accompanied the tea–a bouquet of early blooming flowers, fresh gingerbread cookies, and a book from the library that Gretta said the king thought I might enjoy.

Nicholas' continued kindness to me was a surprise that I grew to anticipate every day. These were such simple, thoughtful gestures, and yet they had a startling impact.

I was startled even further by the news that Nicholas had organized some relief efforts for the people of Valen. This I heard from Nerissa.

Though she insisted I need not stay by her side as often as in those first days after our loved ones' passing, I continued to sit with her during the day and some evenings, reading or working on needlework. One such afternoon, while bright spring sunshine and a soft breeze spilled through the open window, the former queen looked up from her stitching.

"Nicholas is showing himself to be a good king, I think."

"Is that so, Mother?"

"Yes, for a man who never expected to be in this position, he is doing a splendid job thus far. I was pleased to hear of his efforts to help the people of Valen."

Her last statement brought my eyes up. "What efforts?"

"Has he not told you yet?" Nerissa sat her needlework in her lap. "I must say I am surprised. Well, I have not heard the news from his own mouth, but my maid told me what the servants are saying. It seems he has organized a small team of knights to bring food and other needed supplies to those suffering, particularly the very poorest peasants who cannot afford these items themselves. The men are supposed to be distributing the goods once a week for the foreseeable future."

I fumbled my stitch work, the needle slipping and pricking my forefinger. I winced and bought the smarting appendage to my mouth.

Nicholas had organized something to help the people since I could no longer do so? Well, I supposed his motive could have nothing to do with me. But after my anger with him over forbidding me to leave the palace, the action did seem related.

"Nay, he has not mentioned it yet... But I shall have to speak with him about it. And thank him." I looked up to find Nerissa watching my face intently.

Could she see the conflict that existed within me? This pull toward my new husband, and yet the desire to hold to the memory of her son? Just as I had never confided in my mother about my lack of romantic love for Miles, I had never spoken of the matter to Nerissa. As far as I knew, she assumed that I had loved her son very much. Would she not be disappointed in me if I let go of Miles so quickly, allowing this attraction to Nicholas and my esteem for him as a person to have its way?

She had already suffered enough heartbreak. I could not bear to cause another wound to her soul.

Nay. I needed to continue to guard my heart against these emotions. At least... for a while.

I would not wait, however, to ask Nicholas about his efforts to aid the peasants of Valen. The next time he asked me to join him for a game of chess, I eagerly accepted. I waited until the game was underway and Nicholas had drained his first goblet of watered wine before bringing up the subject.

"So..." I cleared my throat, suddenly inexplicably nervous. "What is this I hear about the distribution of goods among the people?"

He finished his play before looking up from the chess board. After two more games together in the past two and a half weeks, he was getting *slightly* better. "Ah, that. Forgive me for not telling you yet. I intended to..." He sat back in his chair and rubbed at his black curls. "Truthfully, I have been preoccupied. These meetings with the Council, the constant learning of what goes into running the kingdom—'tis more taxing than I expected. But yes, I arranged for a team of men to take food and such to the people. In the capital, at least. It feels like a paltry effort. I wish I could do more for the rest of our subjects, but it is a start, nonetheless."

I leaned forward to make my move and offered him a grateful smile. "Thank you, Nicholas."

He glanced away from me with a small shrug. "Of course. 'Tis the least I can do." His face took on a troubled expression. "As I said, I wish there was more I could do at present. I despise feeling helpless..."

Silent moments ticked past until he suddenly sat forward again. "Now, where were we? 'Tis my turn, correct?" Without waiting for my reply, he made his move. A bad one that would cost him. I smirked.

"You know," he said, "we have not kept our usual custom. I am supposed to be asking you questions that you must answer."

"And *I* am supposed to be doing likewise. What do you wish to know?"

"Favorite childhood memory?"

That was a safe question, not too revealing or uncomfortable, but challenging even so. I was blessed to have many happy memories of childhood. How could I pick just one? I sat back, lost in thought for a time, one hand over my middle that still had only the faintest rounding to it.

"There are many I could share. Time spent playing with my siblings–Roland, Gareth, and Matilda. Special moments shared with both of my parents. But… one that stands out to me right now is the first memory I have of going with my mother into Caelrith, the capital of Acuniel, and visiting the orphanage she and my father founded before I was born. You do know she was a peasant by birth, yes?"

His eyes widened. "Actually, nay, I did not. How did she find herself queen of Acuniel?"

"'Tis a long story for another time, but needless to say, her heart has never been far from the people she once lived among.

"When I was around five years old, she took me with her to the orphanage and I played with the children there. I tumbled around in the dirt alongside them, created silly games with them, and they never once treated me like a princess. To them, I was just Adelaide."

I glanced up at him to gauge his reaction to my tale. He gave me his full, eager attention, so I continued. "I have never begrudged my title. In truth, I have always counted it an honor to be who I am. But… at times it is nice to be known as something, or someone, more."

He smiled with understanding in his eyes. "I agree. And what a lovely memory that is. I would like to visit Acuniel someday. And meet your mother."

I laughed. "You would love her, I am sure." *And she would no doubt love you, as well.* But I would not tell him that. "She is a formidable woman–strong, confident, smart, and fiercely passionate about what she believes in. I can only hope to be half as good a queen as she is."

"I assure you, Wife–there could be no better queen than yourself."

I stared, dumbfounded by his words. He did not jest. His face was completely serious, earnest. Before I could form a response of thanks, he spoke again.

"When this accursed plague leaves our land, we can plan a trip to visit your family. I would like to meet them all, of course; not just your mother."

"I would like that very much… Thank you." It was my turn again, so I made my move before saying, "Now 'tis my chance for a question. What is *your* favorite childhood memory?"

He huffed a breath and stretched in his seat. "I should have known you would turn the question back around on me. Let me see…" He paused, tapping a finger against the armrest of his chair. "I would say, the last Christmastide before my mother passed. Mericus and I were eight years old and still had no care for inheritances and titles. We were merely brothers and the best of friends.

"My mother and father gifted us with several things during the twelve days to Epiphany that year, but our favorite gift was a pair of wooden practice swords with our names carved in the hilts. We were finally old enough to begin our training and thought ourselves quite grown up with those so-called weapons."

He laughed in the way one does over a fond memory, his eyes distant, as if looking into the past. "I shall never forget how we gallivanted around the castle, fighting one another for the rest of the day, and the sound of my mother's laughter at our antics."

His mirth faded, replaced by a melancholy that thickened the air around us. "'Twas only a few months later that we lost her and the son she birthed." He met my eyes, pain evident in the sudden tenseness of his jaw. "Not a day goes by that I do not miss her."

My heart broke for him. Young boys should never have to grow up without a mother.

On impulse, I reached across the table, waiting for him to put his hand in mine. His long fingers wrapped around my own, his palm slightly rough, but warm and strong. I had intended to say more, to offer some sort of comfort, even if it was simple. Now I found I had no words to give. Instead, I squeezed his hand and could do nothing more than look at him, hoping my message would get through.

Apparently, it did, for after a long moment, he squeezed my hand in return. Traced his thumb in a circle across my skin. "Thank you, Adelaide."

Chapter 19

Nicholas

HIS HEAD ALREADY POUNDED, AND IT WAS NOT EVEN midday. Nicholas resisted the desire to rub at his temples. It had been a stressful morning spent with the Council. The latest death toll numbers had arrived from across the ten regions of Trilaria, and with each one that Lord Raynard read aloud, Nicholas' stomach had knotted tighter and tighter.

Nearly two thousand lost since the first case of the plague was reported three months ago. Men, women, old, young... So many lives were stolen by this dreadful scourge, and Nicholas could not begin to understand it. Why must such misfortune befall them?

Despite the authority he now wielded as king, Nicholas felt completely powerless against this plague. The food he distributed to the peasants of Valen seemed a dismal effort. He wanted—nay, *needed* to do more. But not even a king can stand against such a vicious unseen enemy as this.

The mood within the meeting chamber was strained all morning, but it stretched tighter upon a sudden urgent knock at the door. A knight standing guard at the entrance stepped into the corridor to investigate the interruption. *No one* disturbed the Council when it was in session.

Unless, of course, there was an emergency...

The guard reentered a few moments later, his face ashen. He bowed to Nicholas, who sat on his throne at the far end of the room. "My king, permission to speak?"

"Please, do."

"A messenger has just arrived from the eastern border region of Dartwell. A contingent of knights from Galiel have attacked and pillaged multiple villages there, along with the manor home of one of Dartwell's lesser nobles. The Duke of Dartwell is requesting assistance in pushing back the invaders."

The tension snapped, exploding into chaos. Voices blended together in a mesh of fear, anger, and confusion. Lord Raynard spoke over the melee, "'Tis just as we feared would happen. Our enemies have seized upon our moment of weakness."

Nicholas stood from his throne, a riot of emotions thrumming through him. "But Galiel? I thought they were our allies. King Theobald's own daughter, Princess Ophelia, was the acting queen of Trilaria for a few days before Prince Carac died."

"The marriage alliance was made in the hopes of strengthening our ties with Galiel. King Theobald has always straddled the line between friend and foe. And clearly, he has decided to cross that line completely, now that his daughter has been returned to him and we are vulnerable."

Nicholas fought to keep his composure in front of the Council. This was the first *true* test of his ability to lead the kingdom. He had to be strong. Keep a level head. His people needed him, and he could not fail them.

"We must take action immediately." Nicholas let his voice ring out over the room, silencing the Council. He looked to the guard still standing across the room. "Please bring Commander Andrew and Captain Stefan here at once so we may organize military reinforcements for me to take to Dartwell."

"*You* take them, Your Majesty?" Lord Raynard questioned.

"Yes, does not a king lead his troops into battle?" He may not be able to stop the invisible disease attacking his people, but he was proficient with a sword and *could* do something about these attackers made of flesh and blood.

Lord Raynard shared a look with his fellow councilmen. "In all due respect, Your Majesty, we must advise against that. Yes, that is the typical way, but with things as unstable as they are, it would be unwise for you to leave the protection of the palace. If you were to be struck down on the battlefield, or catch the plague and die, Trilaria would once again be without a king. Yes, the crown would pass to your brother, but do we really want to risk yet another loss of a monarch so soon?"

The man had a point…

But the thought of remaining behind in safety while he sent other men into a dangerous, even deadly, situation—it turned his stomach.

"Ultimately, the decision is up to you, of course; but that is our advice to you, and I hope you will heed it."

Nicholas clenched his fists at his sides, torn between what his advisors wanted of him and what his people would no doubt expect. Either way, someone would be disappointed by his decision.

"I understand your concerns, Lord Raynard, and will take them into account. I shall think on it until it is time for the men to depart, and then announce my decision."

His wife's face flashed in his mind. What would Adelaide have to say about the matter? Would she want him to stay behind, or would she understand his reasoning for wanting to go? Raised as the eldest daughter of a king and then being married to a crown prince for the past three years, mayhap she would have some wisdom to offer on such matters.

As soon as he finished this meeting, he would ask her opinion.

Adelaide

A knock at my door startled me away from my dressing mirror. It had been another difficult morning that found me once again rising at a late hour, and Gretta had only just left after helping me prepare for dinner. Had she returned for some reason?

I crossed to the door and opened it, surprised to see Nicholas standing there. "Oh! 'Tis you."

"May I come in?" His face was shadowed and tense. A chill of foreboding swept up my spine.

"Yes, of course. Is something amiss?"

He walked past me into the room, eyes lowered to the floor. His steps crunched over the dried lavender and rushes strewn across the stones. "I am afraid so." He rubbed at his temple, eyeing my slightly rounded belly. "Mayhap you should sit down for this."

The chill turned into prickles of unease spreading across my skin. Mutely, I followed my husband to the pair of chairs before my empty fireplace, sinking into the cushions. "What has happened?"

Nicholas rested his forearms on his knees, hands clasped together. "A contingent of knights from Galiel have attacked Dartwell."

My spine snapped straight. "Galiel? But I thought—"

"Evidently your *dear* former sister-in-law returned to her father's house with more than her personal belongings. She has clearly informed him of our weaknesses, and King Theobald has decided to seize upon them. We believe he is testing the waters with this small attack, seeing how we respond. If he thinks he can dominate us, we shall have a full-scale war on our hands."

My blood turned to ice. "What do you plan to do?"

"I have a team of knights prepared to depart within the hour for Dartwell and assist in pushing back the enemy. I have spent the last two hours organizing everything with the Council, Captain Stefan, and Commander Andrew. However, I was hoping you could offer your opinion on something."

"Me?" What on earth could he need my help with?

"The Council believes I should stay here, in the safety of the palace, lest something befall me on the journey or in battle. But I…" He massaged his temple again. "I despise the thought of sending men out to fight while I stay behind. And what will the people think? Will they believe I am a coward because I do not fight? Or will they think it wise of me to protect myself as much as possible, so as not to risk the throne becoming empty again? I am torn, Adelaide. I feel as though either choice could have negative consequences."

He paused to look up at me, his dark eyes intense and troubled. "What do you think I should do?"

Despite his earlier mention of wanting my opinion, the question took me by surprise. Did he truly value my thoughts so much?

I sat back in my chair, stunned. A situation of this magnitude required great care and thought. I could not rush to give him my answer.

I sat silently as he fidgeted in his seat, tapping his heels against the floor. Finally, I folded my hands in my lap and began. "One cannot always trust one's instinct or heart, but in this, I believe following *both* of those would be prudent. Mayhap that tug you feel deep inside is the Lord trying to tell you which path to take?" I tilted my head, studying his handsome, yet troubled, face. "And judging by what you have told me thus far, you already know which direction you are leaning toward."

My husband lowered his head, nodding somberly. "I do. I must accompany the men to Dartwell. Even with the risks, 'tis imperative that I set the tone for my reign, showing the people I will fight for their safety even at risk to myself. I shall not be merely a figurehead hiding behind the walls of his palace."

Pride swelled swift and sure in my heart, startling me with its intensity. But it was well deserved. Nicholas was a good man, and so far, a good king.

He stood up. "I know I said that you mustn't endanger yourself, and here I am, about to put my own life at risk. But you do understand how the two situations are different, yes? I would not want you to think me a hypocrite."

I offered him a small, reassuring smile as I stood to follow him to the door. "Yes, I do understand."

Within an hour, I watched as Nicholas' men prepared to leave the palace courtyard. My husband was stunning in his chainmail and surcoat emblazoned with the royal crest of Trilaria, and a thin, golden crown wreathing his black hair. He went first to his stepmother and sister, wrapping them in a loving embrace.

Eleanor clung tight to her brother, her cheeks flushed and streaked with tears. "Be safe, Brother. Please, you must come home to us. I shan't know what to do if–"

"*Shhh*, Eleanor." He gently grabbed her face in his hands and kissed her forehead. "How can I go off to fight knowing I left you in such a state? Dry your eyes, Sister. All will be well. You shall see." He smiled bravely at the girl, but it did not quite meet his eyes.

Eleanor nodded vigorously before hugging her brother tight once more. Then Nicholas moved on to Nerissa, offering a word of farewell before stepping in front of me and taking my hands in his. "Pray for us, my queen."

"I shall, every day until you return. And you *shall* return." I squeezed his hands tight, staring into his face. "Go with God."

He raised one of my hands to his mouth, kissing my knuckles. "Please take care of yourself in my absence, Adelaide." For a moment, he looked as though he would say more, but then he abruptly released my hand and hurried to his horse, swinging himself into the saddle in one smooth motion.

I felt a hand on my waist and looked back to see Nerissa at my side. I wrapped an arm around her waist as well, noting Lady Clarice and Eleanor drawing closer to stand with us. The team of knights grouped their war horses into formation and trotted through the palace gates, standards snapping in the wind.

For the first time since Nicholas made his decision, fear clamped around my heart. I knew as well as Nicholas did that this was his best course of action. But it was dangerous, nonetheless. Would I soon find myself a widow once more? Would Trilaria lose yet another leader?

My eyes followed Nicholas until he disappeared from view. *God, please keep him safe. Please bring him home to us.*

Chapter 20

Nicholas

IT TOOK EIGHT HOURS OF HARD RIDING TO REACH Dartwell. The men stopped to water the horses but little else. By the time Nicholas and his men rode into the town surrounding Dartwell castle, it was well past dark. Exhaustion threatened on the edges of Nicholas' mind, but adrenaline surged through his body so strong that any thought of rest was kept at bay.

Nicholas pulled his horse to a stop, his men following suit. The scent of smoke from distant fires tainted the air, but the area was surprisingly quiet. "All is still. Has Lord Dartwell already driven the Galielians back?"

"Mayhap..." Sir Benedict, one of his personal King's Guards and second in command for the mission, pulled his steed closer to Nicholas. The man's highly trained eyes studied the landscape. "Or mayhap the enemy has retreated for the night and plans to return."

Nicholas tightened his hold on Castor's reins. There was yet another possibility–that the enemy had already conquered the region.

"This way to Dartwell Castle, Your Majesty." Sir Benedict motioned to crenelated stone walls that were barely visible overtop the thatched roofs of town.

The group spurred their foaming horses onward, thundering through the rutted streets until they reached the castle.

Sir Benedict pulled his horse abreast of the gates. "Open up, in the name of the king!"

The silhouette of a guard appeared at the top of the wall. Was it one of Lord Dartwell's men? Or a Galielian?

The guard turned and called down into the courtyard. "'Tis the king's men!"

The towering gates swung open on creaking hinges, the sound echoing in the deathly stillness. A man dressed in chainmail and a blood-stained tabard stood waiting for them on the other side. "Your Majesty." The man immediately took a knee, fist pressed over his heart. His head bowed in obeisance. "I am Lord Francis, Duke of Dartwell. I thank you, King Nicholas, for heeding my request for aid."

Nicholas leapt from his horse. "My lord, it is our honor and duty to aid you and your people. Please, tell me what has happened here. I do not see signs of the enemy being in close proximity."

Lord Francis stood. "Please, come in and we shall discuss everything."

Nicholas and his party followed their host into the torchlit courtyard. A couple hundred men, women, and children clustered together there, in and among the castle's out-buildings. Many slept, but others sat huddled in fear-laden silence. Their eyes turned to Nicholas when he entered, and every awake, able-bodied person assumed a bow in his honor.

The sight of so many showing him reverence was... unnerving. Would he ever become used to such displays?

Lord Dartwell walked close at his side, leading Nicholas through the castle entrance and into the Great Hall where they could speak privately.

"My king, about seventy Galielians first attacked yesterday morning, crossing our border and ransacking a small village near it. With the number of our enemies and the plague weakening so many of our people, too many lives were lost... However, one young man ran here to inform us of the attack.

"My men and I immediately set out to render aid, but the enemy had already made its way to another village and the manor home of Lord Rupert. We met the enemy just outside of that village and battled in a field. Both sides lost several men. We were forced to fall back, and that is when I sent a messenger to request your aid."

A maidservant appeared in the Hall as the men took seats around a long trestle table, and Lord Francis sent her off with orders to bring the king some water and light refreshments.

"We have been engaged in skirmishes ever since. The Galiel-ians have retreated for the night, but they have not left our lands. They will be back, and I know their goal must be to take Dartwell Castle. They may think if they wear us down with these small con-flicts, then we will not be able to withstand a full-scale assault on the castle."

"How many men do they have left?" Nicholas began calcula-tions in his head, trying to determine the number of enemy men to their own.

"Fifty at least. Still enough to do damage. But the worst of it is, I believe they have reinforcements waiting across the border to join them in the attack. Just think of it… They send in one group to wear down my men as they fight to protect our lesser nobles' holdings, and then bring in another group of men to strengthen their own forces as they begin attacking my castle."

Nicholas rubbed his jaw. "Yes… I see your point. It is certainly possible."

"Which is why your aid is so critical here. I have little doubt that on the morrow, we shall wake to find the enemy at our door. The men I have not already lost to the plague or the fighting are weary, but with the added numbers of your men, we should be able to fend off the attack."

The maidservant reappeared, along with two others, carrying trays of bread and cheese, pitchers of water, and drinking cups. Nicholas accepted the first offering of water, downing it in a few gulps. Then he took a piece of bread and cheese and forced it down his throat. He knew his body was hungry, but too much anxiety knotted his insides for it to willingly accept food.

"As you can see, I have brought all of the townspeople into the castle to protect them. They shall be barred within the keep when the attack comes."

Nicholas swallowed the last of his bread and cheese. "Good. Do you have plans for how the men should be positioned for the battle?"

Lord Francis nodded. "I do, sire." While Nicholas forced him-self to eat more of the food, the duke explained his battle plans. An hour later, both men were in agreement on all of the details and another servant arrived to inform them the king's room was ready.

Lord Francis stood from the table and Nicholas followed.

"Please, take your rest. Your men can bed down here in the Great Hall, and my guards will sound the alarm if the enemy is spotted before we wake at sunrise."

Exhaustion still battered the gates of Nicholas' mind and body, determined to break through. But how could he sleep with so much turmoil going through his thoughts? Nicholas nodded his gratitude anyway. "Thank you for your hospitality, Your Grace."

"Of course, Your Majesty." Lord Dartwell bowed and Nicholas turned to follow the maidservant to his guest chamber.

When Nicholas finally sank into the straw-stuffed mattress, his muscles sighed in relief after so many hours on a horse. Laying on his back, hands tucked behind his head, he imagined what Adelaide might be doing. Was she asleep? Or mayhap still awake and sitting before her fireplace, as she had been just that afternoon when he was in her chamber? Did she still have trouble with nightmares, as she admitted the night he stumbled upon her praying in the chapel?

God, keep my wife and the babe safe while I am away. Let her find peace and rest this night.

Nicholas rolled onto his side, continuing his prayers for his wife, his family, his people, and the potential battle on the morrow. In time, the exhaustion he'd been staving off finally broke through, pulling at his eyelids and dragging him into a restless sleep.

Chapter 21

Adelaide

AN OVERWHELMING SENSE OF DREAD SENT MY EYES FLYing open and my body scrambling out of bed before dawn. My heart raced in my chest, and only one thought pulsed along with my blood.

I must pray for Nicholas.

Something was happening. I was sure of it. And while I knew Nicholas was in danger, there was no way of knowing exactly *how*.

All I could do was pray.

Not even the threat of my morning nausea could keep me from sinking beside my bed and clasping my hands on its edge. My body trembled with urgency. "Oh, God in Heaven, have mercy upon my husband and his men and all the people of Dartwell. Let Your hand go before them and drive back our enemies. Keep Nicholas safe. Let him return home."

I pressed my forehead against my shaking hands, tears filling my eyes. Nicholas was becoming a dear friend, a companion. I had no wish to see him die. And Trilaria *needed* him. *I* needed him… at least for the security he offered both me and my child.

"Lord Jesus, please spare Nicholas. Please keep him safe. Protect him and bring him safely home to us."

Nicholas

"Arrows at the ready, men!" Nicholas held his hand in the air. A score of archers stood around him, poised to volley arrows at the enemy busy erecting ladders against the side of Dartwell Castle.

Lord Francis' suspicions had proven correct.

The Galielians did return just before dawn—with a hundred fresh soldiers in tow.

The battle began raging as the first rays of light tinged the eastern sky. Over an hour later, rounds of arrows still flew from the walls. The defenders picked off more than a few enemy soldiers, but it was not enough to send the invaders running. Even now, they charged forward, and if they succeeded in erecting those ladders, they would soon scale the castle walls.

Nicholas' heart hammered against his breastbone. He had trained in the ways of combat since he was a boy. But never had there been an occasion to put those skills into action. Trilaria had experienced nearly perfect peace since the war with Acuniel ended over twenty years ago. And now... here he was, king of Trilaria, yet untried in battle, and leading his forces in what could be the start of a new war.

What if he failed?

What if he could not stop the invasion and Trilaria was overtaken?

Panic threatened to clench around his throat, his heart, his lungs. But now was not the time for panic. He had to focus. He had to be strong.

"Aim... FIRE!" Nicholas lowered his hand. A score of arrows whizzed through the air around him. Not all found their mark, but those that did struck hard and true, taking out those attempting to brace two of the ladders. The third group continued unhindered, however, and three men started up the rungs.

"The third ladder, men! Arrows ready!" The team of archers surged into motion again, fitting new projectiles on their bowstrings. "And aim... Fire!" The arrows flew, striking two of the men on the ladder and knocking them to the ground with shrieks of pain.

But while Nicholas and his men had been occupied with the

third ladder, the first two were moved back into position. Nicholas looked down, spotting men ascending the ladders with all the speed and dexterity of cats. "Down below! Men on the ladders! Fire at will!!"

Arrows flew. Enemy knights fell, plummeting to the ground, but more came, scurrying up all three ladders faster than the archers could pick them off.

"At the ready, men!" A surge of adrenaline pumped through Nicholas' veins. Heightening his senses. Heating his blood. "Prepare for hand-to-hand combat!"

"Enemy on the wall!" someone shouted.

Nicholas spun to see an invader had indeed reached the allure atop the castle wall and was already locked in combat with one of Dartwell's knights.

"Your Majesty! At your right!"

Nicholas spun back around, finding a Galielian coming over the wall's edge. As soon as his feet touched the allure, the man drew his sword, bloodlust in his eyes.

Nicholas' pulled his own sword from its sheath. Steeling himself, he raised the blade.

The other man was fast, experienced, his weapon flying at Nicholas so quickly that the impact of their blades almost sent him toppling to the ground. With a grunt, Nicholas shoved his opponent back, sending the man stumbling.

Nicholas readied himself, feet braced for the force of the next blow. When their weapons clashed, Nicholas twisted his sword in the move his father taught him as a youth. Pinning his opponent's blade in such a way that Nicholas was able to slide his own sword forward along the length of it and pierce the man's neck. With a gurgling cry, the Galielian dropped to his knees and fell backward, his chainmail clanging against stone.

Nicholas staggered back a step, sweat dripping down his face, onto his lips. The salty taste of it reminded him too much of blood. Bile surged in his throat.

He had just taken a life–for the first time.

Other enemy knights had crested the wall, and the sound of fighting echoed all around. The thud of a battering ram now rumbled below, rattling the very stones on which Nicholas stood.

But all of that faded in the face of what he had just done.

Bile rose again, begging for release. Nicholas braced his hands against his knees. He was going to be sick. He was king, he was *leading* this battle, and he was going to be sick right here in front of his men.

"Your Majesty! Watch out!"

An urgent shout reached him through the mental fog, bringing his head and body upright. But it was too late.

An enemy arrow was already whizzing toward him. Piercing his right shoulder.

He heard another whizzing sound cut through the air right before a second arrow pierced his left leg. With a cry, Nicholas doubled over. Pain screamed from both wounds, traveling along his nerves and wreaking havoc.

"Your Majesty!" Nicholas spotted Sir Benedict fighting his way toward him.

Nicholas had to keep moving. Keep fighting. He limped down the allure, sword raised, eyeing a Galielian soldier even now scrambling over the castle wall.

The force of their colliding blades sent Nicolas toppling, his sword flying from his hand. He tried to catch his balance, but it was no use. He landed hard on his injured leg. Then he felt himself falling backward. Was he about to plummet thirty feet into the courtyard below? But nay, his back slammed against the sharp edge of a stone staircase.

The world turned end over end as Nicholas rolled down the stairs. He felt the arrows digging deeper into his flesh. The shafts snapped. His head cracked hard against one of the stairs and then at last he lay still.

Nicholas could not move, did not *want* to move. His vision blurred.

"The king is down! The king is down!"

The panicked voices and chaos of battle began to fade. His vision tunneled, and darkness crashed in upon him. The last thing he saw before surrendering to the abyss was his wife's sweet face.

Forgive me, Adelaide. For failing.

Chapter 22

Adelaide

I SWIRLED THE GINGER TEA IN MY CUP, THINKING OF the man who normally had the beverage delivered to me every morning and night. In the nearly two days since he left for Dartwell, I had been forced to request the drink for myself…

How spoiled by his kindness I have become.

The weighty feeling of dread had only partially lifted after my time of prayer yesterday morn. Especially since we had yet to hear any news from Dartwell. So far, God alone knew whether Nicholas and his men arrived in time, and if they had been successful in driving the enemy back across the border.

I could not decide whether this lack of news was a good sign… or an omen of doom.

Another prayer whispered from my lips. Then I lifted my cup to drain the last of my tea and stared out my window at the overcast sky.

A sudden knock brought my head around. Gretta paused in her straightening of my bed to answer the door.

Sir Arthur stood outside, his face grave. "My queen, King Nicholas has just arrived. I… I am afraid he is wounded."

I bolted from my chair, sending it and the empty cup on my table clattering. "Please, take me to him."

"Yes, my queen." Sir Arthur bowed and moved aside as I hurried from my chamber. That weight of dread increased tenfold, like a boulder sitting on my chest.

Nicholas made it home… but would he still die, before my eyes like Miles did?

"They have not yet brought him to his chamber. He and the knights that returned with him are still below in the courtyard. But I knew you would want to know of his arrival straightaway."

"Yes, thank you, Sir Arthur." His stride was long and quick, but with the powerful sense of urgency nipping at my heels, I easily kept pace with him. At the palace entrance, we found a pair of haggard-looking knights carrying my husband on a stretcher. Nicholas' form was limp, his face ashen and his head bandaged.

I hurried to his side, gripping his hand. It was dirty, stained with a mix of blood, dirt, and sweat. The rest of him was just as filthy, though it looked as if someone had at least attempted to quickly wash his face. His other arm—the right one—was splinted and bound to his side. Was it broken?

His chainmail shirt and royal surcoat had been replaced with a loose white tunic. Crimson red blood stains marred the fabric covering his right shoulder.

"My king, 'tis me, Adelaide. You are home, Husband." My heart stuttered to see his eyes peek open at me. His gaze was groggy, weak, but at least he remained responsive.

"What happened?" I addressed the men carrying the stretcher, but a King's Guard that had followed them inside stepped forward—Sir Benedict, if my memory served.

"The Galielians attacked Dartwell Castle yesterday morn just before dawn—some one hundred and fifty men. King Nicholas led in the defense of the castle and was wounded shortly after the enemy succeeded in breaching the walls. He sustained two arrow wounds before taking a tumble down a set of stairs and breaking his arm, not to mention gaining a hard blow to the head."

My stomach churned at the mental images the explanation evoked. "Were our men victorious?"

"Yes, my queen. Though it was a battle hard won. The Galielians were determined, striking hard and fast. They scaled the walls and flooded the keep. But our men, though outnumbered, fought valiantly."

I gripped Nicholas' hand tighter. "How many of our own were lost?"

"My queen... Such matters are— That is, I have already said too much. I... do not wish to distress you with even more details."

Was I a child that must be shielded from the world? Or a frail woman who would faint at every disturbance? I had no need for him to protect my so-called delicate sensibilities. "I said–*how many were lost, sir?*"

The knight lowered his eyes, cheeks flushing. "Nearly a third of our numbers, with many more injured, including the king, as you see."

"Thank you for your information. And I must also offer my heartfelt thanks for your brave service to our kingdom. Please, take your men to the garrison and rest. I and the royal physician shall see to the king."

"Yes, Your Majesty." Sir Benedict bowed and departed as instructed, leaving Sir Arthur and myself to accompany the stretcher bearers to the king's chamber.

As soon as we entered the room, I flew into action. "Place the king on his bed. And Sir Arthur, send for servants to come wash him, and for the royal physician to tend to his wounds immediately."

"Yes, my queen." Sir Arthur bowed and hurried back out the door.

As soon as the stretcher bearers finished settling Nicholas, I dismissed them and hovered at his side. "Nicholas?" I gathered his dirty hand in mine once again. "Nicholas, can you hear me?" His eyes no longer peeked open at me. In fact, his face was now completely slack, as though he had fallen unconscious. But his breath moved evenly up and down within his chest.

I smoothed a hand across his brow, brushing back his curls that were matted with blood and damp with sweat. "You are home now, Husband. And I shall stay here, by your side."

A sudden surge of emotion rushed up from my middle, bringing tears to my eyes. I now knew the reason I had awakened in such a fearful panic yesterday…

The battle had begun at the very time I was compelled to pray.

"Lord, I thank You for seeing our people through to victory, and for bringing my husband home. But I ask You—please spare his life. Do not… Do not let me watch him fade away as Miles did. I do not think I can bear it a second time."

Nicholas

Agony. Pure agony burned from his shoulder down to his arm and in his leg, bringing him out of the blissful state of unconsciousness.

Nicholas groaned, shifting where he lay. The stretcher he had been riding home in had gotten considerably more comfortable.

Nicholas flexed the hand of his uninjured arm, feeling the plush mattress beneath him. His eyes fluttered open.

He expected to see an overcast sky above and the bobbing rear of a horse before him. Instead, he saw the shadows of evening candlelight and the intricately carved posts of his own bed.

"Nicholas?" A soft female voice at his left.

Adelaide.

He was home, indeed.

"You are awake! Oh, praise the Lord!" Her hands gripped his uninjured arm, her upper body leaning forward until she came into his view. Her face was angelic in this light, her skin fairly glowing. Her dark hair hung around her face, loosed from the usual pins and coverings that were required when she was in public. He liked her hair better this way…

"Adelaide?"

"I am here."

"How… When did I arrive?" His voice was thick and groggy, as if he had imbibed too much wine. His head pounded like it too.

"This morning."

The searing pain screamed in his wounds again, bringing another groan out of his throat.

His wife's hand settled on his bare chest, rubbing in soothing circles. "*Shhh…* Be still. I know it hurts… The arrows were removed, and your wounds stitched up back in Dartwell, but the one in your shoulder came open on the journey home. The physician had to stitch it again. He also bound your broken arm with a better splint."

"And what of this infernal pounding in my head?"

"Your head was cut, just here, along your hairline. Remember?"

He followed where she pointed and touched the bandage on his head. Snatches of memories from the battle came back to him. Killing the Galielian soldier. The arrows piercing his body. His fall down the stairs. "Ah… some of the memories are rather blurred. But yes, I remember."

"Are you thirsty?"

"Yes. Some water, if you will."

She was already in motion, retrieving a cup of water from the bedside table and bringing it to his lips. "Drink slowly." The softness of her words and the gentle touch of her fingertips as she steadied the cup were almost as soothing as the water.

He sank back against his pillows when he could drink no more, and shifted deeper into the soft mattress. It was then he noticed that not only was his shirt gone, but *all* of his clothes had been removed. "Have," he cleared his throat, "have you been here all this time?"

She sat back in her chair, eyes lowering as if in embarrassment. "I have been with you since you arrived, yes. Though I did leave just long enough for your servants to undress and wash you."

So she had not been around to see him unclothed, but she *had* witnessed the physician sewing his shoulder and dressing his other wounds. She was stronger than she appeared, that was certain. If it had been his stepmother in her place, she likely would have fainted at the sight of a needle piercing his flesh.

"God has shown you favor, my king. You shall not be able to fight for some time, due to the broken bone in your sword arm. And we must pray the arrow wounds do not turn putrid. But, Lord willing, in time you shall be good as new."

Yes, *he* had survived… But how many others had not been so fortunate?

His muscles tensed at the question he must ask. He knew he must have been told the outcome of the battle already, but that too had grown blurred from the head injury and blood loss. "The battle, Adelaide. How did it end?"

She offered a bittersweet smile. "I am told the defense of Dartwell was a success. What Galielians survived retreated to their side of the border. But… our loss was great."

"A victory, yet at heavy cost." Again, he remembered the man he killed. That cold, debilitating realization that he had just taken a life. The life of a man who was doubtless a son, husband, father, and friend to people in Galiel.

So many lives lost on both sides... They piled upon him now, weighing him down just as the numbers of plague victims did. How would he ever bear the weight? And if the plague continued, if more battles arose, the weight would only increase.

"Nicholas?" Adelaide's concerned voice snapped him out of his dark reverie. "Are you well?"

"Ah, yes. Yes, I am well. Only tired." He could not meet her eyes when he told the lie.

"Then you should go to sleep. 'Tis nearly midnight." She pulled the covers higher and tucked them more firmly around him. Even in his pain-filled state, he was highly aware of the way she moved, her proximity as she tucked him into bed like a child, leaning over him in such a way that her long hair fell forward and tickled his face. If only she would lean further still and let him kiss–

He mentally shook himself. *Cease this, Nicholas. You are in no state for such things. And her heart is in no state to accept you...*

"I trust you took care of yourself in my absence? If you did not, I shall find out about it, you know. And speaking of sleep, you should get some rest now yourself."

She finished her ministrations and settled back in her seat, one hand nestled against her middle and the child that grew there. "I was a good girl, I assure you. And I am perfectly content to stay here in this chair."

He would have sat up if his aching muscles would allow it. "Nay, you need proper rest."

"Please, do not make me–"

"I *will*, Wife." He reached out and placed his palm on her knee. He had never touched her thus, and her blue eyes snapped to his face at the contact. "You must sleep. Do try to understand that I only seek your welfare, and that of the babe."

"And I only seek *yours*."

He chuckled low in his throat. She was stubborn as a donkey at times. But he knew better than to compare her to such a beast aloud.

Nicholas turned his hand over, hoping she would catch the hint and place her hand in his. And she did.

Nicholas gently squeezed her fingers. "Please, Wife... For me. If you truly seek my welfare, then take yourself to bed, for that is what will help *me* rest–knowing you are taken care of."

She stared at him for a long, silent moment, their hands entwined, her eyes shining glassy in the candlelight.

Looking at her looking at *him* like that... He nearly suggested she sleep next to him, if she was so determined to stay by his side.

Should he suggest it? She was his wife, after all, so there was nothing wrong in it.

But nay. He could not bring himself to ask her.

Finally, she nodded her agreement. Then she rose, releasing his hand. "Sleep well. I shall leave the door open, so if you require anything, you need only call."

"You have my thanks." He smiled at her, even as another wave of pain shot through his wounds and exhaustion seeped back into his body. "I shall see you on the morrow."

She glided from the room, blowing out the candles as she went, leaving Nicholas in darkness tinged with moonlight. He lay there, listening to her movements as she managed to undress herself rather than calling for her maid. When he finally heard the creaking of her bed as she settled into it, and saw the candlelight disappear from her doorway, he let himself succumb to sleep.

Chapter 23

Adelaide

"YOU ARE A FORTUNATE MAN, YOUR MAJESTY—AS I TOLD your wife yesterday. Your injuries, though severe enough to keep you inactive for a while, are nothing your young body cannot recover from with the proper treatment."

I watched from the foot of Nicholas' bed as the royal physician carefully rubbed a poultice of honey and herbs over my husband's wounds. Nicholas winced at the contact, though he kept his complaints silent.

"It seems God has ordained for you to sit upon Trilaria's throne a while yet."

Nicholas' lips curved in a tight smile. "I am grateful to have been spared." There was a *but* to his statement, though... I could sense it in his expression, the tone of his voice. He wanted to say something more, yet he withheld it.

"The only thing we must truly worry about is that arm. You *must not* use it, Your Majesty. We would not want the bone to heal crooked. Especially with it being your sword arm, you do not want to risk losing use of it."

Nicholas nodded soberly, signaling his understanding and yet not offering any verbal promise to do as ordered. I would have to keep a watchful eye on him then.

"So far, there does not appear to be any infection. The pain shall continue though, as your healing progresses. Especially in your broken arm."

The physician straightened, wiping his hands on a rough piece of cloth. "There. All done for the time being. I will be back on the morrow to examine you–though send for me immediately if you develop a fever."

Nicholas offered his thanks and a polite dismissal to the physician, who then gathered up his instruments and prepared to leave. The man stopped just short of the door, turning back to narrow a gaze at me. "And *you*, my queen. Be careful not to overtax yourself. You are supposed to be resting."

I glanced at Nicholas, catching his smirk and the gleam of satisfaction in his eyes, before nodding respectfully toward the physician. "Thank you for your concern. I shall be careful, I promise."

"Very good. I bid you both a good day, Your Majesties." Then the physician departed with a bow, leaving Nicholas and I alone.

"See? I am not the only one concerned for your health." Nicholas crossed his hands atop his stomach, that satisfied gleam still angled at me. Could the man not pull the bedclothes higher now? The physician had moved them to the lower part of Nicholas' torso during his examination, and it was highly distracting...

I cleared my throat, moving to my chair beside his bed. Taking it upon myself, I pulled the bedclothes up to his shoulders, being careful of his splinted arm. "I appreciate your concern as well as his."

He hummed low in his throat, as if doubting my words. "Shall you stay with me all day again?"

"I stayed with Miles when he was ill." My memories flashed back to the agonizingly slow, fear-filled days spent at his bedside. Watching the color gradually leach out of him until the plague stole his life completely. "I assumed I would do the same for you." And all the while, I would pray this bedside vigil did not end the same way.

"I see... Well, if that is what you wish, I would be happy to have you stay. Though I shall not go back on my insistence that you sleep."

"Understood, Your Majesty." I proffered a small bow of my upper body, drawing a laugh from him.

He groaned, rubbing the place where the arrow pierced his shoulder. "Ugh, it hurts to laugh."

"Then I shall try not to be too amusing." I smoothed my hands down the skirt of my gown. "What shall we do today? Would you like me to read to you?"

And thus began four days of being in near constant company with Nicholas. I had books brought up from the library that I read aloud, while other times, I worked on my needlework as we sat in surprisingly comfortable silence or shared casual conversation. We took all three meals of the day together in his chamber, though he had to eat his in bed—at least until the third day. By then, Nicholas was restless and eager to be up and about. He was not without pain, but his wounded leg could at least bear his weight tolerably well.

The only time I left his side was for him to tend to personal needs with the help of servants and when we went to sleep. And when the Council needed to meet with him in private.

The afternoon of the fourth day, Lord Raynard knocked at the king's door, requesting a private audience for the Council with His Majesty. I allowed the man inside, and when the rest of the advisors arrived shortly after, I quietly excused myself through the connecting door to my chamber. It thudded softly behind me, but the men's voices were still audible through the wood if I stayed close.

I knew I should not eavesdrop... But no doubt they would speak of the conflict with Galiel, and how could I *not* be concerned about the possibility of going to war with the kingdom of my former sister-in-law? If I was not allowed to be present for such a discussion, could I not at least listen from here?

I lowered myself to the ground, curling my legs beneath the folds of my skirt with my ear to the door.

"Your Majesty, while the battle for Dartwell Castle was a success and the Galielians were driven back to their side of the border, we must prepare for war. Our enemies ultimately lost this initial conflict, but you and I both know it was a narrow victory on our part. If King Theobald was brazen enough to send the attack in the first place, he shall no doubt still feel confident that he can overtake us. A full-scale war could be at our doorstep any day."

"I understand, Lord Raynard." Nicholas' voice sounded troubled. "The matter has weighed on my mind these past days. We must do our best to be ready for whatever may come."

"I would suggest sending missives to each of your nobles that still live," another man spoke up, "ordering them to muster their men and begin preparing for battle, so they may be called upon if necessary."

"Our numbers shall be greatly reduced due to the plague," another voice warned.

"Then I would suggest we all beseech the Most High for His favor, for we shall doubtless need it."

"I agree, Lord Gregory," said Nicholas. "Please, have the scribes prepare the letters. The physician should approve my return to normal duties by the morrow, minus the use of my arm. We may begin more in-depth planning then."

"As you wish, sire."

"You are all excused. I have much to contemplate before the morrow."

"Yes, Your Majesty," a chorus of male voices intoned.

I leaned my head against the doorframe with a shuddering gasp. War… Was it truly so imminent? The very thought filled my heart with fear and dread. Our kingdom had already suffered so much these past months since the plague began. Could we truly survive a war at the same time?

God, have mercy upon us all.

My fingers lingered over a pawn on the chessboard as I thought through my move.

"Anytime now…"

I narrowed a glare at my husband. "Now I shall take twice as long just to spite you."

He chuckled, the first bit of mirth I had seen from him since the Council left his chamber earlier in the afternoon.

To prove my point, I sat back in my chair and reached for my customary evening cup of ginger and honey tea, taking a long, slow sip. I sighed in satisfaction, carefully placing the cup next to the remains of the light supper we had once again shared in the privacy of Nicholas' chamber. After tonight, these languid days in each other's company would have to end, and Nicholas would return to his usual schedule.

The thought saddened me more than I cared to admit.

"I never did thank you for having this tea delivered to me every day. And for the other kind gifts."

Nicholas fiddled with one of my chess pieces he had managed to capture. "What makes you think I am the one responsible?"

"Gretta told me. Not to mention, the tea arrived every day until you left for Dartwell. Who else could it have been?"

He smirked, still not meeting my eyes. "'Tis nothing. I am only pleased it has helped you. And that you enjoyed the other items."

Little did he know one of the flowers he sent me even now lay drying on my windowsill. 'Twas foolish, I knew... But I could not bring myself to throw it out.

"*Now* shall you finish your turn?"

"So impatient." I clucked my tongue in mock disappointment and leaned forward to make my move.

"At last!" He tapped his good hand on the table and sat forward to decide his own play.

I studied him over the chessboard. The weight of his conversation with the Council was evident in the creases of his brow, the rigidity of his shoulders. I had yet to see him so troubled. Something within me longed to help him, to relieve that weight. But how?

"Nicholas... Do you truly believe war is on its way?"

His eyes darted up to my face, no doubt discerning I had listened in on the meeting. "I hope not. But... I can feel it in the air. Further trouble is most assuredly brewing."

"Though we did nothing but welcome and love her, I knew Ophelia held little affection for us—that much became evident after Carac's passing. But that she would betray us... That her father would choose to attack us now. It is unconscionable! How could they do this?"

"King Theobald is clearly not a man of honor, since he would break his alliance with us. That is what makes me so certain this conflict is not over. He has already gone so far as to risk the plague spreading to his own people by attacking us once. And that attack was almost successful in capturing one of our castles. Why should he stop there?"

I reached for my tea, taking a long sip in an effort to quell the nausea that had suddenly sprung up, this time more from the conversation than my condition.

"We must be prepared for whatever comes." Nicholas made his move decisively, putting his chess pawn down hard.

The steel flashing in his eyes reminded me of my father, King Rowan. After warring with King Wesley for eight years, my father made peace with the King of Trilaria before my birth, and the kingdoms had been allies ever since. My marriage to Miles was the culmination of years spent mending relations, the pinnacle of the trust shared between our lands.

My father was a powerful and determined man, but loyal and honorable to his core. Even if I were not queen, I had no doubt he would make good on his treaty with Trilaria and come to its aid if needed. 'Twould be a great risk... This plague would surely spread to Acuniel if so many of its men entered our land to fight. But my father was too true to his word to refuse aid, even with the risk. I was certain of it.

"You know," I took my next turn in the game, "if necessary, I can request aid from my father."

"Nay." Nicholas shook his head firmly. "'Tis too great a risk to Acuniel. What if the plague spread there?"

"Nicholas, he would help us, I am certain. He has sworn to aid Trilaria in the event of war, and he will not go back on his word. If we request his help, he *will* come. The plague is likely to spread beyond our borders in time, regardless of our efforts to contain it. Who knows how these things truly spread anyway?"

My husband ran his hands back through his hair with a low growl of frustration. "I do not need the lives of yet another kingdom on my conscience."

There. A portion of what troubled him had slipped out. But would he share more?

"Nicholas... I know 'tis a heavy weight to bear—"

"Can we speak of something else, Adelaide?"

His forceful tone startled me. I blinked. "Of course. Forgive me. I only..." I looked down at my hands, steadying my breathing. "What would you rather talk about?"

Nicholas sat forward and moved a knight on the chessboard. "*Anything.*"

I am back at Miles' bedside. My husband lies there, his skin white save for the areas blackened by the plague, eyes gray, body lifeless.

But then he sits up, reaching for me with cold, dead fingers. "You failed me, Adelaide. You were not the wife I wanted. I should have married someone else."

I scream, tumbling backward in my chair as he rises from the bed. Chasing after me.

I fling myself out the door, expecting to emerge into the usual corridor. Instead, I find myself in the dark hovel of a peasant. The stench of death permeates the air. I look down. At my feet lay a dozen or more peasants, as pale and lifeless as Miles. I scream again. Tears wet my face. "Nay! Nay! No more!"

Then I hear more screams, though not my own. I turn around and suddenly I am on the wall of the palace. All of Valen is screaming, mourning their dead. I cover my face, weeping into my hands.

"Adelaide."

It is Nicholas' voice. But it is weak. Wheezy. I remove my hands from my face and see I am standing at his bedside. The color of death overtakes his skin. He reaches a blackened hand toward me, but I am just out of reach. "Goodbye, Adelaide." Then his body falls slack.

He is gone.

Dead.

Just like Miles. Just like the peasants.

"Nay, please! Do not go!" I launch myself upon his lifeless form with a cry of anguish. It disappears beneath my touch, along with the bed. The darkness surrounding me lifts, revealing an open battlefield with a blood-red sunset streaking the sky overhead.

All around me, men are screaming. Dying at the hands of soldiers dressed in the colors of Galiel.

The war has come.

It is destroying what the plague has not already. All of Trilaria is burning. Every citizen falling under the hand of either an invisible foe or one armed with sword and spear.

I huddle into a ball in the midst of the chaos. I cradle my arms around my middle and the child yet unborn within, weeping for my people, my loved ones, and the future that is dying around me.

A very real moan tore from my throat. A hand clamped around my upper arm, gently shaking me. "Adelaide? Adelaide, wake up. 'Tis only a dream." My eyes flew open to find Nicholas hovering over me. "It was only a night terror, Adelaide."

He was alive. The war had not yet come. And it was all nothing but a horrid dream.

Tears of relief poured out of my eyes. I choked on a sob, surging up from the mattress. I clung to Nicholas, holding him around the neck, weeping into his shoulder.

He had somehow struggled his way into a pair of hose, but not a shirt, thanks to the sling holding his arm secure against his stomach. This realization almost made me pull away in embarrassment, but after the chilling nightmare, he was warm and safe. Like a shelter in the midst of a tumultuous storm.

And I was helpless to resist.

His good arm wrapped tight around my back, his chin against the side of my head. "*Shhh.*" His voice rumbled in my ear. "You are safe. I am here." He rocked gently side to side, as if soothing an infant.

"It–it felt so real. So–so awful." My body trembled against him and a cold sweat dampened my skin.

"You once told me you had dreams about those you have seen die. Was this more of the same?"

I nodded. "It–it haunts me, Nicholas. But this time there was more... This time, I saw the war."

"Adelaide." He pulled me away from him enough to look me in the face. "Forgive me for speaking to you harshly earlier. I did not mean to offend you. 'Tis just that..." His face scrunched with frustration and pain. "So much has been weighing on my mind, and it has grown tenfold since Dartwell. You see–"

His hand tightened against my back. His face turned away from me. Silence and tension stretched tight between us until he at last spoke again. "I killed a man, Adelaide. In the battle."

I stared at him through the darkness, confused. "Killing is a requirement of w–"

"This was my first time." He blurted the words like a confession. "My first battle."

"Oh… Nicholas." My heart broke for him, finally understanding at least some of what had been troubling him so deeply.

On impulse, I placed a palm against his stubbled cheek and brought his face back toward me. I intended to say more, offer words of comfort, but once our eyes collided, my words fled.

But words were unnecessary, it seemed. For suddenly his brows lowered and he leaned in to press his forehead against mine. My breath hitched at the closeness, the feeling of his arm tightening around my back to pull me even closer. I let myself relax into his hold. He needed this. Just as I had needed the security of his embrace just moments ago.

Our breath mingled. Only an infinitesimal gap separated our lips. I could make them connect if I leaned in just so…

My heart sped back up, making my head spin. The sensation was… frightening. No one had *ever* made me feel this way.

The memory of Miles' cold, dead body and the harsh words of his reanimated corpse in my dream sent me pulling back.

I should have felt like this for *him*.

"Forgive me." Nicholas dropped his arm and ran that hand over his face and through his sleep tousled hair. "Here I came to comfort you, and I have instead made this about myself."

"Nay," I shook my head. "Do not apologize."

"But I must. I should not burden you with my troubles."

"Yet is that not what a husband and wife are supposed to do? I will gladly hear whatever troubles you have, at any time. Please, do not withhold them from me."

There was so much more on his mind that needed sharing. I knew it. But would he share any more of this weight he was attempting to carry all alone?

His eyes drifted over my face. "My cousin was a fortunate man… And I am, as well, to have such a sweet creature at my side."

I lowered my head, tears building again. His words were another twist of the knife in my already aching conscience.

"Go back to sleep, Adelaide. I shall see you on the morrow." His weight lifted from beside me, but I did not look up to watch him limp away. And I never could go back to sleep that night.

Chapter 24

Nicholas

THE SOUND OF CLANGING SWORDS SENT NICHOLAS flashing back to Dartwell as he watched the palace knights spar in the courtyard below. He winced, feeling the phantom of pain twinge through his wounds, even though they were well on their way to healing.

Nearly two weeks had passed since the battle for Dartwell, and though the physical pain would eventually disappear, he doubted the memories would ever fade.

Nicholas dreaded the thought of more fighting. But, as he had told Adelaide several nights before, something at his core told him the conflict was only just beginning. It was like the scent of a pending thunderstorm in the air. He could smell the tempest brewing, feel the humid moisture in the whipping wind against his face. It was only a matter of time before the gathering clouds released their fury.

That was why he had to be ready.

He was so certain he had failed Trilaria that night on the walls of Dartwell. Yet graciously, God granted him a second chance.

He could not fail this time.

A sharp whistle from the Captain of the Guard ceased the sparring matches. "Rotate partners!"

The men, already sweaty and breathing hard from an hour of training exercises, obeyed immediately. With another whistle from their leader, the fighting began again.

"Captain Stefan!" Nicholas strode down the palace wall on

which he had been standing and hurried down the nearest stairs. "I would join, if you do not mind."

His captain hesitated, glancing between him, his arm resting in a sling, and the sparring men. "Uh… Pardon me, Your Majesty, but… how–"

"There is no harm in using my left arm. 'Twould do me good to be more proficient with it, in the event I lose use of the right one on the battlefield again."

"As you wish, my king."

"A sword, if you will."

Captain Stefan flicked out a hand to one of the knights, who darted forward to offer his own weapon before leaving to retrieve a new one from the armory. The weapon seemed to weigh more than Nicholas remembered. He twirled the blade in a quick figure-eight. It had been too long since he trained with his left arm, making his movements awkward and cumbersome.

But it was time. He could not wait any longer to begin strengthening his body and preparing for combat.

"Shall you be my opponent, Captain?"

"Of course, sire." The man took a fighting stance in front of Nicholas.

"Do not go easy on me. You understand?"

Apprehension flickered across the man's face, but he nodded affirmatively.

Nicholas attacked first, whirling around to bring the sword down on the captain. The man blocked the blow, the sound of their clashing blades singing through the air. Captain Stefan pressed in and used his full weight to send Nicholas stumbling backward. Nicholas regained his footing, though not as quickly as he would have liked, and surged forward to attack again.

True to his word, the captain did *not* take it easy on him. He attacked with ferocity and Nicholas was hard pressed to keep up. For long minutes they battled back and forth. Pain radiated in Nicholas' thigh, and his broken arm ached from too much jostling. But he pushed through it. He could not let it hold him back. If he was injured in battle again, he must be prepared to keep fighting longer this time.

With a yell, Nicholas spun around for another attack. His

weight came down on his left leg as he turned, and pain screamed through his muscles like a banshee. His leg buckled beneath him and he fell down, hard, on his left knee. Sweat coated his body. His limbs trembled with exertion. Exhaustion.

"Your Majesty!"

"I am well!" He twisted his fingers tighter around the hilt of his sword, trying not to cry out from the pain. He felt the eyes of every man present, watching him. Were they judging him as well?

After all, how could he lead the army and protect Trilaria if he could not even handle a simple training exercise?

Gritting his teeth, Nicholas pushed himself to standing. "As you were, men."

He glanced at Captain Stefan, catching the man's concerned expression. "You heard your king. As you were!"

Obediently, the palace knights took their fighting positions once more.

Composing himself the best he could, Nicholas handed the borrowed sword to Captain Stefan and limped across the courtyard. Once within the shadowed interior of the palace, safely hidden from prying eyes, Nicholas pressed his back against the wall. A pained breath gasped out. Wincing, he laid a hand over the place where the enemy arrow had torn through his thigh.

Fears and doubts swirled in his brain. Mocking. Accusing.

If he had been wounded in his first battle, after killing only one man, who was to say the same would not happen next time? Or worse? With these injuries sapping his stamina, would he even survive another fight?

Nicholas shook his head, mentally shoving aside the torments. He could not think like that. He would get stronger, he would be ready. And he would not fail this time.

Anything less was unacceptable.

Adelaide

> *May 20th*
>
> *Mother,*
>
> *To answer your inquiry about my health, I am feeling well. The nausea of the first stage of pregnancy has finally begun to ebb. I understand it has lasted longer than usual, according to Nerissa, and I dare to hope that it shall soon be gone entirely.*
>
> *Other changes in my body have begun, however, and my condition grows more undeniably obvious by the day.*
>
> *I wish you were here, Mother, to share this time with me. If only Caelrith were not so far away.*

I dipped my quill into the inkwell, dangling the instrument over the container to let the excess liquid drip down. I wanted to tell Mother about the attack by Galiel and ask for her prayers. Heaven knew we needed them. But I knew if I mentioned the conflict, Mother would tell Father, who would likely offer help—which Nicholas had already sternly refused.

I understood his reluctance to bring Acuniel into our borders, thereby all but guaranteeing it would be infected with the plague. The thought of that happening made fear well in my own heart, and in retrospect, I could appreciate his refusal to ask for help.

But by refusing to even request my father's aid, was he dooming our kingdom to destruction?

With a shudder, I put my quill to the parchment.

> *Trilaria continues to struggle through this dark time. And my mind struggles to understand God's allowance of so much tragedy. It makes me fear bringing a child into such a world. But I know what you would say, Mother—that God has a purpose in all things and is still good even in the midst of tragedy.*
>
> *I know you surely pray for us daily, but I ask once again for your intercessions. Especially for Nicholas.*

His anguish the night he came to wake me from my nightmare, the admission of his torment over the life he took... It wrenched my heart to remember.

How much else was he hiding behind the appearance of strength and control he exuded?

My new husband carries much on his shoulders. I know he needs your prayers most of all.

Nicholas

"Another letter arrived for you, sire." Nicholas looked up from his desk and at the knight bowing before him.

"Thank you, Sir..."

"Sir John, Your Majesty."

Nicholas nodded. He was generally good at remembering names, but with so many knights, servants, and nobles to keep track of now, it was proving a little more difficult. "You are dismissed, Sir John."

With a final bow, the knight pivoted on his heel and quit the room.

Nicholas turned the parchment over in his hands. A wax seal marked the front. The crest of Maren.

"Who is it from?" Lord Raynard spoke up from his seat opposite Nicholas. The noble had spent the past few hours with him, going over potential battle plans ahead of their next meeting with the Council.

Nicholas unfolded the document, his eyes scanning the neat script. "The Duke of Maren. He has received our orders to prepare his men and have them ready at a moment's notice."

Nicholas' stomach sank at the words in the last paragraph before the nobleman's valediction. He closed the letter, lowering it to his desk. "The duke also informs me that his daughter has perished by the plague. His son is ill as well, though recovering and expected to live. He vows his fealty and commitment to Trilaria's protection in spite of the sorrow overshadowing his house."

Lord Raynard sighed grimly. "Lord Wilfred of Maren is not my favorite of Trilaria's nobles, but my heart grieves for his family just the same." He shifted in his seat, crossing one leg over his opposite knee. "No word from your brother yet, I take it?"

Nicholas' shoulders tensed, along with his jaw. "Nay, nothing yet." Aguilar was no further away than Maren, so Mericus' response should have arrived by now. Would his brother dare defy him as his king? Regardless of the condition of their personal relationship, Mericus was still bound by honor and the *law* to obey Nicholas' call to arms.

Lord Raynard hummed, displeasure in the sound. "Well, we shall hope he responds soon. I truly would have thought better of the man than to disrespect his sovereign, let alone commit treason."

"My brother is… a man of many facets. There is likely much he is capable of that you would not expect." Nicholas thought of the night he caught Mericus with the maidservant in the library. No doubt Lord Raynard would be shocked by the knowledge of that, as well, especially since Nicholas still suspected the maid had not consented to the encounter.

Lord Raynard sat forward, studying the map of Trilaria spread across the desk and all the markings they had made while planning potential military movements. "Under normal circumstances, our army would likely stand equal with that of Galiel," he said, abruptly steering the conversation in a different direction. "However, our numbers will be greatly diminished by the plague. We shall know just *how* diminished soon, I hope. Once the nobles have had time to gather their men."

The tension in Nicholas' shoulders increased tenfold. "Realistically, based on the number of deaths reported, how many men do you think we will have?"

His chief councilor dipped his chin. "It is difficult to say, sire."

"Answer the question, Lord Raynard. How many men?"

The nobleman hesitated, reluctantly meeting Nicholas' eyes. "At best, twelve hundred knights with a couple hundred able-bodied free men that can be called to service. Unless we wish to force unskilled peasants to contribute as well, as was sometimes done in the war with Acuniel."

Overwhelming nausea churned in Nicholas' gut, and for a moment, he could commiserate with how Adelaide must have felt these past months. "Do you think we even stand a chance? Truly?" He had been careful not to voice his doubts amongst most people, but Lord Raynard he trusted. And he needed to know the man's *honest* opinion.

Lord Raynard rubbed his bearded jaw. "Truthfully, sire... I know not. I hope so. I *pray* so. But all I know for certain is that, if war does come, it shall be brutally fought. Whether we win or lose."

Nicholas nodded, swallowing the bile in his throat. "I suppose only time shall tell, then. But we shall be ready, whatever our fate."

Chapter 25

Adelaide

OVERCAST SUNLIGHT STREAMED THROUGH MY WIN-
dow, illuminating the page of the book in my lap. It was the last
one Miles added to our library before the plague hit—Homer's *Odyssey*. He had always loved the written word, and he was thrilled to
add this beautifully transcribed copy of the ancient Greek work to
our collection.

Had Nicholas ever read the *Odyssey*? I would have to ask him...

Pushing the thought aside, I tried once again to focus my
mind on the text. While I had always struggled to speak Greek, I
could read it quite well. But the foreign words alluded me today,
my thoughts so scattered and jumbled that I read the same page
over and over.

I sighed and closed the book. Mayhap this was not the day for
Greek.

The sound of a door slamming nearly sent the heavy book
tumbling from my lap. I gasped, catching it just in time.

The noise came from Nicholas' chamber. Was something
amiss?

Standing, I closed the book and sat it in the chair I just vacated. A man's shout rang out from under our shared door. I hurried
across the room, heart suddenly hammering. "Nicholas?"

Not waiting for permission, I pushed open the door. My husband stood in the middle of the room, drenched in sweat, and
looking like a man on the brink of a rampage. A chair lay toppled,
as though he had pushed or kicked it over. He wore only a simple
linen tunic, his sling, hose, and boots.

Clearly, he had been training with the knights again. It was not a practice I particularly approved of… but thus far, I had held my tongue on the matter.

"Leave me be, Adelaide." He stalked across his room, no longer limping on his injured leg.

"Nicholas, what happened? Is there anything I can do?" I drew closer, eager to ease whatever upset caused such an outburst. 'Twas uncharacteristic of him, from all I had seen.

He jerked away from me when I tried to touch his shoulder. "Nothing happened, Adelaide!"

"Then *what* has you in such a state?"

He growled and slashed a hand through the air. "I am *weak*, Adelaide! I–" He growled again, looking like he wanted to kick another chair. "I cannot seem to fight with my left arm without shaming myself. I cannot don a garment on my own. I cannot write. I can scarcely relieve myself without assistance. I am utterly useless! There–*are you happy now?*"

I gaped at him. "You are not *useless*. You must be patient and allow your arm to heal. In time, you shall have all of your former strength and skills."

Suddenly, he seized my shoulder with his good hand. "What if we do not *have* time?"

I stared up into his face, so dark and angry and tormented. My mouth opened and closed several times before I found the words I wished to say. "You must not be so hard on yourself. If war does come, you will be ready to lead our people, I am certain. Even if you must lead them from here for a time."

His black brows cinched together as if pulled by an invisible thread. "But what if I am *not* ready?" His breath came ragged, and the fearful desperation in his tone sent a tremble through me. I had seen him vulnerable once, when he comforted me after my night terror. But never like this. This time, it was as though his every thought and insecurity spilled from each movement of his face.

"You shall. I know it." I touched the shoulder of his wounded arm, willing him to take my words to heart. "I believe in you, Nicholas."

Something seemed to crack inside him. His posture lost its hard edges, his head dropping "Truly?"

I nodded, surprised by the tears pricking my eyes. "Truly."

He swallowed, nodding his head slowly. Then his chin lifted, and our eyes met. His dark irises, nearly the same color as his hair, flitted back and forth between my own. As if searching for something in their depths. He still held my arm, but the hardness of his touch faded, leaving only tenderness.

I pressed my lips together, trying to hide how my breathing hitched. Could he feel the way my pulse thumped in my veins?

"Adelaide…" Since when had he drawn closer?

"Yes?" I cursed myself for the way the word wobbled out of my lips.

His eyes darted down, to the very lips that had just spoken.

My heart catapulted into my throat. Nay… He would not, would he?

Suddenly, he sighed and closed his eyes. "Thank you," he whispered.

"For what?"

"For everything."

Then he dropped his hands and the distance between us grew, sending my heart plummeting to my toes.

Was that *disappointment* I felt? Nay. How could I want him to kiss me? I was supposed to be content within the boundary lines he established early on. I was not supposed to desire more.

"If you need nothing further, I shall leave you alone now." Then I turned my back to him and strode out of the room, measuring my strides but wanting to run.

I returned to my chair and my book, but did not bother attempting to read it again. First that moment after he woke me from my nightmare… Now this moment of anticipating his kiss and being disappointed when it never came…

Nicholas said *he* was weak? Well, *I* was the one growing dangerously weak.

Nicholas

He almost kissed her. And part of Nicholas wished he had. But another part said it was not yet time.

For the rest of the day, all through the evening, and into the night, Nicholas replayed the moment in his mind. Adelaide said she believed in him, and he had seen the truth of it in every line of her sweet face. That knowledge had so overwhelmed him, so comforted and strengthened him, that Nicholas had desired nothing more than to kiss his wife.

He could have sworn she wanted to kiss him too. He had felt the shift in her posture. Felt the charge in the air between them. And God help him, he had *almost* done it. *Almost* claimed that kiss.

But... he could not do it. Those fears of rejection, of frightening her away, of not being what she wanted or needed–they had risen again with a vengeance, squashing his desire.

It had not been the right moment. But soon...

Soon.

She was softening, Nicholas was certain of it now. He would not dare assume that Adelaide *loved* him yet, but she was at least opening her heart. And soon, he would try to take the next step in nurturing that growing affection.

Nicholas rolled over in his bed. It was much too hot in this room. Sweat slicked his skin and made it miserable beneath the bedclothes. He kicked them off, sitting up in frustration and running his free hand over his face.

Adelaide's birthday was coming up soon. Would that be the right time to confess that his heart was swiftly becoming hers?

Regardless, he would do his best to make the day special for her. She had been through so much, lost so much, and she endlessly gave of herself to those around her. She deserved to be the one receiving all the care and attention, for at least that day of all days.

His stepmother had offered great insight on the female gender all those weeks ago, and no doubt, she could help him with this as well. Yet part of him wanted to plan everything on his own. Would it not mean even more to Adelaide if it came directly from his heart?

Yes, that was what he would do. He would begin planning her

birthday right away. And God willing, on that day, he would take a bold step that could be the key to opening the door on a deeper relationship with his wife.

Nicholas could only hope and pray that she was willing to take that step with him. And that he did not lose his nerve in the meantime.

Feeling at least slightly more settled now, Nicholas sighed and laid back down. Settling into the mattress, he smoothed a hand over his right shoulder. The skin where the sutures had been was red and puffed, as was the skin over his leg wound. They would make nasty scars, but both wounds were healing nicely. If only his arm would heal so quickly.

I believe in you.

Truly?

Truly.

Adelaide said she had faith in him, and her words provided a much-needed dose of encouragement. But was she correct? Was her belief in him warranted… or a gross misjudgment?

With another sigh, Nicholas closed his eyes. *God, let her not be wrong about me. Let her be right… I cannot bear the thought of disappointing her.*

Chapter 26

Adelaide

I STUDIED MY FIGURE IN THE LOOKING GLASS, RUBBING a hand down the swell of my stomach. There was zero chance of mistaking my condition now, and it seemed the strain on the laces of my gowns worsened each day. I sighed, shifting uncomfortably in my too tight garment.

Nerissa had observed the changes in my body last week over dinner, suggesting I have new gowns made soon. I resisted the idea, hating to cause a fuss and spend valuable funds that could go towards Nicholas' efforts to aid the people. But mayhap Nerissa was right.

"You look lovely, so you mustn't fret. Especially on your birth-day!"

I cast an appreciative but close-lipped smile over my shoulder at Gretta. Someone tapped at my door and the young maidservant whisked away to answer it while I took a seat at the dressing table. My hair still hung in a long braid down my back, and it would take another half-hour for Gretta to arrange its length into a respectable style.

"Oh, Your Majesty." Gretta's voice betrayed her surprise. "The queen is still dressing for the day."

I swiveled on the seat, catching sight of my husband standing in the doorway. The casing framed him like a work of art. And what a lovely work of art he made in his rich blue velvet surcoat that perfectly complimented his skin tone and hair.

God, help me…

"May I come in?"

Gretta looked back at me, waiting for my approval.

I nodded once. "Of course, do come in."

He smiled my way. That broad, genuine expression that made his eyes squint and did inexplicable things to my insides.

Blast that smile!

Gretta moved aside and allowed my husband entrance. Surprisingly, an entourage of maidservants followed behind him. There were five in total, each bearing parcels wrapped with cream linen and tied with blue and green silk ribbons to match the royal colors.

"What is all this?" I stood from my dressing stool.

Nicholas bowed with a flourish of his good arm. "Happy Birthday, Adelaide. I come bearing gifts."

My heart fluttered with surprise and pleasure. "You remembered it was my birthday?"

"And why should I have forgotten?" He rose and instructed the servants to sit the parcels on the floor in front of my fireplace. Then he gently took my hand and led me to one of the chairs before the hearth. "Here, sit. I will hand them to you to open."

I settled into the chair, marveling at his generosity. First the tea, flowers, and book–now all of these gifts.

"This one first." Nicholas placed a gift in my lap before taking his own seat opposite me. He perched on the edge, looking eager as a young boy awaiting a sweet.

Heart fluttering even more, I tugged at the silk ribbon, unfastening the bow that held the folds of linen together, pulling back the wrapping. I gasped. "Oh, Nicholas!"

"I overheard my aunt telling you to have new gowns made the other day, since your others are... no longer suitable. I also noticed you were reluctant to act on her suggestion, so I spoke with the royal seamstresses myself. They have created new gowns that you will be able to wear for the rest of your pregnancy." His face suddenly tinged red. "I hope I did not overstep. Or offend. Especially since... they are not mourning clothes."

I smoothed a hand over the icy-blue velvet gown. My heart felt torn, caught between elation at the beautiful gifts and guilt at the thought of putting away my mourning. Since I was already remarried, *technically* it was not improper for me to cease outwardly mourning my previous husband. But the fact that it was not improper did not necessarily make it the right thing to do...

I swallowed my inner turmoil, at least for the moment. "How could I be offended by such a generous gift?"

His eyes were like smoldering embers, heating me from my toes to my face. "Hold it up to you."

I rose from my seat, unfurling the heavy gown, letting the linen wrapping tumble to the floor. I held the shoulders to my chest while the velvet fell in thick folds to my feet. "'Tis beautiful, Nicholas." The gown had extra panels of fabric that allowed for my expanding middle, and the round neckline, flowing sleeves, and skirt were hemmed with an intricately beaded design.

"'Twas only a sennight ago that Nerissa and I spoke of new gowns. How did the seamstresses have time to create such beautiful garments so quickly?"

"'Twas a feat, I will not deny. But they were eager to do the work for their beloved queen." He nodded to the four parcels still at my feet. "Open the others."

I handed the first gown to Nicholas, who stretched it over his lap, and settled back into my chair to open the other gifts. Each one held an equally breathtaking gown, sewn with love and care that was visible in every stitch.

"Are you pleased?" He sounded so anxious, so eager.

I pushed out a smile. Did it reach all the way to my eyes? I doubted it. "Of course. Thank you, Nicholas."

He stood, hefting up the gowns I had piled on his lap. His left arm had indeed grown stronger over the weeks since his injury. "Shall you wear one for your birthday?"

I found myself on my feet as well, looking into his face. "Would you like for me to?" I remained unsure how I felt about the matter, but...

"Very much so. And if you do, wear this one. For me?" He indicated the ice-blue one with a jerk of his chin. "It matches your eyes."

My mouth opened and closed. Heat seared my cheeks into a rosy hue. It was too long before I was able to get my mind and tongue to work together. "I thank you again, Nicholas. No one has ever been so generous on my birthday. Except my father when I was a little girl. He found *any* excuse to purchase me a new pony."

"The day is still young. Who says this is all I have planned?" He cocked that too-dazzling smile again. "We shall celebrate with great feasting this afternoon."

"There is no need to go to so much trouble. You shall spoil me, my king."

"That is the idea." He tipped his head down, waggling his black brows playfully.

I could bear that smile and the sultry light of his eyes no more. I took the pile of gowns from him and turned away, carrying them to my bed as quickly as I could. "In that case, I shall see you in a few hours."

Nicholas departed soon after, and Gretta returned–I had not even realized she and the other servants left, giving the king and I privacy. "They are most beautiful, my queen!" She reverently touched a navy over-gown with gold details and paired with a red silk underdress.

"They are, indeed."

"The king is such a kind man, is he not?"

"Yes… He is." I smoothed a hand over the pale blue gown–the one he claimed matched my eyes. Had he chosen the fabric himself for that very reason?

It *was* a beautiful gown. One of the loveliest I had ever owned. But was I truly ready to set aside my mourning attire?

To lay aside the outward sign of my grief felt like moving on from Miles. And I had already told myself I could not do that yet. Every time I thought about leaving Miles behind me and allowing my feelings for Nicholas to grow, guilt assaulted me once again. It plunged me back into my nightmare, Miles' accusations ringing in my ears.

"Do you want to change into one of these, Your Majesty? Any of them would look so lovely on you."

I turned at the sound of Gretta's innocent question. She watched me with expectant eyes, patiently awaiting my answer.

Nicholas

Nicholas had not felt this nervous since his midnight wedding. He tapped his heel against the Banquet Hall floor. Where was she? What in Heaven's name was taking so long?

More importantly… had she decided to wear one of her new gowns?

Nicholas knew only three months had passed since Miles' death, but in a way, she was no longer a widow. She was *Nicholas'* wife now, and he was very much alive and well.

Nicholas knew not if he could ever truly replace his cousin in Adelaide's heart. But he did know her leaving widowhood behind was a crucial step in the process of building a life and hopefully… *love* with his wife.

They had made so much progress, building a friendship over these past two months. Yet they would never be able to go any further if Adelaide was unwilling to do so.

Please, God. I yearn to win her heart, to share that tender sort of affection my father shared with my mother and stepmother. Let her continue to open her heart to me.

And let this plan of mine not be a horrible mistake.

The doors to the Banquet Hall opened and his head snapped up. *Bother…* It was only his aunt, stepmother, and Eleanor. He sighed, watching as the trio of women crossed the room to where he and the Royal Council and their families mingled.

But the doors opened again a moment later, and there she was. His *breathtaking* queen.

His heart soared into his throat and then sagged back down with relief. *She wore it.*

The blue gown looked even better on her than he expected. She was radiant, like an angel drifting across the room toward him. The folds of fabric lay across her softly rounded stomach and cascaded to the floor like a waterfall, swishing across the stone as she walked. The color of her eyes—the exact hue of the dress—stood out even from this distance and he was hopelessly lost.

How could any woman be so beautiful?

She made him weak in the knees.

"My queen." He hurried to her side, taking her hand and kissing it. "You are... the loveliest thing my eyes have ever beheld."

Her cheeks flushed crimson. "You flatter me."

"'Tis not flattery if it is true."

He led Adelaide to her chair at the right hand of his and stood with his goblet held aloft. "I would like to raise a toast to my wife, our lovely and gracious Queen Adelaide of Trilaria. Her gentle heart, fierce passion, and unwavering loyalty are crowning jewels unto her." He let his eyes fall on Adelaide, hoping she could see his sincerity. "And *she* is the crowning jewel of all Trilaria."

Everyone raised cheers of, "Long live the queen," and a becoming blush spread up his wife's neck and into her face. She did not enjoy being the center of attention, yet she deserved it more than anyone he knew.

When the cheers at last died down, the feasting began. Nicholas had instructed the kitchen staff to prepare all of Adelaide's favorite dishes, and he delighted in her pleasure at the spread and every happy hum of delight as she ate. But Nicholas himself found it difficult to enjoy the food when all he wanted was to be alone with her. To give her the last and most important gift he had prepared. To see if she would accept it... or spurn it.

When at last every dish had been served and eaten, and the other diners began to disperse, Nicholas leaned close to his wife. "Expect me to come for you at the supper hour. I have more plans for this day."

Her soft floral scent teased his nose as she turned her head toward him. "Nicholas, I believe you have already done enough for one day."

He stood from his chair, taking her hand and kissing it. "Just be ready when I come for you, my queen."

Chapter 27

Adelaide

THE SERVANTS PREPARED A LIGHT SUPPER FOR US IN THE privacy of the sitting room that night, complete with a tray of delectable strawberry tarts–just as I told Nicholas I favored on birthdays. I devoured more of the treats than I should have; but my nausea had ebbed even more over the last few days, so it was difficult to resist all of the delicious food now that I could properly enjoy it.

When we finished our meal and the servants carried away the remnants, Nicholas retrieved the chess board and set it between us. His skill at the game had increased with each time we played, but this night, he played more poorly than ever.

Was he losing on purpose? Or did something else distract him?

Almost immediately after I declared, "Checkmate," he sat forward in his chair, left hand gripping the armrest.

"Would you care to go for a walk?"

The abrupt question took me off guard. We had yet to do such a thing together, but… why should we not? "I would be happy to, if that is what you wish."

"Splendid." He jumped up to assist me to my feet, and I tucked my hand into the crook of his uninjured arm.

Nicholas led me through the winding passages until we reached a door that led onto the palace wall. The sun had long since set, but a warm summer wind still blew across the city of Valen, ruffling my skirts and the veil covering my hair. I relished the feel of the wind against my face, and the panorama this vantage point offered. "A beautiful view, is it not?"

"Breathtaking, actually." The capital city stretched below us on three sides, while a steep hill cut sharply down behind the palace, keeping that side of the city well protected against attack. Beyond Valen's walls lay gently rolling hills and dense forests.

We came to a stop at one corner of the wall, beside a turret rising high into the air. A flag of Trilaria crowned the turret's roof and snapped in the wind. The world around us lay cloaked in night, but dozens of stars dotted the heavens, lending the kingdom an ethereal glow. Aside from the wind, the snap of flags, and the distant pacing of royal guards, all was silent. Peaceful. One could almost forget that a plague stalked the streets of Trilaria. And that enemies may even now be conspiring to bring about our downfall.

"Adelaide."

Nicholas' voice broke my reverie, bringing my attention to him.

"Our marriage began so unexpectedly that I did not even have the time to procure a proper ring for you. However... I have desired to remedy that."

Suddenly, Nicholas lowered himself to his knee, on the leg he had not injured. He stared up at me in the silvery starlight, his face so earnest, even anxious.

I gasped, my heart speeding dangerously. What on earth was he doing?

Nicholas used his left hand to reach into a drawstring pouch on his belt. "I selected this for you from the royal treasury. I thought it would suit you well." He offered up a silver ring that held a large, glittering sapphire at its center. "Adelaide, Princess of Acuniel and Queen of Trilaria... My wife..." He swallowed. "Will you accept this ring as a token of my troth? For though we wed for reasons of convenience and duty, I pledge my life to you forever."

My eyes roved from his face, down to the ring held in his fingers. It was exquisite, artfully crafted and exactly what I would desire in a ring. But... the sight of it–not to mention his startling words–filled my insides with a tumultuous sort of dread. And more than a touch of panic.

I glanced at Miles' gold and emerald ring still on my left hand.

Nicholas had already indirectly asked me to put aside my mourning clothes, and that had been difficult enough. Now he was directly asking me to further cut ties with my first husband by accepting this new ring.

"Adelaide?"

My gaze snapped to his own. He looked so handsome, innocent, even vulnerable kneeling there in front of me. But the mounting storm of confused emotions blurred that alluring image. Fear and curiosity. Pain and elation. Longing and guilt. It all swirled inside me as I stood stuck between two lives–my past that I wanted to cling to, and a future I feared to accept.

"I... I must go, Nicholas. Please, excuse me."

Then I swept around him and all but ran away. Tears streamed down my face, the storm of emotions erupting with lightning and thunder in my chest.

How could he do this? Did he not see the difficulty of what he was asking of me?

I shut myself in my chamber and sat trembling on the edge of my bed. I had spent three years with Miles and never felt any of the things that Nicholas made me feel... I could not understand it. How could I spend so long with one husband and never come to care for him as I wanted to, and yet spend *two months* with Nicholas and feel so... discombobulated by him? He consumed my thoughts, invading every crevice of my mind and heart.

It could not be right, could it? Not when it made me feel so guilty, so traitorous. Miles' face flashed in my memory, then Nerissa's. How could I let go of the father of my child? How could I break the heart of the woman who called me her daughter, by showing more love and devotion to Nicholas than I did her son?

That was just it... I could not. Not yet. And in that moment... I wondered if I would ever be able to.

Nicholas

She rejected his ring. She rejected *him*.

Nicholas sat against the stone parapets, the silver and sapphire ring clutched in his good hand. He had already been here so long that some of the guards stopped to ask if he was alright. He sent each of them off with a vague reassurance and sank back into his own thoughts.

Of course, he had known this was a possibility. He had known there was every chance that offering Adelaide this ring would scare her away, that this step might be too large for her to take yet. But after the moments they shared since his return from Dartwell, and after she arrived at the banquet in the gown he gave her instead of her widow's garb... He had hoped... He had thought...

"I was a fool." Nicholas pressed his fist to his mouth.

The worst of this was, seeing Adelaide run away from him, feeling pain sharper than any blade piercing his chest, made him realize...

He *loved* his wife.

He had come to care for her in ways beyond mere physical attraction, springing from a place deep within his soul. 'Twas a love that was true and hard to put to words, yet so certain he could feel it in his blood.

But Adelaide did not love him in return.

Nicholas had never been easily prone to tears, preferring to keep a stiff upper lip for the sake of his family. But *this* tore at his heart in ways he never could have expected. The tears came, hot and blinding, filled with the pain and embarrassment of her rejection.

All he had wanted was to take care of her and make her happy, winning her love in the process. That had been his goal these past months since their unexpected union. But somehow, he accomplished the opposite–he caused her pain and pushed her farther away.

He should have *known* not to rush her. He should have known not to take this risk. He should have known that she was not ready to leave Miles behind yet.

Mayhap she would never be...

Nicholas swiped at his tears in frustration. Then he gathered the discarded pieces of his heart, pushed to his feet, and forced himself to walk to his chamber. He paused outside Adelaide's room, resisting the desire to knock. No light shone from beneath the door, so she must already be abed.

With a sigh, he entered his own chamber. After his manservant helped him prepare for bed, Nicholas sat before the empty hearth, the ring in his hand once more.

It mocked him. Declaring his foolishness.

He had taken a risk, made his move, and suffered for it. Just like in their frequent chess games, when he could never seem to win, no matter how hard he tried.

Whether he would one day win her heart or be forever doomed to the pain of unrequited love, Nicholas knew not. But he did know one thing—he would not press Adelaide into a deeper relationship with him again. As in chess, he had made his move, and now… he would wait for her to make her own.

Nicholas looked down at the ring again, twirling it between his fingers.

But first… he would do one last thing.

Adelaide

For the first time in forever, it seemed, I woke without any trace of nausea. I no longer required the ginger tea that had been such a comfort to me these last months, but it arrived on my tray that morning, nonetheless.

Wrapped in my favorite dressing gown, I sat down to break my fast. Steam from the cup of tea swirled up into my face, mingling with the scent of porridge, boiled eggs, and fresh raspberries. It taunted me, reminding me of the man who began this daily ritual of mine.

Thoughts of Nicholas had haunted me like a horde of ghosts all through the night. Dark circles lined the bottoms of my eyes, though, luckily, Gretta had made no remark on them.

I knew not which was worse now: the nightmares about Miles, or the tormenting thoughts of Nicholas.

"Oh, I nearly forgot." Gretta finished laying out my gown—an olive green one Nicholas had given me yesterday—and crossed the room to me. She withdrew something from her apron pocket.

"The king gave this to me on the way up and asked me to deliver it."

She held out a folded piece of parchment. A slanted, masculine hand had scrawled my name across the front.

I took the parchment from her, my pulse tripping over itself. "Thank you, Gretta."

She curtseyed before returning to her duties, leaving me to read whatever note the parchment held. No doubt written by Nicholas himself.

All thought of food and tea forgotten, I carefully unfolded it. Something slid out and dropped into my lap.

The ring.

Snatching it up, my eyes moved from the ring to the note, hurriedly reading each word.

> *Adelaide,*
> *The ring is yours to keep and do with as you*
> *will. Wear it only if you so choose.*
> *Yours,*
> *Nicholas*

My back thudded against the wood of my chair. I looked down at the ring in my palm, studying the delicate design the silversmith had crafted along its sides, and the sparkling sapphire at its center.

He would not force me to wear it…

The knowledge was a relief. And yet… it only caused more confusion than before.

"What is that, Your Majesty?"

My fingers snapped closed around the ring, hiding it from Gretta's curious eyes. "Nothing. Just… another birthday gift from King Nicholas."

She grinned, a lone dimple flashing. "He certainly likes to spoil you, my queen. You are quite blessed, if I may say so."

I bit my tongue, offering no comment. Instead, I rose and strode to my desk. If this ring was mine to do with as I pleased, then it would stay here, locked away in a drawer.

Chapter 28

Adelaide

THINGS WERE NO LONGER THE SAME BETWEEN NICHO-las and I. He was still kind as ever, but remained aloof, distant, throwing himself into his daily duties and combat training with greater fervency. We continued our weekly chess games, but while our conversations had once flowed freely and easily, they now felt stilted and strained.

I *should* have felt at peace, knowing he would not press me for more than I was ready to give. But I did not. All I felt was greater inner turmoil than before.

It made little sense and caused even more frustration.

Other changes also came over the following weeks. Lady Clarice and Eleanor decided to return home to Aguilar, feeling obligated to support and assist Mericus in some way. Secretly, I wished the two women would stay in Valen instead. While we did not spend an abundant amount of time together, it was comforting to have more females in residence, especially with things so awkward between Nicholas and I. Besides, I suspected Mericus would not truly appreciate the support of his female relatives.

To compensate for the lack of time spent in Nicholas' company, I made sure to spend more time with Nerissa. I could not help but feel I had neglected her in the past weeks. She seemed happier since the discovery of my pregnancy–it gave her a glimmer of hope to cling to–but I knew she still grieved her losses deeply. Surely loneliness was her constant companion.

So every afternoon following dinner, we sat together to work on needlework. We sewed tiny garments for the babe, which sparked happy conversation about whom it might favor in looks, name ideas, and the like.

Every day, my stomach seemed to grow larger. The flutter and gentle thumps of the child within became a common occurrence. It was both strange and wonderful, and made the knowledge that I would finally bear a child all the more real.

Everything else in the world may be nothing but chaos and confusion, but this babe was a promise… a reminder that life could come from the midst of death. And I had to hold onto that.

Nicholas

Battle plans, death tolls, food shortages… Snatches of his latest meeting with the Royal Council replayed on an endless loop in Nicholas' head. It was enough to drive a man to insanity. Or drink. Or both.

Had ruling the kingdom been this difficult for his uncle? Or was it only Nicholas who could not handle the pressure and stress?

"Nicholas?"

Adelaide's soft voice brought his vision into focus and his mind back to the chess game between them. She stared at him, her face betraying her concern. "Are you feeling well? You look rather peaked."

"Of course; only tired. 'Twas a long day… Much to think about." He rapped his knuckles on his arm rest. "Is it my turn?"

"Yes, I already took mine several moments ago. You were staring so intently at the board that at first I assumed you were thinking through your play."

"Oh. My pardon." He had, in fact, not given any thought to his next move at all. He rubbed his chin. "Let me see…" He selected a knight and moved it.

Adelaide raised a brow in silent question. He had made a poor move apparently. Nicholas winced, but there was no going back now.

Silently, she sat forward to take her turn.

Nicholas had made sure to keep their usual routine of a weekly chess game, despite the dismal failure of his birthday plans. He had distanced himself in many ways, in respect of her wishes, but could not bear to part with these evenings. They were the one bright spot in his stressful weeks.

Except for when they caused more pain than pleasure in his heart.

Sitting alone with her like this, remembering his pain and humiliation, longing for shared love rather than this increasingly tenuous friendship—'twas a thing of torture.

Was he mad for subjecting himself to the agony?

"Oh!"

Adelaide's sharp gasp nearly made his heart stop. He bolted forward in his seat. "Adelaide? What is it? Is something wrong?"

Her hands pressed against her swollen middle, but she did not appear to be in pain. In fact, she looked *elated*.

She laughed, shaking her head. "Nay, not at all. The babe—it just kicked hard. I could feel its foot jab against my side."

He gasped out an incredulous laugh of his own. The process of growing a child was a strange and fascinating miracle. Of course, from the beginning, Nicholas understood that his wife was pregnant; but to know the babe could now be *felt* within her womb made the entire thing more real.

"Oh! There it is again." She looked up at him, hand still pressed against the side of her abdomen. "Would… would you like to feel it?"

His eyes widened. She was truly *inviting* him to touch her, even in a harmless, chaste way?

"Of–of course." He slowly pushed himself out of his chair and went to his knees beside her.

"Here, give me your hand." Nicholas placed his one usable palm in Adelaide's. She flattened it against the lower side of her belly. It was surprisingly firm beneath his touch.

A sudden jolt against his hand startled him. "I feel it!" He stared in wonder. "Utterly amazing…"

She laughed again, the action making her stomach bob. The babe responded with another kick, as if delighted by its mother's laughter. Nicholas looked up at his wife, taking in the sight of her face which seemed to grow in beauty each day that he knew her. How had he been blessed with such a treasure?

Love swelled in his chest, for both Adelaide and this unborn child. Feeling the babe's movement, Nicholas knew more than ever, he loved the child like his own.

But would he ever have a child *truly* of his own blood with Adelaide? The thought that such might never be sent new daggers of pain through his still tender heart.

"Nicholas?" Adelaide's voice pulled him out of his tormenting thoughts. She stared at him, all humor gone from her face and replaced by concern, even some discomfort. "Is... something amiss?"

He reluctantly pulled his palm away. "Nay... Nay, not at all." Nicholas swallowed. If only he could tell her the truth. With everything in him, he wanted to. But doing so would only push her further away, mayhap ruin his chances forever.

He would have to suffer in silence for a while longer yet.

But he could no longer do so this night.

"God's creation is amazing, is it not?" He pushed to his feet. "If you will excuse me, Adelaide, I am afraid I am more tired than I realized. I should go."

Her lips parted, brows knitting together. "O–oh. Very well, then. I shall see you on the morrow."

"Yes, the morrow. Sleep well." Then Nicholas turned and left as quickly as his steps would carry him.

Chapter 29

Nicholas

SLEEP WAS A REFUGE THAT NIGHT, A BLESSED RELIEF from the troubles of his world. For a moment, his mind was at peace, his body at rest.

But an insistent knock abruptly shattered the tranquility.

Nicholas awoke with a start, pushing himself up on his good arm. Darkness still cloaked the room. He could not have been asleep longer than a couple hours–if that.

Nicholas groaned, rubbing at his temple and his eyes. "One moment." Sliding out of bed, Nicholas bemoaned once again that he could not easily dress himself with this blasted broken arm. Glancing around, he grabbed a blanket from the bed and did his best to create some semblance of modesty.

The knock pounded again, this time harder and accompanied by a loud, "King Nicholas? I bring urgent news!"

Nicholas hurried across the rush-strewn ground and opened the door a crack. Captain Stefan stood with Sir Benedict, who had been assigned to guard his door this night. Both men's faces were cold and tense. "King Nicholas," the captain bowed. "My deepest apologies for disturbing you at such an hour. But... a messenger has just arrived, bringing news from the eastern border regions."

The Captain of the Guard swallowed, jaw clenched tight. The man was usually extremely well composed. Whatever this news, it clearly had him shaken.

"It... it is Galiel. They have returned, invading at numerous points all along the border with the full force of their army. Some five thousand in number."

Nicholas' stomach plummeted to his toes. A cold chill of dread swept his body and the last vestige of sleep vanished.

Galiel had arrived after all. War was upon them. And just as Nicholas feared, the men of Trilaria would be horribly outnumbered.

Panic stole up his throat, but he shoved it back down. He had to remain calm. Keep a clear and level head. He had to fly into action and counter the invaders' attack immediately.

"What would you have us do?"

"Summon the Council. I shall meet with them in a half hour." Nicholas fisted his hand tighter in the blanket held around his waist. "And Sir Benedict, summon my manservant to help me dress."

"Yes, Your Majesty." Both men ran to do as bidden while Nicholas waited in restless silence until the servant arrived.

As soon as he was properly clothed, Nicholas dismissed the man. The Council would be expecting him in a few minutes, but there was someone else who needed to hear this news first.

Nicholas hurried to his wife's door and paused with his hand against the latch. "Adelaide?" He gave the courtesy of a knock before he pushed open the door. All was silent within, save for the sound of quiet breathing.

"Adelaide?" He sat on the edge of her bed and gently shook her. "Adelaide, wake up."

A strangled, disoriented sound escaped her throat as her eyes flew open.

"Adelaide, 'tis me."

"Nicholas? Wh–what are you doing here?" She leveraged herself up into a sitting position.

If it were his sister or stepmother to whom he was breaking this news, he would approach it more gently. But he knew Adelaide could handle the straightforward truth. "Galiel has invaded the eastern border. War is upon us."

"God in Heaven..." She clutched a hand to her chest. "What do you plan to do?"

"I must go meet with the Council now to decide the exact course of action, but I know we shall retaliate immediately."

She nodded soberly, rubbing a hand over the swell of her stomach. "I will be praying. Please, keep me apprised of the situation."

"I will, I promise. But you must go back to sleep. 'Tis yet the wee hours."

She scoffed. "How do you expect me to sleep at such a time as this?"

"Please." He dared to reach out and touch her arm. She was warm from sleep beneath the linen of her nightdress. "I have enough troubles to concern myself with, without worrying about you as well."

She ceased her protests, but her lips pressed together, as if holding in those objections. Finally, she sighed. "Very well. I shall *try* my best, but I make no promise that I will be successful."

"A fair enough compromise." A small smile found its way to his mouth, despite the direness of the situation.

If only he could embrace her, feel the solace and strength her arms provided before he headed into this nightmare. Like the time he confessed his torment over the first life he took. He had clung to her like a lifeline then.

Instead, Nicholas sighed and let his hand trail down her arm. "I shall see you soon." Then he stood and hurried out the door.

The mood of the Royal Council chamber was nearly as dark as the night still shadowing the world outside. The gathering of men frantically discussed their next moves, deciding how best to distribute their forces, and dictating letters to exhausted scribes that would be sent to each province posthaste. Riders even now prepared to leave with the all-important letters calling men to arms, along with the knights of Valen, who would leave to join the fight.

"How much longer until our knights are ready to depart?"

"Within the hour, sire."

Nicholas nodded, thinking through the things he needed to do before departure himself. "Good. I trust one of you can ensure the letters are sent. I must prepare to leave." Nicholas stood from his throne.

Lord Raynard blinked. "Your Majesty, I fear I am confused…

You cannot accompany the men. Your arm is not yet fully healed! Even now you wear it in a sling."

"It is healed enough. 'Tis been more than six weeks since the injury, and the physician was scheduled to remove the sling in a few days. Besides, I have been training my other arm to use a sword as well. I shall not stay behind while our men go to fight."

A chorus of protests collided in the air. Lord Raynard and two other councilmen stood from their seats, desperation in their voices.

"My king, you mustn't."

"You shall do more good here until you are well enough to fight safely."

"I beg you to reconsider, Your Majesty."

Frustration boiled within him. This was exactly what he feared. He knew, in his gut, that Galiel was not finished with them, that they would be back. He feared he would not be well enough to lead the fight when the time came. And here that fear was coming true before his eyes.

Nicholas could not stay within the safety of Valen while his men bled and died for their country. He would feel like too much of a coward. As useless as his broken arm.

"Nay!" He sliced his hand through the air, silencing the Council. "I shall leave with the men this very morn."

Lord Raynard stepped closer, his hands clasped entreatingly. "Your Majesty, please. Think on this. Our kingdom needs a ruler that is alive and well far more than it needs a warrior leading the charge into battle. 'Tis in everyone's best interest if you stay here."

Nicholas growled, wanting to rip off his sling and prove then and there that he could use his arm perfectly well. Instead, he turned aside, bracing his good hand on his hip and drawing a deep breath. Could there be a way to do as he desired *and* please his counselors?

"Very well. Summon the physician and have him examine me. Then we may determine what shall be done."

Shortly thereafter, Nicholas found himself back in his chambers with the Council crowded about him and the physician removing the sling and splint from Nicholas' arm. Every movement of his stiff muscles was agony, but Nicholas held his tongue. After a few minutes of careful examination, the aging man shook his head.

"The bone appears sound. However, it shall take several weeks, even months, for your arm to return to its previous strength. I am afraid your recovery is far from over yet."

Nicholas pulled away from the physician. Not the answer he was hoping for, in the least.

Why did he have to be such a dolt as to fall down a flight of stairs and break his arm in the first place? There was no time for a hindrance like this!

"I shall stay a fortnight, but not a day longer."

"Your Majesty, it would be better if—"

"*That* is my decision," he cut off the physician's words. "And it is final. Anyone who attempts to dissuade me shall be in contempt of the crown."

The physician lowered his head. His advisors stiffened, the room falling uncomfortably silent. "You are dismissed. Lord Harold, please see to it that all letters to our noblemen are dispatched. Lord Raynard, please see the knights of Valen off to war."

Low murmurs of assent followed, along with hurried, muted steps, and then Nicholas was alone in his chamber with naught but a useless arm and a boiling cauldron of frustration.

Chapter 30

Adelaide

THE FIRST TWO WEEKS OF THE WAR WITH GALIEL SEEMED an agonizing eternity, full of restless days and equally restless nights, waiting with bated breath for news from the front.

Nicholas was nigh unbearable to be around. He paced like an animal trapped in a cage, desperate for someone to let him out. He spoke little, and what words he shared were short and terse. I knew he slept little as well, for the flickering light of a candle shone beneath our connecting door more often than not when I rose in the night to relieve myself.

I would have begrudged his waspish attitude if it were not for the deeply troubled shadows lurking in his eyes every time our paths crossed. How could I blame him when my own heart was so unsettled?

Most nights, I found myself tossing and turning before finally succumbing to sleep. My nightmares became more frequent again, waking me nearly as often as my pregnant bladder. Frightening images of plague-riddled soldiers fighting and dying by the hundreds haunted me, so disturbingly real that I dreaded going to sleep each night, even as my body cried out for rest.

An even greater darkness than before now stole across our land, threatening to destroy everyone and everything I loved...

How could I *not* be troubled when faced with such a reality?

I desperately wished to describe our situation to my mother, but I knew I could not. If I was to honor my husband's wishes not to seek aid from my father, then my family could know nothing of our circumstances. Or at least not hear it from me. Who knew how fast the news would spread by simple word-of-mouth?

Without my mother's wise words or presence, I often sought comfort in prayer, though it seemed any and all peace was hard won. It felt as though the heavens were blocked to me, with my prayers and the Lord's comfort leaking through tiny chinks in a stone ceiling.

What strength I had, I shared with Nerissa, keeping her spirits bolstered even if mine flagged. I tried to do the same for Nicholas, offering him conversation and friendly smiles when appropriate. But he received little of it, preferring to keep to himself and the dark troubles straining his features and forming knots of tension in his shoulders.

As the fortnight drew closer and closer to an end, a greater sense of fear bore down on my heart. I would never try to bar Nicholas from doing what he felt he must do as king, but I could not escape the worry that his leaving would only end in tragedy.

I once told him that I knew he would be ready for the war when and if it came, but now... I could not help the doubt crowding in on that earlier belief. What if the physician and the Council were right? With a weak left arm and even weaker right arm, Nicholas would be nearly handicapped on the battlefield. How on earth could he possibly survive a war in such a state?

The Lord spared his life in battle once... but would He do so again? Or would my husband's determination to be a good king ultimately be his undoing?

Nicholas

Nicholas swung his sword around, his body whirling with it. All the force of his movement propelled his blade into the wooden practice dummy in the training area of the courtyard. It was late, and he should be preparing for bed. But he had not been able to resist one last practice session alone before his departure on the morrow.

As soon as his blade connected with the wooden form, pain ricocheted up his arm. Nicholas cried out involuntarily before snapping his mouth shut, his sword clattering to the ground. He clutched where his right arm had broken, and bit back a curse until the pain abated.

Had he caught the attention of any on duty guards? Nicholas dearly hoped not.

Stretching his unused arm over the past days had been agonizing–arguably more painful than the break itself. Nicholas quickly realized it would be a daily uphill struggle to regain his former strength. Yet he was determined, his decision set in stone and beyond all negotiation. He would not stay here in the safety of his palace while his kingdom struggled for its very existence. And so, from sunup to sundown, he worked the atrophied muscles in his dominant arm, while also continuing to strengthen his other one.

His efforts were not without any success, but still a far cry from attaining his desired goal. It remained painful to fight, and it would take all his strength and resolve to wield a weapon in the midst of battle.

But Nicholas would not relent… He would not give up. There was far too much at stake for that.

The next morning, Nicholas exited into the dreary morning sunlight, dressed for battle. His curls had been washed and combed into order, a simple gold crown placed upon his head. He was ready for war, even if no one else thought so.

Adelaide stood with his aunt, dark circles smeared like paint beneath her eyes, and her hands clenched in front of her pregnant belly. Why did she look so weary? Was she unwell?

His heart stumbled over a knot of fear, and for the first time, Nicholas doubted his decision to leave. What if something happened to her and the babe while he was gone?

What if he died in battle and never saw her again?

Nicholas crossed the bustling courtyard and reached for his wife's clenched hands. They were cold to the touch, despite the warmth of the summer morning. "Prithee, take care while I am away."

She nodded solemnly. "We shall pray every day for your safe return, and for favor upon our army." She blinked furiously, her chin tucked. Was she fighting back tears? "Your kingdom needs you, Nicholas. Do keep yourself alive and well..."

Her words sent both pain and pleasure through his heart. She genuinely did not want him to die. Did that mean she cared for him in a way beyond friendship?

Nicholas squeezed her hands tighter, feeling the press of Miles' ring against his palm.

He stifled a pained sigh. Best not allow himself to be fooled into seeing love where there was none.

"Farewell, Adelaide."

Then Nicholas released her hands and forced himself to turn away, stride to his horse, and mount up before he did something foolish.

Like declare his undying love for her. Or change his mind about going to fight after all...

PART 3

Chapter 31

One month later...

Nicholas

NICHOLAS HISSED A BREATH THROUGH HIS TEETH AT the damp rag's contact with the gash on his face. The wound ran from just above his left eyebrow, down to his cheekbone. Though not quite deep enough to warrant sutures, it still stung like a dozen bee stings and had bled profusely. The camp physician offered his apologies for the third time before dipping the rag in a bowl of water and dabbing at the wound again.

"'Twill leave a scar, but 'tis nothing serious. It will give you an air of mystery, make your presence more... imposing."

Nicholas chuckled at the physician's attempt to reassure him. "Imposing, eh? We shall see. I am only thankful the dagger's blade missed my eye."

"A fortunate thing, indeed, sire."

Nicholas winced at another sting. So far, he had managed to avoid serious injury, even with his weakened arms. But it had not been easy. Every day of this last month had been a struggle to not only survive, but also project the image that he had all of this chaos under control.

Battles actively took place all along the eastern regions. Villages, towns, and manors were being raided, and two castles were currently under attack–one of them being Dartwell. With their inferior numbers and so many different fronts of battle, the Trilarians were hard pressed to keep up.

"Your Majesty, Commander Andrew is here to see you."

Nicholas looked up at Sir Benedict standing in the open flap of his tent. "Please, send him in."

The knight bowed and moved out of sight. The staggering form of his military leader soon filled the doorway. "King Nicholas, I am relieved to know you are well." The leader of his army bowed low.

"Yes, 'tis nothing but a scratch really. The physician here is nearly finished cleaning me up. Please, take a seat."

Commander Andrew lowered his bulky frame onto a stool, opposite where Nicholas sat on the edge of his cot. "I come bearing the latest reports from our various divisions. I regret 'tis not good news, Your Majesty."

Nicholas' stomach knotted. "Physician, would you please excuse us for a moment?"

Immediately, the man halted his ministrations, set aside the soiled rag and bowl of water, and quit the tent.

"Please, speak freely, Commander."

"First, the worst news… Dartwell has fallen."

Alarm spiked through Nicholas' pulse. "Go on…"

"The castle was overcome, Lord Francis killed. As yet, I know not what has become of his family. We can only hope the Galielians retain a shred of honor and have shown them mercy."

Images of his time in Dartwell flashed in Nicholas' memory—fighting alongside Lord Francis, watching him care for his people who took shelter within the walls of his castle. That man was gone, his castle conquered.

The first of Trilaria's strongholds to fall into enemy hands.

"You said that was the worst news. What other tidings do you bring?"

"The troops from Maren are gravely battered to our north. The plague runs rampant through their men, killing just as many as the war itself."

"What of the Galielian troops? Do we know if the plague has infiltrated their numbers?"

"I have heard no reports yet. But it is certainly a possibility, after nearly seven weeks since entering our borders. We can only hope that it does—and soon. In fact... I can send instructions for the bodies of plague victims to be launched into the enemy lines during the next conflict, if you so desire."

Bile roiled in Nicholas' gut. "Nay. Absolutely not. I shall not dishonor our people's loved ones in such a way."

"As you wish, sire..." The man's tone alluded to his disagreement on the matter, but Nicholas was firm on this.

"Anything else?"

Commander Andrew shifted on the low stool, his large frame clearly uncomfortable there. "The attack on Ferrynsworth Castle continues. Duke Ferrynsworth and his men remain strong—for now. Also, a large division of Galielians have been spotted heading our way. We believe they could be en route to Claimore, now that Dartwell has been conquered. Many of the invaders who took the region shall doubtless be headed that way next, as well."

The region of Claimore lay squarely between Dartwell and Valen, a day's hard ride from Nicholas' camp. Though that was with only a small group of men traveling. When transporting an army on foot, that time increased dramatically.

"Send word for someone to reinforce Ferrynsworth. We shall prepare to meet the enemy and keep them from reaching Claimore as long as possible. Who is close enough to aid us?"

"Your brother and his troops from Aguilar could arrive in a day or so. I can send a rider to them immediately, if you wish."

At the mention of Mericus, Nicholas tensed. Was He ready to cross paths with his twin just now? "Yes, please do."

"I will see to all the arrangements forthwith."

"If that is all, Commander, you are dismissed."

The man stood, bowing low. "Good eve to you, sire."

He departed, leaving Nicholas alone for a blessed moment. Crickets chirruped outside, the sun beginning to set in the west. The direction of home. And Adelaide.

What was she doing just now? Preparing for supper? He prayed she was well, along with the babe.

Nicholas looked out at the world beyond his tent opening. *God, be with her. Keep her safe in my absence.*

The prayerful thought brought his stepmother to mind, and then Eleanor. And then Mericus. He said a prayer for each, lingering on Mericus.

His brother had taken the longest of any of his nobles to respond to the order to raise his troops, but Mericus had shown himself loyal to his country in the end. He immediately responded to the call to war after the invasion, leading his troops to their assigned location. Such actions proved Mericus cared about his country enough not to attempt rebellion and treason, but did that mean he had forgiven Nicholas?

He would know soon enough. Their paths were about to converge once more.

The physician returned then to finish cleaning Nicholas' wound. As soon as the task was completed, Nicholas excused the man, shed his outer garments, and stretched out on his cot. He missed his large, soft bed back in Valen. He ached for Adelaide. But this sparse tent, uncomfortable cot, and daily struggle to lead the army was his reality now.

This was war…

And Nicholas did not see a soon victory in sight.

For two days, Nicholas and his men waited for his brother to arrive. A tense mood hung over the camp, all eyes trained on the horizon. A scout Nicholas sent into the surrounding area returned the evening of the second day with news that the Galielians would reach the River Threin by the following afternoon. They could wait no longer than morning if they wished to surprise attack the invaders from the advantageous higher ground on the river's western edge.

Nicholas gave instructions to have the Valen soldiers set out at dawn, fully expecting Mericus not to arrive. Commander Andrew said his brother could reach them in a day or so, but it had already been over two. Had his brother decided to rebel against his authority after all? Or mayhap the group was attacked on the way and barred from reaching them by another group of invaders… Regardless of the reason, Nicholas could wait no longer.

At first light on the third day, Nicholas emerged from his tent, chain mail and crown in place, his sword swinging at his hip. His squire had already saddled Castor and waited with the beast nearby, rubbing Castor's mane while he chomped on dried summer grass.

Suddenly, someone shouted in the distance. It was too far off for Nicholas to make out the words, but the news quickly spread.

"The flag of Aguilar has been spotted! Lord Mericus has arrived!"

Nicholas stepped away from his horse, the small meal he had scarfed down turning sour in his stomach. He set off at a brisk pace toward the camp's edge.

His twin had arrived. And Nicholas would now face him whether he was ready to or not...

By the time Nicholas reached the edge of camp, the men of Aguilar were fully visible in the pale light of dawn, along with the standard of Aguilar flapping in the breeze. At the fore of the group, Nicholas spotted an all-too-familiar dark head.

When the newcomers reined to a halt, Nicholas hurried forward to meet his brother as he leapt from the saddle.

"Your Majesty..." Mericus bowed, and to most, the words and gesture must have seemed genuine. But Nicholas recognized the underlying sarcasm.

Apparently, his brother had *not* let go of his anger yet after all...

"'Tis good to see you, Brother."

Mericus stood with his hands clasped behind his back. "My men are here and ready to fight. Where do matters stand with the advancing Galielians?"

So no warm greeting then... "A scout has reported that the enemy is poised to cross the River Threin within a day's time. We aim to meet them there and block them from advancing toward Claimore as long as possible. We were just preparing to leave now."

"I will tell my men not to get comfortable. We shall set forth at your word." His brother spun on his heel and, without so much as a "by your leave", left to instruct his troops.

Nicholas turned away as well, heading back into the bustling activity as knights and squires busily tore down camp. He ground his jaw, easing a breath out through his nose. *Why* did Mericus insist on such a wall of hostility between them? Was there even a way for Nicholas to scale it?

Father's heart would break if he could see us now...

Chapter 32

Nicholas

ANTICIPATION, FEAR, BLOODLUST... IT ALL MINGLED TO-
gether in the warm summer air, so strong Nicholas could almost
taste it. The combined forces of Valen and Aguilar, four hundred
in number, lay in wait behind him, two furlongs from the western
side of the River Threin. The sound of marching feet and hooves
thudded in the distance.

The Galielians would reach the river at any moment.

The sun beat down hot overhead, its light rippling across the
gentle flowing waters of the Threin. Waters that would soon turn
red with blood...

Anxiety clawed at Nicholas' stomach so hard he thought he
might grow sick. Sweat slicked his back beneath his mail hauberk
and other battle gear. Unlike some of the men behind him, Nicholas did not relish the coming conflict—as he did not relish any of
the battles he fought over the past month. Every life he took was
like a stone piled upon his back. And he had no wish to add another to that pile.

But he would do what must be done. For Trilaria. For his family. For Adelaide.

God, give me strength! Let me lead us to victory.

Castor shifted beneath him, sensing his unease. Nicholas
rubbed a gloved hand along the horse's neck. "Not much longer
now, boy."

Indeed, less than a quarter hour later, the company of Galielian soldiers came into view on the other side of the river. Hidden
as they were by a small ridge, the Trilarians remained unseen. The

cavalry led the procession of Galielians and halted along the water's edge. A man at the front, seemingly the leader of the company, whirled around and shouted orders that Nicholas could not make out across the distance. The enemy troops began the task of fording the river and bringing their men across.

Comparing the size of the group to Nicholas' own, he would guess the Galielians were at least eight hundred in number. Out manning them by two to one.

Nicholas shifted himself and Castor further behind the stand of trees that shielded him from view, then turned to Commander Andrew and Mericus behind him.

"Commander, tell the men to fall into formation. Once the Galielians cross, I will give the signal to march atop the ridge."

"Yes, sire." His military leader bowed and turned his horse to do as instructed.

Nicholas eyed his brother who still remained behind him. Mericus sat straight and tall in his saddle, the muscles of his arms visible even beneath his chainmail, his body poised for combat. "God be with you this day, Brother." Nicholas meant every word of the sentiment.

Mericus only glanced at him, his silence ringing louder than any shout.

Jaw clenching, heart sinking, Nicholas faced forward in his saddle.

Every minute seemed a small eternity, but at last, their enemies stood on their side of the river. Before the invaders could reorganize their lines, Nicholas raised his arm and motioned forward. He nudged Castor's side and led him out onto the top of the ridge in full view of the enemy. His soldiers moved in behind him in neat lines, first a row of archers, followed by the foot soldiers, with the cavalry flanking the sides. The only riders that would charge the center were himself, Mericus, and Commander Andrew.

Nicholas drew his sword and raised it to the morning sky. "For Trilaria!"

The shout echoed behind him and radiated down the ridge to the Galielians, who looked up at them in alarm. Men shouted orders below and the Galielians scrambled to prepare for the assault.

This element of surprise and the fact that Nicholas' men had the higher ground would be their only advantages. He prayed it would be enough...

The Trilarians marched forth, and once they drew within firing range, Nicholas signaled the archers to send down a volley of arrows. Some met their mark, but the assault primarily hindered the forming of the enemies' battle formation. The archers sent another three volleys of arrows down before Nicholas spurred Castor onward, signaling the men to speed up their march.

When only a short distance stood between them and their opponents, the Trilarians charged full force, ramming into the broken lines of Galiel's forces.

As they had been throughout these last weeks of combat, the Trilarians were outnumbered. But they fought for their homes, their families, for the existence of the kingdom they loved, and no number of enemy soldiers or overwhelming odds would deter them.

Sweat dripped down Nicholas' face, nearly blinding him. He swiped at his eyes with his free hand before whirling Castor around to assist Commander Andrew in finishing off his opponent. The man's horse had been killed out from under him, forcing him to fight on foot.

The Battle at the River Threin had begun well, with his men felling many of the enemy troops in rapid succession. But then the Galielians rallied, better organizing their lines and pressing in from the sides.

Things were rapidly spiraling out of control.

Nicholas stabbed his sword forward, piercing through his and Commander Andrew's opponent. When the body fell, Nicholas turned to quickly survey the scene. All around him, his men fought with feverish desperation. But too many of them were falling, either wounded or dead.

Far too many.

Nicholas sucked in a breath that tasted of sweat and blood. The roar of combat rattled his ears. He spotted Mericus a short distance away. His brother still fought from atop of his solid black steed. His hair, drenched with sweat, stuck to his forehead and cheeks in clumps. A startling ferocity, more vicious than even the day he accused Nicholas of stealing the throne, burned in his eyes.

His brother was a warrior of the fiercest degree.

But even great warriors could be brought low.

It happened before Nicholas could shout a warning–an enemy spear coming from behind and stabbing his brother.

"Mericus!" Nicholas spurred Castor forward, plowing through the melee to reach his twin's side. Mericus' sat hunched over in his saddle, looking as though he would topple.

The world blurred as Nicholas' sword flew as if of its own accord, attacking his brother's assailant.

Panic.

Blood pulsing in his temples.

Raging fear.

A sharp blow to his head.

Fury.

Before he knew it, the spear-wielding soldier was dead and Nicholas was out of the saddle, crouching at his brother's side with no regard for the raging chaos surrounding them.

A crimson tide of blood already soaked the grass beneath Mericus' back. Nicholas gripped his arm. "Brother. I am here."

Mericus said nothing, only writhed in pain, eyes wide.

Suddenly, the noise around Nicholas rushed back into his awareness. The battle. His men. They were losing. They were dying. But he could not let this be the end. They *had* to live to fight another day.

And if there was one thing he learned over the past month, it was the hard truth that sometimes there was only one way to do that.

"Retreat!" Nicholas screamed out. "Trilaria, retreat!" He pushed himself up from the blood-soaked grass, pulling his brother with him.

"Leave me–"

"Nay," Nicholas snapped, using every ounce of his strength to support his brother's weight. "I shan't leave you here."

Miraculously, Castor still stood where Nicholas had left him, though he stomped his hooves and tossed his head in agitation. A pair of Trilarian soldiers covered Nicholas as he managed to heft his brother over the horse's back.

"Trilaria, retreat!" he shouted again.

All around them, his men responded, breaking away to rush through the ever-narrowing opening at their backs as the Galielians continued to hem them in. Nicholas lingered only long enough to ensure all had taken notice of the retreat before darting forward himself. He sprinted as fast as he could, pulling Castor behind him and climbing back up the slope away from the river's edge.

He had been forced to retreat plenty of times in the last month, but this time was different. This time, retreat tasted like a bitter gall on his tongue. Surviving felt like cowardice. And carrying his wounded brother from the battlefield seemed the greatest failure of all.

Chapter 33

Nicholas

THE MOANS OF WOUNDED MEN ECHOED OUTSIDE Nicholas' tent. Dozens of soldiers littered the ground in the sun-baked valley where the Trilarian squires had established camp while the battle raged. Each of these lives mattered, and each weighed heavy on his heart. But here, in this shadowed tent, one life mattered more than any other.

Nicholas tapped his foot anxiously, his bloodied and dirt-streaked fist pressed against his mouth. Blood dripped from a place where the gash beside his eye had split open again. His right arm ached from too much strain and a knot pulsed on his head from the blow he sustained. Yet Nicholas scarcely took note of any of it.

The camp physician looked up from Mericus' ashen form lying on Nicholas' own cot. He shook his head, eyes conveying honest sorrow.

A boulder settled in Nicholas' stomach. He knew. Had known it the moment he saw the spear pierce his brother's flesh, but had refused to admit it...

His twin was going to die.

Silently, the physician rose and departed the tent, leaving the brothers alone. Nicholas knelt on the grass at his brother's side. 'Twas a miracle Mericus survived even this long, so grievous was his wound and blood loss. But Nicholas would waste not a moment longer. He missed his chance to bid Father farewell. He would not repeat that with Mericus.

Emotion clogged Nicholas' throat, and it was several moments before he could get any words past the lump. "Mericus?" Nicholas reached out and gripped his brother's hand. "I am here with you."

"Nicholas?" His brother's voice was dry and brittle as straw. His eyes slowly fluttered open to rest on Nicholas' face.

"Yes, I am here."

Mericus stared at him through glassy eyes. "I told you..." his brother's breath came short, "to leave me... on the battlefield."

"And I said I would not. I could never leave you to perish alone like that." His breath hitched on that lump in his throat again. Was he really having this conversation? "I love you, Mericus."

A breath of a laugh passed his brother's lips. "You... love me? I would not... have known it."

Nicholas gripped Mericus' hand tighter, leaning further over him. "I have loved you every day of my life, and I have *tried* to show it. Have I failed so miserably that you would doubt me even now, at a time like this?"

Mericus tried to pull his hand away, but he was too weak to escape Nicholas' grip. His breath wheezed sharply–the unmistakable rattle of death. "You sought... to take... what should have... been mine."

"Nay! Never. I did not ask for any of this to happen. I only ever wanted to *protect* you, our family, Aguilar, the kingdom. I tried to take care of all of you, Mericus." He had not wanted to cry here, where only the fabric walls of his tent could muffle the sound from any passersby. But the tears spilled anyway.

"You... betrayed me. You... stole the throne. You stole... Father."

"Stole Father? How could you– That is ridiculous. I never *stole* him from you."

"He... always loved you... more than me. I could never... be the heir... he wanted."

Nicholas' shoulders sagged. Was that truly what Mericus believed? "Nay, Brother. Father loved you. I *know* he did."

Mericus shook his head. "I do not need... your attempts... to comfort me... I know the truth." Once again, Mericus tried to pull out of Nicholas' hold, but Nicholas refused.

"Mericus, I–" His breath came fast, the weariness of the day's events setting in, along with an acute sense of anguish. "I know not how to–" He shook his head. "Please, Brother, I beg you. Forgive me for whatever trespasses I have made against you. Please, I have no wish to leave things as they are."

Mericus remained silent, his expression cold.

Did his brother's hatred truly run so deep that he would refuse to make amends on his deathbed?

Nay, this could not be! It could not end like this.

Nicholas would do anything, give anything, to make things right. If only his brother would hear and accept the sincerity of his heart!

"Mericus, please." He hiccupped on a sob. "I am your brother and despite what you may have believed, I love you. I never wished to harm you. But if I have failed in this, I beg your forgiveness. Please, let us leave the past behind."

To Nicholas' surprise, a lone tear dripped from Mericus' eye, running down his temple into his sweaty and matted curls. Mericus swallowed. "Nicholas... I..." Then he hesitated, looking for a moment as though he would reconsider. Extend the branch of peace in the end. Offer a resolution to more than a decade of feuding.

Nicholas gripped Mericus' hand tighter, raising it to his face. "Yes, Brother?"

But it was too late.

In the time it took Nicholas to utter those two words, his twin breathed his last.

"Mericus?" Nicholas shook his brother's hand, as if that could have some effect.

Nothing happened. Mericus' body lay still. Too still. Even the air in the room seemed to have changed.

Nicholas could feel it... that separation from his twin. Despite their many differences, they had always been connected in a way that no one but a twin could fully understand.

That connection was now severed. His brother was dead. And with him, their chance at reconciliation.

Nicholas fell back, catching himself on the grassy earth. His heart crumbled, radiating out in jagged pieces that cut everything in their path. Losing his father without the opportunity to say goodbye had been painful enough—it still haunted him nearly every day. But this... This was so much worse.

This time, he had been able to say what was in his heart, but the words were tossed aside like refuse. They meant nothing to Mericus. Instead, it appeared his brother chose to take his hatred for Nicholas to the grave.

Broken and spent, Nicholas bowed his head and wept.

Nicholas stares as his mother's coffin and that of his baby brother are lowered into the earth. His nine-year-old heart can scarcely comprehend how his beloved mother can be here one day and gone forever the next. Tears had wet his face the night she died, but they could not do so now. From now on, he is not a child. He is a man, and he must be strong.

To make his mother proud.

To take care of his father and Mericus.

He reaches over and grips his twin's hand. Mericus cried when Mother died too. But since then, only anger lines his face. Even now, it darkens his eyes and knots his brow. He does not pull away from Nicholas' hold, but he does not hold tightly in return.

"We have each other, Mericus. You know that, yes? We will always have each other. I will always be here for you."

His brother looks at him, eyes still angry, but with a tinge of his own sorrow peeking through. He opens his mouth to respond.

"King Nicholas?" A hand shook his shoulder, rousing Nicholas from sleep. "Your Majesty, wake up." He jolted, lifting his head to find Sir Benedict crouching before him, sympathy and a touch of uncertainty in his eyes.

Nicholas looked about the darkened tent. Spotting the body still lying on the cot beside him.

Mericus.

So *that* part had not been a dream. His brother was indeed dead.

He winced, feeling the pain in his sore muscles as he sat up. The chainmail he still wore jingled noisily. "Forgive me, it seems I fell asleep. How do our wounded fare? Any other casualties?"

The knight glanced slowly between Nicholas and the shadowed form of Mericus. "A few, sire. But that is not why I am here…

First, we must decide what to do with Lord Mericus' body. And second, I wondered if you wished to inform her ladyship—your stepmother, I mean—and the queen of this occurrence?"

Yes… that. Of course, his stepmother and Eleanor deserved to know as soon as possible. And Adelaide as well.

Nicholas rubbed a hand down his face. "Yes, yes, Sir Benedict. We may bury my brother's body at first light, when a more proper burial may be performed. As for the rest of my family…"

What to do, indeed? With Mericus dead, Nicholas was now fully responsible for the well-being of his kin. And it did not sit well with him to know his stepmother and sister remained home at Aguilar Castle with only the most essential of defenses.

"Lady Clarice and Lady Eleanor must get to the safety of Valen with all haste. We know not when Galiel will set its mind on taking Aguilar. I trust none of my knights more than you, Sir Benedict, to handle this task. Gather a small group of men, journey to Aguilar, and get them safely to the palace. They can inform the queen and my aunt of Mericus' passing, and the four of them may take comfort together."

"As you wish, sire. It shall be done." The loyal knight placed a fist over his chest and bowed his torso, though he still crouched before Nicholas on the ground. Then the man exited into the night, leaving Nicholas alone with the remnant of his brother.

Nicholas stood and pulled the heavy chainmail off his body before sinking back to the ground on weary muscles. He had felt the pain of loss before, when his mother and the babe died, then when he learned of Father's passing. But *this* pain was far greater. This was agony without hope or peace.

Nicholas had promised, all those years ago, to always be there for his twin. And he tried his best to keep that promise. But in the end, he failed. All he managed to do was push Mericus away until his brother wanted nothing to do with him.

It seemed Nicholas' worst fears were coming true before his eyes.

Chapter 34

Adelaide

THE SUDDEN APPEARANCE OF LADY CLARICE AND ELEA-
nor could mean nothing good...

The moment I heard the two women had arrived with a trio of
knights, led by Sir Benedict, I hurried down to meet them. Prickles
of unease chased up my arms. They sent no warning of their coming, and neither had Nicholas.

Had Aguilar been attacked? Even conquered?

God, let it not be so.

Outside, dark storm clouds hung low and thunder rumbled
in the distance–a promise of much needed rain. The wind raged,
tossing my navy skirts hither and yon. Sir Benedict helped Lady
Clarice down from her modest sidesaddle, while another of the
men assisted Eleanor. Both women looked worn through, their
clothing rumpled, and hair frazzled.

Speaking of clothing... They no longer wore the stark white
of mourning, but rather drab gray and brown ensembles covered
by summer cloaks.

The moment Lady Clarice's slippered feet touched the ground,
she hastened to me and fell in my arms. "Oh, Adelaide. Praise God
we have arrived safely! We come bearing such terrible news." The
ordinarily poised noblewoman choked on a ragged sob.

My stomach plummeted, my thoughts instantly darting to
Nicholas. Had something happened to him? Surely the Council
would already know and have informed me.

"'Tis Mericus. He–he was slain in battle."

Shock instantly numbed my limbs.

Mericus, dead?

Oh, dear Nicholas… What pain you must feel.

Eleanor ran up then, falling onto my shoulder with heaving sobs. I wrapped my arms around the travel-weary, heartbroken women and breathed a prayer for strength. For the ability to offer comfort in such a time.

"Nicholas sent Sir Benedict to fetch us from Aguilar and bring us to you." Lady Clarice gathered herself and wiped at her eyes. "We have been traveling nearly incessantly for over two days with naught but these plain clothes and a few items in our saddlebags, so as to attract as little attention as possible."

"You must be exhausted, you poor dears. Come." I turned and steered them toward the palace entrance as thunder rolled overhead. "We shall get you settled, with hot baths, fresh clothes, and a hearty meal. Then we may talk further."

A bath and a full stomach cannot undo the pain of the world, but they can go a long way in relieving it for a moment. They certainly did so for Lady Clarice and Eleanor.

Afterward, I sat with the women in their shared chamber–they had no wish to be separated for the time being–and listened as they shared the full tale of Mericus' death and their harried journey to Valen. My heart broke at the account, aching as they ached.

Lady Clarice said she was told Nicholas was with Mericus at the last. But no one knew how things ended between the brothers. Had they made peace? I dearly hoped so, for both the sake of Mericus' soul and Nicholas' conscience. My husband may not have always agreed with his twin, but I knew he loved him greatly even so.

After an hour or more, Lady Clarice assured me they would be fine on their own for a time. The journey was taxing, to say the least, and she and Eleanor could both use a rest. I did not quibble, instead offering them another embrace before excusing myself.

By the time I sat ensconced in my chamber with Nerissa, the storm was releasing its fury on the world. Thunder rolled and lightning cracked. Were it colder, 'twould have been the perfect evening to sit by the fire with a book and a hot drink. Instead, Nerissa and I occupied ourselves with sewing tiny infant garments. After the day's dark events, our conversation was sporadic, with long pauses of aching silence.

Nicholas occupied the majority of my thoughts, so much so that my needle slipped and pricked my finger on more than one occasion. Thoughts of him, fear for his safety, and even a longing for his return had plagued me since his departure. But this latest news magnified it all until I was utterly consumed.

If only he were here, to not only comfort his family, but receive comfort in return. Knowing Nicholas, he no doubt blamed himself for his brother's death somehow. If only I could reassure him that he had nothing to feel guilty about at all.

Warmth stung my eyes. When had these tears welled?

Hastily, I blinked them away, lest Nerissa notice my distress.

But it was too late.

"Adie? Whatever is the matter?"

I resumed my stitching, cheeks flaming. I blinked back the rest of my tears and forced a smile. "Nothing at all. I am quite well."

"I do not believe that for a moment. Tell me, what troubles you?"

"Mother, please…"

Nerissa narrowed her eyes, lifting her chin in a regal way that bespoke her many years as queen.

I sighed and sat the half-finished infant gown in my lap. 'Twas useless to argue with her. "My heart hurts for Nicholas and his family… That is all."

Nerissa hummed. "It sounds so simple when you say it like that. But grief is not simple at all, is it?"

Silence reigned and I thought the subject finished, but then she spoke up again. "Before Nicholas left, I sensed… Was there some quarrel between the two of you?"

My nerves jittered at the unexpected question. The babe turned within my womb, as if recognizing and responding to my discomfort. "Why would you ask that?"

"The two of you seemed to be growing close, and then something abruptly changed. As if a wall had been erected between you."

The room suddenly felt too hot. I resisted the urge to fan my face. Were things between Nicholas and I really so obvious as all that?

"I... He... 'Tis hard to explain." I had no desire to share the wedding ring incident with Nerissa. Or the war taking place on the battleground of my heart. As far as I knew, Nerissa knew nothing of the ring, and she certainly could not know the truth about my feelings for her son.

"Please, Adie. Explain it to me, as best you can." She sat there, patient and attentive as could be.

I fiddled with the tiny linen garment still resting in my lap. "Nicholas and I... We are friends, but not husband and wife in the way one would think... if you understand my meaning." My cheeks flamed hotter. "He tried to present me with a wedding ring of his own on my birthday, and I told him–" In truth, I had not told him much of anything. I ran away like a coward. "Well, I did not accept it."

Nerissa's eyes widened. "Whyever not?"

"Because..." Oh, why must the woman pry such deeply buried truths out of me? I had never planned to speak of this to her, to admit how Miles' death haunted me.

"Because it is too soon, of course. Miles–God rest him–has only been buried a few months. 'Twould be a dishonor to him."

"How would that dishonor him? Nicholas *is* your husband, no matter how soon or not soon it is since Miles' passing. In seeking to honor Miles, are you not, therefore, dishonoring the man who is your husband *now*?"

"You do not understand, Nerissa. It feels wrong... I feel... I feel too guilty."

"And what on earth do you have to feel guilty about?"

I rubbed circles across my belly, drawing strength from the comforting closeness of my child. Miles' child.

The tears from moments ago returned, in spite of my efforts to hold them back. I shook my head, swiping at one that escaped down my cheek. "Because I should have been a better wife to Miles. He deserved more than what I was able to give. He deserved–"

Nerissa's brow furrowed, her lips turning downward in a troubled frown. "Adie... You were an excellent wife to my son. I have told you so."

"'Tis just it. *I* do not think I was. I think he would have been more pleased with someone else. And… I did not love him." The confession seemed to break the dam on my secrets and the full truth spilled forth in a rush.

"Miles was a good man, a kind husband, a dear friend to me, but I never felt more for him beyond that, no matter how I wished to. Not like you loved King Wesley, or my mother loves my father. And Miles *deserved* to be loved in the deepest way possible. But I never could give him my full heart. And I never seemed to earn his, for he never told me so. How can I feel so differently about Nicholas when I have known him so little? How can I give him my heart when the man whose child grows within my womb never even possessed it?"

I expected anger, hurt, or at the very least, shock. But all I received was, "Oh, my dear girl…" And then Nerissa knelt before me on the tapestry rug. She took my sewing work from my lap, laid it aside, and gripped my hands tight. "Adie, I already knew how you felt about Miles."

My jaw fell slack. "You did?"

"My hair may be turning gray with age, but I am not *blind*, Adelaide. I have spent too long in a royal court to be fooled by much, and I have learned to deduce much of what you try to hide from me for what you deem my own protection. I could see there was mutual respect and esteem between you and my son, but no… spark. I still think love could have formed between the two of you, as time continued to pass, and you were united in love for your child." Her eyes grew heavy with sadness. "But such as it is… You *were* a *good* wife to Miles, my dear.

"You may not have loved him in the romantic way you always envisioned. But you loved him in the ways that mattered most. Love is more than just passion and heady emotions, though those things *are* a blessing to experience. Rather, much of love consists of our daily actions. You served your husband selflessly, you were his companion, his confidant, you were faithful and loyal and good until the end. Now you have the chance for a different love, one like what you once desired. Why deny yourself that chance?"

The tears ran in rivulets down my face now. I shook my head. "But Nerissa, how can I do this? He was the father of my child, for goodness sake. I cannot simply move on—"

"Adelaide. Listen to me." Nerissa stared earnestly into my face, touching my cheek. "You say Miles deserved more? Well, I say *you* deserve more. *You* deserve to be loved and cherished for who God created you to be.

"If your heart is truly not ready to love, then by all means, take your time. But if the man you are now married to awakens something special and true in your heart, then embrace it, my dear girl. Nicholas is a *good* man, as I am certain you have learned. Do not bar him from your heart for the sake of what you *think* you should be doing. And certainly, do not do so on my account."

I hiccupped on a sob I could no longer hold in. Nerissa wiped my tears away, and then she embraced me. A hug so full of care and affection that I crumpled and wept on her shoulder until my head began to ache.

At last, we pulled apart, and Nerissa smoothed gentle hands across my cheeks again. "Tell me the honest truth… Do you love him?"

That was the all-important question, was it not? *Did* I love Nicholas? Until now, I had not even allowed myself to consider the question.

"I… I know not."

"My dear, 'tis not wrong to have joy even as we mourn. I am having to learn that as well…" Nerissa rested a hand against my stomach. "It is at times difficult to embrace the joy in the midst of loss. But I would miss out on so much if I did not. There are great blessings to be found, even here."

I placed my hand over hers. My child kicked against our hands and we both laughed through our tears, lightening the heavy moment. Nerissa stood slowly, using my chair to help herself to her feet. "I suggest you pray, search your heart and learn it. And if your heart is leading towards that of your husband, then please *follow* it, my dear. I know my son would want you to be happy. And I want you to find happiness as well."

Chapter 35

Adelaide

LATE INTO THE NIGHT, I SAT BY MY WINDOW, SHUTTERS open to the late summer breeze, and watched moonlight cast a silvery sheen on the world. The storm had since passed and left in its wake that distinct petrichor scent I loved. The wind toyed with my hair and snuck through the fabric of my nightdress, prompting me to pull the wool blanket higher on my lap.

Somewhere out there, Nicholas lay beneath the same moon and stars. Was he asleep? Or did grief and troubling thoughts haunt him as well?

Prayer still felt like a futile thing of late, but I returned to it once more. I knew of no other way to sort through my tangled emotions. "Lord God, comfort Nicholas' heart this night. Be with him and give him strength. Protect him and bring him safely home to us."

I wrapped my arms around my pregnant belly while the babe kicked wildly. How would Nicholas look holding this child one day? I could just picture the joy on his face, the light in his eyes.

I sighed a weighted breath. "Do I love him, Lord? *Can* I truly love him?"

Nerissa's words echoed inside me ever since our conversation earlier in the evening. She claimed Miles would have wanted me to find happiness, and that *she* wanted that for me as well. She did not expect me to cling to the memory of her son for many years before opening my heart to someone new. To Nicholas. She said to discern whether or not these feelings within my heart were love.

She claimed I had been given a chance for deep, lasting love with Nicholas, a gift from God alone.

But were any of those things actually true?

Could I embrace this joy even in the midst of so much sorrow?

A Voice seemed to carry in on the breeze, whispering straight to my heart. *I have given you hope and a future, Daughter. Do not fear to accept my gift.*

A chill traced along my arms. I snuggled deeper beneath my blanket, tears rising in my eyes. Memories flashed–the moment Nicholas agreed to my proposal, how he looked at me as he said his vows, the tender way he comforted me when I was ill the next morning. Every single moment of kindness since then. Every touch, every look, every time I found myself longing for something more… For his kiss, for his embrace. For him.

Slowly, I removed the self-inflicted inhibitions on my heart and allowed the dam to break. With each passing moment, the flood grew stronger, flowing from a place deep within my soul. It was both a relief and an agony, experiencing this release.

Finally, the flood waters of my heart finished their flow, leaving me with one bone-deep realization.

I *did* love Nicholas.

I loved him as I had never loved anyone else before.

A gasping breath left my lips and instantly, tears began to drip down my cheeks. For too long I willingly made myself blind to the true condition of my heart, never acknowledging it had become Nicholas' own. And I hurt him in the process, pushing him away when he gently asked me to take a step closer to him.

Had my actions ruined any seed of love that had taken root in his own heart?

Oh, God, let it not be so.

All my life, I yearned for a romantic sort of love, and had hoped to find it with Miles. Yet when my chance for it at last stood before me, I had spurned it. Crushed it beneath the weight of my guilt and fear and regret.

I swiped at my tears, sucking in a deep breath. The moonlight flashed on the emerald of my ring as I lowered my hand. I paused, staring at the symbol of my union with Miles.

'Tis time.

I sobbed anew, a part of me breaking all over again at the memory of my first husband. All we had hoped for and dreamed of, all we were never able to share, especially the child in my womb. 'Twas unfair. And I knew every time I looked at my child, I would ache a little inside.

But God had provided a chance for another life, one that just might be even greater than my childhood imaginings. It was time to accept it. I had to put aside my fears and guilt and everything I thought I should have done differently and find joy in the here and now.

I rose from the chair and crossed to my desk. With trembling fingers, I opened the drawer and found Nicholas' ring. It was as beautiful as I remembered. A carefully selected gift from a man that was worth more than all the jewels in the royal treasury.

Placing the ring on the wooden surface of my desk, I looked down at the gold and emerald one I had worn since Miles placed it on my hand three years ago. A fresh wave of tears fell from my eyes. "Farewell, Miles... I shall always remember our time with fondness. And I shall *always* treasure the greatest gift you ever gave me—our child. How I wish they could know you..."

Then I slipped the ring from my finger. I felt the last severing of my ties with Miles, like a thread being cut. The sensation hurt, but it no longer felt like a horrid betrayal.

I pressed a kiss to the ring and placed it in the drawer.

Nicholas' ring called to me, this new symbol of my new life with the man who held my heart. I would wear his ring with pride. And when, Lord willing, he returned home one day, I would confess my love.

Then I picked up the ring and slid it onto my finger. I smiled. A perfect fit.

Chapter 36

Nicholas

DAYS OF FIGHTING BLENDED ONE INTO THE OTHER AS Nicholas and his men struggled to hold back the invaders. His sword seemed an extension of himself, battle becoming unsettlingly familiar. With every day, the weight of Nicholas' grief pressed harder upon his heart, but he blocked out the pain as best he could. If he dwelled on it too long, he would surely crumple into a heap and never rise again.

So he pushed through each day, fighting and repressing. But in the dark watch of night, the spectre of grief haunted him, refusing to be banished. It lurked in the shadowed corners of his tent, whispering accusations and regrets as he lay awake longing for the refuge of sleep.

Had he truly failed so miserably that his brother would not even forgive him before he died? For a moment, there at the very end, Mericus' countenance had changed, and he seemed on the verge of accepting Nicholas' desperate apology. But the fact remained that Mericus never completed whatever statement he intended to make.

And that sentence left unfinished would haunt Nicholas for the rest of his days...

After a sennight of struggling to hold or push back the Galielians, Nicholas had to face the reality that his efforts were futile. He and his troops were now only a short distance from Claimore, with the enemy not far behind. 'Twas in their best interest at this point to make for Claimore Castle and prepare for a confrontation there.

The morning of the eighth day, Nicholas and his men rode

hard and fast for Claimore. They arrived by afternoon, just before the late evening sun approached its final descent into dusk. A shout rang from atop the castle wall as he and his company galloped into view, the flag of Trilaria snapping in the breeze. When they reined in their horses outside the gate, Commander Andrew shouted up to the guard. "Open in the name of King Nicholas of Trilaria!"

The gate creaked open, and Nicholas and his men hurried through. He was off his steed in seconds, looking around the courtyard for Lord Byron, Duke of Claimore, or anyone who could take him to the man.

"King Nicholas!" He whirled around to see the Duke of Claimore striding toward him. The nobleman–tall and still lean even in his forties–bowed low, one fist pressed over his heart.

"Lord Byron, the Galielians are heading this way," Nicholas said, eschewing formal greetings. "They shall be intent upon taking your castle. We must prepare with all haste, for they shan't be far behind my men and I."

"Of course. We shall begin preparations immediately. However, there is something I must tell you, my king. Please… may we speak privately?"

Nicholas glanced at the chaotic bustle of soldiers moving all around them. Something about the man's question, the tone of his voice, set Nicholas' nerves on edge. "Certainly, Lord Byron. Though, if you do not mind, I would like Commander Andrew present. Anything you need to tell me may be shared in his hearing."

The nobleman nodded quickly. "Of course, Your Majesty."

Nicholas turned to request the commander's company, and the pair soon followed the duke into the castle keep.

Within the Great Hall, all was quiet and deserted, the silence deafening when compared to the activity of the courtyard. It only further strained Nicholas' nerves "What is this matter of such import?"

Abruptly, Lord Byron swiveled on his heel to face them. "My men intercepted an enemy scout three nights ago. It has taken much… *convincing*, if you will, to get the man to speak, but we have at last succeeded in gaining information from him."

The duke's lips clamped into a hard line. "The man claims King Theobald intends to lead his troops to Valen and lay siege.

He believes, with the plague ravaging our people and resources, and the cold months approaching, we shall be easily conquered by such an attack."

Commander Andrew spat a curse.

Nicholas took a quick steadying breath, absorbing this distressing news. "Has the soldier given any indication of when this plan shall be enacted?"

"Not exactly, sire. He only said King Theobald intends to attack the capital as soon as he can converge his army there. These lesser conflicts are meant to wear us down and strain our kingdom further. But King Theobald is not interested in a prolonged war, or merely winning and losing land along the border like King Rowan once was. Nay, he aims to strike straight at our heart and bring us to as swift a surrender as possible."

Now Nicholas wanted to mutter a curse of his own. He fought the urge to comb his hands through his wind-tousled curls. "We must be prepared for this siege as much as possible. The longer we have to prepare, the better our chances of outlasting the Galielians as winter sets in."

"Someone must notify the Council immediately," Commander Andrew spoke up. "We have not a day to waste."

"My thoughts exactly. The decision of how to proceed lies with you, of course. But–if I may be so bold as to suggest it–my advice would be for you to return to Valen. Prepare to lead the city through this coming conflict, and leave us to defend Claimore."

The stress of this sudden decision caused a painful thumping at the sides of Nicholas' skull. It felt wrong to leave Lord Byron and the others to defend the region alone. But he could not hesitate to warn Valen and the Royal Council about the impending siege. And who better to oversee the city's preparation than himself?

Nicholas growled low, bracing his hands on his hips. "I see the wisdom in your suggestion, Lord Byron." His muscles spasmed at the thought of more hours spent on Castor's back. "I have no wish to abandon you here… but you are correct–I must see to the capital's defense."

He turned to Commander Andrew. "Please gather a small group of men and inform them of this latest development. We shall rest for two hours, share a meal, and be on our way. But you shall stay to assist Lord Byron."

"Yes, Your Majesty." The commander bowed low and hurried to do as instructed.

"I would be remiss if I did not ask at least one thing of you before you depart." The Duke of Claimore's controlled demeanor slipped, revealing a hint of the fear beneath. "Would you consider taking my wife and daughters with you? My sons have just taken their vow of knighthood and shall remain here to defend our home, but… I would feel more at ease knowing my wife and daughters are in the capital. Even with the possible siege."

Nicholas could well sympathize with the man's fear for his loved ones' safety. Even now, thoughts of his own family threatened to distract him from the matter at hand. How could Nicholas refuse the duke's earnest request?

"Of course. We shall protect them with our lives and ensure they make it to Valen unharmed. They will have plenty of company among the women of my family and the Council's wives."

Lord Byron's shoulders drooped in relief and he bowed. "I thank you. I shall see they are ready for the journey."

Exactly two hours later, Nicholas and a half dozen knights, along with Lord Byron's wife and two adolescent daughters, rode away from Claimore Castle as the day faded into evening. The brief nap and scarfed meal had not been enough to restore his weary body. And the worry over Claimore's fate and that of Valen kept his insides in tangled knots.

He should be happy he was headed home, poised to reunite with what remained of his family, and with Adelaide most of all. But somehow, the prospect brought no pleasure. Seeing his loved ones would only twist the knife of grief deeper and remind him all the more of everything he stood to lose if he failed again.

Chapter 37

Adelaide

"HIS MAJESTY HAS RETURNED, MY QUEEN." MY SPOON clattered into my bowl of porridge at Gretta's announcement. After delivering the morning meal, I sent her to retrieve a cup of ginger tea–my nausea had resurfaced in the last several days. But clearly the girl returned with more than just the requested beverage.

"You are certain?" My stomach fluttered like a hundred butterfly wings.

"Yes, Your Majesty. Everyone is speaking of it. He and a small group of knights have just arrived in the courtyard, along with a woman and two girls near Lady Eleanor's age. I know not who they are or why they are here."

"I see…" My hand shook, sloshing my tea as I lifted the cup for a long drink. I swallowed the hot liquid and realized too late that I should have taken a smaller sip. "And where is the king now?"

"Heading to see Lady Clarice and Lady Eleanor, from what I understand."

"Thank you, Gretta." I set aside the tea and pushed back my chair. "I must go to him straightaway."

Gretta nodded and hurried to secure a veil over my hair before I abandoned my half-eaten meal and fled the room as quickly as my pregnant girth would allow. A whirlwind of emotions drove me forward. Elation, fear, anticipation, curiosity, excitement–a heady mix that left me woozy.

Nicholas was alive. Home. But *why*? Who were the women he brought with him? And most importantly, would I have a chance to tell him the truth of my heart?

My pace did not slow until I reached my destination, breathless and pressing my hand against a pain in my side. The door to my in-laws' shared chamber stood slightly ajar, voices reaching me from within.

I hesitated just outside the door. Would it be an intrusion to walk in now, when Nicholas was likely comforting his family in their grief? But I *had* to see him. I would not shout my love to him in front of his family, of course… but I had to at least see for myself that he was truly whole and hale.

With a bracing breath, I pushed open the door.

My eyes sought him above all else, drinking in the sight like water to a thirsty soul. Nicholas stood with his arms wrapped securely around Lady Clarice and Eleanor, facing the door. His head lifted and his eyes met mine with the force of a lightning strike, sending a jolt straight to my toes. His beard had grown thick in his many weeks away, his features hardened by war. A long, scabbed-over gash marred the left side of his face, near his eye. The change in his appearance was startling, but not altogether unattractive.

For the briefest moment, his face softened, his eyes sliding over my form in one quick movement. Then a veil seemed to fall into place, his emotions hidden and his focus solely on the weeping women in his arms.

I self-consciously smoothed a hand across the folds of my lavender gown. Did I look well to him? I should have paused long enough to check my appearance in the mirror.

At last, the women lifted their heads from Nicholas' shoulders, sniffling and wiping at tears. Eleanor turned and saw me first. "Oh! Adelaide. We did not hear you enter."

My lips twitched into an uncomfortable smile. "My pardon. I heard Nicholas returned."

"He has indeed, God be praised." Lady Clarice turned inquisitive eyes on her stepson. "What I am wondering is *why* he has come home to us."

"We shall speak on that later. I must meet with the Council first."

Her lips frowned, but she did not protest. "Very well, then. But prithee, tend to yourself first, Nicholas." Her petite nose wrinkled. "You smell something terrible."

Ordinarily, Nicholas would have laughed at her gentle teasing.

This time, he only nodded, blank-faced. "I suppose a bath would do me good. I will see you both soon."

Then he stepped past the women, heading toward me. My heart leapt. I looked up into his face as he paused before me, opening my mouth to offer my sincere condolences, but he beat me to the first word.

"And how do you fare, my queen?"

His deep, rich tone wrapped around me like an embrace. How had I made it so long without hearing that voice? But his words and expression–or lack thereof–were too stiff, too formal. Was he not pleased to see me at all?

"Quite well. Thank you." I boldly reached out to touch the wound on his face. "What happened–"

He pulled away from my touch. "'Tis just a scratch, nearly healed. Do not trouble yourself on my account."

I blinked, pulling away my hand. Heat suffused my cheeks. "My apologies... I only..." Hurt stung my heart. He had been distant before he left for war, but this coldness...

Surely my love was not reciprocated if he behaved this way.

I swallowed. "I suppose I shall see you later as well."

Then he was gone, his footsteps retreating down the corridor, leaving me under the concerned scrutiny of his stepmother and sister.

Nicholas stayed behind closed doors with the Council for hours, missing dinner entirely. At last, shortly before supper, I heard him enter his chamber to dress for the meal. I waited, hoping he would knock upon our adjoining door and explain what was going on. I nearly knocked on the door myself to demand he tell me.

But fear stayed my hand. After his rebuff earlier, self-doubt reared its ugly head. His actions before my birthday, the sweet gestures, gifts, near-kisses... They convinced me over the past several days that he had, at least at that point, felt some tender affection for me. But seeing his demeanor towards me now, I feared my rejection had crushed any and all fondness, let alone love, he once felt.

So, like a coward, I did not enter his room. Instead, I found myself sitting at his right hand at supper, picking over my roasted pheasant with disinterest and casting surreptitious glances his way. Would he not even notice I began wearing his ring?

Gloom darkened the mood of the gathering, and tension stretched the atmosphere tight. Much of the delicious food prepared by the kitchen staff remained uneaten on the table. It seemed I was not the only one with a low appetite.

A wave of lightheadedness overtook me, and I resisted the urge to rub at the pain throbbing in my temples. I should make myself eat more. Though I could barely stomach the thought of food at the moment, mayhap a lack of sustenance was the reason for my discomfort.

Nicholas cleared his throat and lowered his wine goblet to the table. "I know many of you are still wondering why I have returned when the war yet rages." His eyes slid to his stepmother and Eleanor before looking down the table at the rest–Nerissa, the Council, their families, and the new trio of women I recognized as the Duchess of Claimore and her daughters. "I fear I have come with grave news. We intercepted information stating the Galielians intend to work their way to Valen and lay siege."

Lady Clarice gasped, placing a hand over her heart. "God in Heaven!"

Similar murmurs and exclamations of distress spread down the table, but I remained silent, my hands beneath the table. A siege upon Valen could be devastating under any conditions–'twas my father's plan to finally put an end to the war between him and Trilaria decades ago. But with a plague among us, depleting our economy and resources, and lowering our numbers of fighting men, 'twould almost certainly spell our doom. Especially if the siege began or lasted through the cold autumn and winter months. Such an attack would be risky on the Galielians' part, since their own supplies could run out before the battle was won. Though it could also work perfectly in their favor, forcing the cold, hungry, plague-riddled defenders of Valen to surrender or starve to death.

God, have mercy upon us all...

I looked to Nicholas, waiting for his next words.

"I have returned in order to personally oversee the siege preparations. The more supplies we accumulate before the Galielians arrive, the better our chances of surviving. Our greatest hope is to outlast the enemy through the autumn and winter. We shall at least have proper shelter; they will not. If we can hold out long enough, they may fall back, or even abandon the war entirely."

Eleanor whimpered, leaning onto her mother who fanned her face as though she might faint or panic. Some of the Council wives were doing the same, and the poor Duchess of Claimore looked positively ill.

Again, I thought of my father and the aid I knew he would be willing to render. But I could not broach that subject here, in front of so many witnesses. 'Twas a conversation best had alone.

"We shall pray without ceasing that God will give us favor in this." I leaned forward, pitching my voice for Nicholas' ears alone. "May I please speak with you privately, when you can spare a moment?" Then I could not only ask him about sending a message to Father, but also, if I could work up the courage… tell him how I felt.

Nicholas' dark eyes fell on me at last, for the first time since the meal began. "Of course… when I can spare a moment."

That "moment" did not present itself as easily as I expected.

For three days, Nicholas kept himself busy, locked away in his study or with the Council. And every time I attempted to go to him, a guard informed me the king was not to be disturbed.

Frustration made me testy and tense. Was he truly so intent on avoiding me?

When our paths crossed at mealtimes, my husband kept that stony demeanor firmly in place, but I *knew* he was hurting. I had seen plenty of stress and grief on his features since our wedding, but this… This was different. *He* was different, and it frightened me to see the change.

I longed to offer what comfort I could, to get to the heart of what troubled him so. But would he *ever* give me a chance to do so, let alone speak with him about the siege? And what about telling him of my love? At this point, I feared such a profession would be thrown back into my face in disgust…

But the longer he avoided me, the more I became determined to *make* him talk to me. He could not avoid me forever. I would not stand for it.

Sitting at dinner on the third day of this maddening interlude, I stabbed at my venison. If only I could force him to say something to me now. But how could I with so many others once again present?

Another headache pounded in my temples. It had pestered me since yesterday morn without relent. Nausea continued to come in waves as well, reminding me of those miserable early days of pregnancy. 'Twas likely a result of all this frustration and stress. I forced myself to breathe deep and take a small bite of the meat on my trencher, glancing for the hundredth time at Nicholas.

I could not no longer wait for him to deign to speak to me. I needed to act today, lest I go mad.

I will have to force his hand…

The phrasing of that thought sent a solution racing to the forefront of my mind.

Of course! I barged into his chamber in the middle of the night once before, offering myself as his bride and pleading with him to wed me in order to force the Council to name him king. I could do much the same again, except this time, I would offer my love and the comfort he was too stubborn to ask for himself.

It had been a monumental risk then, and it would be so now, though it was no longer my reputation at stake. Nay… This time, it was my heart that weighed in the balance. He could fulfill my every hope and dream, or crush it all with one word.

But this love in my heart… 'Twas worth any risk.

Chapter 38

Adelaide

I RUBBED AT THE PAIN THROBBING IN THE UPPER RIGHT side of my belly. Then I took a deep breath, trying to fill my lungs that struggled for air. My headache had grown in intensity throughout the evening, as had the nagging feeling of nausea. But I could not let it stop me. I *had* to speak with Nicholas this very night.

Besides, it must only be my nerves making me ill. Once I got this weight off my chest by speaking to Nicholas, all would be well.

"Almost finished, Your Majesty." Gretta released a coil of my hair from the iron curling tongs she heated in my fireplace, letting the ringlet fall down my back.

After curling a final few locks, Gretta retrieved a sheer white veil and secured it to my head with an ornate silver circlet. "There you are." She giggled quietly and whispered, "His Majesty will be pleased, indeed." Gretta had discerned by now that my marriage with the king was not what most would assume, and she was delighted by my rather scandalous plan.

To my chagrin, we discovered Nicholas chose not to retire to his chamber immediately after supper, instead hiding himself away in his study once again. But that news had not discouraged me. He would have to return to his room eventually–and I would be there waiting.

With my ensemble complete, I lifted the heavy folds of the blue gown Nicholas favored and stood from the dressing stool. The room spun, my vision blurring for a startling moment. My body listed to the left.

"Your Majesty!" Gretta caught my arm, steadying me. "Are you well? You look frightfully pale."

I rubbed my temple, wincing at the pain wracking my head. "Yes, of course. Only a bit of dizziness."

Gretta's brows furrowed dubiously, but she made no comment. I gently withdrew my arm from her hold and made my way to the door adjoining mine and Nicholas' chambers. Another wave of nausea struck, but I breathed through it, willing my stomach to settle. I could not allow this malady to hinder my plan.

Inside Nicholas's room, I quickly lit a candle to chase away a measure of darkness. Placing the light on the mantelpiece, I took a seat in a nearby chair. Two hours had already passed since supper's end. Surely Nicholas would retire soon, but if not, I would wait as long as necessary.

With each passing minute, however, the nausea in my stomach intensified, no matter how much I tried to settle it. A cold sweat broke out on my forehead, my body churning with the need to retch.

I knew this sensation only too well...

I pushed to my feet, hastened across the room, and sank to my knees before the blessedly empty chamber pot. Seconds later, the contents of my stomach made their reappearance. But this bout of vomiting was worse than even the earliest days of my pregnancy. The strain of it made my head swim, squeezed my lungs so tight I could not breathe.

"My queen?" Gretta's alarmed tone echoed dully from the other side of the door. Thank God she had not yet left! The door creaked open and I heard her soft, hurried footsteps enter the room. "Oh!" She sank to her knees beside me. "Oh, I *knew* you were not well!"

I cradled my stomach, frightened by the pain shooting through it, now even worse than before. This was not mere nerves or a product of stress. Something was dreadfully wrong.

As soon as my sickness subsided enough for me to speak, I reached out and gripped Gretta's hand. "Have someone fetch the physician."

Nicholas

Adelaide was ill.

Everything within Nicholas seized with fear the moment a servant brought him the news. Instantly, he left the work in his study and sprinted upstairs.

He avoided her these last few days, he was ashamed to admit. The anguish of Mericus' death was so acute, deeper than even the loss of his father or mother, that he had no wish to speak of it with Adelaide just yet. She had a way of making him want to open his heart and share the deepest parts of himself. He knew the moment they were alone, he would be helpless to hold in the grief any longer.

So he kept her at bay, ensuring no opportunity for that arose.

But now… those things holding him back from her could do so no longer. Adelaide was sick and the very *thought* of something happening to her was enough to make him crumble. He had to see her *now*. He had to hold her hand and make certain she was well. He had to tell her–

Nicholas heaved out a weighted breath.

Was he truly ready to tell her everything, despite the risk of facing her rejection again?

When he finally reached her chamber, one of Adelaide's guards stood outside the door. He bowed at Nicholas' approach. "My king. The physician is examining Her Majesty. He asked that he not be disturbed. Unless, of course, you… insist on being present."

Doubtless, Adelaide would not appreciate Nicholas' barging in at such a moment. Even though his nerves were a tangled mess and he wanted to see her immediately, he would respect her privacy and wait.

Nicholas sucked a deep breath through his nose, shaking his head. "Nay, I shall wait here and speak to the physician when he exits."

The guard nodded and resumed his protective stance beside the door. Nicholas, however, could not stand still. He paced the corridor, hands on hips, heart thudding like the hooves of a dozen stallions.

What is taking so long?

Just when Nicholas thought he would burst, the door opened, and the physician exited with his bag of instruments and tonics in hand.

"How is she? What has happened? Is it the plague?"

The physician put out a placating hand as Nicholas rushed at him. "'Tis not the plague. She is… well enough, for now." He sighed and glanced at the guard, as if afraid to speak in the man's presence.

"Speak freely, man," Nicholas spat in his impatience.

"It seems the queen has developed a condition I have seen a handful of times in other women. The cause is unknown, but in some women, the symptoms of headache, severe nausea and vomiting, abdominal pain, blurred vision, and other maladies can develop. The women who display such symptoms struggle greatly with their labor, at times even falling into fits and seizures." The physician turned a sorrowful eye on Nicholas. "Almost always, the mother does not survive."

A battering ram may as well have crashed into Nicholas' chest. All the air fled his lungs with one fell swoop of the physician's words.

"My deepest apologies, Your Majesty. I wish I had better news to share, but alas, I must speak the truth. There is still a chance that she will birth a healthy child and both she and the babe survive. But she is most certainly in grave danger. You both should be prepared for the worst."

Of its own accord, Nicholas' mind flashed back to the day his mother died in childbirth, following her stillborn infant boy into the arms of their Lord.

Horror overwhelmed him. Nay… The same *could not* happen to Adelaide. She could not die! She had to live, both her *and* the babe. How was he supposed to live without them? Surely, he would perish from the heartbreak.

"I have given her strict orders to rest. She must stay confined to the family quarters on this floor only—no climbing stairs, no venturing anywhere else in the palace. She must get plenty of sleep and must not participate in strenuous activity of any kind." The man lifted his brows pointedly at Nicholas.

He nodded. "I understand. I will ensure she follows your orders to the letter."

"Very good. Please, let me know if anything with her condition changes."

"Of course. Thank you."

The physician nodded and the guard led him away, leaving Nicholas shaken and drenched in fresh grief. There was still a chance Adelaide could live, but he would not risk missing his opportunity to confess his love. He had waited too long to make things right with Mericus... and he *would not* repeat that mistake with his wife.

Chapter 39

Nicholas

SHAKING, NICHOLAS KNOCKED ON ADELAIDE'S DOOR.

Moments later, it opened, revealing his aunt's worried face. "Nicholas. Please, come in."

He entered the room, his eyes immediately gravitating to where Adelaide sat propped against a collection of pillows. Her face was pale, and fear glistened in the depths of her blue eyes. The sight nearly broke him then and there.

"May I have a moment alone with my wife?"

"Of course." His aunt moved to kiss Adelaide on the forehead. "Goodnight, Adie. Please send Gretta for me if you require anything." Adelaide nodded and Nerissa left, leading Gretta out with her.

The door thudded softly shut. Silence descended, broken only by the rapid thumping of Nicholas' pulse. Could Adelaide hear it too?

He scanned the room, suddenly as nervous as a young lad. He took in the various candlesticks lighting the room, the furniture with a distinctly feminine air to it, the ornately crafted bed, and finally, the woman occupying it. Her hands rested on her swollen middle, her eyes wide and intent upon him. Her hair fell in thick ringlets around her shoulders. Strange. He could have sworn her hair was not curled at supper time.

"You came to see me." It was both a question and a statement.

"Yes, of course. I came the moment I heard." Gathering his courage, Nicholas strode forward and settled his weight on the edge of her bed. He took her right hand and held it firmly between both his own.

"Adelaide..." He hung his head, wrestling for the right words to say. "Forgive me for keeping you at a distance since my return. 'Tis a long story I promise to tell you soon, but my brother's death... 'twas more difficult than I ever expected. I avoided you because you have this uncanny way of making me want to share my innermost heart... even if I would rather it remain hidden."

She said nothing, so he forged ahead.

"But when the physician told me—" He paused, swallowing against the rising tide of his fears. "I knew I could not let myself stay at a distance any longer. I had to come to you and tell you that—" He looked up into her eyes, so wide and luminous, and still shining with a raw fear he had never seen in her before. He stared deep into those windows to her soul, willing her to hear the sincerity behind what he had to say next.

"I *love* you, Adelaide. You are my very heart, the greatest treasure I could ever possess. I know not how I ever lived without you before, and I know not how I would live without you now." Fervency heated his blood, causing him to grip her hand tighter. "If there is *anything* good that has come of this wretched plague, it is that I was able to marry you. I love you most ardently, and I shan't ever cease telling you so... if you will allow me."

She stared at him, eyes even wider than before. Then suddenly, she hiccupped on a sob and burst into tears.

"What–what is it? I did not mean to make you cry." He rubbed the back of her hand. She was supposed to be resting, and now he had gone and upset her. Had he made a mistake in speaking to her about this right now?

"You—you truly love me?"

He lifted her hand to his mouth, pressing his lips to each of her trembling fingers. "Truly."

She sobbed again, but this time it sounded almost like a laugh. She lifted her left hand and held it out to him. "I have been trying to find a moment to tell you ever since you returned. I finally resolved to wait for you in your chamber and *make* you listen to me. *I* love *you*, Nicholas. My heart is *yours*. Every piece of it."

He finally looked down, his gaze landing on her outstretched hand. The silver and sapphire ring he had given her sparkled on her fourth finger.

She had chosen him, chosen his ring. She *loved* him.

Wonder flooded his soul. Somehow, his efforts to earn her trust and affection succeeded, fulfilling his every hope. Nicholas had won her heart and now she offered it to him freely. And he would accept that offering with reverent gratitude. He would cherish it with everything inside him for as long as he lived.

"You truly love me?" The smile breaking forth on his lips could not be helped as he repeated her own words.

She nodded vigorously, tears flowing down her cheeks. "Truly."

The word broke down any remaining doubt. A tether seemed to pull him toward her, and he could not resist. Nicholas moved close enough to take her into his arms.

"Adelaide…" He cupped her face in his hand, her cheek soft and dampened with tears. "I know not how I could be worthy of your love. But I thank you for choosing me."

His eyes lowered to her mouth. The memory of kissing her at their secret wedding had tormented him for so long. He wanted—nay, *needed* to kiss her again. He pulled her closer, feeling the firmness of her pregnant belly bump against him, lowering his hand to the side of her neck.

Her breathing of his name was all the request he needed.

Nicholas lowered his face to hers, capturing her lips. Heat shot down him like fire. Her lips kissed him back, hands reaching out to grip his tunic, inviting him closer, deeper. He accepted the invitation, pressing into the kiss and breathing her in. Absorbing her into his heart.

Oh God, I love her… I have never loved any person so much.

Nicholas sank his hand into her dark hair, fingers weaving into the curls. He would go on kissing her forever if he could, yet he knew he needed to stop.

Nicholas forced his lips away from hers. His breath came ragged, scraping out of his chest. His entire being longed for the woman in his arms. But he had to think about *her*. The physician already warned him of her need for strict rest, and to take this moment any further would be reckless and selfish.

"Adelaide… My love." He pulled his hand from her hair and

gripped her arms instead, willing himself to push her away. "We must stop."

"But Nicholas…" Her voice was breathy. Pleading.

"Nay." He put a finger against her lips that were reddened by his kiss. "Do not tempt me, Adelaide. *Please.*" She stared at him, her color high from their passionate embrace. "'Twould be selfish of me. Dangerous of you. After what the physician said–" He shook his head, nauseated at the thought of the man's grim prognosis. "I shall not jeopardize your health in *any* possible way. I would rather wait for you a couple more months than risk losing you for a lifetime."

The tears returned, brimming in her eyes. "I am frightened, Nicholas."

He pulled her close again, wrapping his arms tightly around her shoulders. "*Shhh…* I know, my love. I know." Fear burdened his own heart, tainting the blissful moment they just shared. "All will be well–you will see. It *has* to be. For I shall *not* lose you, Adelaide." He pulled back enough to lift her face upward. "You understand me?"

She nodded, lips pressed tight against a sob.

"Very good. There now, cease these tears." He gently wiped at them with the pad of his thumb. He let his fingers linger on the line of her jaw and felt a shudder course through her. God help him, he wanted to kiss her again.

"You should go to sleep." He sat back, reluctantly pulling his arms away.

Sniffing back the last of her tears, she nodded and moved to lie down. He helped her get situated, realizing for the first time just how much her belly had grown in his absence.

Tucked beneath the covers, her hair spilling across her pillow, his wife took his breath away. "Stay with me a while?" Her voice was hopeful, vulnerable. "I would prefer not to be alone at the moment, and… I missed you so much while you were away."

He placed a hand on the top of her head, stroking her dark curls. "I will happily stay right here until you go to sleep."

She smiled, clearly satisfied.

Nicholas pulled a chair up close beside her bed and settled into it. He took her hand and stroked her fingers, up her wrist, along her arm. She sighed in contentment, settling deeper into her pillow and staring at him through sleepy eyes. "Thank you... for everything."

Her words to him on their wedding night, before she went to sleep at his side

Nicholas' heart swelled with love once again. How on earth had God blessed him with her for a wife, let alone allowed him to win her heart?

"You are most welcome." He stroked her arm again in gentle circles. "Sleep well, dearest. I promise you, mine will be the first face you see on the morrow."

She hummed happily through her exhaustion. "I could grow accustomed to that."

In little time at all, his wife's chest rose and fell in the gentle rhythms of sleep, her face relaxed and full of peace. Nicholas pulled his hand from hers and placed a gentle kiss on her forehead. "Goodnight, my love." Then he retired to his own room, leaving the adjoining door open lest Adelaide awaken and require anything.

When at last Nicholas crawled into his bed, he sagged against the mattress, weary in body, yet full in heart. Adelaide loved him, and that knowledge gave him the strength to face whatever the morrow held.

Chapter 40

Adelaide

NICHOLAS LOVED ME.

Every morning when I awoke, the wonder of that knowledge struck me anew. The man I begged to marry me for the sake of my child and the kingdom had not only become my friend, but my love.

Why had I not allowed my heart to admit it sooner? Then I could have enjoyed loving him longer.

For days, Nicholas and I basked in a lovesick bliss, spending as much time as we could together. But two glaring black spots marred our happiness: the fear of what would become of the babe and I, and the fear of the coming siege.

Of course, death was always a possibility in childbirth; yet in this case, the physician had all but guaranteed it. And while it frightened me when I fell ill with the plague, this time was different. *This* fear went bone deep. Because it was no longer only my life at stake, but also that of an innocent babe.

I could not help but also fear losing the future with Nicholas I had only just begun to explore. For so long, I dreamed of a love like my parents shared. And now that I had it… would it slip through my grasp like sand?

As each day passed, my joy over being loved by Nicholas grew. But the sense of doom grew in equal measure, especially as I watched Nicholas' burdens also multiply by the day. I found myself turning to prayer and reading of the Scriptures multiple times a day, desperate for at least a measure of peace.

"I will extol thee, O Lord; for thou hast lifted me up, and hast not

made my foes to rejoice over me. O Lord my God, I cried unto thee, and thou hast healed me," I read the words quietly to myself, sitting in bed one night.

The Psalm was the very one I read to Nerissa right after the loss of our loved ones, and the words struck my heart just as they did then.

"For his anger endureth but a moment; in His favor is life: weeping may endure for a night, but joy cometh in the morning."

I lowered the book to my lap, tears welling hot in my eyes. The psalmist cried unto the Lord and received the help and healing he so needed. But would God incline His ear unto *me*? What of our mourning, and the bleakness of our night? Could He truly turn all this into joy?

None of it made any sense. Why should so many lives be lost? Why should our kingdom be invaded by someone who was supposed to be our ally? Why did Nicholas have to lose two people he loved, so close together? Why had I been forced to wait so long for a babe, only to likely lose my life in the birth?

I hiccupped on a sob and pressed a hand against my mouth to muffle the sound, lest Nicholas hear and hurry to investigate. *Why, God? Why must so much darkness and pain overshadow us? Why must I watch the life I have come to love disintegrate around me?*

No heavenly voice came in the night, but suddenly, I remembered wise words once spoken by my mother. "God's plans are higher than ours, my darling. We may not always understand what is happening around us, but He is working things to a perfect end even so. He may allow our hearts to break, but He promises healing in the end. Our world may grow dark, but He promises light on the other side of the night."

I rubbed a hand over my stomach. "God in Heaven, help me to believe that is true. Help me... help me not to be afraid." More tears flowed down my cheeks, running down my neck and dampening the edge of my nightdress. "Help me to hold on to the promise of the morning. Help me to surrender my future, my babe, my husband, my kingdom... into Your hands. I know you are strong enough to bear their weight, even if I cannot."

Once again, I heard no response, but my raging nerves soon settled, my tears dried, my eyes grew heavy. And that night, I slept more soundly than I had since the war began.

Nicholas

Nicholas turned the page in his book—*The History of the Kings of England*, which he had finally gotten around to reading. But his mind was far from focused on the words. They blurred, swimming across the page. Siege preparations consumed his thoughts, as they had nearly every moment of the last few days.

The one high point in his new routine was spending the evening with Adelaide after many hours of work and stress. Oftentimes, like now, sitting together in the quiet of the family sitting room, he could almost imagine that their world was at peace. That he did not stand to lose absolutely everything at any moment. That it was just the two of them alone in the world and nothing else mattered.

Nicholas sighed and reached over to take Adelaide's hand, which rested upon the arm of her chair beside him. She looked up from her own book, brows raised. "Yes, dearest?"

"Do you ever wish we could just… run away?"

She giggled for a moment before sobering, apparently realizing he did not speak in jest. At least, not fully. "If I am being transparent, then… yes, sometimes. While I have never begrudged the life I was born to, there are days when I wish I could be someone different–wish I could disappear and live a simple life."

Nicholas hummed low in his throat, eyes going unfocused. He never wished anything of the sort before becoming king. He would never, could never forsake those he loved and everyone who counted on him. Yet how could he not long for an easier existence?

"How do your stepmother and sister fare? You did visit them earlier this morning, yes?"

"They are well. Or as well as they can be, I suppose. Both of them still greatly mourn Mericus' loss."

Adelaide squeezed his hand tight, her sympathy palpable. The morning after they confessed their love, Nicholas made sure he was the first to greet her upon waking. It was then he allowed himself to share the painful story of Mericus' death–the horror of those moments, the resolution never quite reached. Adelaide wept with him, as he had known she would, holding him and offering reassurances.

Then Adelaide shared her own painful story of why she hesitated to let him into her heart–and how he had stolen into it anyway.

He could hardly believe his ears. How could any man not fall hopelessly in love with her? Nicholas supposed he should be grateful *he* was the only man to ever possess her love, despite his former beliefs to the contrary. Yet, Nicholas could not help but doubt his late cousin's sanity.

The former Princess of Acuniel was a jewel of the greatest price. She was soft and sweet as an angel, with a gentle voice and unrivaled grace. But a framework of iron lay beneath her surface, lending her a strength that was contagious to those around her.

The only thing harder to understand than Miles' inability to love her was the fact that Nicholas had somehow been worthy of *her* love and devotion.

"Oh!" Adelaide suddenly gasped, startling Nicholas from his reverie. "My, he is active today." She giggled and set aside her book to press her hand against her ribs. "First, I feel a kick on this side, and then the other. He must be turning flips in there!"

Nicholas closed his own book, leaning forward to place his palm to her stomach. Sure enough, sharp thumps hit against his hand, warming his heart with love and wonder.

"You know, I was thinking," she rubbed the back of his hand in a circle, "we ought to decide on a name for the babe soon."

That familiar wave of conflicting emotions rose up again. It had become his near constant companion, appearing every time he thought about the coming child. He already loved the babe as his own and longed to hold him or her in his arms. But he also balked at the idea of something happening to Adelaide.

"We? You would like my help in choosing the name?"

"This shall be your child too... even if not by blood."

Her thoughtfulness evoked his first genuine smile of the day. "I would be honored. Do you have any in mind already?"

"Nerissa and I have spoken of the matter a few times. I... would like to honor those we have lost with the name, especially if it is a boy—which I feel certain it is. Miles' full name was Miles

Alexander Wesley. And of course, his father was Wesley. So at least one of those names should be used."

"I agree. Though why not use Miles' entire name? And if you do not wish to call him Miles… then we could call him… Alexander, mayhap?"

"Hmm… I would be agreeable to that. It only seems right, to honor Miles so." A shadow flickered in her eyes for a moment. But then she smiled. "I have been having a harder time with a girl's name."

Nicholas rattled off a list of names that came to his mind. She scrunched her nose and shook her head at each and every one.

"Oh, I know. What was your mother's name?"

"Juliana." A lump formed in Nicholas' throat to know Adelaide would even consider using the name.

"Juliana…" she drew out the syllables, as if testing them on her tongue. "'Tis perfect."

He rose from his chair and sat on the edge of her chaise, bringing his head to her eye-level. "You are wonderful–do you know that?"

"Hmmm. You often say so, though I know not whether to believe you." She smiled impishly, focusing on his lips.

Nicholas obliged her silent request, lowering his mouth to hers. Her kiss tasted better than any fine wine.

He pulled back and placed a kiss against her forehead. "Are you tired? I can help you back to your chamber to rest, if you like."

She shook her head. "Nay, not yet."

Before he could say anything further, the door to the sitting room opened and Lord Raynard entered. Nicholas bolted to his feet. "Yes, my lord?" The councilman never appeared in the family quarters without invitation.

Lord Raynard bowed. "Pardon my intrusion, Your Majesties, but I fear I must bring grave news."

Nicholas' muscles coiled tight. He swallowed, bracing himself. "What is it, Lord Raynard?"

The nobleman glanced at Adelaide, a silent question in his face.

"Please, fear not for me, my lord. You may speak freely." She reached out and took Nicholas' hand, offering silent support.

Lord Raynard took a deep breath. "Well then… I regret to

say that we have just received word that both Ferrynsworth and Claimore have fallen into enemy hands. The Lord of Ferrynsworth is dead, but Lord Byron is believed to have been captured. Commander Andrew is unaccounted for, as well."

Nicholas bit back a curse and spun away, ripping his hand from Adelaide's grasp. He knew it! He *knew* if he left Claimore, it would fall. "Anything else, Counselor?"

"Nay, sire."

"Then you are dismissed."

The door thudded softly shut and Nicholas stalked to the fireplace. With a roar, he pounded his fists against the wooden mantle. "I knew this would happen! If I had not left, then–"

"Nicholas. You mustn't blame yourself for this. If you remained behind in Claimore, the castle could have still fallen. And you would most assuredly not have been allowed to live. Then where would we be?"

He was startled by a touch on his shoulder and realized Adelaide had managed to stand and waddle to his side. He spun to face her. "You should not be on your feet. You are supposed to rest as much as–"

"Oh, hush." She frowned and placed a hand against his cheek, now clean shaven. A thick beard was not to his liking, he had decided. "I shall rest soon enough. But *you* must listen to *me* at the moment. You cannot dwell on what might have been–trust me, I know. You must only prepare for the future and move forward."

He frowned, wanting to pull away from her touch, yet also hopelessly drawn to her comfort. "I cannot help but feel accountable for each and every soul in this kingdom, Adelaide. 'Tis my responsibility to protect them. I must do everything possible toward that end."

She stared hard into his eyes. "And you *are*."

Then she tapped her fingers lightly against his cheek, glancing away. "Well, there is one thing I have been wanting to mention since your return, but I have had a difficult time finding the right moment."

She lowered her hand to his shoulder. "Nicholas, *please* let me send a letter to my father requesting his aid. He will come, I know it, and it is likely we will be able to push back the Galielians with our combined armies."

He stepped around her, out of reach. "Nay, Adelaide. I already told you I shall not bring your father and his people into this. I shall not risk the safety of Acuniel for our sake."

"But is that not what allies are for? To assist in times of war? My father has sworn to help defend—"

"*Nay*, Adelaide! Enough!"

She blinked, back thudding against the mantle behind her. Had he ever yelled at her in such a way?

Nay, he had not.

Nicholas sighed, his shoulders sagging, ire fading. "Please, my love. I know you mean well, but… do not speak of the matter again." He stepped closer and cupped her cheeks in his hands. She said not a word, only stared up at him with wide, glassy eyes, her body tense. He knew not whether to be reassured by her silence or frightened by it.

"I should go, Adelaide… I have some things I must attend to before supper." Then he pressed a swift kiss to her temple and hurried from the room.

There were plenty of things he needed to do, that was true. But more than anything, he could not stand a moment more under the silent scrutiny of his wife.

Chapter 41

Nicholas

NICHOLAS SQUINTED IN THE AFTERNOON SUN FROM his place atop the city wall, surveying the workers digging a series of trenches around the perimeter of Valen. He had been home for a fortnight now, preparing the city for siege–which included overseeing this digging project. The team of peasant men had nearly completed the task, and these simple ditches would go a long way in staving off enemy attack. The Galielians would be forced to either fill or bridge the trenches before they could bring their siege engines or towers to Valen's walls.

Over the last several days, every man not ill with the plague or working on the trenches was tasked with some other sort of preparation. Fletchers crafted arrows by the hundreds and blacksmiths forged and sharpened blades, while others gathered and organized food stores in central locations to aid in rationing. Some worked to carry the sick to the town hall, which, along with the cathedral, would be barricaded and protected in the event Valen's walls were breached.

Satisfied with the progress, Nicholas turned and strode down the allure to one of the spiral staircases housed in a tower. Sir Benedict and Captain Stefan flanked him, his escorts through the hectic streets.

Before the war, Nicholas had not interacted with the common folk like this, having been sequestered in the palace's so-called safety by the Council's pleading. But in his mind, war made those wishes obsolete. He would no sooner have allowed someone else to oversee the siege preparations than he would have remained behind from battle—no matter how much his advisors disapproved of either decision.

"How goes the weapon preparations? Are they almost complete?"

"The Master of the Blacksmiths Guild lives just around this corner." Captain Stefan motioned up ahead. "Would you care to check with him on the progress yourself?"

"Excellent. Yes, do take me to him."

Captain Stefan nodded and took the lead, guiding the group to a blacksmith shop beneath a modest two-story house. The sound of a hammer against steel echoed from within. "Frederic of Valen! Your king wishes to speak with you!"

The hammering stopped as Nicholas and his companions entered the shop, ducking beneath the lintel. A man stood at an anvil, his back to them while he hurriedly quenched a glowing blade in a barrel of water. Hissing steam filled the air in a thick cloud. As soon as the blade was cooled, the man withdrew it and set it on the anvil with a clank.

Turning to his guests, the blacksmith offered a bow of reverence. "King Nicholas." His voice betrayed his surprise. "To what do I owe this honor?"

"I wish to hear of the progress you and your fellow blacksmiths have made in the weapon preparations. Are they nearly complete?"

"Yes, sire." The man straightened from his bow, revealing an angular, bearded face marked by light wrinkles and striking green eyes. Light brown hair touched with faint streaks of gray crowned his head. "Right this way."

The master blacksmith turned and led Nicholas further into the low-ceilinged shop, where a substantial collection of swords, daggers, and spears had accumulated. "We have repaired and sharpened all of the old weapons that were brought to us, and forged as many as we have the resources to make. I have enough steel for only one more sword after the one I am making now. All of the blacksmiths in the guild bring me their work when complete. I inspect the quality and, if they meet my approval, store the weapons here. I can attest that you will find no finer work in all of Trilaria, Your Majesty"

The man offered his explanation with a steady but enthusiastic tone as Nicholas and his companions inspected the cache of weapons. Nicholas thought he detected a foreign accent in the man's voice–very similar to Adelaide's, except fainter, as if worn away by time.

"Is that an Acunielian accent I hear, Frederic of Valen?"

The blacksmith stiffened, eyes widening in surprise. "Ah, yes, sire... I am Trilarian by birth, but my family moved to Caelrith, Acuniel, when I was a boy of eight years. I lived there until the final days of the Trilarian-Acunielian war. My father and grandfather were blacksmiths, so I have continued in their trade."

"And have worked your way up to Master of the Guild. Quite an accomplishment."

The man ducked his chin, seeming humbled by the praise. "I was an impetuous man in my youth. 'Twas several years before I finally settled into the life I was meant to live, but I have been blessed since then. A wife, three children–all of them alive and well. Good, honest work I enjoy. What more could a man ask for?"

"Indeed." Nicholas smiled, liking Frederic already. "You have done excellent work here. I thank you for your service to our kingdom. I shall see that you and your fellow blacksmiths are rewarded handsomely for every weapon."

Frederic of Valen bowed. "I thank you, sire. You are most gracious, though we do not expect a reward. 'Tis the least we could do to serve our country."

When the man straightened, he tilted his head and hesitated before opening his mouth again. "I... I would like to congratulate you on your marriage, and on the coming babe. May you be blessed and happy. And... I hope Queen Adelaide is faring well?"

Nicholas raised a brow at the question. He appreciated the man's kind words, and his interest in Adelaide seemed harmless enough. But something about his tone and the earnest gleam in the man's eye, as if he had a personal reason for wanting to know, piqued Nicholas' curiosity.

"Thank you, Frederic. The queen is... well enough. Though we appreciate any prayers offered on her behalf." That uneasy twisting appeared in his gut at the mention of Adelaide. The subtle request for the man's prayers did not even begin to convey Nicholas' true feelings. But he could hardly stand here and confide in this peasant he had only just met.

"I see. Forgive me if my question seemed forward, Your Majesty." The blacksmith's face took on a sheepish expression. "'Tis only… I knew the queen's mother… long ago."

This revelation sent Nicholas' eyebrows arching high. This man knew Queen Arabella?

Nicholas opened his mouth to ask about the connection between this man and the peasant queen of Acuniel, but Captain Stefan stepped forward. "We should be going, Your Majesty. We must check the security of the food stores before heading back to the palace."

"Certainly." Nicholas cleared his throat and took a step back. "Good day to you, Frederic of Valen. I hope we shall meet again."

The man bowed deeply, offering his thanks once more as Nicholas and his companions departed.

Much like the weapons, the food stores had been well-organized and there was nothing left to be done. Nicholas ordered the storehouse locked with thick chains and placed a guard at the door. It felt wrong to bar his people from all of the food left in the city. But how could he make their already low supply last as long as possible if he did not strictly ration it each day?

With a churning gut and restless heart, Nicholas made his way back to the palace as a cool September wind rushed down from the north. There was no guarantee the city would survive this siege. But he had done everything he could think of to prepare his people.

Now, they could only hold their breath…

And wait.

Adelaide

A trumpet of alarm shattered the stillness of night.

I gasped a strangled cry, pushing myself up in bed. Darkness still cloaked the world outside my window and hung heavy in the room. But there it was again, that blaring sound of a trumpet–nay, *many* trumpets, ringing from somewhere outside.

I managed to climb out of bed and waddle to the window. The sight that met my eyes froze every drop of blood in my veins.

"God, have mercy upon us all."

Down below, the Galielian forces surrounded the city of Valen. Their ranks lay in tidy squares a furlong from our walls, their torches shimmering in the dark like thousands of fallen stars. 'Twould have been a pretty image if it did not foreshadow our almost certain doom...

Chills tingled along my arms, both from the fear still freezing my blood and a lack of warmth in the room. The cold of the autumn evening had settled in while I slept, and the fire Gretta lit after supper had dwindled to little more than embers. I rubbed at my skin, willing warmth back into it.

This was it. The siege the captured soldier had spoken of three weeks ago, was at last upon us.

Our enemy had us surrounded, trapping us within the city.

"Adelaide?" Nicholas pushed through our conjoining door, making his way to my side. "You have seen them then..." His arms came around me from behind. They wrapped around my chest and pulled me against him.

I gripped his forearms with shaking fingers. "What do you think they plan to do? Shall they attack us right away? Or... attempt to starve us out?"

"I am uncertain." Nicholas' voice rumbled in his chest against my back. Tension filled his muscles that held me close. "And I know not which to hope for."

The digging efforts done by many of the peasant men would aid in our defense, and many of our troops had managed to reach us, bolstering our number of defenders within the walls. We had stores of food, and weapons enough to arm much of the peasantry, if needed.

But would it be enough?

I wanted to believe so... I wanted to trust that God would spare us from destruction, but...

I turned in Nicholas' arms and pressed my face against his shoulder as he tightened his hold on me. *Heavenly Lord, please protect us. Protect my husband. Protect our family and our people.*

"I love you, Nicholas." I lifted my face and looked into his eyes. "I love you with my whole heart, and I always will. No matter what happens."

He swallowed and pressed a kiss against my forehead. "I love *you*, my darling. And I will protect you and the babe to my last breath." He placed a hand against my stomach, chasing the chill from my skin. "I give you my word."

Nicholas

"I believe they mean to starve us out, Your Majesty." Lord Raynard stood at Nicholas' side atop the palace wall, gaze trained on the Galielian encampment.

After their initial arrival and threatening show of strength the night before, the enemy troops pitched their tents around the city and stationed a guard outside the walls and gate. They had not yet begun filling the ditches separating them from the city; and based on this and a lack of other movement, it seemed the army of Galiel was in no hurry to attack.

Nicholas breathed deep, his breath fogging before his face. "Begin rationing food immediately. We must, by all means necessary, hold out longer than the Galielians."

Lord Raynard made no comment, but there was no need. Nicholas knew the man shared his own fears and doubts.

The number of plague victims had increased in the last weeks and would only continue to do so with the added population of their troops, the crowded quarters, and lowering temperatures. And thanks to the unwelcome guests encamped outside, the people of Valen would have nowhere to bury or even safely burn the dead...

As people perished, their bodies would pile up in the street, no different from discarded rubbish.

Nicholas cut off this line of thought, too disturbed by the mental images to let them continue. He turned away from the disheartening sight of over four and a half thousand troops surrounding them, and headed for the sanctuary of his palace.

God, spare us. Help us to outlast our adversaries. Please, do not let my people suffer and die before my eyes.

Nicholas could not stomach the thought of watching anyone else he loved die, knowing he had been helpless to save them. If that happened… it might just kill him as well.

Chapter 42

Adelaide

NEARLY A MONTH... THIS DAY MADE THE TWEN-ty-eighth since the Galielians arrived and the siege against Valen began.

I squinted at my needle, trying and failing to thread it in the sitting room's dim light. Nerissa, Lady Clarice, and Eleanor sat with me, keeping their own hands busy with needlework as we sought to pass the time. It felt wrong to be tucked away within this cozy, firelit room, twiddling away at such meaningless tasks while our people suffered in the autumn chill. They stretched their fuel as far as they could, ate only enough to survive, while we sat here and *embroidered*.

'Twas enough to make me want to scream!

I longed to do something useful, to help them in some way. But I was utterly powerless, especially in my condition, and with my lying-in set to begin only two days hence.

My malady only seemed to worsen in the last few weeks, the pains in my stomach growing sharper and more frequent, much to the physician's distress—and my own.

One shot through me even now, forcing me to abandon my needle and press a hand against my belly. It was hard as a rock beneath my touch. I breathed deep through my nose, waiting for the pain to pass.

"Adelaide? Are you well?" Eleanor's gentle voice spoke up from my right.

I nodded through the pain, unable to speak until it passed. "Yes, yes. Nothing to worry about." I forced a smile to reassure my companions, but looking up at Nerissa, I knew she at least remained unconvinced.

"Do you think Nicholas shall have more news for us soon?" Eleanor paused in her sewing, wringing the edge of her project with worried hands. "About the last skirmish between our troops and the Galielians?"

Shortly after the siege began, the remainder of our troops arrived, coming in behind the enemy lines. They held no hope of completely defeating the invaders, but they began engaging groups of them in small skirmishes, slowly eliminating enemy numbers. The two sides had clashed again today, according to what we heard from the servants. But Nicholas had yet to bring us any news on the outcome.

"I hope so, Eleanor."

The girl sniffed, no doubt fighting back tears again, and tried to refocus on her work. The poor dear had been immensely distraught these last weeks, still struggling with grief over Mericus and now fear of the siege. And who could blame her? Tension ran taut as a bowstring throughout the city, as we all prayed and waited for the outcome of this dreadful conflict.

Already food and fuel were dwindling. And the number of sick had increased dramatically, not only among the peasants, but the fighting men as well.

It was nearly impossible *not* to fear... Though I tried.

Another sharp pain gripped my middle. Except this one held on and would not let go. I gasped and bit my lip, tensing in my chaise and gripping the arm rest.

"Adie? You are *not* well." Nerissa plopped her work into her lap. "You should lie down and rest."

"Mayhap you are right..." I could no longer deny my discomfort. "A rest might do me good."

"Of course, it will. I know 'tis hard to sleep with so much turmoil all around and being so physically uncomfortable." Nerissa helped me to my feet. "But remember what the physician said?"

I did remember—we all did. Only too well.

I gripped Nerissa's arm as we navigated down the corridor to my chamber. With my swollen feet and ankles and ponderous belly, our steps were frustratingly slow. Another pain gripped me when we reached my door, and I had to pause to grip the door-frame.

Unease pricked along my spine. These pains were not like those I experienced over the last weeks. These were different… Stronger. Deeper.

Could it be that my labor had begun?

But the babe was not due for another month! Surely it was not ready to come *now*!

"Adie? You are starting to frighten me. Your face has gone white as snow." Nerissa placed a hand against my back. "We shall summon the physician and have him examine you immediately."

All I could do was nod and allow her to lead me into my chamber. Gretta hurried forward to unlace my gown, Nerissa assisting her. I clumsily stepped out of the heavy garment, using the post of my bed to steady myself. When Gretta turned to lay aside my gown, I moved to the edge of the mattress, intending to sit on the edge and push myself back onto my pillows.

Suddenly, I felt a popping sensation within my stomach. Warm liquid ran between my legs and soaked my chemise as though I had not been able to hold my bladder. "Uh… Nerissa…"

"Adie?" She gasped. "Oh Lord, have mercy!"

I gripped the edge of my bed with trembling hands, staring with horror at the liquid in a puddle around my feet. A month early it may be, but my time had most certainly come.

The babe was on its way.

Chapter 43

Nicholas

NICHOLAS PULLED HIS CLOAK TIGHTER AROUND HIS shoulders, attempting to ward off the crisp wind blowing between the dwellings on either side of him. With it came the scent of death and decay from the piteous plague victims, along with the usual stench of waste. Bile rose in Nicholas' throat, and it was all he could do not to cover his nose. He refused to show such weakness in front of his people. 'Twas not their fault their loved ones were dying, and they had no place to bury them.

If anything, the fault lay with *him*. For failing to protect them all from this invasion in the first place, or at the least, for not preventing the siege.

Sir Benedict walked with him along the narrow street, their footsteps crunching among the sounds of children crying and people coughing. Around the next corner lay the storehouse that held the city's food supply for the siege, where a long line of peasants had already gathered to collect their evening rations.

The guards distributing the goods noticed him first, snapping to attention. "Hail, King Nicholas!" The line of peasants stopped to bow in his direction, hushed whispers passing between them.

Nicholas and his companion halted outside the storehouse door. "At ease, men. I would like to know how we fare."

The guard in charge of the operation stepped forward. "Your Majesty, may I speak with you… privately?"

The man's cautious tone and the way he glanced around nervously made Nicholas tense. "Of course." He led the way out of earshot of the peasants. "Please, speak freely, sir."

The man glanced around and pitched his words low. "Rats have gotten into several bags of grain and other goods, damaging them beyond use."

Nicholas bit back an oath. "How does this affect our stores?"

"Truthfully, sire? We have enough to last another fortnight, at best. We can cut rations back and try to make them last longer. But if more food gets damaged…"

Nicholas knew they could last a few weeks without food, thanks to water wells within the city that would keep them alive. But he also knew if they reached that point of desperation, the people could turn to anarchy, thievery, even unspeakable acts of violence in an effort to survive. He had heard many accounts of prolonged sieges where all sense of order and humanity was lost.

God, let us not come to that…

Nicholas clapped a hand on the knight's shoulder. "Thank you for your hard work. Please, see that the rations are cut by half. And if any more food is damaged, let me know straightaway. The palace has its own stores that will be rationed and distributed when these run out." Though even those would not last long. But no need to alarm the man further.

"Yes, Your Majesty." The guard bowed and hurried back to his post and the waiting line of peasants. Nicholas started back on his path towards the palace, leaving Sir Benedict to catch up. He had not seen Adelaide since early that morning, and after this frustrating and discouraging day, he knew even a few minutes in her company would do wonders.

In the distance, Nicholas heard a low thud. Like the rumbling of thunder. It brought him up short, looking to the sky for signs of a storm. Then another thud sounded, this time from a different direction.

Sir Benedict paused at Nicholas' side. "Did you hear that?"

"Yes…" Nicholas' muscles coiled tight. "I thought it was thunder, but…" Another thud sounded. "'Tis not a storm. The sky is clear overhead."

"Trebuchets." Sir Benedict's voice echoed Nicholas' own suspicions.

"They have begun the bombardment." Nicholas hastened into a jog, heading for the nearest tower filling a corner of the city wall.

"Do you think they wish to intimidate us into surrendering

faster? Or mayhap they already grow tired of waiting and wish to take Valen by force."

"Only time shall tell." They reached the stairs and barreled up them, onto the wall. All the knights on patrol here stood watching the Galielian forces in the distance.

"Your Majesty!" Nicholas pivoted on his heel to see one of his men hurrying toward him. The knight stopped at Nicholas' side and bowed. "They have begun hurling boulders at the city. However, our walls are strong and thick–it will take days to wear them down enough to cause a collapse."

The walls *would* hold against the stones, at least for a while. But the missiles could and would still cause damage, and more than anything, fear.

"Any damage done yet?"

"One section of crenellations has been crushed, but no men were struck."

"Good."

"Watch out!" Nicholas and his companions turned to see a boulder hurtling toward them.

"Everyone, down!" Nicholas dropped to his stomach along with every other man standing nearby, shielding his head with his hands as the boulder sailed overhead. Wood splintered and crashed, raining down on them in shards. Nicholas raised his head. The boulder had crushed the roof of the tower he and Sir Benedict just exited.

"We should tell the Council, my king." Sir Benedict tugged at Nicholas' arm as he pushed up to his feet again.

With a nod, Nicholas followed Sir Benedict, reluctantly leaving his men to weather the bombardment alone for now.

The massive boulder had plummeted through the tower's roof and, along with debris, blocked the stairwell, forcing the pair to take an alternate route. They ran towards the next nearest tower, racing against time and the inevitable strike of another missile.

Another stone flew through the air, but struck lower this time, against the side of the wall. It rattled the stones beneath Nicholas' feet, causing him to stumble, yet he kept moving, following behind Sir Benedict until they reached the tower. They raced down the steps lest a stone strike the roof as it had the other tower.

When they reached the ground level, they found a small crowd of peasants staring up at the city wall, panic in their voices as they spoke amongst themselves. A thin woman in a patched gown clutched a small boy to her side, fear drawing her features tight.

Nicholas put out his hands to reassure them. "All is well. Our walls are strong and shall not crumble beneath such an attack. Please, be at ease and return to your homes."

His small speech worked well enough. The crowd turned and dispersed, heading for the shelter of their dwellings. With a muted sigh of relief, Nicholas resumed his trek home at Sir Benedict's side. They no longer ran, though. To do so would only alarm the populace unnecessarily. Instead, they set a leisurely pace that nearly drove Nicholas mad until it eventually brought them to the palace gates.

Inside the courtyard, Nicholas spotted Sir Arthur running away from the palace entrance. The knight's eyes widened when he spotted Nicholas. "My king! I was just coming in search of you."

The urgency in the man's tone froze Nicholas where he stood. "What has happened?"

"'Tis Her Majesty." The man swallowed, gulping for breath. "She–she has begun her labor."

"*What*? Now? 'Tis not her time yet." That frozen sensation spread into his blood, seeming to still even the beating of his heart.

The knight shook his head. "Forgive me for being the bearer of such news, but 'tis the truth. There is no doubt. The babe is coming–early though it may be." Sir Arthur's face flushed with embarrassment over such a private topic, but the fear in his voice was unmistakable. He served as the lead King's Guard assigned to Adelaide's protection and held her in high esteem.

"Thank you, Sir Arthur." Nicholas patted the man's shoulder before sprinting ahead. The fire of urgency now replaced that chill in his blood. He must get to Adelaide. Ensure she was well. He had to… to… to do *something*.

Please, do not take her from me, Lord. Let her live. She must live!

His mind flashed back to that dreadful moment when the sounds of his mother's distress suddenly ceased. And the moment not long after when his father informed him and Mericus that she and their infant brother were gone.

The same could *not* happen to Adelaide.

It was unthinkable.

Adelaide

My chamber lay cloaked in darkness, save for the roaring fire. Since my lying-in had not yet commenced, the servants had to work in a flurry to prepare my chamber for the sudden birth. They hung tapestries over the window, stoked the fire until it blazed, and replaced the rushes and dried herbs on the floor. It was considered imperative that the birthing room be dark and snug, similar to the womb from which my child would emerge. They accomplished their goal, for the room felt positively stifling.

The physician had arrived in the midst of all this chaos, examining me and confirming what I already knew—the babe *was* coming early. He had then turned me over to the hands of the capable midwives who served anyone in Valen that could afford their services. They, along with Nerissa and Lady Clarice, had hovered around me ever since, tending to my slightest need and making other preparations for my labor.

The constant chatter—even if kept to a whisper—the swirl of activity, and the continued pain contracting my body stretched my nerves dangerously thin. I longed for nothing more than peace and rest, but royal births were not simple affairs. As the queen birthing the potential heir, I would have no shortage of witnesses to this, my moment of greatest physical and emotional vulnerability. Such as it was, I should be thankful there were not *more* people packed into my chamber. If not for the plague, I would have selected ladies-in-waiting from among the nobility by now and they would be in attendance as well.

I breathed through another pain, tensing against my pillows. Sweat beaded on my brow and anxiety twisted relentless knots in my stomach.

I had been preparing for this moment that could well steal my life. I *thought* I was ready. But now, when faced with it head on, and sooner than expected, I realized I was *not* so prepared after all.

Fear held me in a vise grip. I was not ready to die. I wanted to live, wanted my child to live. I wanted to serve my kingdom along-side the man I loved, and enjoy a long, full life together.

Oh, Nicholas… Had he been notified of my labor yet? How fearful he must be now, if so.

Suddenly, commotion sounded from the hall. "I care not if it is not done!" My heart jolted at the familiar voice. "I am the king, for heaven's sake! And I said, *let* me in that chamber *now.*"

The door flew open, banging against the wall. My myriad of attendants gasped, whirling to face the person who dared disturb my sanctum.

"Nicholas." I breathed a sigh of relief.

He hurried to me, raw fear twisting his features as he reached my side and gripped my hands. "My love, I am here."

"How does the city fare? The siege? What is the latest news?"

He shook his head emphatically. "Let me worry about that. What you should be focused on is *this.*" He glanced around the chamber, taking in the sight of the scandalized midwives and the disapproving looks of Lady Clarice and Nerissa.

"Please, take care." He leaned forward to kiss my hands. "I need you, Adelaide. I need you and our babe." His throat bobbed as he swallowed, his eyes glassy.

Tears flooded my own eyes and I nodded. "I shall… I prom-ise."

Nicholas leaned close and pressed a desperate kiss to my lips, paying no heed to our audience. The kiss tasted of salt–from my tears or his own? I savored it anyway, soaking in the furtive expres-sion of his love, drawing strength from it.

He pulled away too soon, pressing a gentle hand to my flushed cheek. I wanted him to stay, but… childbirth was the domain of women. Men had no place here, and he was needed elsewhere. There was still a war on, after all.

"You should go."

He opened his mouth to protest but I reached out and gripped his arm. "Go, Nicholas. I have plenty of capable women to attend me, and I shall be well." I prayed my words sounded convincing enough, for I knew not if I believed them myself.

I forced out a small smile. "You shall better serve me by pray-ing for our babe's safe delivery–and by tending to the kingdom. Our people need you."

His shadowed eyes searched my face, jaw rigid. Finally, he nodded. "As you wish." He pressed a final kiss to my forehead and whispered, "I love you, Adelaide. I shall see you soon."

"And I love you," I whispered back.

He pulled away from me then, hurrying from the room like fire chased at his heels.

It was all I could do not to call him back.

Chapter 44

Nicholas

A KINGDOM RIDDLED WITH PLAGUE AND RAVAGED BY war, his capital under bitter siege, and a beloved wife at risk of death as she struggled through childbirth...

God, let this nightmare not get worse!

Nicholas massaged his temples, leaning against the chapel's altar rail. A monstrous headache took up residence in his skull, no doubt a product of the stress bearing down on him, pushing him to his wit's end.

Adelaide had been in labor for an entire day, and still the babe was not here. He knew enough to know that the longer the labor, the higher the risk became. And with Adelaide's already precarious condition–

Nay. You mustn't think that way. Adelaide will be fine. She shall birth a beautiful, healthy child.

His body ached and his eyelids drooped with exhaustion, but he could not sleep. Any time he tried, he only tossed and turned in misery, his mind fraught with thoughts of Adelaide and the conflict taking place outside these palace walls. Instead, he found himself in the chapel, on his knees, beseeching Heaven on behalf of the woman and kingdom he loved so well.

Looking up now, at the evening light streaming through the stained-glass windows, his mind drifted back to the night of their secret wedding. The way Adelaide looked in all her finery, her dark hair framing her face, her beryl blue eyes shining in the candle-light. The feel of her lips as they shared their first kiss at the priest's behest.

But above all, he thought of the vows he made to her.

He had determined, then and there, to keep every word of his vows to serve, honor, and protect her. To love her as a man ought to love his wife. He had strived to do so ever since, and in the process, had indeed fallen in love with her.

The reality of that love far exceeded his wildest imaginings. Adelaide was the love of his life, more precious than the throne or any riches this earth held.

She was a priceless gift from God.

He could only pray God would not take that gift away from him...

Adelaide

The hours blended one into the other, linked together by agony and exhaustion. I had known pain before, but not like this.

This made one forget all but the pain itself, forsaking all sense of usual propriety or modesty. The presence of the many women in my room and the vulnerable nature of the birthing process had long since ceased to bother me. All I wanted now was this ordeal to be over. To hold my child to my breast and soak in the sight of his face.

But would I ever see his face?

With every passing hour that the babe did not appear, I began to fear I would not.

Concern lined the expressions of my attendants, as well, though they did not voice any such concerns aloud—at least not in my hearing. Nerissa sat at my bedside, allowing me to grip her hand through the contractions and offering words of comfort. When not doing that, she whispered prayers, as did Lady Clarice across the room.

It was now the morning hours of my second day of labor, according to one of the midwives. I almost wished she had not informed me of such, for knowing just how long I had been at this task sent fear and discouragement rattling through me.

Nerissa mopped my brow with a length of damp cloth. "Fret not, my dear girl," she whispered, as if reading my thoughts. "Your babe shall be here soon. You mustn't give up."

Before I could form any sort of response, another pain gripped me. I tensed, clenching my teeth to hold in a cry.

"You must push, Your Majesty!"

I bore down, unable to hold my tongue any longer and crying out in pain. Tears leaked from my eyes, streaming down to my jaw. *God in Heaven, help me!*

"I can see the head, my queen! Not much longer now!"

My limbs trembled with exhaustion, my hair and specially sewn birthing nightdress drenched with sweat. But the midwife's words gave me hope. When the next pain came, I bore down again.

"Almost there!"

My heart raced, a potent mix of fear and adrenaline rushing through my veins. *God, have mercy. Please. Please, help me do this.* Rallying a final burst of strength, I bore down again, clutching Nerissa's hand in a grip that surely crushed her fingers.

I felt the release as the child rushed forth and into the waiting arms of a midwife. Cries of exultation filled the air. I sagged back against the pillows in exhaustion. Then the most glorious sound filled my ears.

My babe's first cry.

Chapter 45

Adelaide

TEARS OF JOY AND RELIEF POURED DOWN MY FACE. I held the infant, already swaddled tight in a length of soft cloth, against my breast.

A daughter.

I could scarcely believe it. I had been *so* certain 'twas a boy I carried, and a part of my heart broke at the thought that Miles would have no heir to carry on his legacy after all.

But how could I be truly disappointed when looking into that sweet face? The babe was so tiny and delicate, I feared I would break her. But she seemed hearty enough, and she certainly had a strong pair of lungs. From the moment air first touched her skin, she began squalling… at least until I coaxed her to suckle. Then she settled right down, snuggling against my skin.

Ten tiny fingers and toes, a pert nose that called Miles to memory, full lips, eyes and cheeks still pinched and puffy from the ordeal of entering the world. She was utterly perfect in every way.

My daughter.

Juliana, as Nicholas and I decided just a few weeks ago. Though, of course, the name would not be official until her christening.

Such love filled my being, I could hardly breathe, and the agony of my labor already began to fade. This child was worth every moment of it.

Nerissa sat close at my side and wrapped an arm around my

shoulders, pressing a kiss to my temple. "Oh, Adie! She is beautiful!" Nerissa sobbed happily. "Miles would be so proud."

A fresh wave of tears burned my eyes. Dear Miles… If only he were here to meet his daughter, to see what good had become of our union, such as it was.

But I had Nicholas now… And he would be just as pleased to meet this child that he loved as his own.

I sniffed back my tears. "Someone must tell Nicholas."

Nerissa patted my cheek. "We shall send word to him in just a moment. The midwives must attend to a few other things first, before he can come." Even now, the team of women buzzed around me like a hive of bees.

Suddenly, another sharp pain gripped my middle. I gasped, jostling the babe still nestled against my chest.

"'Tis only the afterbirth. It shall pass soon." Nerissa patted my shoulder soothingly.

The gaggle of women at the end of my bed crowded in close, furtively whispering amongst themselves. They examined me and the lead midwife's head soon snapped up, eyes wide. "My queen, I–I– 'Tis not merely the afterbirth. You are bearing *twins!*"

"*Twins?*" Nerissa and I cried in unison.

"They do run in the family," Lady Clarice remarked, drawing nearer.

New fear surged up in my heart, stealing the joy of holding my daughter. My breath grew short, fresh sweat beading on my skin as panic set in. I rejoiced at the thought of *two* children after so long of waiting for even one. But the thought of going through labor all over again eclipsed that pleasure.

"Breathe, Adie. Breathe. All will be well." Nerissa placed a hand against my cheek, bringing my eyes to hers. "You are *strong*. You *can* do this."

A midwife came to my other side and took Juliana away from me. I reached after her, not wanting to be separated from her so soon.

"Nay, let her attend the babe. You must focus on bringing this second one into the world." Nerissa pressed another kiss to my head. "Just think, Daughter. *Two* babes! Oh, God has blessed us, indeed. He has brought great joy from our mourning!"

I nodded vigorously, sucking in calming gulps of air. I had to focus on that. The great blessing we were receiving even in the midst of so much pain and loss.

But more loss could yet come...

So far, I had managed to survive the arduous labor process. But could this next babe be the one that stole my life?

I hated the tears that burned my eyes and ran down to the neckline of my soiled nightdress. I was supposed to be strong, I was supposed to be brave–for my children, for Nicholas, for Nerissa. But such terror reached its claws into my being, robbing me of my courage. My body trembled uncontrollably as though I were caught in a frigid wind.

I grabbed Nerissa's hand and gripped it tight, turning bulging eyes on her. How I wished my mother was with me right now. If not for the plague, I knew she would have come weeks ago. But God had blessed me with Nerissa, and her comfort was as good a substitute as I could ask for.

"Pray. P–please pray." My voice warbled out of my lips that were dry for want of drink.

Nerissa nodded, tears in her eyes, and bowed her head. Her voice lifted in quiet, earnest prayer, speaking peace over my terrified heart.

The contractions began again in earnest. The darkness of the room, the heat of the fireplace, the voices of the midwives, Juliana's pitiful wail–it all blended together into a swirling blur.

Nerissa supported me from behind, holding me up since I could no longer do so myself. The exhaustion ran bone deep now. *Help me, Lord. I cannot do this.*

I am with you, Daughter. Do not be afraid.

But I am afraid. So afraid.

Be at peace. Your life is in my hands.

My pulse raced at the sound of the Lord's voice, so clear in my mind it was as though He sat beside me.

He was right. My life belonged to Him, and I could only

trust that He had everything firmly in His control. Even if my fear wanted me to believe otherwise.

"Not much longer. The babe is nearly here."

I bore down again, finding strength for one more push.

Fresh pain.

The hot surge of blood.

Startled cries from the midwives.

And then I began to tremble violently. Except this time was different. This was not mere exhaustion or fear. I felt my eyes rolling back in my head, my body beginning to seize.

"Your Majesty!"

"Adelaide!"

My life belongs to You, Lord. Please, take care of my children and Nicholas.

Then all went hazy and faded to black.

Nicholas

An insistent hand shook him awake. "Nicholas." He jolted, lifting his head from the altar rail. When had he fallen asleep?

Lady Clarice hovered over him, her face pale and eyes lined with dark, bruise-like shadows. "Stepmother? What are you doing here?" He pushed himself upright, head spinning from the sudden change in position after being slumped over so long. "What time is it? Has the babe come? How does Adelaide fare?"

"Nicholas... She..." His stepmother's lips trembled.

He shot to his feet, nearly collapsing when he discovered his legs had gone to sleep. Needles of pain pricked all along his skin. He grabbed his stepmother's arms. Dread weighted his lungs, making it difficult to breathe. "What has happened. Tell me, now."

She swallowed, tears shining in her blue eyes. "Your wife has born not one, but *two* beautiful babes. *Twins*, Nicholas, like you and your brother. Except this time, a girl and a boy. They are small, though seemingly healthy. But Adelaide..."

Nay… Nay. Nay. Nay.

"Is she—"

"She is alive. But— Oh, Nicholas, 'twas terrible! As the second babe–the boy–emerged, she fell into a seizure. Then more fits overtook her. Several, one after the other, before Adelaide had time to recover." His stepmother shook her head. "She had already been bleeding, but the seizing escalated the issue. The midwives are making progress in stanching the blood, and the seizures have ceased. But… she has not yet awakened."

"Nay." Nicholas stepped back, raking trembling hands through his hair. "Nay!" It was the only word he could get out. The only word repeating endlessly in his brain.

He must go to her. Now.

Even with his numb legs, Nicholas turned and sprinted for the door, his pace never slowing until he reached Adelaide's chamber. The same two King's Guards stood outside, their faces drawn and troubled, much like Lady Clarice's had been. This time, they did not attempt to prevent his entrance to the birthing room. They mutely stepped aside, and Nicholas plunged through the door.

The scene he walked into was nightmarish. The room was dark and lit only by the roaring fire, as it had been when he was here at the start of Adelaide's travail. But now the gloom felt eerie and oppressive, the heat suffocating. The team of six midwives bustled around the room, their voices kept to soft whispers as they gathered up stained towels. The salty tang of sweat and blood tainted the air.

His wife lay on the bed, covered by a light sheet up to her waist. Her skin was ashen save for dark half-moons of exhaustion beneath her eyes. Her hair lay tangled and wild against her pillow, still damp with the sweat of labor.

The sight of her blurred in Nicholas' vision. This… could not be happening.

"My king." He turned at the sound of an unfamiliar feminine voice. It was one of the midwives, clad in a plain gray gown and white wimple. "The physician has been summoned and should arrive any moment. We have done everything we can to help Her Majesty. Though we were able to staunch the flow, she has lost much blood. Once the physician comes to offer his insight on the situation, we shall wash her and make her as comfortable as possible."

He nodded slowly. "Th–thank you."

She offered him a sorrowful lift of her lips. "The Lord be praised that you have two beautiful babes, one a son to inherit his grandfather's throne. They appear healthy thus far, but they shall need a wet-nurse as soon as possible. They are small things and shall require constant care and nourishment."

Twins. He could hardly absorb the shock of it.

A daughter. And a son–an heir.

Everything they had hoped for, and more…

But as much as he wanted these precious gifts, he wanted his *wife* also.

"Nicholas." His aunt stood from her seat across the room. She looked as exhausted as everyone else, and tears glistened on her cheeks. His eyes traveled to the bundles held in each of her arms and a breath gasped from his lips.

His aunt drew nearer, giving him the first full view of his children. "They are beautiful, Nicholas. So beautiful–just like their mother." Her lips trembled in a bittersweet smile. "God has given us a double portion of His blessing this day."

Nicholas stared in wonder at the tiny infants, their pink faces and petite features, their eyes closed in sleep. It had been so long since he had seen, let alone held, such a delicate creature. Would he even know how to handle them?

"You should hold them, Nicholas."

"What if I hurt them?"

His aunt chuckled low, the sound so at odds with their surroundings. "You will not hurt them–I assure you. Here, come sit."

The former queen moved to Adelaide's bedside and sat on the mattress' edge. Nicholas slowly made his way to the bed and sat next to her, mere inches from where Adelaide lay unconscious. Then Nerissa carefully passed one babe into his arm. When the child was settled safely, she passed him the other. "This here is the boy," she indicated the babe in his left arm. "And that is the girl."

Alexander and Juliana, as he and Adelaide had decided. They

were light as feathers in his arms. He snuggled them against his chest, tears blurring his vision again. How wondrous it was that such beings could come from a union between a man and woman.

Love poured from his heart, overflowing until it filled every part of him. He *loved* these children as if he had been the man to help form them. He loved his wife even more now, for how she so bravely brought these beautiful creatures into the world. Even at the cost of herself.

Nicholas shifted to better see Adelaide's pale and unresponsive face. A sob welled in his chest, begging for release. But how could he allow himself to unravel before so many witnesses?

He hung his head, the pain of grief screaming through him as he held the twins close. The world crumbled around him relentlessly, despite how hard he tried to hold it up.

Chapter 46

Adelaide

THE FIRST THING I KNEW WAS PAIN. IN MY HEAD, MY limbs, every inch of my body. Pain, and then a weakness so consuming I could not summon the strength to do more than open my eyes–and even that took effort. At last, they fluttered open and stared up into the dark shadows above me.

Memories came flooding back then, and with them, a disoriented panic. *My babes.* Where were they? My heart and body cried out for them. I needed them. And they needed me.

I willed my mouth to speak, but nothing came out save a gasp of breath. My fingers clenched in the bedclothes, bumping into something hard. And hairy.

"Adelaide? Dearest?" Nicholas lifted his head from my bedside, his voice thick and groggy. He looked as terrible as I had ever seen him–hair a wild disarray, eyes bloodshot and swollen, face pallid. How long had he been sitting here?

"Oh, my love, I thought– I feared–" He gripped my hand in both his own, pressing a fervent kiss against my fingers.

I opened my mouth to speak, but once again nothing came out.

"Here, let me…" Nicholas all but knocked his chair over in his rush to retrieve a cup of water. He held it against my parched lips, hand nestled behind my neck, and coaxed water into my mouth. It was all I could do to swallow without choking, and even this simple action seemed to wipe me of my strength.

Short of breath, I sank back against my pillows. At last, words formed. "The children…"

"Are with a nurse, my love." Nicholas smoothed a calloused hand over my cheek, his eyes shining with unshed tears. "I shall have them brought to you if that is your wish."

As soon as I nodded, he leapt into action. Within minutes, both babes lay nestled on my chest, sleeping soundly.

"We have two beautiful children, Adelaide. Juliana... *and* Alexander."

An heir for Miles after all.

Tears stung my weary eyes and gratitude poured from my heart even as overwhelming love filled it. The Lord had granted me the son I hoped for *and* so much more by giving me a daughter as well.

Thank You for this gift, and for allowing me to see their sweet faces at least this once. And surely it would be this once. For I could feel my strength draining more by the second. 'Twas a strange feeling, like water leaking from a vessel, and I knew there was only so much water left and no way to replenish it.

"We feared you were lost to us. 'Tis been half a day since the birth and you have not opened your eyes 'til now." He smoothed the hair back from my face, his touch tender and full of love, then rested his palm on Juliana's back. "Our family has been notified and will be here any moment. We have summoned the physician as well, and he should arrive soon to assess you."

"Nicholas... the war?"

His eyes flashed with a worry he could not hide in his exhausted state. "It rages on. But fret not. You must focus only on getting better. Leave the siege to me."

But I could see in his demeanor that all was not well. Our days were numbered, and Nicholas knew it, even if he would not speak it aloud.

Lord, only You can save us now. Let my husband not be too stubborn to ask for Your help. Let him place his trust in You more than himself.

A new wave of exhaustion crashed over me, making my vision shift in and out of focus. "My love... I need you... to listen to me."

"Of course, Dearest. What is it?" Nicholas rubbed my hand between his war-roughened palms.

"You must not... despair. You must continue to fight... and let God's will be done. If you survive the siege... make certain my parents... know the twins. But please, do not... give them up. *You* are their father. They belong with you." I sucked in a breath, my strength sapped further by so much talk.

"What nonsense is this? You speak as if you shan't be here."

I shook my head, a tear dripping from the corner of my eye and running down my temple. "My love… you cannot stop this. I know, in my heart… my time is over."

"Adelaide, nay–"

"*Listen*, Nicholas. You must listen. You cannot save everyone. You cannot save me. But that is alright… God shall carry me into His rest and you… you must accept that. You must release me, Nicholas."

He gripped my hand with bone-crushing fierceness. "Nay. I shall not hear a word of this. You shall get well. You will see. The physician shall arrive any moment and he will agree. You shall recover and we shall live our life and–"

"*Shhh.*" More silent tears dripped into my hair. Had I the strength, I would have pulled out of his hold to smooth my fingers over his tangled curls and stubbled jaw. I would have wiped at the tears running down his cheeks. "Please, my love. For your sake and mine… let me go. And be at peace."

I stared at the babes lying on my chest, longing to wrap my arms around them. My sweet children for whom I had longed these past years. Would they ever understand how much I loved them, even though I knew them so briefly?

"Adelaide, please. Do not say these things." Nicholas leaned forward in his chair, bringing his tortured face closer to mine.

That water draining from the vessel of my soul flowed faster now, my strength waning. My vision tunneled for a moment and I sought Nicholas' eyes before blackness could enclose. "I love you, Nicholas… Loving you, even for a moment… has been a gift."

The crushing sorrow in his eyes was the last thing I saw before I sank back into oblivion.

Nicholas

Not dead, but not truly alive either–that was what the physician said when he examined Adelaide. She had fallen into a deep unconsciousness, yet she still clung to a thread of life.

There was no telling how long it would be before that thread snapped. A few days, a few hours… It was all down to a matter of waiting now.

But still Nicholas held onto hope, with all the tenacity of a man drowning and desperately clinging to a piece of driftwood. He would not accept Adelaide's fate. No matter her fervent pleas and the physician's counsel, he *would not* accept it.

For hours now, he had sat here at her side, willing her to live. Willing her to open her eyes again and say his name. She looked perfectly at peace lying there in her fresh nightdress embroidered with tiny flowers along the neckline, her braided hair falling like a thick rope across one shoulder. She would make a lovely picture, if not for the sickly pallor of her skin.

Nicholas pressed his fist against his mouth, leaning on the bed's edge. Outside, the stones from Galiel's trebuchets continued to batter the city walls, instilling fear and anxiety into the hearts of the people. More crenellations and another tower had been damaged, a few of his men either wounded or killed. Thus far, the wall continued to hold, but how long would that remain the case?

If the wall did not give out first, their food supply certainly would.

Nicholas shuddered, despite the warmth of the room.

His world truly was falling down around his ears.

What a miserable king I have turned out to be.

How did he ever think he could run a kingdom? He was an incompetent fool, barely able to hold *himself* together, let alone a nation. He could hardly go into battle without getting sick to his stomach. And he could not even seem to protect those closest to him.

He growled and braced his head between his hands. He was alone with Adelaide at present, and the sound of his frustration pierced the silence like a knife. "Why would You allow me to become king if I cannot succeed as a leader?" He spat the bitter words at Heaven. "Mayhap Trilaria would have been better off with Mericus after all."

But if his twin had become king, then Nicholas never would have married Adelaide. She might have been cast out of the palace, and her infant son would never have had a chance to take his place on his father's throne.

And Nicholas never would have known the love of the Princess of Acuniel.

Nicholas reached out to grip Adelaide's limp hand between both of his. Her sweet face was slack, the clever mind he loved so well lost within the recesses of unconsciousness. Could she tell he was here? Could she hear him?

If she *could* hear him, mayhap she would heed his plea to stay.

"My love, I know what you said, but... hold on. Please... you *must* hold on." He squeezed her fingers, hoping the pressure would rouse her somehow. Tears burned his eyes, hot as the fire still glowing in the chamber hearth. "You have two beautiful babes, and they need their mother. The kingdom needs you." His tears flowed for the hundredth time in the past day, it seemed, dripping down his nose and chin. "*I* need you, Adelaide."

Nicholas choked on a sudden sob. He tried to muffle the sound against their entwined hands, but there was no holding back his grief. It came bursting out of him like a river too large for its banks. "I need you more than you know, my love. I know not how I could possibly live without you!"

He lifted his face and stared at the dark ceiling above, as though he could see past it into the heavenly realm. "Lord, please do not take her from me! Please, spare her life. I cannot lose her. I cannot–"

Nicholas shook his head and leaned over, weeping into the bedclothes. He lost his mother in much this same way when he was just a lad–a lad that still desperately needed her. He lost his father when he was not even there to bid him farewell. He lost his brother before they could have a chance to rebuild what years of hatred and bitterness had torn down. The thought of losing Adelaide as well was a soul-crushing blow from which he feared he would never recover.

Nicholas tried so hard to win her heart, to love her well, to protect her. He had sacrificed his own desires for her sake. He had done *everything* he could to prevent this from happening. And yet here he was, watching his wife fade away. Watching as the future they had only just begun to dream of slipped through his fingers.

His face pressed deeper into the bed. "God, I beg of you! Spare her. Please, have mercy!"

Release her to me.

Nicholas' sobs quieted. He lifted his head, the hair on his arms standing on end. The deep, but soft Voice sounded clearly in his spirit.

Release her to me, my son.

But he could not. He could not give her up. He could not let her go!

Nicholas shook his head, a war waging within his soul. "Nay. I cannot. I *will not*."

You wish to protect and serve those you love, but you can only do so much. I can do all things. Release her to my hand and to my will.

Nicholas bowed his head, trembling with the pressure of another sob building within him. He had never heard the voice of God before, not in such a clear way, but he knew without a doubt it was the Lord speaking to him. His presence charged the very air, as though He stood there in the room. Even the nearby fire seemed to grow still and quiet in the hallowed atmosphere.

Nicholas knew, deep down, what he needed to do.

And yet...

He ground his teeth, fighting against the agony of his grief. "But it shall tear my heart asunder, Lord."

I am near to the brokenhearted and bind up their wounds.

Nicholas squeezed his eyes shut, wrestling with the words. Could he really do it–surrender his heart, his love, his longing for a future with Adelaide into the hands of God? Could he possibly bear the pain if God chose to take all of it away? Even if the Lord said He would be there in the midst of it.

"I want to believe what You said... But how can I?"

No answer came this time, but Nicholas knew the answer just the same.

All he could do was make the difficult decision to *just do it*. Just trust that God knew all things.

Nicholas released the pent-up sob. It came out more like a yell. A cry of pain. Raw and full of anguish.

He pressed a kiss to Adelaide's cold, limp fingers. "I love you with all my heart, my darling."

Nicholas remembered her tentative question of, "Truly?" when he first confessed his love for her, and it brought a tearful smile to his mouth. Yes, he truly did love her as he had never loved another.

As he would never love another again.

Nicholas leaned forward and tenderly kissed Adelaide's forehead, her nose, her cheek, her lips, tasting the salt of his tears each time. He could feel the ripping of his heart as he released Adelaide's hand and placed it on the bed.

"I give her to You, my Lord. I give You my wife." He bowed his head, feeling the remainder of the ripping taking place inside him. Not just the ripping of his heart, but the ripping away of his control. "Let Your will be done."

Chapter 47

Nicholas

IT WAS ALL NICHOLAS COULD DO TO LEAVE ADELAIDE'S side. He wanted to stay with her every moment, but he knew doing so right now would not help him release her fate into the hands of the Giver and Taker of Life.

He had to flee that place of despair and find another place where he could better clear his mind.

Nicholas found himself once again in the palace chapel, kneeling at the altar railing with his hands clasped and head bent.

He could not fully protect Adelaide, no matter how hard he tried.

He could not force his brother to take honorable actions or heal the rift between them, no matter how much he had wanted to.

He could not fully protect or defend his kingdom, no matter how much training and preparing he did.

He could not stop a plague that man could neither see nor touch, no matter how earnestly he wished to.

All of these matters were ones that, ultimately, he had been powerless to handle on his own. He *had* failed, just as he feared he would. But was his failure because of some innate incompetence? Or was it because he insisted on bearing every trouble solely on his own shoulders?

The events of these last months had shown him just how weak and powerless he was.

But God? Had the Almighty not told Nicholas He could do

all things? The Lord was strong enough to bear these weights, even if Nicholas was not.

One by one, Nicholas took the burdens he had struggled to carry since his coronation–or rather, since his mother's death–and laid them at the feet of his Sovereign.

Fresh tears poured down his face, except these felt like a cleansing. A washing of his soul. A refreshment he had not even known he needed.

"I cannot carry this weight any longer. Please... I give it to You. Do with it as You will. I know not if You shall see fit to save us from our enemies. I know not if You shall rid us of this noisome pestilence. But I ask that You guide me in Your will. Grant me wisdom to do what is best for my people. Lead me in this dark hour, for I know not which way to turn anymore."

Slowly, like a languid tide washing in, peace stole over his mind. The heaviness lifted. He could breathe again.

That same hallowed presence permeated the room, as it had done in Adelaide's chamber, and all Nicholas could do was stretch himself prostrate on the cold stones of the chapel floor. He pressed his face into his hands and let himself drift on the holy tide.

He is with Adelaide, on a sunny hilltop dotted with vibrant wildflowers. A spring wind swirls across the grass until it appears to dance. His wife is radiant in a pale green gown, looking almost like a wood sprite as she turns and casts a playful grin at him. Moments later, she is in his arms, her face lifted to his, that grin still stretching her full lips wide with joy.

"I love you, Nicholas," she says before kissing him. Her lips are sweet as fresh honey.

A gleeful shriek sounds behind them and they turn to see two children toddling toward them. Juliana and Alexander. They are the very image of Adelaide, with echoes of his cousin in the shape of their eyes and in Alexander, the color of his hair.

Adelaide breaks away to open her arms to them, and they run into her embrace, wrapping tiny arms around her neck with more bursts of delight.

She looks so blissfully happy… It makes Nicholas' heart swell with joy and a longing to take her into his arms again and kiss her until the world fades away.

Nicholas crouches at her side and opens his arms to the children. They giggle and throw themselves into his chest. His arms close around them and his eyes fall shut.

Who knew such beauty and light could exist in so dark a world as this?

Nicholas' eyes opened, and instead of the windswept hill and the faces of Adelaide and his children, all he could see was the chapel floor.

'Twas nothing but a dream.

A beautiful, tantalizing dream.

Nicholas pushed his weight up from the floor, cringing at the pain in his chest from laying so long face down on the hard stones.

Instead of the overwhelming ache, knowing Adelaide lay on the brink of death, he still felt the peace of hours before. Or *had* it been hours? Mayhap only minutes? Surely not a full *day*.

Nicholas turned and sat with his back against the altar railing, legs bent, hand rubbing at his sore chest. The weight of his troubles remained absent as well, leaving his mind at peace for the first time in far too long. He rubbed a hand through his tangled curls and sighed.

The weight may be gone, but he was no closer to knowing what to do about this war with Galiel.

He could only pray guidance would come when he needed it most.

Nicholas looked up and noted the soft light streaming through the stained-glass windows. Apparently, he had slept until dawn.

As much as he wished to stay in the tranquility of this room, there were matters to attend to. Nicholas rose and left the chapel. He needed to freshen up and change his clothes, then check on Adelaide and the twins.

And then, check on the state of the siege.

He did the first task, finding a fresh pitcher of water at his washstand, left by some servant, and using it to wipe the sleep and dried tears from his face.

Clad in fresh, unrumpled clothing, he exited his chamber and wavered between who to check on first–his children or his wife. His heart called out to be at Adelaide's side again, but his love for the infant twins tugged him just as strongly. Especially after that dream…

If Adelaide were awake, she would tell him to see to the children's care above her own.

He turned his steps toward the nursery, suddenly aching to hold the tiny infants in his arms again.

Just before he reached the door, hurried footsteps echoed behind him. "Your Majesty!" He paused and turned to find Sir Benedict jogging toward him. "My king, we have been looking for you everywhere. Captain Stefan and the Council must speak with you forthwith."

Nicholas stifled a sigh, lips pressed tight. The duty of the crown called… and he must answer.

And as much as it pained him, his wife and children would have to wait.

Chapter 48

Nicholas

THE GALIELIANS ARE UNDERMINING A PORTION OF THE city wall. Nicholas kneaded his forehead, elbow resting on the arm of his throne in the Council's meeting chamber. *God, grant me wisdom.*

The patrol of soldiers on the wall's southern portion had noticed the activity going on below at daybreak and hurried to inform Captain Stefan. The work could have only just started that morning, or it could have been going on for a few days without their notice, thanks to the distraction caused by the trebuchets. There was really no way to tell how much progress had been made.

"It appears we have two options," said Lord Raynard. "Either we can have a team of men start digging at the other end and meet the enemy in the middle. Or we can place an extra guard over that area so we will be prepared the moment they break through the surface."

"The more likely scenario is that, once they are squarely underneath the wall, the Galielians will build a bonfire and compromise the structure of the wall," Captain Stefan pronounced gravely. "It will collapse, causing chaos and casualties, while offering them a path into the city."

"If their missiles do not damage the wall first," a councilman said, arms crossed over his brawny chest.

Voices rose in dispute and an underlying feeling of panic swelled in the room.

God, I know not what to do… Lead me to the right course of action.

Nicholas drew in a deep, slow breath, calming his buzzing nerves. He remembered Adelaide's suggestion, that he request aid from her father—and his staunch refusal to do so.

It was true, he did not wish to endanger any more lives by bringing the Acunielian forces into their diseased borders. But much of his refusal stemmed from his determination to handle all the troubles of the kingdom alone. He wanted to prove he could be a wise leader and stand firm. Yet a wise leader knows when to seek counsel... And when to humbly request help.

Lord, what if I doom Acuniel to destruction as well by bringing them into this conflict? What if this plague ravages their land? What if Adelaide's family falls ill and dies? I could never live with myself knowing that.

***Kings and kingdoms rise and fall at** my command and no other.*

A chill passed over his arms at the words echoing from deep within him. Nicholas took another calming breath and nodded. Though it terrified him... he knew what he must do.

"Silence, my lords!" Nicholas' voice bounced off the arched ceiling of the chamber, immediately shushing the fervent debate. "Captain Stefan, organize a rotation of soldiers to keep watch over the area where the Galielians are digging, in case they do decide to tunnel all the way through. We shall not expend the precious energy of our men by digging a tunnel ourselves.

"In the meantime, I shall send a message to Acuniel by one of Queen Adelaide's carrier pigeons. The bird will reach Caelrith in a fraction of the time it would take a man to ride the distance. I shall request King Rowan's aid, and if he is so willing, he should be able to arrive with reinforcements in a few days."

"But Your Majesty—what of the plague?"

Nicholas swallowed, the question still nagging at his mind as well. "We shall leave that in the hands of God."

"How do we know King Rowan shall even deign to help us?" one of the councilmen asked. "I know he is our ally, but so was King Theobald before he turned on us. King Rowan once warred against us himself for *eight* years!"

"I have not had the honor of meeting the King of Acuniel yet, but his daughter, our queen, is a woman of the best character. Such is usually the result of equally good parents. Not to mention,

Queen Adelaide was the one to first suggest I ask her father for aid–she firmly believes he will keep his vow of allegiance and help us."

"The king may indeed come, sire." King Raynard's brows furrowed. "But on such short notice, how many reinforcements can we even expect?"

That was a valid concern… "King Rowan will not be able to bring the full might of his army. But this, as well, we must leave in God's hands. He knows how many men we need to turn the tide of this conflict."

The room fell silent for a beat, two, three… Then Lord Raynard spoke again. "At your word, sire. It shall be done as you say. Is there anything else you would like us to do?"

Nicholas leveled his gaze at each of the men, feeling stronger and more certain as a ruler than he had since his coronation. "Call the people to prayer. Rally the troops and have them prepare for battle. We shall pray for the life of our beloved queen," a lump formed in his throat and he had to swallow past it, "and for the Lord's deliverance of our land."

To the Esteemed King Rowan of Acuniel,

I, King Nicholas of Trilaria, husband of your daughter, Adelaide, Princess of Acuniel and Queen of Trilaria, humbly ask for your aid as our ally. Our land is under attack from the Kingdom of Galiel, and due to the plague still afflicting many of our people, we are ill-equipped to fend off the assault. Valen is under siege and I fear we shall be overcome without reinforcements. I understand the risk this would bring upon your kingdom, thus I do not expect you to help us and will hold no ill will against you if you choose to remain neutral in this conflict. But I do humbly beseech you, as your ally and a man who loves your daughter and your twin grandchildren that she has just delivered… Please, come to our aid with all haste.

Also, it is with a broken heart that I must in-form you of Adelaide's grave condition. There were complications with her early labor that may prove fatal. Only the Lord can save her now.

Yours Respectfully,
King Nicholas of Trilaria

Nicholas mulled over the words as long as he dared, knowing time was of the essence, but also wanting to convey the message clearly. It was with an anxious stomach that he watched the carrier pigeon dart from the palace walls and fly over Valen. He waited with bated breath, praying the Galielians would not notice the bird and shoot it down.

When at last the bird passed safely over the enemy and disappeared from view, Nicholas breathed a sigh of relief and allowed himself to leave the wall. The tolling of the cathedral's bells echoed through the streets, calling every citizen to prayer, including Nicholas. Although this time, he would do so in the company of his children and their mother.

He had yet to hear any news on Adelaide's condition, but he supposed no news was good news in this instance.

When he reached Adelaide's chamber, she lay in the same state as before. But unlike last night, Nerissa sat in the place he had occupied.

His aunt looked up from her lap where there rested a well-worn book. Her face was pale and drawn from too many sleepless nights—the same as everyone in the palace these days—and tears shimmered on her cheeks. "Oh, Nicholas. 'Tis you." She sniffed and dabbed at her face with a delicate, lace-edged kerchief.

He took a seat on the bed beside Adelaide, facing his aunt. "What are you reading?"

Nerissa looked down, smoothing her hand over the open page. "The royal psalter." She gave a teary laugh. "Adie read passages to me when I was ill. I thought I would do the same for her."

His aunt reached out and lovingly stroked her former daughter-in-law's arm. "I know not what I did to deserve her. She has been better than a daughter to me."

Nerissa paused for a silent, weighted moment. "I tried to get her to leave, you know. Shortly after Carac passed and it became clear an heir would have to be found outside our immediate family. I told Ophelia and Adelaide to return to the homes of their fathers and leave me to suffer in what I thought was the Lord's judgment."

His aunt's mouth lifted ruefully. "Ophelia wasted no time in fleeing this place, and now I can clearly see the girl held no affection for any of us. But Adelaide?" Nerissa shook her head. "She staunchly refused. She vowed she would never leave my side, my people would be her own, and where I died... so would she." His aunt hiccupped on a sob and pressed a trembling hand to her mouth.

Nicholas' heart reached out to the woman, and a fresh wave of his own grief threatened to overtake him. Instead of giving in to it, he moved nearer and placed a comforting arm around Nerissa's trembling shoulders.

When her sobs subsided, she wiped at her face with her kerchief. "Why must so much suffering exist? Why must our hearts break so continually? I cannot fathom it, Nicholas."

The same questions ran endlessly through Nicholas' own mind. "I wish I fully understood it myself..." He thought back to every tragedy and trial of the last several months, flinching at the pain-soaked memories. So much of these events still did not make sense to him, but in some ways, the meaning behind them was becoming clearer. "The best I can make of it is that... our world is simply... *broken*. And, like with my arm, when something is broken, it hurts."

Nicholas paused to swallow against the hard truth forming a lump in his throat. It was not easy to accept, but it was true, and he could deny it no longer. "The pain of this broken life reminds us we are ultimately not the one in control. It turns–or at least it *should* turn our eyes to the One who *is* in control. Who promises light on the other side of this dark and broken existence."

Nerissa squeezed Nicholas' hand. "Very true, Nephew. And there is light to be found even in the *midst* of this darkness–though it can be difficult to remember that. Our Adelaide has been a light in our lives, and she has given us two beautiful new lights to cherish."

The former queen dabbed at her tears again. "The Lord is still good and gracious, even in our sorrow. I suppose all we can do is hold onto the bits of light we have now, as we hope for more in the future."

Nicholas nodded his head in solemn agreement. He had to hold onto the light he had been blessed with, even as he struggled through the darkness of grief.

It was hard to fathom how the world could ever hold any more light without Adelaide in it…

But that, as well, he would have to leave in the Lord's hands.

Chapter 49

Nicholas

NICHOLAS' BREATH FOGGED BEFORE HIS FACE IN THE morning air. His chainmail armor weighed heavy on his shoulders and the cold made his scars beneath twinge with pain. But energy coursed through his veins, providing a heady distraction from the discomfort.

With the morning light, two days after he sent the messenger bird to Caelrith, the Galielian forces moved into action.

He spent yet another restless night at Adelaide's side, watching her fade farther and farther away. The physician had said just last eve that she may have but a day, if that, left—unless she awoke long enough to take water or other sustenance. When the news arrived that the Galielians had formed battle ranks and were moving closer to the city walls, it was all Nicholas could do to pull himself away from her. He could not bear the thought of returning from battle—if he returned at all—to find her gone.

But he had no choice.

There was a city full of innocent lives to protect. And he knew if Adelaide were able to speak to him, she would tell him to go.

So he forced himself to give her one last kiss, then hastened to dress for battle. With every piece of armor and weaponry his manservant helped him don, another weight had settled in the pit of his stomach.

He knew not what the outcome of this day would be, but he would charge forward anyway.

God above, grant me wisdom. Nicholas uttered the desperate prayer in his mind for the hundredth time that morning. *Give me the strength to lead my people through this, and to face whatever may come.*

He stood with Captain Stefan on the wall above the city gate, watching as the Galielian troops marched toward Valen in perfect rows. The sound of their pounding feet echoed like thunder.

"When they are within firing range, order the archers to begin shooting."

"Yes, Your Majesty."

Boulders continued to batter their walls every few minutes. And that noise, combined with the rumbling of the enemy's advancement, had the entire city bound in tense, fearful silence.

Nicholas spared one more glance toward the horizon. *Lord, if it is in Your will to spare us this day, let King Rowan arrive.*

The sun stretched orange and pink fingers across the horizon. But no activity stirred the forested hills to the south—the direction in which Acuniel lay.

For now, at the very least, they were on their own…

Nicholas took a fortifying breath and steeled his gaze on the enemy marching towards him. At last, the first row of Galielian foot soldiers drew within firing range.

"Trilaria at the ready! Aim… FIRE!"

A volley of arrows zipped through the air and into the enemy ranks. Some found their marks, but not all. The archers shot another wave of arrows and prepared for a third. As they did so, Nicholas saw the Galielian archers raise their own bows towards the city. But at least half of the projectiles were not *ordinary* arrows.

"Flaming arrows! At the ready, men!" Nicholas shouted, even as the missiles launched toward them.

Several arrows found their mark in the chests of his men. Flames of fire arched over the wall into the city below. Most landed on thatched roofs, setting them ablaze.

"Fire! Fire!"

Alarm bells rang from somewhere below and men rushed to put out the flames. Women and children shrieked in fear.

"Steady, men! More arrows!" Captain Stefan shouted to the archers.

Arrows rained down, striking the enemy ranks, though many of the invaders raised their shields to fend off the attack. Still, onward the Galielians came, swarming like ants around Valen's walls.

The acrid scent of smoke and burning wood and thatch stung Nicholas' nose. Behind him, peasants continued to battle the flames, even as more arrows flew overhead and set new fires or killed those trying to stop them.

The fires of anger burned in Nicholas' gut. This war was no longer just taking the lives of his men or nobles, it was taking those of helpless innocents.

This shall not *stand.*

Determination strengthened his resolve. He would fight to the death for his people, for his soldiers, for his dying wife, infant babes, and other family back in the palace—God so help him.

If any Galielian soldier crossed into this city, they would do so over Nicholas' dead body.

A boulder flew through the air and struck the wall directly below where Nicholas stood. It rattled the stones beneath his feet, threatening his balance. An arrow flew past and struck a man at Nicholas' left. The knight cried out, clutching his shoulder and staggering backward.

The Galielians were in no rush to scale the walls. Apparently content to continue the barrage of arrows and boulders, they fired upon the city in waves for over an hour, picking off soldiers when possible and causing general chaos.

Fires continued to ignite in the areas bordering the city walls. Valen only had so many wells, and the only way to draw the water was with single buckets. Therefore, the amount of water needed far eclipsed what the people were able to produce.

It did not take long for several blazes to spread down the street, eating up the wooden structures and discarded plague victims.

Smoke from the nearest fire clouded the air so thick Nicholas could taste it. Soot streaked his sweaty face and ash peppered his hair. His men were rattled–he could feel it. But they could not let these fires deter them. That was what the Galielians wanted, was it not? To burn them into surrender, since starving them out had not yet succeeded?

There was also the tunnel to consider... Nicholas' men stationed on that section of the wall had reported the digging was still underway. They had managed to pick off many of the under-miners with arrows, but the Galielians were persistent and, so far, refused to give up.

A knot suddenly wrenched tight in Nicholas' gut.

The arrows, the fires–it was all a distraction. A means of bringing their focus away from the tunnel.

"Captain Stefan! We must–" Nicholas' shout was cut off by the most horrifying noise slicing through the sounds of fire and fear. The rumble of stone against stone, like a mountain being moved from its place.

He spun around in time to see a portion of the city wall crumble and crash inward. A massive cloud of dust flew into the air, mingling with the smoke already darkening the city.

Captain Stefan ran to Nicholas' side. "Shall I lead a portion of men to the site of the collapse?"

"Nay, you stay here. I shall go." Urgency sent Nicholas sprinting to the nearest tower. Captain Stefan shouted orders behind him, and soldiers ran after Nicholas to follow him to the breached wall. He took the stairs two at a time, his sword slapping against his leg, his chainmail jingling.

When he pushed open the door at the bottom of the stairs, a cloud of smoke assaulted him. It invaded his lungs. Stung his throat and eyes. Nicholas coughed and covered his face with his arm, left with no choice but to wade blindly through the cloud.

"Your Majesty!" A soldier shouted behind him.

But Nicholas pressed on, choking and coughing, until he emerged from the smoke, gulping in a somewhat clean breath of air. He was still several blocks from the site of the collapse. Gasping in another draught of air, he sprinted forward. From multiple directions, more of his soldiers appeared, heading to the same destination.

The moment Nicholas turned the corner near the site of the collapse, the cloud of dust and smoke swallowed him. Nothing but a gray haze met his vision. He choked on the air, dust and dirt scraping the inside of his throat. For a panicked moment, he thought he might suffocate.

Nicholas pressed his nose into his arm, wading through the haze. He knew homes lined this street that dead-ended into the wall. Had they been destroyed? Were people even now trapped in this choking cloud, beneath the rubble? Nicholas' ears strained to listen for cries for help, but all he could hear was his own coughing and that of the soldiers entering the cloud behind him.

At last, the dust began to settle, fading enough that he could see his surroundings. It was a ghostly landscape. Dust covered everything, including the soldiers around him, making them appear like ashen phantoms.

Nicholas squinted through the haze. Up ahead, a portion of the wall wide enough to fit fifteen to twenty men had fallen into a heap of rubble. Piles of stone made the path through the opening a precarious trek. Yet he knew they had mere minutes before the first enemy soldiers would dare to make the climb while others worked to clear the path.

On either side of the opening, Nicholas saw exactly what he feared. Large stones had crashed into the nearest buildings, turning their wooden frames into heaps of rubble.

Nicholas spun around, searching for signs of life. Mayhap the residents of this street had sensed the danger and vacated the premises in time. *Lord, let that be so!*

"Someone, search these homes. Take anyone you find to safety immediately."

A young soldier hurried to do Nicholas' bidding, his booted feet stirring up dust as he ran.

Nicholas wiped sweat, soot, and dust from his eyes and turned to face the other soldiers behind him—about a hundred in number by this point. "The Galielians will be upon us at any moment. Assemble into ranks and prepare for battle!"

The men immediately did as they were told, falling into place and blocking off the street. Swords left their sheaths in a chorus of metal on metal.

Nicholas' pulse thudded in his neck, his own sword drawn and clutched in his right hand. How many soldiers would the Galielians bring through this breach? As long as the numbers stayed low enough, he knew his men could hold them back, picking off each soldier as they entered the narrow street. But if the Galielians cleared the debris enough to flood this opening with hundreds of soldiers...

The Trilarians would be overrun in no time.

Lord, grant us strength. Go before us in this fight.

On impulse, Nicholas ran toward the mountain of rubble. His boots crunched against the crumbled stones as he climbed just high enough for the soldiers to see him. He turned, stabilizing his weight and raising his sword into the polluted air.

"Our enemies have succeeded in breaching our walls. But hope is not yet lost." He let his eyes travel over his weary and dust-coated troops. "Yes, we are outnumbered, our supplies are depleted, our bodies are weary, and our capital burns at our backs. But we cannot let these things hinder us from facing our enemies with courage.

"We are fighting for much more than our own lives. We are fighting for our homes, our livelihoods, our *families* and all those we cherish." His voice caught on the last phrase, his mind darting toward Adelaide and the twins. Nicholas jabbed his sword at the fire and smoke rising from the city. "Let all of *that* serve as the fuel we need to fight these invaders and drive them from our lands!"

A cheer arose from the men.

"We may not live to see the morrow. Yet if we die, let it be in the defense of our liberty and the safety of those we love!"

Another cheer filled the smoky sky, this one louder and longer than the last—even with the likelihood of death staring them in the face.

"For Trilaria!"

Nicholas stabbed the air with his sword, letting his own shout rise until his throat burned and his blood ran hot with determination.

"Your Majesty! Look out!"

Nicholas spun around. Up above, a trio of Galielian soldiers had reached the top of the heap and were climbing down, swords in hand.

Nicholas ground his feet into the rubble and readied his blade.

The real battle had just begun.

Chapter 50

Nicholas

THE ARCHERS ON THE CITY WALL RECOVERED FROM the shock of the collapse and began firing on the intruders from above, but that did not deter the Galielians. They continued through the opening like infesting vermin.

The first soldier that dared reach the bottom of the rubble met the end of Nicholas' blade. Then another came, and another. Nicholas fought them without fear, with no thought save his desperate desire to protect his land and all it held.

Jab, slash, stab, repeat. Fighting became a deadly dance, his sword an extension of himself.

The sounds of battle clashed with that of raging fire, clanging bells, and cries of fear. All around him, his men fought with the same ferocity, the sort motivated by deep convictions and raw desperation.

Nicholas knew... and he suspected his men did as well...

This was their last stand.

They had this and only this moment to either win or lose. But they would not give up the battle, even if they had to fight to the very last man.

Nicholas' blade collided with that of another attacker. The man recovered from the blow and shoved Nicholas back with all his might from his higher vantage point on the crumbled stones. Nicholas took a quick step backward, but his boot met only air. He tumbled end over end down the dusty hill of debris. Rocks sliced his skin. Dirt and blood mingled on his tongue. At last, he landed in a heap of chain mail.

Nicholas groaned and rolled onto his back. Pain screamed in his side with every breath. A bruised or broken rib? He ground his teeth, hissing through the pain. There was no time to sit and nurse whatever wounds his tumble had inflicted. An enemy blade could find its home in his flesh at any moment.

With a growl, Nicholas pushed up from the ground and onto his knees. His sword was gone, lost somewhere during the fall, but a dagger hung in a sheath on his hip. He pulled it out quickly, noting the enemy soldier heading toward him.

The man eyed Nicholas as he came to his feet, taking in the dirty and bloodied Trilarian crest on his chest and the golden circlet that had fallen at his feet in the tumble. "Are *you* the one they chose as king?" The man sneered, dust coating his face. He was older than Nicholas by several years, broader and bulkier through the chest.

Nicholas did not deign to offer a response. He only gripped the silver hilt of his dagger tighter and held it at the ready.

The Galielian scoffed. "You should give up now, while you may still save the lives of most of your men. Yours is a fool's errand."

Again, Nicholas did not dignify the words with a response. Instead, he charged forward up the hill, knife poised for attack. The soldier was ready, though. He deflected Nicholas' dagger before swinging his sword around in a wide arc, aiming for Nicholas' neck.

Nicholas arched back just in time to evade the death blow, leaping from the pile of rubble, his weight jarring against the ground. The Galielian bounded toward him again, sword raised beside his head with both hands. The glow of a nearby fire glinted off the blade.

Nicholas *needed* a sword. Unless he managed to knock the weapon out of the soldier's hand, he knew he would not be able to avoid the farther reach of his opponent's blade for much longer.

He quickly searched his surroundings, holding his dagger at the ready.

There. A sword lay beside a fallen Galielian soldier some twenty feet away.

Nicholas took three sideways steps toward the sword. But his opponent was no fool. His eyes darted toward the weapon and surmised Nicholas' intent, for he suddenly charged forward, teeth bared and gaze murderous. The steel blade sliced the air, coming for Nicholas' head again. He ducked, using the moment to edge closer to the discarded sword.

His adversary jabbed at him, missing once more. While the man recovered from the momentum, Nicholas swept up the sword. He brandished the weapon at his opponent and ran forward. The man dodged what would have been a fatal blow, but still caught Nicholas' sword in his shoulder. He growled a curse and stabbed his own blade forward into Nicholas' thigh.

Nicholas cried out in pain, feeling the weapon slicing through the same muscles he injured in Dartwell. When he tried to put his weight on that leg, he buckled and sank to his knees.

Nay.

He could not stay down like this. He had to rise and fight. The Galielian was already closing in for the kill.

Nicholas gripped his sword and rammed it upward with a fierce yell just as the Galielian reached him. The blade sliced through the links of the man's mail armor and sank into his gut.

Nicholas pulled his sword back out and rolled away as his opponent fell forward into the street to breathe his last.

Nicholas used his sword to push himself back onto his feet. Pain screamed through his leg, and he could already feel the blood seeping through his hose. Nicholas panted, steeling himself against the pain. He pushed his sweat-soaked curls out of his eyes and surveyed the battle still raging all around.

The Galielians had succeeded in removing much of the rubble, making it easier to send troops through the opening. They were practically a swarm now, attacking with unrelenting ferocity. His men fought valiantly, but they would soon be overwhelmed.

"Your Majesty!"

Nicholas' head snapped up, searching for the source of the voice.

"The gate!" His gaze snagged on an archer still fighting up above them on the wall. "The Galielians are battering the gate!"

Once again, their enemies had used one tactic to distract them from their plans to use another. If the Galielians managed to break down the city gate and enter by that route as well, the Trilarians would be completely overtaken in moments.

Part of him wanted to run straight for the gate and ensure its defense, but Captain Stefan was there, and the man was far more experienced and no doubt already handling the situation.

Nicholas could not get distracted. He had to focus on *this* moment, *this* front of battle.

Nicholas shook himself and prepared for a new opponent. The adrenaline pumping through his veins now eclipsed the pain in his leg, fueling his body and giving him the strength to press on. He met the next soldier that attacked. Then the next, and the next, and the next.

With every man that fell, a part of him broke inside, knowing he took the lives of men with loved ones waiting for them in Galiel. But Nicholas had loved ones waiting for him too. He had an entire kingdom counting on him this day.

God, give me strength. Help me to defend my people. Help me carry the weight of this responsibility.

Onward he pressed, pushing harder and harder until everything became a blur of smoke and death, sweat and blood.

Then his current opponent sent a swift kick to his wounded leg. Nicholas cried out and buckled beneath the blow. He fell to his back and nearly lost his grip on the hilt of his sword again. The earth knocked the breath from his lungs, leaving him gasping for air.

The soldier stepped over him, blood-stained sword poised to kill. Nicholas could not breathe. Could only stare up at the man who looked to be the same age as himself.

Was this it? Was this the last moment of his life?

Would he and Adelaide soon be in the heavenly realms together?

The blade lowered, aimed for Nicholas' heart.

If You will it, Lord. My life belongs to You, just as Adelaide's does.

Then a sharp trumpet blast split the air.

The soldier paused, startled by the sound.

Get up, Nicholas.

Breath swelled back into Nicholas' lungs and he rolled out of his adversary's reach. He pushed to his feet, sword in hand, and looked to the horizon beyond the opening in the wall. He could not see anything there from this vantage point, but the trumpet call sounded again.

King Rowan.

Help had arrived after all.

Chapter 51

Nicholas

"THE ACUNIELIANS HAVE ARRIVED!" THE JOYOUS SHOUT
from the wall reached Nicholas below, confirming what he already
knew.

Shock held both the Trilarians and their enemies in place, taking in the unexpected news, as though a momentary truce had
been declared.

It could not last long, however. The Galielians would rally and
resume the attack any moment.

"My king! You should come see this!" A soldier shouted from
above. Nicholas took the advantage of the lull in battle to turn and
sprint toward the nearest tower. He barreled up the stairs, blocking
out the pain pulsing in his thigh, and burst through the door onto
the city wall.

The bodies of a few of his archers littered the allure, but most
men remained standing. Their shooting had ceased, however, as all
eyes focused on the horizon.

Nicholas shielded his gaze against the afternoon sun and
looked to the south. There, a multitude of mounted knights had
emerged from the wooded hills. The red and gold standard of Acuniel snapped in the chilly wind, and sunlight glinted off the armor
of a man riding at the forefront.

King Rowan.

His father-in-law.

More soldiers flowed from the trees–more than a thousand in
number, if Nicholas had to guess. How on earth had King Rowan

amassed such a number on a couple days' notice? 'Twas impossible. Yet… his eyes were not mistaken.

Nicholas breathed an incredulous sigh.

The battle was not over yet.

Nicholas lifted his sword with a shout, and every Trilarian soldier near enough to hear followed suit. Hope swelled and surged, shifting the atmosphere from one of despair to renewed determination.

"For Trilaria!"

The shout became a roar as the realization of the Acunielians' arrival spread throughout every corner of the city.

"Keep fighting, men! Fire!"

The archers leapt back into action, firing at the Galielians still outside the city. Below, fighting resumed at the breach in the wall.

Nicholas strode down the allure, rallying the men, calling orders. Squires and peasant men hurried past him, carrying armloads of more arrows to replenish the archers' stock.

To the south, the Acunielians reached the army of invaders, who were now forced to divide their attention between the city and the attack from their rear. The remaining Trilarian troops who had engaged the invaders in small skirmishes throughout the siege, regrouped to join the army of Acuniel.

Nicholas continued shouting encouragement to his troops as he headed back toward the thick of the fight. They had a long way yet to reach victory, but Nicholas could feel it deep in his soul…

The tide was turning.

As the first touch of sunset tinged the horizon, Nicholas heard another unexpected sound.

Long, loud blasts on a trumpet.

Nicholas pulled his sword free of the last unfortunate man to meet death by his hand and spun around. He had returned to the wall breach, where he and his men continued to do whatever they could to hold back the invaders. The Galielians steadily pushed them back, gaining ground in the city, but Nicholas and his men had refused to give up.

Now, however, the fighting once again gradually came to a halt as everyone took notice of the trumpet blasts.

"What does it mean, sire?"

Nicholas opened his mouth to respond when a distant shout cut him off.

"Galiel surrenders!"

Nicholas nearly sagged to his knees in shock and relief. Could it be true?

"King Theobald is captured! Galiel surrenders!"

His men lifted a victorious shout, weapons brandished to the sky. The Galielian soldiers shared looks of disbelief, and for a moment, Nicholas feared they would refuse to comply with the order to surrender. But at last, weapons clattered to the ground. His men immediately moved in and held the surrendered soldiers in groups at sword-point.

"Your Majesty!" Nicholas spun, finding the Captain of the Guard running toward him, his face streaked with soot and sweat. He came to a stop before Nicholas and gave a quick bow, his chest heaving for breath. "Sire, the Galielians have flown the white flag of surrender. King Rowan rides toward the city as we speak, along with a group of men in the colors of Acuniel. There is another man in tow, whom we believe to be King Theobald. The battle... it is over. We have *won*."

Nicholas gripped the man's shoulder. "Are you certain?"

"*Most* certain." A relieved smile lifted the man's lips.

Nicholas squeezed his eyes shut. Thank God. *Thank God.* Somehow, against all odds, they had come out victorious.

"My king, your leg!"

Nicholas opened his eyes and looked down. Blood soaked the hose on his left leg, below the hem of his long chainmail tunic, turning the fabric a garish dark red. As the rush of battle drained from his body, weakness struck. His head swam.

"Your Majesty." Captain Stefan caught him by the arm. "We should get you back to the palace forthwith. King Rowan will be wanting to meet you there, and we must tend to that wound."

Nicholas nodded and followed Captain Stefan away from the

scene of battle, away from where too much blood had been spilled on both sides. The ache of loss hung heavy within him.

But God delivered them from their enemies, and that was where his focus must rest. There would be time enough to mourn later.

Chapter 52

Nicholas

NICHOLAS PUSHED AWAY THE PROBING HANDS OF SIR Benedict. "Leave me be, man."

"But sire, your leg must—"

"Nay, not now." Nicholas shifted his weight off his injured leg, stifling a wince at the pain throbbing both there and in his ribs. Sir Benedict ducked his head in subservience, though his jaw clenched tight. Nicholas knew the man meant well, but there were far more pressing matters to attend to than a wound that was not imminently fatal.

The palace gates swung open and a half dozen horses and their riders trotted into the courtyard, garbed in Acunielian red and gold. The man leading the group sat taller in his saddle than the rest, with an unignorable air of authority about him and a golden crown glinting atop his head.

Without question, this was King Rowan of Acuniel.

Nicholas' gut clenched. It struck him now that he was meeting his wife's father for the first time. A strange thing since, had theirs been a usual marriage, Nicholas would have first sought the man's permission to marry Adelaide.

The formation of horses broke apart, revealing a man led by a rope tied around his hands. Blood streaked one side of his face from a gash at his hairline. His mail armor was finely crafted, his tabard bearing the crest of Galiel, and a crown sat somewhat askew atop his graying hair.

The defeated King Theobald of Galiel.

The Acunielians and their captive reined to a halt before Nicholas in the courtyard's center. Immediately, King Rowan swung down from his saddle, his face all hard lines and intensity. Adelaide always spoke so highly of her father, claiming him to be a kind, affectionate sort, but this man appeared to be a warrior through and through. Not at all how she made the king sound.

He strode toward Nicholas, his chainmail rattling and boots thudding heavily across the ground. One of the Acunielian knights dismounted and led the disgraced king of Galiel forward.

"King Nicholas of Trilaria." His father-in-law's voice was deep and strong, arresting the attention of any who heard it. He bowed, his face still a mask of severity. "It is an honor to meet you."

Nicholas bowed in return, ignoring the fresh wave of pain in his leg and side. "King Rowan of Acuniel. You have my utmost gratitude for responding to my request for help. I know 'twas no small feat to rush to our aid on such short notice, and I know it comes at great risk to your own people. Though, I must say I was taken aback by your numbers. We did not dare hope for so many reinforcements."

"Ah, that. I shall gladly explain later. But do think nothing of it. Allies must help each other in times of crisis. That is, unless you are this dishonorable blackguard here."

The Acunielian knight drug King Theobald forward and forced him to his knees. The knight's sword was out in a flash and pressed beneath the king's chin.

King Rowan's brow furrowed darkly over eyes that were unsettlingly similar to Adelaide's. "I spared his life on the battlefield, for it is not mine to take. The judgment of his fate belongs to you."

Nicholas turned his eyes on the man who had betrayed his vow of allegiance and invaded Nicholas' kingdom. King Theobald's face, though bloodied and smudged with dirt, was defiant. Yet thus far, he remained silent. Cold.

For a moment, anger flamed in Nicholas' heart. This man had nearly destroyed them all in his greedy quest. How could Nicholas *not* be angry? Could anyone blame him if he wished for revenge?

But something deep inside said that taking King Theobald's life in restitution for his treachery would not solve anything. It would only create more problems for both kingdoms. And add further weight to Nicholas' conscience. The faces of the men whose lives he had taken in this war would haunt him enough already…

Nicholas stepped forward on a limping gait. He withdrew his sword in a smooth motion, despite his exhausted muscles.

King Theobald's eyes flashed with anger, his lips a grim line.

Then Nicholas rammed the sword into the dirt, inches from the king's body. He leaned forward onto the hilt and brought his face close to King Theobald's. "Your life does not belong to me, either. Consider yourself fortunate indeed to receive such mercy, for I am certain you would not grant me the same."

Nicholas leaned closer and spoke through gritted teeth. "You and your army shall return anything and everything you have taken from my people, and then you shall leave these lands and *never* return. If you *dare* cross my borders again without my invitation, mercy shall not be so easily handed out."

Nicholas pushed himself upright, wrenching his sword from the ground. "May God deal justly with you, according to His will."

King Theobald's jaw fell slack, eyes belying his astonishment at this ruling. "I… thank you… for your mercy, King Nicholas." The man looked a bit green as he forced out the words. Cleary, his pride was more wounded than his body.

"Thank not I, but God. And believe my word, King Theobald—we are no longer allies of any sort." Nicholas straightened and tossed a hand at the knights gathered round. "Now get this man out of my sight!"

The Acunielian grabbed the rope securing King Theobald's hands and jerked him to his feet, away from Nicholas. King Rowan stepped around them to reach Nicholas' side. "My men shall escort King Theobald and his troops out of your lands and ensure they leave peaceably. I have further reinforcements on their way, led by my sons, in case there is more trouble."

Nicholas nodded his thanks, but before he could form any words, the King of Acuniel spoke again, his hand clamping down on Nicholas' shoulder. "I must commend you for showing mercy to such a snake as King Theobald. It takes a stronger man to show mercy where none is deserved than it does to exact vengeance. Your uncle, King Wesley, was such a leader, offering even greater mercy to me after all I did against his kingdom in my youthful folly."

Nicholas stared at his father-in-law, taken aback by his words.

And, once again, by the stunning similarity between his and Adelaide's blue eyes.

"I thank you, King Rowan. And once more, I must thank you for coming to our aid."

"I confess, I feared trouble would arise since I first heard of the plague in your kingdom. So I have been preparing my troops for some time already–several months, in fact–and kept them near the border. I would never dare to overstep by arriving uninvited, but I wished to be prepared at a moment's notice, in case you did petition aid."

Nicholas pushed out an incredulous breath. That explained the seemingly impossible number of soldiers.

Relief, gratitude, and an overwhelming wash of humility tumbled over him. The Lord had been making a way for their deliverance all along–far before Nicholas even knew they would need it.

"I could never leave such a close ally, let alone my own daughter, to weather such an invasion alone." The king's eyes flashed with a myriad of emotions–fear, anguish, love, anger. "Please, tell me. Does my daughter still live?"

Nicholas swallowed, fresh grief oozing in his broken heart. "As of this morning, yes. I... know not what has become of her since, however."

King Rowan's brows furrowed again, in a way that Nicholas thought must be a habitual thing for him, based on the permanent wrinkles that had formed there. "Take me to her."

Nicholas nodded and turned to call Sir Benedict to his side. He gave the knight instructions to confer with Captain Stefan and see that the fires were put out, the wounded tended, and the civilians of Valen looked after in the wake of the battle. Then he led his father-in-law toward the palace entrance.

"Your leg. It looks quite painful. You should have a physician look at it soon."

Nicholas shrugged off King Rowan's concern. "'Tis nothing," he said, even as his head swam again from the blood loss.

When they reached the warmer, shadowy interior of the palace, King Rowan drew to a sudden halt. He skewered Nicholas with a steely gaze. "There is something else we must discuss for a moment. I allowed my eldest daughter to marry the Crown Prince of Trilaria because I knew it was what our kingdom needed at the time, and because she was *willing* to do so. However, since then, and since realizing my daughter's marriage was not all I hoped it would be for her... I have come to regret my decision."

The hardened warrior persona was gone, replaced by the role of a protective father. "I want my daughter to be happy, and to be cherished as she deserves. So I must know now, *King* Nicholas of Trilaria, do you love my daughter? Or did you only marry her because it helped secure you the throne?"

Nicholas flinched beneath the king's penetrating gaze and frank words. But he did not have to think for a moment about what his response should be.

"I married your daughter, not for the sake of the power it could possibly provide me, but for the good of Trilaria and the sake of protecting both Adelaide and her unborn child—or children, as it turned out. Ours was not a love match, but I determined, from the moment I spoke my vows, that I would be a true husband to her. I would learn to cherish her. Protect her and serve her until my dying breath.

I have done everything in my power to do just that, and I can tell you with utmost certainty that yes, I *love* your daughter. Adelaide matters more to me than any crown, any amount of land, or wealth, or power. She and the twins she bore are gifts far greater than I could ever deserve. And if God has chosen to take her from me..." Nicholas paused to swallow his emotions and catch his breath, "then I shall have to live every day upon His mercy to survive such pain."

King Rowan stared hard at Nicholas for several long, agonizing moments. Then, at last, he clapped Nicholas on the shoulder, his hard edges softening and lips lifting in a sincere smile. "In that case, I am honored to call you my son, Nicholas. Please, call me Rowan."

Nicholas blinked, stunned by the shift in the man's countenance. "Thank you... Rowan."

His father-in-law's smile melted into sorrow. "Now, let us see what has become of my daughter."

Chapter 53

Nicholas

ANY REMAINING HARDNESS FADED FROM KING ROWAN'S visage the moment he stepped into Adelaide's chamber. Those striking eyes turned soft, his shoulders dropping as he hurried over to her.

Nerissa sat at Adelaide's bedside once again, and her head snapped up at the sudden intrusion. Her mouth formed a small O, shock evident in her face as she bolted to her feet. "King Rowan! You came! And Nicholas!" Her eyes darted down to his leg. "You are wounded! Is the battle over? Are we safe?" Her words came out in a breathless rush, tumbling one over the other.

Nicholas placed a reassuring hand on her shoulder. "We are safe. King Rowan's reinforcements made all the difference. A truce has been declared."

She pressed a hand to her heart. "Oh, God be praised!"

"How does Adelaide fare?" Nicholas' eyes settled on his wife's face. Relief crashed over him to see her still alive. He had truly feared he would return from battle to find her gone.

"She remains the same. Alive, but… not truly here."

King Rowan picked up his daughter's hand and gripped it in both his own.

"I should give you some time alone with your daughter, Your Majesty." His aunt moved toward the door. Nicholas reluctantly turned to follow her.

"Nay, Nicholas. Please, stay with us."

Nicholas nodded, slowly moving back to Adelaide's side and

sitting in the chair Nerissa had just occupied. His leg and ribs sighed at the respite.

King Rowan smoothed back stray pieces of Adelaide's hair. "My dear girl… I am here. Father is here." Tears filled his eyes and he pressed a kiss to her limp fingers. "I nearly had to lock your mother in the dungeon to keep her from coming with me." He breathed a tear-laden laugh.

Nicholas had yet to meet the Queen of Acuniel, but he had heard enough stories to imagine how difficult it must have been to convince the headstrong, passionate queen to remain home.

"We all love you, dear one, and we do not want you to leave us." King Rowan bowed his head, seeming to struggle over his next words. "But we shall not keep you here if the Lord wants you elsewhere. He gave you to us… and we must give you back."

Nicholas bowed his head, battling against the grief his father-in-law's words drew to the surface, knowing he was right. They could not cling to something that was not truly theirs to begin with. As much as he adored his wife, she belonged to God far more than she belonged to him.

King Rowan sniffed back his tears. "I shall not leave until… Well… *until.*"

Nicholas nodded, wiping at his face. Should his eyes not have run out of tears to cry by now? "Of course, you are welcome here as long as you like. I will see that our best guest chamber is prepared for you right away." He pushed up from his chair to do just that.

"*First,* you should have that leg tended. And I have a feeling you know just as well as I do that Adelaide would tell you the same thing." King Rowan turned a fond smile on his daughter. "She is stubborn and unrelenting in her care of others, like her mother."

Nicholas could not help the smile that came to his own lips.

King Rowan rubbed a gentle hand down Adelaide's cheek. "I shall stay here with her. You take care of yourself, and when you return, I would like to meet my grandchildren."

Adelaide

A babe's squalling cry broke through the darkness enshrouding me.

Alexander? Or was it Juliana?

Give me my babe. I tried to speak the words aloud, but my lips would not move.

"They truly are beautiful. They look so much like her–especially Juliana." A voice I had not heard in ages sent a jolt of recognition through me.

Father? My father is here?

"I fear my wife shall never forgive me for forbidding her from accompanying me. And that woman's ire is not one I relish." Father paused for a moment, no doubt shuddering at the thought of Mother angry with him. "But I would not risk bringing her into the danger of your war with Galiel."

The war... It seemed Nicholas had heeded my suggestion after all. He summoned Father for help. Did that mean the siege was over? Mayhap even the war? Had we won?

"A wise decision, even if a difficult one." My heart leapt at the sound of Nicholas' voice. It had reached me in snatches since I sank back into the dark abyss–tearful pleas and prayers, fervent words of love. I tried to respond to him, but always found it a fruitless effort.

I attempted again now, wanting to let him and my father know I could hear them, but still my mouth would not cooperate. It seemed almost glued shut, completely incapable of moving no matter how hard I tried.

A familiar, loving hand touched my own. Strong fingers wove together with mine. "It is agonizing, seeing her like this." I attempted to squeeze Nicholas' hand, but failed at that as well. "The physician expects her to leave us soon... He said that without water, her body cannot sustain itself much longer."

How long have I been unconscious? Time blurred, making it impossible to tell how many days had passed since I urged Nicholas to let me go. In truth, when I first felt my mind slipping into the depths, I thought *that* was the end. Instead, I lingered in a sort of netherworld–not fully present with those I loved, unable to re-spond to them, but still clinging to life.

I had been prepared for death, resigned to it. But here I was, still hanging on. Could God's plan be different than I had come to believe?

Once more, I tried to open my mouth to speak. Nothing hap-pened. Frustrated, I wanted to cry, but my body would not re-spond to even that.

God, I know my life rests in Your hands alone. I will not seek to wrestle it from Your grip. But please… if You so will… allow me to stay. Allow me to live my life at Nicholas' side, caring for the children You have blessed me with. In my heart of hearts… I am not ready to go.

No answer came, no voice like I heard during the twins' birth when my heart and body were torn asunder by fear and pain. But that same peace washed over me. The holy touch of the Creator.

If You so will, Lord… I uttered the fervent prayer in my mind once more.

Then I tried, one last time, to squeeze Nicholas' hand.

Chapter 54

Nicholas

NICHOLAS NEARLY FELL OUT OF HIS CHAIR WHEN HE felt the gentle squeeze on his hand. "Adelaide? Can you hear me?"

"What is it? Did something happen?" His father-in-law strode across the room, the twins snug in his arms. Alexander squalled uncontrollably, his face puckered and mottled red, and no amount of shushing or bouncing from his grandfather made a difference.

"She squeezed my hand! At least, I believe she did." He had not imagined it, had he?

Nicholas leaned over the bed, tentative hope rising. "Adelaide? I am here, my love. Can you hear me?"

There. There it was again. A gentle squeeze upon his fingers.

A gasp of shocked relief pushed its way out of his lungs. "Oh, thank God." He gathered her hand in both of his, pressing a swift, grateful kiss to her skin.

"N... Nicholas?"

His name had never sounded so sweet in all his life.

"I am here. So is your father, and the twins. Your father came to help us, just as you said he would."

Her eyelids flickered and then slid partially open.

Nicholas had begun to believe he would never see those lovely gem-like irises again.

"Praise the Lord!" He and his father-in-law exclaimed the words together, both crowding over her in an elated rush.

"W... water. P... please."

"Yes, of course." King Rowan still worked to calm the wailing

Alexander, so Nicholas spun away to fetch something for his wife to drink. Water. Where was some blasted water?

There was none to be found in the room now–the servants must have given up hope that she would wake to drink any. He would have to summon someone to fetch it then. Nicholas rushed out into the corridor, startling the guard standing watch at Adelaide's door.

"Your Majesty? Is–is the queen–?" The knight, Sir Arthur, stared at him with troubled eyes, his face haggard after endless hours protecting Adelaide's door while the battle raged outside.

Nicholas grinned and clasped the guard's shoulder, startling the man further. "Nay. The queen yet lives, and she has awakened! Please, fetch a servant to bring water for her immediately. And have someone inform the Ladies Nerissa, Clarice, and Eleanor of the joyous news."

Sir Arthur's eyes misted, his lips pinching tight for a poignant moment. Then he swallowed. "God be praised... God be praised."

Nicholas squeezed the man's shoulder and nodded. No further words were necessary.

Then the knight turned on his heel and hurried away while Nicholas ducked back into Adelaide's chamber. King Rowan sat on the bed next to her, Juliana still held in his arms, though he had placed Alexander on Adelaide's chest and even now helped her cradle the infant close.

Nestled against his mother's chest, the babe soon quieted and lay there in perfect contentment. Adelaide gazed down at him, her face still betraying the continued weakness of her body. Yet the light of love and gratitude was visible in her eyes, along with a renewed sense of life he could not ignore.

It was as though the resurrecting power of Christ Himself had flowed into her body. An undeniable miracle that left Nicholas awed and trembling.

"My son..." Her voice was still thick and gravelly from disuse.

Nicholas settled at her side, smoothing his palm over the top of her head. "He is the most beautiful boy I have ever laid eyes upon. Though how can he possibly compare to his sister?"

A tremulous smile lifted the corners of Adelaide's mouth. She ran her fingers across the babe's cheek. "Who knew such love existed?" A tear glistened in the corner of one eye.

"Indeed…" Who knew he could love this woman in the way he did? And who knew he could love two children so much?

Nicholas kissed her forehead, overcome with gratitude for the wonder of this love. For the wonder that she and the children were still here with him.

Gretta came bustling in then, a cup and pitcher of water in hand, her movements frantic and her voice shaking with emotion. "Praise God! I—we thought we lost you, my queen."

The maid soon fed the water to Adelaide in minuscule sips, while the door burst open to reveal his aunt, Clarice, and Eleanor. The women instantly surged into a sea of chatter, but Nicholas could not begrudge them. This was a moment for celebration.

Their beloved Adelaide was still with them. And after seeing that renewed spark of life in her countenance, Nicholas knew she would not be leaving anytime soon.

Adelaide

"We rejoice that you are alive, my queen." The physician stood at my bedside, where I remained ensconced in mounds of blankets and pillows. His face still bore the signs of shock that marked all those who witnessed my miraculous turnabout. "'Tis surely God alone that has allowed you to live, for I know not how you could have rallied otherwise."

Nicholas squeezed my hand, all of his relief and gratitude in the touch.

"I know 'twas God's mercy that gave me another chance." My voice remained rough from days of disuse, but as I continued to sip on water and warm, nourishing broth, it slowly regained its usual tone and strength.

"However…"

Nicholas' hand tensed around mine at the slow word from the physician, who then tucked his chin, looking hesitant to say what he knew he must.

"However… I fear you may not be able to bear another child.

After struggling to conceive these children, your body may be incapable of another pregnancy, let alone sustaining it to term. And even if you *are* able to conceive, I must warn that it would be extremely precarious."

The physician offered a genuinely sympathetic expression. "You shall recover from this ordeal, but you may never have your full strength again. In fact, I highly doubt it. And another pregnancy would almost certainly take your life."

My heart sank, fracturing with pain. I loved Alexander and Juliana with every part of my being, and I knew Nicholas did as well. But I had hoped–had assumed–we would one day have a child *together.* Mayhap another son, this time one who could inherit Nicholas' family land and continue *his* lineage.

I looked at Nicholas, finding my shock mirrored in the drooping lines of his mouth and the grief-stricken look in his eyes.

Tears gathered and I covered my face with my hand.

"Forgive me, Your Majesties, for delivering such news. But I must speak the truth."

"We... appreciate your honesty." Nicholas' voice was dry, flat. "Please, may we have a moment alone?"

"Of course." The physician began gathering his tonics and instruments, returning them to the satchel he used to carry them. "My work is done here. Though I shall be back to check on you daily, for at least a sennight."

Neither of us responded, only watched the man pack his things and depart from my chamber with a reverent bow. Silence hung in the room. Thick. Heavy.

I averted my gaze from Nicholas, unwilling to see the shocked disappointment in his face again. "Nicholas... I am... Forgive me, I..."

What could I say? That I was sorry he married a woman who could not give him an heir? That he should annul our still unconsummated marriage, find himself a better, healthier wife, and beg him to still abdicate the throne to his cousin's son?

No matter how hard I tried, I could not bring my mouth to form those words.

I felt his weight settle beside me, his grip on my hand turning insistent. "Adelaide... Please, look at me."

I shook my head, a sob welling in my suddenly constricted

throat. The guilt and inadequacy that plagued me following Miles' death returned like an unforeseen tempest, drenching me through.

"Nay, *look* at me." Nicholas' fingers found my chin and turned my unwilling face in his direction. "*Please.*"

I finally allowed my eyes to open, staring at him through a watery veil of tears.

"It matters not to me. Yes, this news is painful. But I *love* you, Adelaide. I love you and Alexander and Juliana, and I will love all three of you until my dying breath, no matter whether or not I ever have a child of my blood. As far as I am concerned, Alexander and Juliana *are* my own." He gently wiped at the tears running down my face. "Please, my love... Do not cry."

"But Nicholas–" I shook my head, still unable to accept it, despite his gallant speech. "'Tis not fair. You shall resent me for it in time–I know it."

"Do you truly doubt me? Do you actually know me so little that you would believe I would act thus? I could *never* resent you for something that is completely out of your control. This is no fault of your own."

I looked back into his eyes, searching. All I found was sincerity. No guile, no bitterness or anger. Just a desperation for me to believe his words.

But how could I allow him to consign himself to such a future? He deserved more than this...

"Nicholas, you deserve better than what I can give you."

"*Nay.* Do you hear me? 'Tis *I* that does not deserve *you.*" He cradled my face in his hands, drawing closer. "My love... You are more than I ever could have hoped for in a wife. You are the queen of my heart, my dearest friend. And I will gladly face *any* future that awaits us, good or bad, if it means you may remain at my side."

He leaned in to kiss my forehead, my temple, my cheek. "Do you not remember the vows I made to you? After you burst into my chamber in the dead of night and practically forced me to wed you?" His tone was teasing, and I could not help the anxious burst of humor that made its way past the lump in my throat.

"I pledged to have and hold you for better or for worse..." He gathered my hands in his and kissed the back of one finger. "For richer or poorer." He kissed another. "In sickness... and in health."

Another. "I vowed to love and cherish you until death itself parted us. Not until difficult seasons came our way, but until the very end." He made his way to where my ring sparkled on my left hand and stopped.

"I meant those words, Adelaide, even then. And I mean them still. I shall not break my vows to you. Do not ask it of me."

I stared at his beloved face, my heart in a melted puddle. "Nicholas... I love you and I want to live every day at your side, but–"

"Then that is all that matters. God shall see to the rest. Do you not believe that?" He squeezed my hands tight. "I have tried too long to balance the weight of protecting all those I care for. No matter how hard I tried to keep them safe, to be what they needed or wanted me to be... It has only ever ended in frustrating failure.

"You told me that I must release you to God. And I did. But He did not take you. He instead returned you to me and took care of every other impossible situation that I knew not how to solve. So that is what we must do again, my love. Do you not believe that only *He* holds our future in His hands?"

Your life is in my hands...

The words the Lord spoke to me in the midst of my labor, when the overwhelming panic and fear consumed me... I could hear them, could *feel* those words again now.

Only God controlled whether I lived or died, if I birthed another child or not, or when this plague would end. The list could go on and on. And knowing that offered peace, *not* fear. It offered the opportunity to press forth and remember His promises.

Though we might taste the bitterness of suffering now or in the future, He promised sweetness in the end. He promised to bind up our wounds and make our broken hearts whole. He promised joy on the other side of mourning, light on the other side of even the darkest night. He promised not to forsake us in our suffering, but meet us in the midst of it.

Fresh tears dripped from my eyes and I fell forward onto Nicholas' shoulder. Like Nicholas' vows to me, God's promises were true and unbreakable.

How could I *not* believe in those promises? In both God *and* the husband He blessed me with?

I wept into Nicholas' tunic, staining it with my tears. It was not long before my body felt drained by the exertion. My head pounded and my limbs trembled.

"You ought to rest, love. You mustn't make yourself ill with these tears." Nicholas gently pulled me off him. I felt suddenly as weak and helpless as my own infants, who were currently tucked away in their room under the wet nurse's care. Nicholas helped me lay back against the pillows and then tucked the bedclothes snuggly around me.

"Are you cold? Hungry? I can have Gretta come back in and feed you more broth. She has been waiting outside in the corridor like a faithful puppy."

I shook my head, snuggling beneath the warmth of my covers. "Nay. I need nothing just now... save you, here with me."

He hovered above me, his smoldering look flooding my stomach with warmth. Suddenly, the longing to be united with him as a true husband and wife was overwhelming. But of course, he would never let that happen until I fully recovered.

In the meantime...

"Will you lie next to me?"

One black brow rose in surprise at my question. But a delighted smile spread his mouth wide. "As you wish, my queen."

He went around to the opposite side of the bed on limping steps—a product of his wound in yesterday's battle—before climbing up and settling at my side. The warmth of his body next to mine was a balm to my soul, releasing all the tension in my aching muscles and weary mind.

Nicholas wrapped one arm across my stomach, which remained awkwardly misshapen from pregnancy. Then he laid his head beside mine on the pillow.

I turned my face to look at him, finding it only inches away. His eyes were full of love, yet slightly hooded, as though already fighting off sleep. After the events of the last several days, surely he was as exhausted as I was—mayhap even more so.

"I love you, Nicholas." My heart swelled with fresh gratitude over having another chance at a future with him. Even if it would look differently than I originally hoped. "I would rather navigate life's sorrows and trials with you at my side, than face a lifetime of perfect days without you."

He sighed and moved even closer. "And I love you." He kissed me, deeper and sweeter than ever before. A kiss that held a million promises.

When at last he pulled away, leaving us both breathless, he snuggled closer and rested his head on my chest, with his ear over my heart.

That night, we both slept more peacefully than we had in months. Many things about our world remained uncertain. But our kingdom was safe, the fires consuming the city had been stamped out, my children were alive and healthy, Nicholas and I were together… And it was enough.

Epilogue

Two and a half years later...

Adelaide

A SPRING WIND CARRIED THROUGH THE TALL GRASS and made it dance. I breathed in the invigorating air, scented with the vibrant wildflowers dotting the ground, and let out a contented sigh.

My strength was not what it once was, my body prone to tire from exertion quickly—but I could still enjoy outings such as this.

"You are radiant this day, my love." Nicholas approached from behind, and I tossed a playful grin over my shoulder as he neared. The pale green silk of my gown swirled against my legs in the wind.

My husband of nearly three years—strange to think so much time had passed already—wrapped his arms around me and pulled my body against him. I lifted my face to his, a joyful grin stretching my mouth wide. "I love you, Nicholas."

Then I kissed him, relishing in the familiar and ever delightful feeling of his lips.

Suddenly, a gleeful shriek sounded from behind us and we turned. 'Twas Alexander and Juliana, now two years old and full of life and vigor, toddling up the hill toward us. Their nurse followed behind, her face flushed as she chased the mischievous little creatures.

My heart squeezed at the sight of them. They still looked like me in many ways, but there were echoes of Miles in the shape of their eyes. And in Alexander's case, his hair color.

I crouched in the grass and opened my arms to them. They ran the rest of the way, flinging their tiny bodies into me. Small arms and hands clung to my neck and giggles of delight made it impossible not to giggle in kind.

Nicholas crouched beside us. "No hug for Father?"

The twins laughed again, nearly tackling him. My husband's arms wrapped around them and squeezed tight, his eyes falling shut. The hug lasted longer than the twins' liking, and they soon wiggled free, jabbering in the way they did—a mix of intelligible words they learned and others that seemed a language all their own.

The nurse caught up to us and gathered the twins' hands. "I beg your pardon, Your Majesties. They are slippery little things. Pulled right out of my hands to run to you, they did."

"Nothing to worry about, Charlotte," Nicholas assured her. "They are children, after all. Let them have their fun."

The nurse, who we hired to replace the wet nurse once the children were weaned, bobbed a curtsy and turned to occupy the twins with picking wildflowers.

"Adie, darling! Do come back soon. Our meal is ready!"

I squinted my eyes in the bright sunlight and looked down the hill to where my mother waved at me. She and Father, along with my siblings, were staying with us in Valen for a few weeks—a much needed visit after a particularly harsh winter that kept all of us ensconced in our homes, even for Christmastide.

It did my heart good to be with my loved ones again. 'Twould not be long before my siblings–Roland, Gareth, and Matilda–began marrying, no doubt leading to further separation.

Nicholas called to the nurse, instructing her to steer the children down the hill. Then he took my hand and tucked it in the crook of his arm. Together, we meandered back down the grassy slope to where the small team of servants arranged a picnic amongst the rainbow of wildflowers. My family, along with Nerissa, Lady Clarice, and Eleanor, found their places on the collection of blankets spread across the ground.

I settled in beside Nerissa, with Nicholas on my left. The mother of my heart reached over and took my hand. "Just look at this, Adie." Her face, once lined with grief, now shone with the light of peace. I followed her gaze, taking in the sight of all my family members united in this picturesque setting. My children's laughter carried on the breeze as they continued picking wildflowers nearby. My brothers teased one another and made Tillie laugh, while my parents sat close together, hands intertwined and looking utterly content. Nicholas conversed with his stepmother and Eleanor, who also no longer bore the marks of daily sorrow.

"When we found ourselves widows together, I never thought to experience *this* again. Love. Laughter. Family." Grateful tears gathered in Nerissa's eyes. "I thought myself forsaken, yet in these years since, the Lord has proven me wrong."

The past two and half years had not been perfect by any measure. Full of rebuilding efforts following the war, a difficult recovery process for myself, and the plague's spread into Acuniel and Galiel before finally dying out... They were long days that frequently tested our strength, patience, and faith.

But through it all, God had seen us through. We, along with our kingdom, had risen from the ashes stronger than before, both in earthly riches and in spirit.

I squeezed Nerissa's hand, gratitude flooding my own heart. "He has proven many things, Mother, and been far more gracious than we deserve." I laid my head over on her shoulder, suddenly reminded of my long-ago vow to never leave her side. How glad I was to have kept that oath, for how much different our lives would look had I not.

"So true, my daughter." She lovingly patted my cheek and leaned over to kiss my head. "From our mourning, He has brought dancing."

"And from our sorrow, He has brought great joy."

Author's Note

I didn't set out to write a story that mirrored the recent events of my own life and our world, but it subconsciously evolved that way. At first, when I realized what I was inadvertently doing with this story–having it revolve around so much heartache, loss, and turmoil brought on by a *plague*–I inwardly groaned and thought, "No one is going to want to read about this!" And part of me still fears that, I must confess. Yet at the same time, I believe this story was *supposed* to be this way and written at this time, which is why I never could discover what Adelaide's story should be sooner. This story was one *I* needed in order to process recent events in our world and in my personal life (namely the loss of both of my grandfathers, just five months apart). I hope it has given you, as the reader, an opportunity to examine some of the things *you* have gone through in the last couple years, and that you found encouragement and healing as I have.

I watched the Lord of the Rings movies for the first time while in the middle of writing this book (Shocking, I know! How could I call myself a book nerd without having watched or read these stories?) and I was deeply impacted by something the brave and loyal hobbit Samwise Gamgee says to Frodo. The theme of my book was already well established by this time, and I could not help but think how fitting this particular quote is for it.

> *"It's like in the great stories, Mr. Frodo. The ones that really mattered. Full of darkness and danger,*

they were. And sometimes you didn't want to know the end. Because how could the end be happy? How could the world go back to the way it was when so much bad had happened? But in the end, it's only a passing thing, this shadow. Even darkness must pass. A new day will come. And when the sun shines it will shine out the clearer. Those were the stories that stayed with you. That meant something, even if you were too small to understand why. But I think, Mr. Frodo, I do understand. I know now. Folk in those stories had lots of chances of turning back, only they didn't. They kept going. Because they were holding on to something."
~ J. R. R. Tolkien, *The Two Towers*

Those words perfectly sum up not only Nicholas and Adelaide's world, but our own as well. We may wonder how things can ever turn out good, and how the sun can ever shine again. But it will. Even darkness must pass eventually. And that thing we are holding on to that's worth fighting for? That is *hope* in the One who is strong enough to bear every burden, heal any broken heart, and drive back any darkness!

Thank you, thank you, thank you for taking the time to read this book of mine! I know there are so many books out there in this world, TBR piles are unending, and a reader's time is highly valuable. I hope Nicholas and Adelaide's story has not only entertained you but ministered to your heart as well.

BUT WAIT... THERE'S MORE!

Before you go, there are a few historical notes I would like to make. While the kingdoms my characters live in are purely of my imagination, they are supposed to be located within our own reality. That said, I tried to stay true to history, especially when it came to some key things that play crucial roles in this story. Beware if you are reading this before reading the book–there are spoilers ahead!

The Plague: While the most infamous outbreak of Bubonic Plague took place about a century after my story, there were two other pandemic-level outbreaks of the plague recorded—the first one in the mid 500's and the third one in the late 1800's. Also, it stands to reason that there were random cases or localized outbreaks of the disease at other points through time that did not make it into our history books. In fact, while editing this book, I heard on the Stuff You Missed in History Class podcast that just recently in Italy, bodies of plague victims were found that predate the pandemic of the 14th century. All of this is why I chose for the "plague" in Trilaria to be the Bubonic Plague.

Mourning Attire: When we think of "mourning clothes", we tend to think of societal norms that actually originated in the 1800's. Prior to that time period, black dye was very costly and not widely available, so for much of history, it was not expected for you to wear all black. In the medieval period, *white* was actually the typical color of mourning, though nobility, and especially royals, would also wear black or purple on occasion. There was also no strict, standardized time period for the wearing of mourning clothes at this point. In Victorian times, people wore mourning attire for over *two years* and went through different stages of mourning (i.e. full mourning, half mourning), but such was not the case in the medieval era.

Medieval Wedding Ceremonies:
You may have noticed a lot of similarities between modern wedding ceremonies and Nicholas and Adelaide's. Believe it or not, many aspects of Christian weddings, particularly the vows, haven't changed much since the Middle Ages, hence the reason for the familiar words and rituals. However, I will note that there were a few details of a traditional medieval wedding that were skipped over in this book just due to the circumstances surrounding the ceremony itself.

Medieval Childbirth Practices & Pre-Eclampsia: You may have noticed some odd details included in the childbirth scenes. Did medieval mothers really give birth in dark, blacked-out rooms with a roaring fire heating the room to "simulate" the feeling of the womb for the baby? Yes! Did royal women really have a large audience witness this ordeal and a group of women chanting and praying around their bed? Yes! There were even more strange practices I read about that didn't make it into the book, but these were the main ones I felt should be mentioned. I know one thing, I'm glad I'm not a medieval woman!

Also, the condition I describe Adelaide as having is pre-eclampsia, which of course was not named thus in those days. Today, this condition is still dangerous but survivable, thanks to modern medicine. However, such a condition was very likely a fatal one in the 13th century.

If there are any other historical details that you're curious about, feel free to reach out to me! I would be happy to chat about it!

Acknowledgments

While my name is the one on the cover, the creation of this book would not have been possible without a whole host of individuals:

My husband, Austin—I thank you for putting up with my sitting in bed late at night with my headphones in, working away at this book. Thank you for always supporting me, giving me space to work when I really need it, and telling strangers about my books. Not to mention, I know I can always turn to you for advice on weapons, battle scenes, and how to wound my characters badly but not *too* badly. Nicholas' tender and loving heart is largely based on you, my very own handsome hero!

My family—thank you for believing in me even when I didn't believe in myself. You never cease cheering me on, and thankfully never groan when I talk your ears off about my writing projects! I'm especially thankful for the support of my sister, Addison (who shares a nickname with Adelaide). You were my first "fan-girl", and often just talking to you about my stories helps me work through roadblocks in them.

Natalie—thank you for being my editor once again! I could not have polished this book up as much as I have without your keen eye! #BookAuntieForLife

To my Bookstagram friends—thank you for praying for me during this process, checking on my progress, and supporting my work so enthusiastically. This was my first book to write with the book community at my back, and it made such a difference. I'm so glad to have found "my people"!

Fellow authors Anna Augustine and B. R. Goodwin—I owe you a BIG thanks for beta reading this book for me! You guys were my first beta readers to ever work with, and both of you helped me so much! Your feedback made this book better, and your love of the story gave me the encouragement I needed to get it out into the world.

Roseanna M. White–thank you for once again creating the book cover of my dreams and handling all of my typesetting! You are amazingly talented in so many ways, and it was an honor to get to work with you again.

Aidan Turner and Liv Tyler–thank you for being the actors that play my characters in my imaginary movie, though you have no idea this book even exists. I love you as Ross Poldark and Arwen Undomiel… but you'll always be Nicholas and Adelaide to me.

Lastly, but more importantly than anyone else… Jesus. Thank You for helping me get this story onto the page. For a long time, I feared I would never write another book. Then the inspiration for this story hit me like a lightning strike and it was as though You flung the doors on my imagination wide open. This book poured out of me like no other story has, and I know that's all You. I write for Your glory above all else, and I pray You take my "loaves and fish" and do what You will with it, for the furtherance of Your Truth and Your Kingdom.